THE
VOYAGEURS

DISCOVERY IN HAVENSWOOD VALLEY

A novel by

BRIAN JAMES
SIDDONS

To Excel In Life - Andover, Minnesota

Published by To Excel In Life
763-350-9272
BrianJamesSiddons.com
Andover, Minnesota

ISBN 978-0615954103

Printed in the United States of America

The fruits of our labor
taste so sweet
when shared.

For my wife,
Jeanette,
and our beautiful children,
Jackie, Spencer, and Harrison.

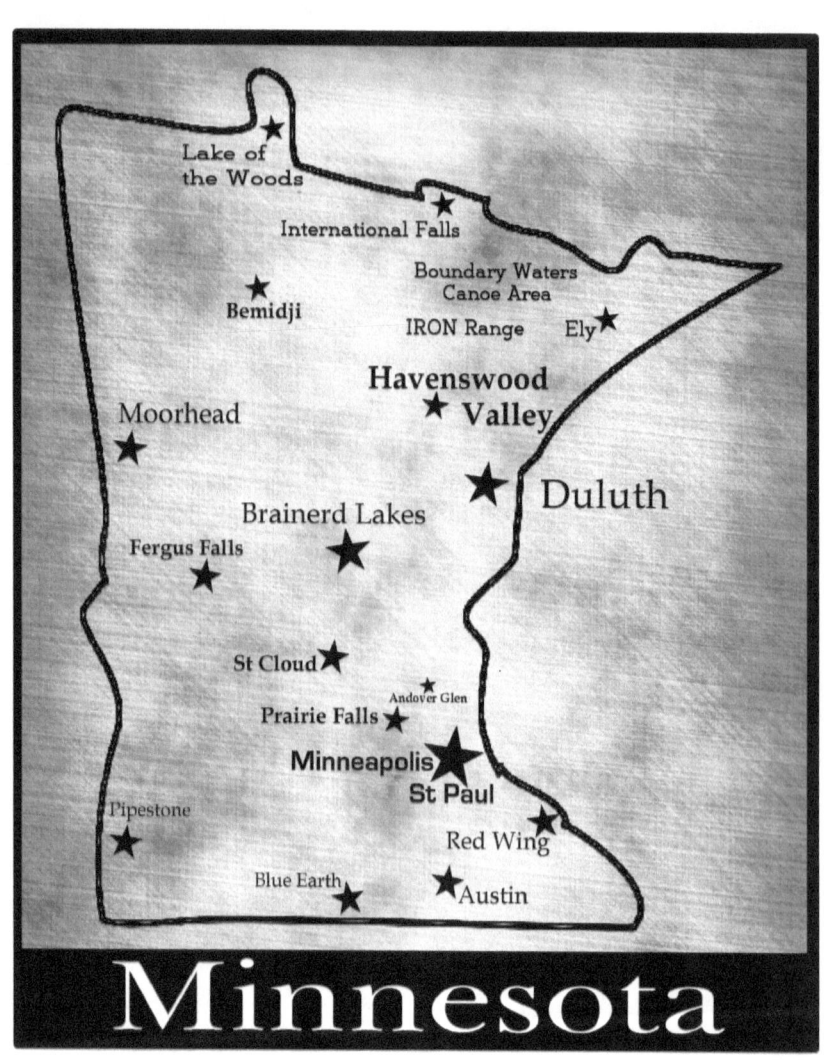

Minnesota

PROLOGUE

Marcus Jennings was four years young at the time, not quite old enough to enable a vivid recollection in his later years, but certainly aged enough to brand the event onto a few memory cells. Although faded like an old tattoo, once in a while a visual flash, nearly as intense as the night it happened, would burst into his consciousness.

Marcus was raised in a rural-suburban area where open acreage was common, lakes and parks abundant, yet shopping and chore runs were no big deal. He was always within a short driving distance to visit relatives, hang out with friends, get to school, participate in sports, and in general lead a pretty normal life. Home was a modest rambler on a three acre plot, built with compassion in the framework and family life in the floor plan. Heading home to 452 Alpine Lane was usually a quick drive from anywhere, unless of course a freight train was passing through the city of 30,003 citizens. An abundance of homes had nestled into many of the prime lots and the growing population had caught up to this once very rural region, increasing the parade of autos stuck behind the dropped railroad crossing arms. Not usually a big deal, but many drivers that had been stopped and forced to wait until the last rail car had disappeared down the track would let their minds wander and eventually get to thinking that it was about time the trains quit running so much during peak drive time.

When it happened, Marcus was nearly asleep. His heavy eyelids were fluttering shut, and the bobbing of his head was in a rhythm of motion synchronized with the vibration of the oncoming engine. His father was distracted by the cars on the other side of the tracks making u-turns. He didn't have a clue as to what was about to happen. Marcus, tired as he was, felt the shiver of needles run up his back, forcing him to fight the straps and sit up as straight as possible. His eyes popped wide open, suddenly totally alert, absorbing everything. Sights, sounds and movement outside of the truck transfixed the young boy, his

1

attention finally settling on the huge object to his right. There, not more than fifty feet up the tracks was a giant, glowing, beast of a machine barreling down upon them from the woods! He saw huge, glowing eyes, a wide, smirking mouth and a plume of white smoke rising above and trailing back behind the monsters head! It was a nightmare racing toward them and then, without warning, young Marcus did what most people would do when faced with eminent danger; he let out a frightful scream, filling the cab of the truck with a high pitched shrill that should have obliterated the windows.

In less than a minute, it was over, Marcus was out of steam and too tired to hold his head up. He cried himself to sleep on the short drive home. His father, heart beating faster than the pistons under the hood and at a loss for the hysteria of his son, put the truck in gear and tried not to let the situation get the best of him.

"I can't stop shaking," said Troy. "It was the freakiest thing. The crossing arms were down across the road, red lights blinking, bells ringing same as any other time we've been stopped there. Everything pointed to a train coming, I even saw some cars driving off, not wanting to wait. The next thing I know Marcus is screaming bloody murder." He sat down, got up, then sat down again. "Holy crap, I thought all hell had broken loose and a train was going to roll right over us."

"But Troy," his wife, Anna, said in as calming a voice as she could, "The way you explained it, there's no reason to think you put the two of you in a dangerous spot. Marcus is just a baby and must have been startled in the darkness."

"I know, it was just so darn un-nerving. I felt totally helpless." Troy stood up again. "And the weirdest part is that there never was a train! The crossing arms just lifted, not a train in sight!"

"Honey, sit down," said Anna. "Let me get you a glass of wine while you take your boots off. We'll sit by the fire, I'll massage your legs and you'll relax. I know it's easier said than done, but you didn't do anything wrong. I'm sure Marcus will sleep it off and that will be the end of it."

At 3:15 am, Marcus gave Troy and Anna a vocal reenactment of his earlier performance at the railroad crossing. At 8:30 am that very same morning, when Nurse Anna Jennings was making her first set of rounds at the hospital, she would learn a new

2

patient in the ICU was the lone survivor of an early morning auto-train collision. The deadly impact had occurred at 3:15 am, not more that six miles from the Jennings' home.

Anna couldn't get to her cell phone fast enough. "Troy," the tears welled up in her eyes as soon as she spoke. "Oh my God, Troy, you're not going to believe what happened last night."

With a bird's eye view of the four season log cabin, you could easily imagine an artist sitting on the nearby hillside, sketching the outdoor scene for a Christmas card. A light October snowfall, early for Havenswood Valley, was slowly coating the copper colored metal roof of the log cabin and the rest of the Washburn property; an outbuilding where most of the tools and equipment were stored, a rock rimmed fire pit, the open field that kept the forest at bay, mowed short for winter, and the long dirt driveway, edged with towering blue spruce trees, began to look like cinnamon toast being covered with sugar. The picture-perfect look was topped off with evergreen branches accepting the snow flakes with ease, and a thin wisp of smoke that was now leaking upward from atop the stone and mortar cabin chimney.

Like squirrels in the fall preparing for winter, the temporary occupants were moving steadily between the parking area and the cabin, quickly filling their northern Minnesota hideaway with the trappings needed to make it through the next three days. "I love coming to the cabin, Sam. Why don't we do this more often?" Allison, a young woman of twenty-six, loved coming to the cabin in Havenswood Valley. "I never get more than a run in the park at home, and this kind of weekend makes me wonder why I don't move away from the city. It's so beautiful up here."

"Too beautiful for me," Sam joked. "I enjoy more of the urban lifestyle to keep me sane."

"Sorry, Sam, but I couldn't disagree more. The snow is so pretty it makes me want to pull out the who-wuzits and plee-dunkits for game time tonight." Allison, all 6'1" of her lean self, was thinking of holiday movies, and of course had brought some with her since TV stations were off limits for the weekend. Her softer side was so transparent it made it hard to imagine the intensity she showed on the volleyball court, a passion she excelled at from middle school through college. Long black hair tied tight, bright green eyes focused, she dominated the game and struck fear in her opponents when she went vertical to strike the ball. Yet there was no missing she was nearly as kind to strangers as she was to friends. A simple act of kindness was the norm for Allison, and her brand new job as a nurse was a natural calling.

"Oh, goody" was the only reply Sam could muster up. She wasn't sour on fun, or jokes, she just needed people to dig deeper to reach her humorous side. Lighthearted banter was akin to decaf coffee, the taste is there but there's no kick to get your attention. Pretty much the way Sam, a 5'7" trim yet curvaceous brunette and occasional rock band lead singer summed up her life at the moment. She did well as a Tech Responder for the software company she managed, but there had been a lull at work and she was ready for a boost. She knew her potential was much higher than the current position she held, it was just a matter of gearing up and going after something more challenging.

The cabin tradition fell into place every year, and was a favorite time for all. It started as day trips back when most of the group had been friends in high school, and then turned into overnights in college. Finally, when nearly everyone was out of college the overnights tuned into two night weekends. The friendships grew stronger, and a day or even two was just not enough time together. Even the guys wanted more time to talk, listen, and enjoy being in the company of lifelong friends. Work had become more demanding for most and this long weekend was becoming a cornerstone in their lives. It was something they all needed, for different reasons, and was an experience they could not achieve with anyone else. In fact, no one was allowed to join unless the entire group agreed, which so far had not happened. No one in the group had married, and when girlfriends and boyfriends of the group were informed of the tradition, they were asked to deal with it. Only once, when a particular boyfriend of Sam's drove up to try and crash the gathering, had they needed to really enforce the rule. It got ugly, but Sam enjoyed the outcome. She had wanted to break up with the guy, and relished the opportunity to provide a grand send off. It comes up at some point during each trip, and Sam still smiles when she recalls the applause and hugs her friends gave her as her suddenly ex-boyfriend drove off. The motto still holds fast; friends don't let friends date jerks!

"Hey, let me give you a hand with that." Thomas saw that Nick couldn't get the box all the way to the cabin without spilling the goods onto the ground. Thomas was always one to help out, and it came naturally. He didn't need thanks or praise, it was just something he liked to do. It was part of the reason so many people were drawn to him, and yet Thomas had kept to himself for most of the last year. He had broken up with a longtime girlfriend just before last year's trip, and although he had attended that weekend, he was pretty distant from the group. Over the past year he had focused on his health and well being, and today he looked and felt fantastic. He was in better shape than his basketball playing days, his 6'2" frame, topped with wavy brown hair and enlivened with large brown eyes, had matured well. His gym workout sessions were more body balanced and his eating habits definitely healthy. With a steady job as an apprentice in a financial analyst's office, all was good in the world for Thomas.

"Thanks, this one is heavier than I thought." Nick was losing the strength in his left arm faster than the doctors had initially expected. The impact of the wound had taken a bigger bite than any of the medical staff in Arizona had projected for such a vibrant young man. At 5'10" tall with a solid build and good diet he was a prime candidate for a quicker recovery than most. But something in Nick's blood had turned against him and instead of starting to heal his immune system had started to drain the muscles and tendons of their function. As a delivery driver, he had been wearing a brace lately, but didn't want to wear it this weekend. The rattlesnake bite was a trauma that continued to impact Nick's life, but he would not let it take over how he lived. If he felt down, he'd look at the eight rattles hanging from his key ring and remember that he got the better end of the encounter.

"Holy wardrobe closet, what didn't you bring with you?" Marcus had known Roxie forever. They, along with most of the group, had grown up in the same second ring suburb of Andover Glen, Minnesota and even now lived near one another. They hung out frequently, and although the emotional draw to each other was strong, had decided to keep things at a friendship level, for now. Roxie liked life in black and white, and a gray relationship that might damage their friendship wasn't worth the trade out.

"Just a few hundred pieces of clothing. A girl can never have too much to wear." Roxie's bag was really filled with photo albums she put together from previous cabin trips and a few extra bottles of wine. Roxie, 5' 7" tall and twenty-seven years old, recently took her first trip to California and had fallen in love with a particular Merlot she discovered in Solvang. She had also fallen in lust with a budding wine expert that suggested the bottle to her and Jenna at dinner one night. Her outgoing nature and athletically slender figure, crafted from years of running, must have been as intoxicating to the sommelier. Although nothing romantic took place she ended up with a few extra bottles of wine. Roxie grabbed her shoulder length, dark brown hair and held it in a bun on the top of her head, "Didn't you get the message about dressing for our formal dinner?" and laughed.

"Uh, no, I missed that message. Guess I should have checked my email before I packed," Marcus smiled. He enjoyed social networking, but he'd rather pick up the phone or drive over to talk, face to face. His job as a Parks System Manager kept him in touch with a wide array of personalities, and he loved the vibrant activity that meeting people brought him each day. At twenty-seven he was slightly above average in every way; 5' 11" tall, slim build, healthy looking. The kind of guy that you would want to chill with, and someone the girls had always wanted to date. His wavy brown hair was neatly trimmed, and when he was seen running down a bike path during a workout, car horns were sure to sound. He filled his work day with plenty of internet and phone contact, but the best part was being out in the field working on projects.

The unloading went on like this for an hour or so, everyone pitching in when another member of the group arrived, to help get the food, gear and bedding into the cabin before it got too late. The drive up was fairly short, and with an early start they were unloaded and starting dinner by 4:00 pm. It was going to be a great weekend!

The first to bring up the subject of a spring trip was Jenna, at twenty-eight the oldest of the group. While she enjoyed the fall trip as much as anyone, and since summer was out due to keeping the calendar clear for everyone's personal vacations, Jenna's heart was in spring. Warm weather, new beginnings, all the classic verbiage so often spelled out in magazines and books fit perfectly for this somewhat petite, blonde haired, blue eyed girl. She put up with winter, but longed for a time when she would live in a warmer climate that would be less demanding on her life than the five months of a Minnesota winter. So how would she begin to test the feedback for the group to meet at the cabin in spring? She needed solid reasoning: spring would be a great time of year to be in the woods, the snow would be gone and they could be outside more, explore more. They had always been here in fall, the time when most things are going to sleep, or dying off. To Jenna, fall was an ending, not a beginning. She spoke up, nervous, but to the point. "Has anyone ever thought of coming here in spring? Don't get me wrong, I really like this trip, but we might want to try a different time of year."

"I think it's a great idea!" Jenna was startled by Kevin's response, but he had also been thinking of an additional trip for the group. He would be a spark for this and felt if they tried it, there might be a new chapter in their lives. Kevin, by all respects was a normal, twenty-eight year old guy; book smart, in good shape, 5'8" tall, serious but with a sense of humor. He needed the group more than most of them knew, and he'd do all he could to put this in motion. "I'll check on reservations, timing, you know all the basics." When Kevin was onto something, he wanted to see it all the way through. His thick, somewhat disheveled hairstyle belied how meticulous he really was. Just ask anyone from his office, where he worked as a surveyor for the city. The task matched him perfectly, and everything would be in line, on time and under control. He'd make sure the spring trip happened.

"I'll never stop coming here in the fall. Warm fires, wine, good food, friends, what could be any better?" Allison really did love the last blast of fall.

"It won't be too cold," Nick offered, "and we won't find anything better, it's just that life will get more complicated. Marriage, jobs, kids, stuff we really don't have to deal with right now. Let's check out the spring option."

"You always did like spring break, Nick," said Axel. He liked to stir the pot and joke often with his friends. "Think you can remember much about any of them?"

"Very funny, Axel," Nick replied. "I'm just saying let's see what we can come up with for a trip here in March or April."

The draw to Havenswood Valley was strong. The friends had fallen in love with the area on their first trip and a second season might be just as enjoyable.

"Great! I'll get started when I get back and let you all know what I find out." Kevin was already thinking of places and dates, and would pick their brains throughout the weekend to make sure he had as much info as possible to make plans for a perfect spring trip.

As tides flow high and low, so do the challenges that take place in our lives. Kevin would never get a chance to plan the spring trip, because nature, and other forces at work in the world, make plans no one can reschedule. In less than forty-eight hours, Kevin would not be thinking about trips of any kind. His friends would rewind what had happened during their weekend together at the cabin, trying to come up with answers.

Why one of them? Why Kevin? Why in Heaven's name did it happen at all?

Aglow with the warmth of light and life, the dining area was now filled with food, friends and a touch of frenzy. Located just off the kitchen, the centerpiece of the room was the table. One that, due to its large size and ornate woodwork, had most likely been reassembled inside the cabin after it had been built. The design and craftsmanship was magnificent, and spoke of some distant ancestry that told stories with their hands and tools.

"This table is incredible. It would be the centerpiece of my kitchen." Karen, 5'8" tall with long, auburn colored hair, was already an established marketer in the restaurant business at twenty-eight. She loved the intricate look of this new addition to the cabin.

"It's in great shape. Not like new, more like it's been worn in by plenty of family gatherings," said Roxie.

"Whoever made it, wherever it came from, I'm really thankful it's here. We've never had a table that would fit us all so easily, and even with the centerpiece decoration there's room for all of us and our meals." Allison smiled, "No kids table needed!"

All agreed the table would get plenty of use, and since it was time to prep for dinner everyone began doing their part. Mostly it was the women in the kitchen and getting the rooms ready and the guys doing a variety of outside chores. There was wood to be brought in, the cars had to be rearranged in the parking area, and a general once around the grounds checking on stuff. Guys loved to check on stuff.

Thomas was in the great room starting a fire and making sure the fireplace insert was pushing heat into the room, rather than up the chimney. But Thomas wasn't the only one looking for a way to heat up the room.

"Thomas, you really have a way with the new fireplace. The flames add a wonderful touch to the ambiance." Allison laughed at her over emphasis of ambiance. "Thanks for getting it started."

11

Allison had the makings of a serious crush on Thomas, and while she really did appreciate the fire, her comment was more of a way to see if there would finally be a return volley to her serve.

"My pleasure, *mon ami*, Allison. It's going to be a cold one tonight and the sooner we get the chill out of the room the better. I may end up sleeping in here to keep the fire going. Wouldn't want the inside temp to get too low." Thomas knew Allison had liked him on the trip here last year, and had been thinking about her for some time.

"Sounds cozy. I've got dibs on the couch if the girls' room is too cold." Allison wasn't shy about bringing out her true feelings. She had missed opportunities in the past, and had recently made a pledge to herself that being upfront, to a point, was the way she would lead her life. If she had told her professors her desire to be a doctor, maybe she'd already be in medical school. Allison was building confidence into her lifestyle and wasn't ashamed to act on her convictions.

"Okay, then, I'll make sure the fire keeps the couch area nice and toasty." Thomas liked Allison's idea instantly, and decided that no matter if the new insert kept the room temperature warm or not, he would be camped out on the floor in front of the fireplace tonight. Thomas felt good about his life, and including Allison would be a wonderful addition. He'd waited too long to let her know how he felt, but his decision to wait until they were together at the cabin was the path he had chosen, and in his heart he knew it would work out fine.

"Awesome, Thomas, thanks." What Allison really wanted to say was; It's a date! See you when the room clears out. She smiled and plugged her phone into the sound system Kevin had brought. Music filled the air and the mood within the cabin rose to a new level of harmony, country style.

The headcount was ten for the weekend. Farthest to travel was Karen, who flew in from Sedona, Arizona and had the wildest time getting in. Flight delays, rental car mix up, and the usual traffic heading out of Minneapolis. No problem for Karen. She was a master at making sure she was compensated for her troubles, and picked up a free flight coupon, was upgraded to a new larger vehicle and to celebrate, made an extra stop at a great bakery for, what else, more treats!

"If the rental was smaller I'd buy one as soon as I got home. I love it, but it's just too big for my needs." Karen led off the first group conversation just before dinner, as it was a natural question from Kevin to ask about her travel to the cabin. She continued, "We'll have to head into town tomorrow and you can see what the drive is like. It has room for a bunch of us to go."

"I'd be lost without my truck. All I need is a seat and plenty of hauling space for my work and toys." Nick loved the outdoors, and heading north for a weekend, or out west for a week, was his way of going to church. "Of course you have to respect the comfort of a well built car for a family, but right now I'm a solo cowboy and it's nice to be able to saddle up at a moments notice."

"Yee haw, Tex! Guess the music has got to you. Seriously, Nick, next time you're getting ready to head out on an adventure, give me call, will you? I need a little outdoor time once in a while and I never seem to make plans. Maybe a spur of the moment trip is the best way to make it happen." Thomas was serious, and he hoped Nick would take him up on his offer. They had done a few things together over the years, but it had been a while.

"Me too, Nick. I get bored easily and would love to go," said Sam. She did love the outdoors, and had started to take a liking to Nick, too. He was a sweet guy, smart, and would do anything for you. She'd known him a long time and as of late, when they had met for coffee or gone bowling with friends, she felt more than just friendship for him. Neither one was dating anybody at the time, and she got the feeling Nick was interested in her as much as she was in him.

"All right, looks like I'll have to set up some trips for us." He smiled at Sam, but kept the conversation focused on group expeditions. "Ice fishing should be first on the list, I'll let you all know what to bring for a minus thirty degree night!"

"I may have to miss that event, Nick." Sam gave him a sly look, "Let me know once you set up something hotter." And with that comment she gave him a wink and walked to the kitchen.

"I get the feeling it would be plenty warm if you took Sam ice fishing, Nick." Thomas had gone out with the group a few times and had seen the chemistry starting with Nick and Sam. "Don't let me interrupt travel plans, but I'm still open to a trip some time."

"Uh, sure, uh, no problem, Thomas." Nick wasn't completely stunned by Sam's comment. They had enjoyed each other's company recently, but this was the first time either one had been so direct. The effect of her words would take a while to sink in, but eventually he'd absorb them and break into a smile just thinking about it.

The group gravitated to the table, and in a short time they were seated on a variety of chairs, stools and benches. As was the custom, dinner the first night was simple and this year it had all been prepared at home. There was plenty of food, and as the pasta, sauces, salads and breads were passed around everyone was in a good mood. As they say, you can't pick your family, but you can pick your friends, and they had all made very good choices.

Once the plates were full and the glasses had been filled, the toasts began. With so much to catch up on, every occasion to impart a couple of thanks and good wishes was taken advantage of. Some serious, some funny, but each toast would certainly be from the heart.

CHAPTER

3

It had been the perfect evening of food, conversation and dessert, and afterwards the friends settled into playing cards and relaxing. This year was the first time in three years the entire group of ten had gathered together, so there was plenty of catching up to do. During a lull in conversations, Samantha began a discussion dealing with a very tough subject, directed mainly at the ladies.

"I'd like to say thanks to everyone for the cards and flowers you sent for my mom's funeral." Sam was normally a pretty stoic young woman, having been dealt a few tough blows on the road of life. Her mother, Sandra, had an aneurism after getting out of bed one morning and in a matter of minutes Sam was without her mother. A heartbreaker the others couldn't get their arms around, nor could Sam. "Our whole family went into shock, myself included, and I just went through the motions of getting through the funeral planning, the ceremony and trying to find my way back to normal. It was good to see you come by, but I know I was pretty withdrawn. By the time I was ready to talk about it, I figured I'd see everyone here."

Most of the friends had met Sandra during high school. Sam was a senior when she started hanging with them, and as friends do, they eventually migrated to her home a few times to meet for a night out or grab a meal. The next bit of the evening was spent reminiscing about times at Sam's with her mom. Whether it was a group of kids coming over after a game at school, or just a sleepover, the girls were always welcome. Even the guys could stay pretty late as long as the lights stayed on and it didn't get too quiet downstairs. Senior Prom was the most fun. Sandra had bought each of the girls a picture frame with the words 'Friends Forever' etched in, for pictures of their group. After she died, the girls added photos of themselves with Sandra into their frames.

"Thanks, girls, and guys, I really appreciate this. I didn't know how it would go, but I feel so much better." Sam did feel a true sense of relief. "I know my mom will watch over us all."

Sharing such an emotional experience capped the evening for most of the group. After the talk about Sam's mom, the only parent that had passed on, thoughts about the importance of family and friends settled everyone down.

The bedrooms began to fill up. Marcus, Axel, Nick and Kevin had bunk beds in the first bedroom, leaving two rooms for the girls. Roxie and Jenna shared one, Sam, Karen and Allison took the other. Thomas took the floor near the fireplace. After a batch of good-nights were exchanged, things became pretty quiet inside the cabin. It had been a long day of travel and activity.

"It sure does get dark in here when the lights go out," Allison was looking around the cabin as she was talking with Thomas. Except for the glowing embers in the fireplace and a couple of nightlights, it was pitch black. "Maybe another log on the fire would be a good idea." She had kept her word to Thomas about taking the couch near the fireplace for the night, and was content with this closeness.

During dinner Thomas and Allison had made some time to catch up. They had been in touch a few times during the last three years, but with Thomas having a girlfriend for some of the time, and then being somewhat distant this past year, there was not a lot of meaningful conversation between the two. They had known each other briefly in high school, joining the group at about the same time. Their time together in college had been enjoyable, two years of seeing each other often, but never actually dating one on one. Mainly group outings, sometimes the two of them grabbed a meal or a movie together.

"Got one right here," answered Thomas. "Just big enough to add some light and keep the temp up." He was settled in on the floor, near the couch where Allison had lain down, and placed the log into the fire. Now he, too, was ready for sleep. He'd fall asleep thinking about the time wasted not acting on his feelings for Allison, yet very happy for the opportunity to discover her now as more than a friend, when they were both ready.

"Thanks, Thomas." Allison was smiling now, "Sweet dreams."

"Sweet dreams to you, too." Thomas was calmed by Allison's voice.

Out in the woods, on this quiet fall night, one that had been sprinkled with a quick melting snow, it was very still. No wind, no precipitation, just a dark night when even the summer bugs had long since fled. While most of the friends had fallen asleep due to a long day, a big dinner, a few drinks and the effects of plenty of fresh air, Karen was struggling to slumber. Having flown in from Arizona, she felt the effects of being tossed into a new time zone, and adding in the fact she was in the restaurant business and kept late hours didn't help matters any. It wasn't about the business, her staff was highly qualified so she had little worry over how the *Rojo Mesa* would function during her absence. Nearly a year and a half removed from a serious relationship, and very glad to be so, for some reason she thought about her old boyfriend. Her ex was a nice guy, but they soon realized when both halves of a couple are working in the restaurant biz, it was one half too many. After so many late nights alone they decided it was time to part ways. No kids, no home, they had rented a condo for a couple years, and no fouls called.

At 3:15 am she finally got up and silently made her way through the darkly lit maze of cabin style furniture, in search of some tea. How cozy, thought Karen, as she looked over at Thomas and Allison, now laying along side each other in front of the fireplace hearth. "Maybe some day that will be me and my mystery man," she mused to herself. The embers glowed red and cast an orange light over the two cocoons and extended into the great room. A dim glow filled the kitchen area, and Karen was able to make her way along the last part of the trek. She hoped a quick minute of the microwave heating water would not be too loud to disturb her cabin mates. While searching the pantry for tea bags and a cup, she froze when she heard the noise.

"Who's awake?" whispered Karen. Someone was walking across the floor in the great room. "Who's there?" The noise grew louder but no one answered. "Hey, it's me, Karen. Who's there?" Suddenly she realized the noise that sounded like two people chasing each other was coming from the front porch. Someone else was already up, and Karen smiled while thinking of sharing tea rather than sneaking around on her own. She walked to the large wooden entry door that led to the porch, but felt a chill as she reached for the handle. The door was still locked from inside! Karen jumped back, knowing that none of her friends could be outside...it was someone, or something, else.

"Thomas, Thomas wake up," Karen was trying to stay calm. She had dealt with some rowdy types in the early morning hours at work and this sounded like a couple of locals caught up in scaring the visitors from the city. "Thomas, wake up!"

"Hey, yeah, I'm up, what's going on?" He was groggy, but definitely awake.

"Someone's outside, on the porch," Karen still had one ear tuned into the noise.

"Thomas, what's wrong?" Allison was awake now.

"I don't know. Karen woke me up and said..."

"Someone's on the porch," she finished his sentence. "Listen."

The porch sounded like a chase scene from a crazy cartoon. Back and forth they went and then all of a sudden, it stopped. Deadly quiet.

"You guys extending the party?" Kevin had awakened from the noise. Since the incident, he had become a super light sleeper. His girlfriend of three years had never returned from a quick drive to the local convenience store for a late night snack the two had been craving. She was killed in a car accident and Kevin beat himself up time and again about not going that night. He still didn't sleep well, or for very long. "Who's outside? Did they leave?"

"Don't know, the noise stopped, just now." Karen strained to hear any sound at all.

It was then their hearts nearly stopped. The sound was not loud, not long, just the most eerie, deathly sickening howl they could have ever imagined.

"Oh, my, God...that sound, what is it?" Roxie was leading Jenna into the great room when the incredibly penetrating vibration let loose through the air once again.

"Sounds like someone is killing a wolf by pulling it apart, slowly, piece by piece." Axel was now entering the room, along with Marcus.

"What in the world was that awful noise?" Nick had come into the room with Sam right behind him.

"Listen!" Karen said. "The porch! What about the noise from the porch?"

Everyone strained to listen. Nothing for nearly a minute.

Bam! The front porch exploded with noise and everyone either screamed or tensed up.

Marcus, Axel and Nick ran to the front windows and thought they heard the sound of something running away from the cabin. Whatever was responsible for making the noise was getting away! With a couple of large flood lights on the grounds, it might be possible to see them leaving.

Instinctively, the three pulled open a small area of the shades to look outside and saw a rustle of leaves and twigs and dust moving across the property. The porch was empty and the outside lights were on. They ran for the door, Roxie pulling it open as they approached.

"Geez, what the heck was that?" Nick was scanning the meadow. "I don't see a thing."

"Nothing to see," Axel said. He had jumped off the porch and was looking around the area for tracks. "Nothing here now. Man, that was a double dose of morbid howling and porch busting action. Too bad this place doesn't have cabin-cam."

"Guys, look at this," Marcus was examining the porch. "These stains were not here today. What do you suppose this stuff is?"

Nick went into CSI mode, "Looks like blood, or mud. I don't know but we should wait until daylight to do anything else."

"I don't see any new footprints." Marcus joined in the hunt for tracks and ground clues. "Kinda weird. There are some animal tracks, looks like raccoon, and maybe some dog. Could be a dog was attacked by some raccoons and that's what we heard howling. Can't tell how old they are, but with the snow melt we had, they must be pretty new."

"Well, we didn't really see anything we could identify," Nick recalled, "just motion and dust and leaves flying along the ground. But, the mud, or blood, got up here somehow."

"We know something was on the porch, but what about something being shot onto the porch? Like a bottle rocket? It would have sounded a lot louder at night, and the echo on the porch would make it even louder-er." Axel smiled at his added 'er' for levity.

"Good thought," Kevin said from the doorway. "Maybe they were trying to set up a Halloween prank and it backfired on them. Or, maybe it was a bunch of wild raccoons."

"Guys, come back in! We want to know what you found." Roxie wanted to get everyone in and lock the door. "Come on, everyone is kinda anxious."

"Yeah, we'll be right in," answered Marcus. "I don't see traces of anything other than the animal tracks. The snow didn't stick around long on the warm ground, so tracks would be tough to make, especially at a fast clip by man or animal. Let's check the cars and trucks, take a quick look around then head in and get Karen's story since she was up when it started."

When the three came back in, the group talked about the noises, the mess on the porch and what the three had seen looking out the shades. Was it a den of wolves, or just a couple of rabid raccoons? Maybe it was just some teens getting their Halloween scare on early. No one was convinced either way.

"I am so creeped out right now. Did you hear that cry?" Sam hated the howling. "How are we supposed to sleep tonight?"

"Sleep?" asked Allison. "What about even staying here?"

After a brief discussion it was decided the guys would stand watch, making sure at least two were awake at all times, until daybreak. It was already 4:00 am, so this meant only a few hours of guard duty. Coffee was put on, food was brought out and it became apparent everyone would still be awake at sunrise.

The rolling tires on the hard packed gravel could be heard clearly from inside the cabin, and Marcus knew it must be the sheriff pulling off the long driveway and into a parking spot. Whether it was a bear, raccoons, or some locals pulling a prank, it had been decided a call to the sheriff's office was in order, first thing in the morning. It wasn't the damage that was done, they had figured out the stains were mainly river mud spread all over the porch and could be cleaned off, but the group wanted to do their part and report the incident.

"Good morning, Sheriff, Marcus Jennings. I'm the one who called this morning. Thanks for coming out so quickly."

"Morning, Marcus. Sheriff Glen Anderson. Glad to meet you." A hearty handshake was exchanged between the two. "Pretty quiet around town, so once I got the call I finished up some paperwork and drove on out." Sheriff Anderson enjoyed meeting people and was very personable, especially for a sheriff! After twenty-seven years spent working his way up the ladder, with the last fifteen as sheriff, he knew just about everything that was going on in Havenswood Valley. He wanted to make sure these seasonal visitors were feeling safe.

"Thanks. If you want, I can show you the porch, but whatever you want to do, just let me know. Everyone's still here this morning, so you can talk to whoever you like." Marcus had never needed to call a sheriff before, so he was somewhat nervous, but glad they had called. It was odd to see a sheriff at the cabin. The innocence of the group's trip felt intruded.

"Okay, glad everyone is still here, then. How 'bout we go inside and I get a rundown on last night from everyone? We'll just go through it like it happened, and then I'll have a look around." Sheriff Anderson wasn't in a hurry to rush through this. He'd met some of the kids in the past when they'd come up. Seemed like a nice group, never any trouble or complaints. And they spent a little money in town doing some souvenir and food shopping. If everyone acted like these kids, his job would be a lot easier.

"Sure, come on in." Marcus led the way into the cabin, up the four wooden steps where the sheriff would take a quick glance along the porch and see the mess left from last night.

Didn't seem like much, but Sheriff Anderson would not rush to judgment. Maybe things got out of hand and the renters made such a mess that a sheriffs report would absolve them of any claims by the cabin owner, his good friend Robert. He'd have to consider everything, but for now it was time to hear their story and find out why it was so important for him to drive out.

After introductions, Karen went first. "It was a little after 3:00 am. I had been trying to sleep, but I just wasn't tired enough, or maybe I was overtired. I got up to make some tea in the kitchen, and as I was just about to open the pantry door I heard the noise. I figured it was someone still up, but when I went to the front door and saw it was locked, I woke up Thomas."

"About what time was that, Thomas?"

"3:21 am. I looked at my watch when Karen woke me up, and I remember it because it was three, two, one. Like a countdown."

"Good recall, I'll note that. Karen, did you think that maybe someone from your group here was outside for the night, and the door had locked behind them?" Sheriff Anderson wanted to get the group's thoughts moving away from what they may have already discussed.

"Not really. I didn't think about anything other than the noise outside was something I hadn't heard before and I was scared. Thomas was by the fireplace, so I went over to wake him up." Karen had just reacted last night, and she wasn't about to second guess what she had done.

"Thank, you, Karen." The sheriff was satisfied with her explanation. "I know it must have been frightening at such an early hour. When things like this happen, we all pretty much go with our instincts. Waking Thomas was a good idea."

It was then Thomas' turn, and after his explanation about the events of the early morning, Sheriff Anderson asked him a couple of questions, made some notes and then continued the same process with the entire group. It took about an hour. Amid the calmness in the room, coffee being served and morning snacks placed on the table, Sheriff Anderson realized that something had really rattled this group of kids. Well, young adults, he corrected himself. He'd do his best to sort it out.

"Okay, then, seems like a good time to stretch the legs. I'd like to take a look outside and walk around in the direction where a few of you thought you saw some movement." Sheriff Anderson needed some time to review what he had heard from the group, and getting outside by himself was the best way to do it. Especially if his instincts were right about the howling.

"Marcus, if you, Nick and Alex, I mean Axel, could come with me for a couple minutes as I get started. Thank you all for your time. Once I get back to the office I'll nose around and see if I can pick up on any goings on around town last night. It is getting close to Halloween and if it was some of our local kids messin' around, I'll find out in a hurry."

After a round of thank yous from the group, Sheriff Anderson, Marcus, Nick and Axel headed out to the porch. It took about fifteen minutes of looking over the stains, taking a few photos and a last couple of questions for Sheriff Anderson to shake hands and say goodbye. He'd be looking over the rest of the property on his own. If he did have any more questions, he'd be back.

"Thanks again, Sheriff, we appreciate your time. It's made us all feel a lot better." Marcus was glad the sheriff came out, whatever the reason for the noise and the mess, it was nice to know they had an ally like Sheriff Anderson.

"No problem, just part of my job." And with that the sheriff turned and walked to the meadow. He would spend a good forty minutes looking over the grounds around the cabin and the section of woods where the guys thought they had seen something. Maybe it was a good strong wind, he thought, but it was a direction to work on and the sheriff wanted to do a complete investigation. He'd learned from the best in his early days, and part of that was remembering you just never know when something that looks like wind in the dark can turn into a real, live, critical situation.

Driving back to his office, Sheriff Anderson figured it was nearly twenty-five years ago to the month when the town had experienced a few occurrences that, to this day, were still not fully explained. It was just after his rookie year, and he wasn't allowed into the inner circle of the situation. He knew it was something the mayor, sheriff and others didn't want broadcast any further than their meetings. Rumors were discreetly discussed about a missing person and some sightings and events of travelers from out of the area. It was hushed up very quickly, and never made the sheriff's report. Even when he had become sheriff and took an afternoon to check into it, he found nothing in the files. He wasn't a reporter, so he ended up figuring that without any records, nor anyone to talk with, there was nothing else he could do but forget it. One thing Sheriff Anderson did not need now was a repeat of that kind of situation with this group of vacationers in his town. Especially since the locals depended on tourism, and news of trouble would travel fast should anything happen. That, thought the sheriff, is not going to happen on my watch.

When the guys came back into the cabin, the rest of the group was ready for a short game of twenty questions. "Did the sheriff say anything? Does he have any clues? What does he think it was? Has this happened before? Have there been any murders around here lately?"

The room became quiet with the last question.

"He mainly asked the questions, and, well, we really didn't ask any," Nick replied. "Guess we were trying to answer the best we could and it didn't dawn on us to ask him any. Sorry."

"That's okay. We didn't think about it till two minutes ago. Guess we're still trying to figure out how this works. It's nothing like TV." Allison didn't want the guys to get the impression the rest of the group thought they had goofed up by not getting any info from the sheriff.

"We did learn the sheriff thinks we're telling the truth, and he said the local businesses have given him good reports on us. Plus the fact he's never had to come out here and handle any problems." Marcus relayed to the group.

"If he had to guess," inserted Axel, "he'd bet it was a couple of big raccoons that made the mess. They get pretty aggressive if they know there's food nearby. He said the mud might be from an area the raccoons had been feeding."

"What about that awful howling?" Sam gave herself goose bumps just saying it out loud.

"He wasn't sure," answered Marcus, "but he said things will sound a lot worse and carry farther at night."

"Or farther-er," said Axel to the slightly amused group.

Marcus didn't miss a beat and continued speaking, trying to use the sheriff's exact phrase. "Lots of echo effect in this area, he told us. Makes it sound fuller and, well," he then inserted Sam's favorite word, "creepy."

"Main thing was not to worry, he'd do some digging around town and then check back with us later today. This town's really big on Halloween, maybe it was just a few guys having fun at our expense." Nick knew the others wanted to know what the plan was. "So, we should either hear from him by phone, or if he's able to, he said he'd stop by. If it was some local kids that did this, having the sheriff's car around the area during the day would let them know they're being watched. That should be enough to keep them away for the rest of the weekend."

"Can raccoons read? 'Cause if they see that the sheriff is hanging around, I'm sure they'll high tail it back to the woods." Thomas was trying to spin a little comedy into the situation.

"So if they can't read, they'll be back?" asked Karen.

"Masks and all, I'm sure of it." Thomas appreciated Karen's support of his dry humor. "They're bandits!"

At this point the conversation went downhill fast, but the mood rose to one of fun and adventure for the day. Plans were now being made to fill a warm Saturday afternoon. The weather was predicted to cooperate, with a big helping of clear skies and temps in the upper 60's.

Kevin, Karen, Sam and Nick were going to head out for a walk on the two mile loop. It was a nice path through the area, and with a pair or two of binoculars they were guaranteed to get detailed views of many different birds. The woods provided birds with housing and safety, and the meadows and water were excellent sources for food. Last trip, one of the birder's highlights was identifying a Pileated Woodpecker. Not uncommon to the area, but always a bonus when you see one. Sam brought along her camera in hopes of capturing a few scenic images. With the trees in full fall colors there would be plenty of opportunity.

Marcus, Roxie and Thomas were going to get a run in, somewhere around six miles at a medium pace. It was so nice to run in this valley, and they were in no hurry to get back. Marcus had his GPS with him, so they were free to take any path and still be able to track their mileage and pace. All were seasoned runners, and enjoyed running in local events, everything from 5k's to marathons.

Allison and Jenna would head into town. Axel, who always enjoyed hanging with Jenna, went along as driver. They'd pick up a few more things for dinner and probably take time to grab a snack. These two girls especially loved milling around the small town of Havenswood Valley, which had been settled in 1858. Many of the downtown buildings, circa early 1900's, were still in great shape and now served as home to a variety of businesses, shops and restaurants. The trio would spend a couple of hours kicking around after they did their supply shopping, then head back to the cabin.

The roads they drove into town were filled with leaf hunters looking for the perfect grove of trees, or possibly that perfect tree, to photograph or just admire. The Stonebrook Apple Farm was a popular stop in town on a day like this. Freshly harvested apples were sold by the bag, and it appeared that everyone in town had a tan, S.A.F. re-useable shopping tote with them. Allison, Jenna and Axel made sure they had plenty of apples to bring back to the cabin, along with two perfect apple pies.

"This town is so cool! I really like coming in, even if it's just to look around. I wish we had something like this where I live." Jenna lived in a suburb without an original downtown business district and loved seeing Havenswood Valley still using such old buildings for everyday use.

"I know. There's just something comforting about an old downtown area. And I can't believe how cool all the Halloween decorations are! They look so authentic, not like all the plastic stuff we see back home." Allison loved the small town feel that came from a century of mixing the original settlement buildings made from stone, brick and lumber with a dedication to town events, holidays and traditions. Sections of the street had been peeled back to expose original brick set in place decades ago. The old growth trees capped sections of the city, matching the height of the church steeples and creating a beautiful canopy.

"Hey, check out that shop over there! Looks like one we should go to." The eclectic, hand painted sign above it's doorway caught Axel's eye as they were headed to the grocery store. "Tres Azure. Let's stop in on our way out."

"Sure," was the dual reply from Jenna and Allison.

It was a quick shopping stop for the cabin supplies, which allowed them extra time for lunch and an excursion of their own. They ordered to-go at the Firehouse Diner, then walked along the stone and brick sidewalk while they ate. A block down the street they came to the Tres Azure store and walked in, Axel holding the leaded glass door open. As they entered, the scent of burning incense was the first thing to trigger their senses, followed quickly by the background sound of 1950's jazz. The three friends stood in place, soaking up the incredible mixtures of sights, sounds and scents.

"Welcome to Tres Azure! The music is very blue, with treasures all around. Thank you for coming in!" Norma loved greeting new customers. "Please, take your time. If you have any questions on our offerings, or if you are in search for something in particular, come and let me know." This usually put her guests at ease, and allowed them the freedom to browse the shop at their own pace.

"Thanks. It was your storefront that captured our attention." Allison loved unique shops. "We didn't see it last trip, and figured a new store meant we had to stop and see what it was all about."

"Wonderful! Yes, we are fairly new, just under a year in Havenswood Valley. We fell in love with the downtown area long ago and knew it was a natural location for what we wanted to do." Norma did love the town, and most anyone that came in felt her store was a perfect fit. "I hope you enjoy your experience."

Tres Azure

Inside our minds, time does not exist. It is a product of the external environment we inhabit allowing various omissions of context as we move through our daily lives. In turn, time will raise questions to ponder as we simply try to recall a recent event. It happened in an instant as three friends left the confines of a small shop in downtown Havenswood Valley, on what was, up to that time, a perfectly normal day.

"How can it be nearly five o'clock?" asked Axel. "We were only in there a few minutes."

"No way it's almost five! I looked at my phone when we walked in and it said three forty-seven," added Jenna. "What's going on?"

"I don't know, and right now I don't care," Allison bit her lip to control the anxiety that was creeping into her central nervous system. "It's getting late. Let's get out of here and back to the cabin."

Allison was still in a fog as Axel steered into the parking area at the cabin, feeling as if the car had driven itself back. All the while her head had been spinning, trying to remember what had happened. She recalls the three had walked into the new store on Main Street, Tres Azure, and while they had enjoyed looking around, had, it seemed, not spent more that fifteen minutes inside. Once out, she remembers they all talked about how freaky the store owner was, that they had felt uncomfortable inside, and had no intentions on going back to the store.

"I feel like I'm trying to remember a dream, but I can't get all the details back. I know we went in the store, bought a few things, then left. It couldn't have been more than fifteen or twenty minutes." Allison headed to the cabin, her head beginning to ache. "What happened in there?" she asked out loud.

"In where?" Marcus was sitting on the porch and answered Allison.

"Huh?" Allison looked up and saw Marcus. Seeing him brought her some clarity, her mind beginning to bring things into focus. Marcus had come to be a confidant in Allison's life. Just being near him poured a dose of calm and comfort into her soul.

"You said, 'What happened in there?', and I asked, in where?" Marcus looked at the trio as though they had just ejected themselves out of a local pub. They walked kind of wobbly, and had been gone longer than everyone figured. "We were beginning to worry about you guys. You said you'd be back at four o'clock, and it's well after five. Too much fun in town?"

"Sorry, dude, but we were kidnapped by a crazy woman. I think she held us captive without us even knowing it." Axel was all over the lost hour and wanted to talk about what had happened. He walked past Marcus and was already briefing the group when Jenna and Allison walked into the room with Marcus.

"Jenna, Allison, what the heck is Axel talking about? Are you guys all okay?" asked Kevin.

"Yeah, this is no time to go bonkers on us after last night," said Thomas. "Only one scary event per weekend allowed."

"Sorry, I'm still trying to figure out what happened," replied Allison. "I just lost an hour this afternoon, and I do mean lost. I can't say why, but I do know it wasn't because I was drinking the afternoon away."

"I know what happened. We walked into the store, the incense made us pass out, and that lady brainwashed us for an hour." Axel had an explanation all set. "We bought things we didn't even want, and I bet she programmed our brains to shop there when we hear certain words."

"Axel, come on, you know that didn't happen. Think back guys, what exactly do you remember?" Kevin wanted to get a clear picture of the shopping experience. He had been through enough tragedy for someone so young, and was always ready to lend a hand when others were in need or distress. Kevin did not sweat the little stuff, and always found a way to help out when big things did arise.

The three downtowners took turns explaining what they remembered, finally piecing together a time line they could agree on. Trouble was they kept coming up short on time, losing about forty-five minutes with their scenarios.

"Let me ask a question, because I see a gap in your story. Each version has you walking into the store, being greeted by the owner, buying something, and then being outside and talking about the eccentric owner." Sam had a way of cutting through the mud, literally, and getting to the bottom of a situation. Working for a software company in a management position kept her on her toes, and troubleshooting was a daily challenge. "Am I correct?"

"Yes, your honor, I plead guilty," was the reply from Axel. "And I am sure my co-defendants will concur." Allison and Jenna laughed and smiled in agreement. Everyone loved Axel, and even though he would take off too quickly on some tangent, his heart was in the right place. Any time you needed help, Axel would come to the rescue.

"Thank you, if I may continue. Ladies and gentleman of the jury," Sam addressed the group, "we have heard testimony about a shopping experience at a local business. A visit inside that was short, yet did allow for a few items to be bought, however we are not hearing the entire story. We did not hear about an exchange of monetary tender, so how could these purchases have been made?" Sam was warming up now.

"Nor is there any discussion about how this group exited the premises once their transaction was complete." Sam continued, "I therefore deduce these items were not actually purchased at the store, but were instead stolen from Tres Azure!"

"Heresay!" yelled Jenna.

"You'll never take me alive, Copper!" added Axel.

"Holy crap, Sam, I think you're right!" Allison was trying to focus. She shut her eyes and tried to trace her steps backwards, talking out loud. "We were excited about the new store, and the sign outside made it look enticing before we even went in. I remember the owner greeting us, the smell of incense and then, barely, I see us looking at some items in the store. Then the owner is helping us learn about the stuff we are looking at." Allison stood up and began acting out her recollection.

"Oh my God, Allison, she did help us!" Jenna stood up, walked over to Allison, and grabbed her left arm, "Norma came over and took your arm, just like this, looked you in the eyes and said something to you I couldn't fully understand."

"Norma?" asked Thomas.

"That's right, that's the owners' name! I couldn't think of it for the life of me until Jenna just said it," said Axel. "Then Norma talked to Jenna for a minute, and then, oh jeez, I can see her eyes like she was right in front of me, staring at me...son of a gun...I've got goose bumps talking about this."

"Sam, I think you're on the right track." Marcus wanted to keep the flow of this conversation going, and he was right, Sam was getting somewhere.

"At this point," Sam jumped back in, "we have our three heroes standing in the store, with few, or possibly no other customers in the store, leaving the villain, Norma, in full control over Jenna, Allison and Axel. And when I say full control, I'm talking about our friends here being hypnotized by this freaky owner!"

"No way!" said Nick. "You guys are pulling our legs and I'm ready for dinner."

"Me too, I know we had a rough night, but come on, this isn't downtown Weirdville. You three and Sam have had enough fun with this." Karen was also ready for dinner and knew they would have to come clean soon, otherwise this act would get old quickly. She walked to the kitchen to help with dinner.

"I'm neutral, but I'm hungry, too." Roxie joined Karen in the kitchen, with Nick and Thomas.

"Sam, come on, are you serious?" Kevin was willing, but not able, to buy into Sam's explanation. The practical side of Kevin's brain kept him from getting in too deep, too soon. "I know some people can do this, some kind of momentary mental eclipse, similar to being hypnotized, but isn't that pretty daring for a small store in a tourist town?"

"I have no idea, Kevin, I'm just going on a tangent and seeing where these three lead us." Sam wasn't sure either way, but she kept on and turned back to Jenna. "Jenna, I think Norma had you three pegged the minute you walked in. Since you were the only ones in there, she had a free game to play."

"So let's say this lady can put us in a short, hypnotic trance, if you will. What's she got to gain? We bought three little oddities in there. If we were totally conscious, maybe we would have spent even more?" Allison was now sitting and had closed her eyes again to get her thoughts back on track. "I don't see any value in her doing this to us."

Kevin was the first to answer, "Maybe she was bored and wanted to have some fun, or to keep her skills up."

"I could see that. A small town, quiet day in the off season," concluded Marcus. "She sees three healthy young adults come in, doesn't see any harm in honing her techniques and does her thing. She knows it will wear off soon and no one will be hurt."

"So we didn't steal the stuff," Axel surmised. "Norma just jolted our brains, had some fun, maybe made us do something goofy and then we left."

Sam was a couple of steps ahead of Axel, "Maybe, but I'm feeling she did want to use her mental skills on you three, but not for fun. As Kevin said, in a small town that relies on tourists, it's a risk she couldn't afford if word got out she was hypnotizing customers. Can you imaging the implications, the lawsuits? And what if Norma had been a 'Norman' - some psycho guy hypnotizing women?"

"He would have taken us up the hill to see his mother in her rocking chair." Axel squealed; "Eeee, eeee, eeee, eeee!," and stoked a good laugh to lighten up the mood.

"Nice, Axel, I guess you'd be right," Sam continued with a smile on her face. "So, let's say she knows the risk, but does this anyway. Why are you three so special? And what the heck did you end up buying?"

The three hadn't shown their purchases yet, and up to now hadn't thought about them. The trip, the drive home, it was all much more impactful than the actual purchases they had made. They each pulled out small bags to show the others.

"Well, here's what I bought," Jenna had hers in a Tres Azure paper bag that was decorated in the same design and colors as the sign on the front of the store. Bold yet muted colors, an almost custom font for the words Tres Azure and a woven, hemp-like handle.

Jenna held out her hand and in it was a small, metallic orb, about the size of a baseball. "Wow, this is really cool. I don't even remember picking this out." There were etchings around the entire surface, as well as a thin ribbon of die cut metal along the middle, like an equator, where the ball would open up when unlatched.

"Me either." Allison was holding up a metal figurine, possibly made of tin, something that would be described best as from the

1700's. It wasn't a doll, but it held enough features to mimic some kind of person. About ten inches tall, it looked like a decoration or symbolic item of some type of group.

"What in the world did I buy?" Axel was truly perplexed, as was the rest of the group. It had five very old looking keys, connected by a ring to a rectangular block of dark wood. Possibly used to open the strangest locks you could imagine. On the other hand, it might have been a Swiss Army knife before there was a Swiss Army knife.

"I have an idea," offered Sam. "Each of you hold your item, stare at it for a minute, then close your eyes and think about Norma and when she first approached you. Like Jenna said, when she came over and touched Allison. See if that triggers anything."

"Great idea, Sam." Marcus liked this approach. "We'll just sit back and watch."

"I'll check on dinner," offered Kevin. He left the room, not sure what to think.

Jenna, Allison and Axel felt weird, but did as Sam suggested. They held up the items and just, well, just stared at them. Looked at them closely, held them, felt them and even smelled them. "It's been three minutes," said Sam, quietly, "now close your eyes, picture your item, and then recall Norma as she came to you. See what that brings."

It was less than thirty seconds and Allison started to cry, softly at first. Jenna began to sniff at her item, and Axel started coughing and fell to the floor. Jenna started to wobble and wave her left arm like a traffic cop! Allison's crying became louder and at this point the entire group was in the great room, watching in disbelief. No one in the room was prepared for these reactions.

Thomas was the first to approach Allison. "Allison…Allison, everything's good, you're here with friends. Don't cry." He put his arms around her and began to gently rock her awake. "Allison, open your eyes, it's Thomas." Thomas was now a believer that the three had been through something in town, and he couldn't wait to drive in and have a talk with Norma.

At the same time, Marcus pulled Axel to his feet and Sam got Jenna to open her eyes.

"Hey, this is way too weird," Nick stated the obvious. "We have got to call the sheriff back and put in a report on this lady at the store. What in the world did she do to these three?"

Allison, Jenna and Axel looked at each other, and in unison burst out laughing! A really deep, nerve releasing laugh session that brought tears to their eyes instantly.

"I closed my eyes and thought this was just stupid, no offense, Sam, but we're not bringing back the dead here tonight." Allison could hardly talk.

"I knew you were faking it, but all I could think of was to act drunk," were the words Jenna could barely get out.

"You two left me nothing, I coughed because I was going to laugh if I did anything else," Axel could hardly see through the tears that filled his eyes.

"You jerks!" Sam laughed.

By now, everyone was laughing! It was like a scene out of a bad scary movie. The absurdity of it even got to Sam. It was a good release for everyone and they joked about it as they all helped pull dinner together. Time now to relax, feast on some steaks and discuss other topics over beer, wine and dessert. There would be plenty of time to think about the hypnotic lady at Tres Azure later.

CHAPTER

7

Whether it was a light breakfast or a multi course dinner, every meal at the cabin was heartily enjoyed by the group. Preparing a meal was a social event from start to finish, with the group taking their time to enjoy the process. Over the years they had perfected this ritual, with everyone taking part in one way or another.

"It sure is nice that everyone helps out with dinner. I've been to some gatherings and it's women doing all the chores and the guys watch TV or hang out and drink beer." Sam was eager to help, and enjoyed the fact meals were a group effort. Everything went quicker when they all participated, but it was more than just having everyone help, it had become part of the bonding this group enjoyed.

"I think it's changed a lot over the years," Kevin said. "Helping out is pretty much the way I was raised, so that's what I do. I don't understand when guys think it's beyond them to help. Heck, some of the best chefs in the world are men and they certainly know how to cook and clean."

"No doubt about it, my favorite part is the eating and drinking," said Thomas, "but it only seems fair to help with the prep and clean up. It's no big deal."

"Speaking of dealing, are we playing Girls Always Win tonight?" asked Roxie. "I haven't been able to play that game in a long time."

"Sounds good to me!" answered Allison.

"Only if we get to play charades afterwards!" It was Nick's favorite party game.

The day had been a full one, filled to the brim with activities. An early start, a busy afternoon with some weirdness tossed in, and now a great dinner with lively discussions, lots of laughter and not a word about the oddities of the previous night or this afternoon. Plenty of time left for playing games and having a normal evening.

"All done here at the sink! Time to step outside and catch sunset by the tail." Thomas and some of the others had noticed the sun was about to set as they were drying the last of the pots and pans from dinner. "The long shadows of fall are here, let's watch them stretch out."

"The golden time of day, my favorite hour to be outside," offered Marcus. "I've been in a few places across the country at this time of year and it's amazing how different it is, yet how similar. So many people think you need to be on a coast to get the fullness of a sunset, but I think an inland sunset during fall is pretty tough to beat. One of my most memorable was in, of all places, South Dakota. Just outside of Mitchell, where the world famous Corn Palace is located. There are acres and acres of sunflower plants that just glow under these golden rays."

"The desert, now that's an awesome sunset!" countered Karen. "Such vivid colors, long views, stark contrast between the sand, rocks, sun and sky. And when there are clouds, oh my gosh it's incredible." Her words convinced at least one person in the group to think more about Arizona.

"I've never seen a desert sunset, sounds like something I should put into my travel plans." Although Kevin was speaking to the group, the words were meant for Karen. It was no secret the group had seen certain members melding into couples. There had been closeness between some of them in the past, but this weekend everyone seemed more mature, more inclined to express feelings they had held back. Karen and Kevin had spent most of the day together, first during the walk with Sam and Nick, and then later the two put a lunch together and enjoyed relaxing near the stream.

"It's a pretty easy flight to Phoenix, unless of course your flights are delayed and the rental car you reserved has been rented out already." Karen gave Kevin a warm smile, it was an offer he would eventually take her up on.

"Sounds like it would be worth it, I'd take my chances." Kevin returned Karen's smile, his flight was as good as booked.

"What about a bonfire tonight?" asked Jenna.

"Oh yeah, we've got to do a bonfire," Nick loved bonfires. It was a love-hate relationship now, due to his encounter outside of

Tucson. "Of course, someone else will have to grab the wood from the stack. If I even get a glimpse of a piece that looks like a snake, I'll have a heart attack!" Nick and Thomas had been out to visit Karen and do some hiking for a weekend during the spring, and they had built a nice bonfire one evening. Everything was going fine until Nick walked over to grab a few logs to put on the fire. As he reached down, a log literally sprang to life and pierced Nick's skin with its fangs, deep into his right forearm. It had been months since the bite, but his arm looked worse, not better.

"Gotta watch out for those live logs," joked Thomas. "Never know when they'll magically come to life!" Thomas was one person that could let a remark fly and no one would take offense. Nick knew he was kidding, and the subject was over and done with in two quick retorts. No one knew what was going to happen to Nick's arm, but a little humor was the best medicine for now. The two shared a respect for each other that went back to their high school days. They both loved the outdoors, and knew a sudden, life changing accident could happen to even a seasoned outdoorsman.

"Yeah, yeah, I get the hint. I'll start the fire." Axel was fine with being the designated bonfire starter, "I'm kind of a pyro anyway."

"Word must be getting out already about the bonfire, looks like we have company coming to crash our party, or stop it. Is that the sheriffs' car?" Marcus had been looking at the sunset, which is the same direction as the county road. He saw the vehicle as soon as it turned onto the long driveway that led to the cabin.

"That is the sheriff, and it looks like he has some friends in the car with him." Nick could pick out a small doe in thick woods, so seeing a passenger was matter of fact. "Maybe they caught someone from last night."

"Wouldn't doubt it," added Thomas, "not many places to hide in Havenswood Valley." It was the sheriff, and he did have company, but it wasn't the rowdy locals they had expected.

The headlights were still on as the squad pulled up to park, and the brightness caused a momentary blinding of everyone on or near the porch. Between the sun sitting low in the sky and the headlights beaming, eyesight among the group was, at the least, like trying to look at skiers on a sunny, snow covered slope without wearing sunglasses. Watery eyes with hazy vision and what looks like yellowish dots floating in the air make for a tough ID at forty paces. About all anyone could make out were the three silhouettes, but only the sheriff was moving.

"Good evening, folks. Sorry about the lights, those halogens are murder on the eyes." Sheriff Anderson was always sure to put the people he served at ease, even temporary constituents. He had learned that speaking with someone in a non-confrontational way would gain him more knowledge than a heavy handed approach. He had also learned over the years to address people with respect for as long as they deserved it, but not a minute longer.

"Wanted to get out here earlier today, but I had to follow up on a few pending items. Hope you don't mind me stopping out tonight. So, I've got some things to talk with you about, and a couple people for you to meet and, well, listen to a few things they have to say. Won't take too long and we'll be on our way. Okay with you, Marcus?"

Marcus could see better now, as could everyone else, and was already scanning the people standing next to the squad car. However, with the sun so low behind them, they looked more like one-dimensional cutouts, not people.

"Of course, Sheriff, anything works for us. We were about to start a bonfire but could move inside if you like."

"Thanks, Marcus. I think on a Saturday night like this, on vacation, a bonfire is something you really have to do. It's going to be clear skies, a light wind. Perfect for a nice group like you have here to be outdoors for a while. Why don't you go ahead and get the fire started, once it's going we'll talk."

"That's my cue," said Axel. "Jenna, do you think you and Thomas could give me a hand with some of the wood by the pole barn? I cut up some kindling earlier. We can get that and some logs for the fire."

"Sure," they replied.

"I'll help, too." Allison followed the trio to the stacks of split wood.

Sheriff Anderson walked back to his squad car and spoke with the two people he had brought with him. They hesitated, but joined him as he headed back to the fire pit.

"Everyone, this is Norma Brookings, owner of Tres Azure, one of our shops in town. And this is Robert Washburn, he owns this land and used to live here. They are not involved, directly, with what happened here last night, but there is something I'd like all of you to know about, and these two are the best way to give you the message."

Marcus wasn't sure what to say. "Sure" was all he could muster. The others at the fire pit nodded their heads in agreement, not sure what to make of the request. They figured the sheriff had found the kids that had come out to scare the group, and was making them drive out and apologize to the cabin group. Never would they have thought the hypnotic lady from Tres Azure would make an appearance. Especially when the four wood collectors walked up to the fire!

"Hey! What is she doing here?" Jenna yelled as she came closer to the fire pit, her arms full of wood.

"It's Norma, from the store today!" Axel exclaimed. "Sheriff, did Norma come here last night to scare us away?"

The sheriff remained calm. He knew from speaking with Norma there would be reactions to her presence.

Allison came into the fire pit area last and stopped cold as she noticed who it was. "Why is she here?" And with that comment Allison dumped her load of wood at Axels' feet, one piece tipping over and hitting his ankle.

It took a few seconds to settle Axel down, no damage was done, and it was more of a nervous reaction to Norma than being hurt. A nice diversion nonetheless from the discussion the sheriff would soon be having with the group. Much as he'd rather not be here on this night, it was his duty, and some would say his obligation, to reveal a chapter of Havenswood Valley history only a select few people even knew about. He was going to open up the proverbial can of worms, and he felt about as confident as a fat turkey in early November that everything would go smoothly.

No time like the present, he thought, and as the fire began to warm the group, Sheriff Glen Anderson started a discussion that could never be taken back. It had been a real event, and now the people gathered before him would be informed of the secrecies of a twenty-five-year-old murder that the police had not been able to publicly solve. A murder that Norma and Robert, the only other surviving persons involved in the inner circle, knew would never be investigated in the manner it truly needed. There would be no CSI, no FBI, and certainly no local investigative reporter. It was a cold, hard fact, that the murder Sheriff Anderson was about to reveal was much more than a killing. It was a warning. Norma and Robert understood, now, but back then they were frightened and would not believe what they felt in their gut. Each would regret it forever.

"This morning, after I came out to meet with you all about the noises you heard last night, and the mess on the porch of the cabin, I said I'd get back to you with anything I found out." The sheriff was standing, facing everyone as they were mostly seated around the fire pit. "Everyone is still here, and at the fire, am I correct?" he asked to no one in particular.

"Yes, Sheriff, everyone's here," answered Kevin.

"Good, thank you. Before I introduce the two people I brought with me, I have to ask a favor. What I'm going to discuss took place over twenty-five years ago, just as I began my service in the sheriff's department. Early on the event was rarely talked about. Eventually I got to know Robert and then Norma, and after I became Sheriff we began our own investigation. The favor I ask is that you keep this information among your group. I can't legally stop you from talking about the details, but I'm confident you'll be discreet."

The fire was burning nicely, and the light danced among the crowd and trees, giving the impression of movement in the woods. The outside area of the cabin had been cleared for the parking area, and then the expanded fire pit. It could easily fit twenty people. The fire pit was made of field stone stacked two feet high and four feet across. Circling the ring was a layer of river rock that meshed with the firm red soil of the natural ground. You could park and walk either to the right and up to the cabin, or left and to the fire ring or the pole barn and back door of the cabin. To the far left, past the fire ring, was a large field, about half the size of a football field. Great for a family day of playing games and a nice buffer from the woods that surrounded the rest of the cabin. From the two lane highway you could see the cabin and field for about thirty feet, but everything else was woods. Quiet, secluded, and currently becoming increasingly creepy to the weekend guests.

"It would have been easy to come here tonight and tell you we had rabid raccoons, or cougars, or bears and that you'd have to evacuate immediately, no questions asked. But that wasn't the case. I poked around town, stopping into shops and restaurants, asking if anyone had been hassled the night before by any of the locals, and ended up at the same place a few of you did today, Tres Azure. It was after you three had been in, and while I stepped into the store as a sheriff, I left realizing there were some things in this world that a simple sheriff has no business dealing with."

"Sheriff, we were pretty scared last night," interrupted Thomas, "so if this is your way of saying gotcha, I'd rather you pass on the drama and let us get on with our bonfire."

"Patience is a price we must all pay, son," offered the tall, stoic man the sheriff had brought with him. "It's a wise investment for each of you tonight. Listen first, and then ask your questions."

The group became rigid, not with fear, but with respect, and maybe a little bit of fear. Who was this man, and what was going on? Was this an elaborate trick to frighten them again, or was the sheriff serious?

"Thank you, Robert" said the sheriff. "As I was saying…"

"Excuse me, Sheriff." Marcus stood up off the ledge he had been leaning against. "I agree with Thomas, this is pretty dramatic, especially after last night. We're here to relax and enjoy a weekend together. If this is a Halloween prank just let us know so we can have the rest of the night to ourselves."

Sheriff Anderson paused for a moment. It was cricket-free silence, even the fire was holding back the usual crackling of burning wood. Thomas and Marcus had just called out a sheriff, in front of the group and the two people he had brought with him. It was a pretty bold move for both of them, and the group wasn't sure what would happen next.

"Thomas, I'd like to say that I applaud you for speaking up. Yes, you did have a scare last night, and while it might seem like too much drama tonight, I assure you I'm speaking from the heart and I have no intention of messing with you and your friends. Marcus, I'm glad you also spoke up with your concerns, and I repeat, my message tonight is something that is true and affects everyone here. It definitely is not a Halloween prank."

"I'm ready to hear more," Roxie was very interested in getting to the bottom of the sheriffs discussion. "Sheriff, please continue and we'll do our best to listen and hold our questions until you're finished."

"Yeah," said Sam, "let's hear the whole story."

"Okay, then, I'll continue, thank you." They were now as attentive as if they were in a college class waiting to hear clues to an upcoming test. On the edge of their seats and positioned around the fire pit, everyone, including Norma and Robert, was full of anticipation as the sheriff started the story once again.

"I was in my second year on the Havenswood Valley Sheriff's Department, low man on the totem pole. That meant when anything happened that needed to be kept real quiet, I was not included in the briefings. The Sheriff's Department had a small inner circle that included the sheriff, and one Senior Deputy, so I do mean a small inner circle. It was no surprise, then, that when the missing person report came in it was handled by the sheriff, and he was the one who conducted the interviews and put out the press release." Sheriff Anderson stood up and started pacing as he spoke.

"It happened so quickly, my head was spinning trying to keep up. The report came in, the release of information was made public, and the boy was found. All told, it was about thirty-six hours from the report to the recovery. Cause of death was listed as drowning in the stream not far from here, and that was pretty much the end of the police work." Sheriff Anderson sat back down and paused a minute before continuing.

"I've never forgotten about it, and like I said earlier, even tried to open the case back up but there wasn't anything to go on. I guess I felt like the real truth was never told because we had a few things happen around that time that could have been connected to the death. The resolution just seemed incomplete, so once in a while Robert and I would get together, then when Norma moved back the three of us started working on the details. This area, very nearby, was where we set up the search team for the boy and it was where the body was brought once found."

"Oh my God," a loud whisper came from Allison, "did we have a ghost here last night?"

"I'm never going to be able to sleep tonight" said Karen in a soft voice.

"Not right here, mind you, but nearby. We were over near the meadow, where the stone wall is located. I believe the stones are the last remnants of the original 1867 old log home, is that right Robert?"

"Yes, Glen, that is correct." The tall man was short on words.

"So, then, all we knew for certain, up until today, was that a boy had fallen into the stream, drowned, and his body had been recovered. Found mainly because of Emily Brookings, Norma's mother. She was called in to help because she was a seer, and had been successful finding people on other occasions. Being able to find the boy as only a seer can, she told the sheriff where to look. At the time I thought we just got lucky and found him. Now I know different. Back then I wondered why there wasn't more information put out about the accident, but it wasn't my place to question how to handle the situation. I did hear talk about some strange events around town, but every time the discussions started, the sheriff would close his door or he'd move outside. I received very little information on the case."

"What about the boy's parents, didn't they want to know more? Why didn't you tell them you thought something was wrong?" questioned Nick. Everyone was thinking the same thing, but Nick was the first to bring it out in the open.

"No excuses, but I was young and figured I was way off base. The boy's mother was dead, God rest her soul, and his father was still in mourning for his wife. Now with the boy gone, he was devastated and there was no way I would chance talking with him about something I had no proof of. Sorry, Robert, but I had no appreciation for what you were going through, otherwise I would have come to you with what little I did know."

Everyone turned to look at the tall man named Robert. It was his son they were talking about! No one could breath.

"Sheriff, I hold no grudge against you. There was not a clue that pointed to anything other than a drowning had occurred." Robert was calm and found a chair to sit in. "I withdrew, and had I been of stronger will then maybe we could have worked together and found the true cause of my son Michael's' death."

"Thanks, Robert" replied the sheriff. "Why don't you go ahead with your story?"

Robert Washburn was tall, thin and very solid for a man of 60 years old. He'd worked most of his life outdoors, was never still for too long and took excellent care of himself. His diet was basic, as was his way of life. Losing a wife at age 30, after five years of marriage, and then your only child five years later, will put the brakes on nearly every emotion a man has. He still had a big heart, and gave generously to church and community, but the organ that pumped blood and oxygen through his body was only that, an organ. He hadn't cried in twenty-five years, not because he didn't want to, but because his heart, his emotional heart, was crushed like limestone under the weight of a ten ton road roller.

His life had turned into a long journey to reunite with his wife and son one day in heaven, but he was a man of God and would not bring himself to take the shortcut of suicide. Robert now kept to himself most of the time. After he worked out a rental deal for his cabin and farmland with a local realtor, there was enough income to retire. He didn't leave his small, downtown house much. Once in a while he'd walk to the bank and deposit a rental check. As part of the sales agreement, and while Robert was alive, no further development could be made to the farmland, only planting and harvesting. Only the cabin rental, some organic farming and the occasional tree harvesting were options.

Tonight, however, Robert had left the comfort and solace of his home to join Sheriff Anderson and Norma to meet with the group that had rented the cabin for the weekend. His life had been changed on this very land due to a strange night so many years ago, and it was his hope to help keep his personal nightmare from entering the lives of others.

"I'd like to say to each of you here tonight, twenty-five years ago I had no interest in much beyond my faith, family, and farming. I was a pretty simple man and saw most things in black and white, good and bad, right and wrong." Everyone was at least breathing again and listening intently to Robert. "Sometimes we get dealt a tough hand, and when I lost my wife, Ellen, God rest her soul, I figured it was my cross to bear. My duty was to raise our son Michael as best I could, and hope he would grow to be the man his mother knew he could be. It wasn't going to be easy, but I had the inner strength of Ellen with me and I knew things would be fine. I couldn't have been more wrong."

"I look at each of you here tonight, and you all look so young, so innocent. All I can say is that you must open your eyes to more than you see. Things will happen, and if you don't see, I mean really see what is out there, you'll spend most of your life missing half of what the world has to offer. If I hadn't been so stubborn, so limited in what I would open up and accept in life, maybe Michael would still be here."

Now Robert had to take a breath, he was showing more emotion than he wanted to. "Good and bad is out there, and if you wear blinders every day, some time when you least expect it the bad side of life is going to take away that which is most important to you. For me, it was my son Michael, my only child and the son my wife Ellen and I had together. Yes, he did drown, but how he came to be in the stream, how he came to be outside at all is no mystery. It was evil."

Robert was finished talking, the sheriff knew him well enough to know. "Thank you, Robert, I know this is tough for you to call up such a terrible event from your past. I will always wonder if I, too, could have done more to help save Michael." Sheriff Anderson started to explain more of what has happened since. "So, then, over the years Robert, Norma and I have talked and met about the night Michael died. We had felt there was something else going on, and after having spoken with Robert and Norma about last night, it was decided we would come together this evening and discuss the drowning with you. I realize that although you made plans to be here based on friendship, this area has a draw that can only be explained as, uhmm, let me find a proper way to say this. This area of Havenswood Valley can best be described as, well, captured by evil."

This comment from Sheriff Anderson took the group by surprise. While it seemed at first to be a joke, he and his guests were not even close to laughing. It had exactly the opposite effect, in fact. The cabin group shifted in their chairs, some stood up, and others scooted closer to the fire. Everyone was feeling the weird mood that had enveloped the bonfire. With a very dark night coming up, they were anxious to get to bed behind the thick, wooden, locked doors of the cabin.

"So, then, you've heard some background from me and Robert on the night of Michael's' sudden death. Now we'll fill you in on how this connects with last night and this area in general. At least, how we feel it connects. I'd like to officially introduce Norma. As you know, she owns Tres Azure, and grew up here until about age seventeen. Her mother, well, I'll let Norma explain."

Norma looked at the group and smiled, a younger version of her mother, Emily Brookings, a woman that had lived in Havenswood Valley and was not only the owner of a local bakery, but also a seer. Emily read Tarot cards and tea leaves and did past life hypnosis in her apartment above the bakery. She helped people find pets, predict future outcomes and even clear up misunderstandings and rumors. Although there were many skeptics around town, those that sought out Emily were usually very satisfied with her readings, suggestions or predictions. Emily was called in and did help find the boy, but it was too late. He was found dead. She was heartbroken, feeling that she could have helped more if the sheriff had contacted her earlier. Emily moved away with her daughter, Norma, soon afterwards. Norma was told about Michael from her mother about a month before she died from brain cancer. Norma had always had the gift, and maybe, her mother had said, some day Norma would accomplish what she could not. Tonight was the beginning of Norma's chance to make good on her mothers dying wish.

CHAPTER
8

"Hello, everyone. I have so many emotions about this subject. I've only told a few people bits and pieces about it and now, here, in front of all of you, I feel my mother's presence and I know it's the right time." Norma had held in the information surrounding Michael's death since her mother had told her. There was never a reason to tell a soul other than when she spoke with Sheriff Anderson and Robert. "I trust in your decisions, Sheriff Anderson. Thank you for having such confidence in me. And Robert, it's been so good to have had more time to spend with you this past year, I can't begin to know the depth of your suffering, and I pray that the burdens you carry will grow more tolerable through the years." Norma took a deep, relaxing, yoga breath. She was ready to proceed.

"My mother had lived in Havenswood Valley for many years, most people knew her as the owner of the Havenswood Valley Bakery. But, her true calling in this life was that of a seer, a gift she grew into and used to near perfection. This wonderful blessing enabled my mother to help others throughout her life and was passed along to me. When she told me the story of little Michael she knew that one day I would be called upon to continue the work she did, and in particular the one mission she was not able to complete. My mother foresaw there would be a return of the evil that took the life of Michael; evil that has been released again, twenty-five years later."

The bonfire did not provide near enough warmth to prevent the sudden chill felt by the entire group. Evil is such a strong word. Being used by Norma, Robert and Sheriff Anderson on this night, in these circumstances, had a huge impact.

"Evil?" Thomas asked.

"Yes," replied Norma. "I can tell you are all surprised by my dramatic choice of words, but I assure you my intention is purely to speak the truth."

"And I can assure you, there is no need for Norma to stray from what actually happened. The reality of the night Michael died needs no added fiction," Robert said.

The group had become entranced and was eager to hear what Norma would say. She led a discussion about Michael's disappearance, with some help from Sheriff Anderson and Robert to fill in parts of the story.

Michael, age ten, had strayed outside. By the time Robert realized his son was missing, the boy was nowhere near the cabin. Robert immediately called the sheriff's office. It was October 31st, Halloween, and Michael had planned to go to a friends house for a party. Dressed as a scarecrow, he was very excited about going door to door for candy at some of the homes and stores in town. He never made it.

Unlike the delay that may take place in a large city, Sheriff Donahue came at once to the Washburn residence, leading the convoy of a car full of deputies and a couple of trucks loaded up with locals wanting to help search. They spread out and spent the next three hours searching until word came in that Michael's body had been found in the stream. It was the saddest news Havenswood Valley had known in many years.

The cause of death was listed as drowning, but there was no reason for Michael to have gone into the stream by himself, much less fall in and get stuck in a swirl hole. He was raised around the water and respected its power. Looking back, this was the first clue the incident was more than a young boy falling into a stream. His little body was trapped by logs and branches, as if he had been locked in a watery jail with no chance to escape. The stream was running fast and high, so it took another hour to retrieve the body for fear of losing one of the fire and rescue squad members.

Robert stood by, watching every step of the rescue, and when Michael's body was laid on a gurney to be sent to the mortuary, he stepped up and prayed over Michael, gave him a kiss on the forehead and bowed his head, unable to watch them load his son into the ambulance. No marks of foul play were found on the body, although it was hard to discern what may have been a wound inflicted by someone, and a wound from the raging water.

After a few questions for the trio, the group felt, sadly enough, that they knew the history of the incident. Now came the next logical question.

"So what does all this mean for us, tonight?" asked Marcus. "You said the evil has returned, but we really need to know exactly what you're talking about. There isn't anything that much out of the ordinary going on now. And nothing like what we heard about Michael's death."

"For some, this weekend won't be anything more than a quirky couple of nights worth of ghost stories. One being a noisy night at the cabin last night, and the other spent learning of a terrible family tragedy, things you read about in the newspaper." Norma was not interested in playing games and wanted to give straight answers. "For others, what you are hearing about will change your lives. Forever."

"I have to ask," Jenna had been sitting on this one for a while. "Today, when Axel, Allison and I went to your store, did you hypnotize us and make us buy things we didn't even want?" There it was, just as Norma liked it, right to the point.

"The short answer is yes, I did. For reasons that will become apparent later, I took the liberty of making sure a few items, from the Pentavichi region of Europe, made their way to the cabin. Don't expect to understand this right now, and I strongly suggest these pieces be left at the cabin and not taken to anyone's home."

Sheriff Anderson stood up and spoke. "Okay, then. Before we get to the heart of the reason we are here tonight, let's take a short break. Maybe a snack or something to drink if you need it, and at this point I'd wager most of you do." Everyone gave a nervous laugh, and agreed it was time to stretch the legs. "Let's take ten minutes and then we'll let Norma finish her talk. After that I'll wrap things up and we'll be on our way."

"On your way?" asked Allison. "Aren't you all going to stay here tonight?"

"Oh, you'll have some company tonight, it just won't be us." The sheriff continued, "I have some events and obligations to attend to, but I have arranged for a couple of my deputies to be posted at the cabin. I don't expect anything to happen, but I'm betting you will all sleep better knowing you've got sheriff deputies on guard."

"Count me in, I'm looking forward to a good night's sleep. I am beat," replied Axel.

"Me too! Last night was a nightmare, really!" Karen was also very tired and was relieved to hear the deputies would be at the cabin. "I'm feeling sleepy already."

The break was just what they needed. Most of the group felt uneasy with how tense they had become while sitting and listening. They made their way into the cabin and prepared a few snacks, poured some drinks and exchanged a few comments about the story. The break was short and they quickly gathered back around the fire. Making a few adjustments in the seating arrangement, the group would listen not only to the last discussion of the night, but to the beginning of a new chapter in their lives.

Norma had pulled them into the beginning of her story in a dramatic way. From the fact her mother was a seer involved in a still unsolved mystery, all the way up until she admitted to hypnotizing the three friends at her store today. A few in the group shared some last minute comments before Norma began speaking.

"I don't know what to think, Karen. They all seem so secretive about an old accidental death case. Doesn't everyone know about it already?" asked Sam.

"That's the whole problem. It wasn't listed as a murder, it was a drowning on the sheriff's report. These guys all think something else happened, and now they're going to tell us about it." Karen had listened intently to everything Sheriff Anderson, Robert and Norma had said. "I'm thinking we're going to help solve a murder case this weekend."

"No way," interrupted Nick. "This is a classic case of townspeople that can't give up on the horribly tragic death of a young boy. Especially since, according to more than one person, it could have been prevented."

"That's pretty heartless, Nick." Kevin didn't have patience for anyone that dealt with death so lightly. "None of us can feel how the pain of this boy's death affected so many people, and we shouldn't pretend to know what's going on here."

"You're right, Kevin. Sorry, that was a pretty broad brush comment. I don't know these people so I shouldn't be so callous." Nick did feel bad about his comment, and knew part of the edge in his words came from dealing with his own life-changing event. He wasn't sure how the snakebite was going to affect his health in the long run, and sometimes he took his pent up anger out on unfair targets. In his heart, he knew better. "I've never had to deal with something like this, and I shouldn't make sweeping statements about a tragedy like the one they all went through."

It was quiet at the fire. Norma stood up and the group was more attentive than before the break, ready to hang onto her every word. She radiated her strength of spirit into the gathering and it reached out to the group like the warmth from the bonfire. Later, after they had gone back to the cabin, the closest word they would all agree on to describe her would be hypnotic. Right now it was time to hear what Norma had learned from her mother, ready or not.

"Most documentation shows Havenswood Valley has been around for one hundred twenty-five years, which is true if you are strictly speaking of modern documentation of the geography bordered and named as such. Originally inhabited by travelers looking for a place to rest, and in some cases hide, many fell in love with the area and stayed on. Of course, not everyone passing through was a candidate for a spot on the chamber of commerce. From the beginning of settlement times, Havenswood Valley has been in a battle of good versus evil. This land, this part of the world has been here for thousands of years, no, millions of years. I'm no anthropologist, but I know that just because people can't read about something, that doesn't mean it didn't, or can't, happen." Norma was walking around the bonfire, moving very slowing, but beginning to become highly animated in her telling of the story.

"Our little slice of time here in Havenswood Valley is just that, a slice in the history of this area. And in this time period you can look back and find many events that are tied together, but only if you look, as Robert said earlier, only if you look past the normal, everyday view and open your eyes to what else is out there. Sheriff Anderson, Robert and I have put together a scrapbook of events that have happened in this area over the last one hundred years, and discovered a few events that took place even earlier. We're just getting started on the older history notes, so most of our information is on the last seventy-five years.

Now, I don't want you to think we're like those people looking for crop circles to explain that aliens are on the way to take over the world, it's not like that. But we are finding out that many events; deaths, disappearances and strange sightings, have occurred over the history of this area that were similar in nature to Michael's, and some similar to what you have experienced. Yes, some do have explanations to what we term the normal world, but they also have connections to darker events. Things like location, time of day, or night, and the one we have seen over and over, the date of these events. Since they happen so far apart, sometimes it's only years, but mostly it's decades apart, so no one has connected these occurrences. But we have! We've worked through the single events and tied them together, with the final string that pulls them all in being the dates of the events. Every one of these events happened in the fall, within forty-five days of Halloween."

"Yep, I'm done. I'll be in the cabin getting ready for bed. I appreciate a good scare around Halloween, but this one's way too elaborate, even for me. Thanks for the great entertainment, but I'm too tired to stay for the ending." And with that Kevin was off to bed as everyone sat slack jawed watching him head to the cabin.

"Kevin, wait a minute." It was Karen, and as Kevin stopped and turned around she said "I'll keep you company," and she was right with him.

"If those deputies you have staying outside tonight wake me up just to scare me, I'm really going to be upset." Sam then stood up, glanced at Nick and started on her way to the cabin. Nick leapt up and walked with her.

At this point Sheriff Anderson jumped in and spoke to those who remained at the bonfire. "It's all about what you choose to see, and I do believe those young folks have seen enough. That's fine, and if anyone else would like to head in, please, take this moment to call it a night, you certainly won't offend any of us. We've been at this for many years on our own, and a few naysayers won't stop us."

"I'd love to hear the ending, but I only get a few days a year with these guys. If I want a little more conversation with my friends tonight I'd better head in and get in some time with Nick and the others. Allison, how about you?" Thomas was on his feet and ready to go.

"Sure, Thomas, I'll go in with you. Good night, all."

And just like that, the bonfire group was down to Marcus, Roxie, Axel and Jenna. Sheriff Anderson, Robert and Norma looked like they had expected this exodus from the start of the evening, and not one of them had tried to stop anyone from leaving, nor did they make any excuses to those still at the bonfire. Robert tossed another couple of oak logs on the fire and asked, "So, you four are going to stick around?"

"I'm not going anywhere. I'm in," answered Roxie. The other three agreed.

CHAPTER
9

It was now just after 9:00 pm. Although there was a crisp chill in the air, the warmth of the bonfire was enough to keep the now smaller group nice and toasty. Talk would be softer and more eye contact could be made. The woods, however, became louder as the wind rustled leaves along the ground and pushed tree branches around, noisily scratching one another. The quick scattering of nocturnal animals was also heard from the bonfire. It was a perfect fall evening for either the ending to a fantastic Halloween scare, or the unraveling of a decades old mystery.

"I have to hand it to your friends that went inside, they know when to cut their losses. This is the last night of their trip and they sure don't want to waste it with an old story they have no interest in. Why are you four still here?" The sheriff wanted to know how steadfast this group was in hanging onto the outcome of the mystery.

"I take most people at face value, until I'm shown otherwise," replied Marcus, "I have no reason to feel this is a hoax. In fact, I'm sure you're telling the whole truth, as you see it. Maybe it's slightly exaggerated, or a bit too dramatic." At this point an owl let out a very clear hoot-hoot, "Ah, nice timing, but whatever, I'm in for the whole telling."

"This is new for me," added Roxie, "I've never had an experience like this, so I'm in it for the intrigue, the social interaction, and just learning from others about how they see life and its twists and turns."

"And you two, Axel and Jenna," asked the sheriff, "how about it. Why still here?"

"I'm Marcus's backup, I can't leave him out here on his own, wouldn't feel right leaving him to be scared out of his wits."

"I just love a good ending," said Jenna, "and after being at Tres Azure today, I want to know what the heck would bring you all out here. It has to be more than a few raccoons running around on the porch last night. I want to know what you found out, and more about Michael, what he was like and why he went out on his own that night."

"Well thank you, each of you, for your honest comments. I appreciate you staying out here with us and your interest in our discussion." The sheriff was ready to move ahead, but stopped speaking and tilted his head to the left. The others noticed and went quiet, not moving a muscle. "I believe we are about to be startled by your friends, seems they are planning to run at us from behind the cabin and the woods over behind the parking area."

Robert had already slipped over to the sheriff's car and held the portable spotlight, waiting patiently. He saw Nick crawling slowly from around the back side of the cabin and into the yard. Robert hit him with the high beam on the first try.

"Awww, jeez, I can't see! Okay, okay, you caught me, can you cut the light now?" Nick was dazed by the impact of the beam, but managed to wobble back to the cabin unhurt.

Robert then noticed Thomas at the far side of the cabin and let him have the same treatment. "Whoa, I'm hit, I'm hit. Dang that thing is bright. I'm going back in!"

"Nice job, Robert. You're still pretty good with the spot."

"Thanks, Sheriff. This one has a lot more candle power than the one I have on my truck. They sure come in handy once in a while, don't they?"

The front door opened and Karen stepped out. "The guys have had enough and beg your mercy. They promise to behave and will not be trying to scare you again. Oh, and thank you for putting them in their place!"

Laughter came from the bonfire and Norma added, "You bet they'll behave, otherwise we'll send in a few raccoons and bears to keep them in line!"

The distraction over, Sheriff Anderson picked up where Norma had left off. "So, as Norma was saying, there are similar parts to many occurrences in Havenswood Valley around the end of October. For our event we know Michael was getting ready to go out on Halloween, he's putting on his costume while Robert is finishing up dinner dishes and getting a few things together for Michael to spend the night at a friend's house. Pretty normal stuff, but a little bit hectic. Robert comes into the kitchen and can't find Michael. The back door is wide open and part of Michael's costume, his mask and hat, are on the kitchen table. Robert, would you like to continue?"

"Sure, Glen. I went out back to look around and the first thing I noticed was the smell. It didn't really register, I must have thought it was a skunk, so I kept walking around the house trying to find Michael, calling out his name, looking for any signs of him. Then I saw the haze, we don't normally get any fog in here, but that night there was this sort of blue haze around the meadow. Thinking back, I'm sure it came from the woods, and I'm sure the smell was not a skunk. It was worse, like a stench from something that had spoiled, something rotten. Maybe a dead animal stink, that's about the closest I can come to explaining."

Robert took a breath. "It was then I saw movement in the woods. It was hard to tell for sure, but there were three, maybe four of them. Fast, almost floating through the woods and past where I could see. Scared me nearly to death, and then thinking about Michael out there I could barely speak into the phone when I called the sheriff. I felt there was a power in the woods, a power that I could not explain but something that would easily be able to pull a small boy from a farmhouse into the woods. Oh, God, I had never felt so helpless in all my life."

"It's okay, Robert." Words of heartfelt comfort came forth from Norma. "Don't beat yourself up again. You know there was not a thing that could have been done. Those evil beings were waiting, watching for just the right moment. It was going to happen sometime."

"I know, I know, it's just different when the three of us have talked about it. But now, out here, talking with people we don't really know, it's more real and brings back the night more clearly than I've remembered in a while." Robert was pretty upset now, he had to stand up and walk around the lawn. He came back and sat down, his eyes staring into the bonfire, his mind not ready to continue talking. Sheriff Anderson picked up the explanation.

"After Robert called into the sheriff's office we got here as fast as we could. Robert was one person you'd believe even if he said the sun had fallen from the sky. And with his son missing, well, you know how adults get when kids are in trouble, they act fast and drop whatever they are doing to help out. Since it was

Halloween we had more staff on duty, myself included. I came out with the sheriff and all the others. Robert was just going around in circles, yelling for Michael, looking at the woods, in the house. He would not accept his son was gone, and the things he had seen in the woods put him over the top, emotionally. As a God-fearing person, he knew evil was in the world, he just felt his little farm was far enough away from anything that even evil wouldn't find it."

"I am so sorry for your loss, Robert," said Jenna. "My little sister went missing for two days. She was lost in the woods during a camping trip with a friend and I thought my parents were going to die if they didn't find her. I was more scared than I had ever been in my life. They found her, but my parents needed a long time to get over it."

This woke Robert from his stare. "Thank you, Jenna. I know parents lose kids every day, but it is the toughest thing for a parent to live with. You'd give your life in an instant to trade places with your child."

Sheriff Anderson continued. "When we all unloaded from the cars and trucks we took direction from Sheriff Donahue. He had us spread out and head toward the woods and across the meadow in a grid he put together. Pretty standard stuff, and we went at it full of hope we'd find Michael. Nobody talked much, but I do remember the other men asking about the smell, and making comments about the fog. We tried to focus on the search but the stench made it hard to breath and the fog made walking slow. Flashlights didn't do much good, and looking into the woods and meadow, with the men yelling out locations, it really was a strange night. Then the dogs showed up, and, well, that made matters worse, not better."

"That's right, Sheriff, those dogs acted like someone was ready to run them over with a big truck. Couldn't find a scent, wouldn't take hardly a step into the woods or meadow. I'd never seen anything like it." Robert's recollection of how the dogs acted was so authentic, you could almost hear the whining, barking and howling. "We all thought there were just too many men around, but fact was, those dogs knew more than we did at the time. They sensed something was wrong in the area and weren't going to challenge something unknown. It wasn't until we changed the search direction on the grid and headed to the stream that the dogs finally left the cabin area."

"Looking back there were so many signs something else was going on, something more than a lost boy, but like Robert has said, we didn't see well enough to notice. So many clues, so many clueless men." The sheriff looked disgusted with himself.

"You see, my young friends, there is a power out here, somewhere in the area, that is full of forces we know very little about." Norma had the look of a college professor leading an important class lecture. "That night, and many nights just like it that we have found in our research, the power comes and takes people, kills people, causes accidents that cannot be explained. The power comes once every few years, or it may skip decades before we find that something happened, something evil. Most times it happens in the fall, around Halloween. We don't know why, other than to say evil, darkness, and death may be a power that has it's own source, and it's own schedule."

"When we found Michael, it was like he was locked into a cage on the stream. Not a real cage, but the logs, limbs and rocks where he drowned looked as if someone had made a cage to trap him. The county officer took pictures of the scene, but I swear it was not a coincidence where he was stuck in the water." Sheriff Anderson looked very upset. "As we have found out in our research, this region has had numerous unexplained deaths and evil happenings, but seeing one, in person, well, you think a lot about God afterwards, and you count up your blessings more often. By the time we came back the next day to try and see how he could have gotten locked in, the entire area was cleared out, like someone had swept the water with a giant rake. It was strange."

"I'm getting freaked out just listening." Axel seemed to speak for everyone.

"Well, if you were to hear all the information we have from the past one hundred plus years, it would totally freak you out. You'd be worried that the little disturbance last night might be signs of something very evil on the way. And if you were the sheriff, you'd make sure that people were notified and extra deputies would be on hand for the night."

These comments struck a cord with Roxie and Marcus, both of whom raced to ask the next question, Roxie won but Marcus was right behind her.

"Are you saying the things in the woods might come back tonight?" asked Roxie.

"Robert, have you seen those things in the woods since that night?" asked Marcus.

"I can't say if they will come back, and no, Marcus, I haven't seen them since that night. I have no idea if they have died, or what their powers might be now. Maybe stronger, or maybe older and slower, like me." Robert got a nervous laugh from the bonfire gang for that line.

"Sheriff, are we in danger?" Axel went straight to the big question.

"I don't think so, but I do know that if this power comes back, and if those shapes appear in the woods again, you will all need to stay indoors. Tonight, and in fact for the next few nights, Robert, Norma and I will be spending some time searching the woods for any signs of the shapes Robert saw so many years ago. Plus, I have three deputies scheduled to be here at 9:00 pm, so they should be arriving any time now. They'll sit here by the bonfire, take some walks around the area and check on the cabin. The three of us will head out onto the trail along the woods and stream, seeing what we can see, always within earshot or via walkie-talkie. If something comes up at the cabin we can be here in a flash." The sheriff seemed to be ready for an encounter with the forms. "The deputies are nearly here, so unless you have any other questions, how 'bout you four call it a bonfire and head in to wrap up the night?"

"I'd just like a recap for our sake," said Marcus. "As I have it in my head, on Halloween, Michael is somehow called outside by these dark forms in the woods. On a night that also has a strong odor in the air, as well as a rare haze or fog. Robert is outside looking for his son when suddenly he sees something in the woods; strong, fast moving shapes that he is unsure of and very uneasy with. Once at the cabin, there is a reading from Emily that this power called Michael into the woods, and when he goes in his life was at risk. Somehow he ends up in the stream where he gets caught up and drowns, but it's more like he was dead already and the water was just a way to dispose of the body.

In my book that's definitely an explanation of evil, but it doesn't mean a lunatic wasn't in the area. Robert, is there anything else?"

"There was something else, but I've said all I can and will let the sheriff finish. You kids, I'm sorry, young adults, please take care of yourselves and always be aware in your daily life of the simple things, because sometimes simple things turn into complicated events." And with that Robert walked to the sheriff's car, opened a back door and sat down inside.

"I'm sure you can understand Robert having to leave, this was really one of the few times I've heard him discuss his son with strangers, and I believe he had his fill. But yes, after Michael was found and taken to the hospital, the doctor noticed some striking marks on his skin. They looked like claw marks, talon marks to be exact, as if a very large bird of prey had picked Michael up and carried him away. We had a couple of experts look at photos of the marks and they said it couldn't have been from a bird, as the bird would have been larger than anything known to man."

There were a couple of moments of silence as the four friends soaked up what had just been said. They had no reason to doubt the story of Michael, and as the deputies that were to stand guard pulled in, they felt it was time to call it a night. But Roxie had one more question.

"Sheriff Anderson," Roxie asked, "why don't you send us home? Are we bait tonight?"

"No, in fact with the deputies here you are safer than if we had sent you all home. Our research shows that there has never been an incident that occurred to groups of people or when the evil was being searched for. I doubt we'll have anything happen tonight, but the three of us are still going to wander around, and these deputies are here until 6:00 am, then two other deputies will come in to relieve them."

"So why did we have the noise on the porch last night if they, these forms, don't do anything to groups?" asked Axel.

"We found some dead animals pretty torn up in the woods and in the stream. We think they may have been trying to hide on the porch or were being attacked. Not sure what was attacking what, but your explanations of what happened had a number of similarities to our research on the historical happenings; the noises, the mess on the porch, seeing some movement in the woods. It sounded just like some of the articles we've read in old newspapers and journals." The sheriff turned to Norma and nodded for her to continue.

"I had seen some signs in my meditations over the past week that there was danger and evil in our midst. When some of you came into my store," explained Norma, "I knew it was your group that needed help, and that's why I had to assist with the purchases. You need the items here with you. In fact, most everything in my store is there to help someone, not just eccentric items in a strange store."

"If you are wondering about the media," added Sheriff Anderson, "we don't talk about Michael's death. They can read the official report. It's out of respect for Robert that we don't discuss our private work on the case, but once in a while the story gets pulled out, mainly because it happened on Halloween. As far as the history of the area, there was one book written on the topic of the weird events and sightings. It was mostly geared for selling the area as a place to visit on Halloween, although we did find some information we used in our research. The town council has chosen not to promote it as a Halloween haunt; they aren't comfortable with that direction due to the fatalities. Havenswood Valley is a beautiful area and does just fine without a spooky hook for the tourists."

"Wow, it still hasn't sunk in that there truly is such evil in the world, especially in a place like this. Since we really didn't see anything, and no one was hurt, I guess our group will have some good debates about the events of this weekend." Marcus felt his questions were answered, for now.

The visitors said their goodnights to the sheriff and Norma, and passed along their condolences for Robert. As they made their way to the cabin they couldn't help but take a more wary look into the woods. Could there really be something out there? Could Havenswood Valley be the home to an evil that was capable of pulling a young boy from his home and into the woods? Discussing an evil that would kill, over decades and possibly longer, for no apparent reason would become a major part of the weekend's final night.

Once inside the cabin, the trio received a volley of questions. It was late, but the group was vibrant and ready for debate. Long into the night discussion raged on about life, love, right, wrong, good and evil. Religion, faith, hope, God and the devil were also hot topics. It was a night to remember, and no one wanted to miss a minute. Of course, no one would admit they were too scared to sleep!

Outside, the deputies had a very boring night. It was a peaceful night full of stars, the moon low in the sky and unable to effect the brilliant display overhead. The deputies were there to watch for any locals that might drive in to taunt the tourists, and make sure there weren't any animals coming in from the woods that might deface the cabin or cars. The good deputies were on alert all night and did a fantastic job keeping the occupants of the cabin safe.

As for Sheriff Anderson, Robert and Norma, well, they too came up empty-handed. A walk on the trails near the cabin was tense, but uneventful. Norma said to the sheriff and Robert that she had a feeling there was something watching them, but it was not strong enough to pinpoint an exact location. The sheriff and Robert replied that they trusted her intuition, and also felt something in the woods. They wanted to know what she was thinking.

"I'm afraid we have not seen the last of the evil, and maybe it has come back not only stronger, but also with more knowledge. If we all felt it, something was out there, it just wasn't ready to attack, or it is going to attack someone else," said Norma.

Sheriff Anderson was at a loss to explain his feelings. "The trouble I have is that I don't know the enemy, I have no idea what we are up against. I just know that if it could pull in a young boy twenty-five years ago, who knows what it can do now."

"Only God knows. We humans seem to have such little experience in the ways of good versus evil. We'll need help, I know that much." Norma said. "I hope we find it soon enough to make a difference in our lifetime."

"We are making a difference," said Robert. "Michael may be gone, but his death will keep life within others. Maybe we saved someone at the cabin this weekend. If so, that's enough for me. I don't need to kill evil, I just need to keep it away from innocents." Sheriff Anderson and Norma agreed. Evil may stick around, but they'll do what they can to keep it out of Havenswood Valley.

Havenswood Valley

For Kevin, his favorite part of the weekend was the Sunday morning rise and shine ritual. It began a couple of years ago when he had to leave early in the morning on the last day. It seemed just as he had said so-long, someone else woke up and came out to say goodbye. This went on for some time until, in fact, everyone was awake and were all waving as Kevin drove off. From that trip on no one left early, but everyone had to get up by 7:00 am and start the day together with a group activity.

Today it was to be a walk along the two mile loop, made more interesting due to the discussions of the previous night. Seems no one had slept very well and although the sheriff had assured them they were not in danger, there was still an uncertainty in the air about the whole story surrounding little Michael. There was sadness about his death, sorrow that Robert had been dealt such difficult blows in his life, and trepidation about coming back to the cabin in the following years. It was hard to believe all of it taking place in such a beautiful landscape, near a town that softly dotted hillsides and lakeshores with modest homes, lived in by regular Joe's and Jane's. How in the world could evil survive in such a place as Havenswood Valley?

Kevin and Karen were up first, as planned by the two. They both enjoyed early starts and wanted to get the coffee going, fruit prepared and pastries warmed up. The two had become close during the weekend and had already set a date for Kevin to visit Karen in Arizona. It was a perfect time in their lives to see if the romance that blossomed during the weekend was truly something to nurture.

"Coffee's ready, should we take a cup out to the deputies?" asked Karen.

"I'm sure they'd appreciate the gesture. Plus, it's just starting to get light so the temp's probably dipping down some." Kevin pulled out three cups for Karen to pour the coffee into.

"Good morning, Deputies. Thought you'd like some hot coffee this morning." Karen held two cups for the men and handed one to each of them. Kevin held one for an absent third deputy.

"Thanks, this is awfully nice of you." Deputy Owens didn't expect anyone out this early, and was nearly asleep when he heard the cabin door open.

"I have another cup of coffee. We thought there were three of you out here." Kevin said.

"Deputy Long wasn't able to join us this morning. He's got the flu. When we called in to talk with the first shift they said two of us would be plenty." Deputy Stevens felt like he was making an excuse for being one deputy short, but he wasn't going to apologize. "We were fine, nothing going on out here except a few raccoons and owls, maybe a wolf or two in the distance."

As if on cue, everyone turned as they heard it. In the woods, right across the open area of the cabin yard and beyond where the bonfire had been, a crashing sound blasted the group back into the reality of why the deputies were there in the first place. It was as if a bulldozer was blazing through the trees!

Both deputies jumped up and Deputy Stevens headed to the woods, not at a run but in a manner in which he could pull his high beam flashlight out and walk quickly in the direction of the crashing brush. Halfway to the woods he stopped, which had only taken about ten seconds, and looked back at the group.

"Bull moose!" the deputies said to each other in near unison. The tension in their posture released. Kevin and Karen could just make out the image of the large mammal as it made its way through the woods in the early morning light. Kevin began walking into the meadow to get a better look. He passed Deputy Stevens who said, "Not too close now, you never know when they'll turn on you." Kevin nodded yes, but did not say a word, he was amazed by this large beast. He watched for thirty seconds or so and then the moose was out of sight.

The relaxed atmosphere didn't last long, as the small group now saw why the large mammal was running. They heard them first, but just barely. In stealth mode, moving quickly and easily through the underbrush and broken timber, they saw one, then three, then maybe five large wolves running through the woods on the same path as the moose. They were well on their way to pulling down a huge feast.

"Wolves" Kevin said aloud in a weird, hypnotic tone. "Woooolves" he drawled. In awe of these magnificent animals he thought to himself about their agility, their size! They must be 70, 80 maybe 90 pounds apiece and all muscle! The four legged creatures churned the ground and maneuvered through the woods, but all Kevin could hear was their breathing; a rapid, yet paced, in and out that was part exhale and part snarl. Kevin's ears filled with the beating of their oversized hearts, built strong from years of chasing down live meals. The sound became louder and caused Kevin to divert his attention from the wolves as they began to disappear from his view. Turning his now glazed-over eyes to the true cause of the mesmerizing rhythm.

Just within the edge of the woods was a unique darkness. Kevin had not noticed it before yet there it was, floating above the ground, filling the space between the trees. It looked beautiful and yet felt dangerous at the same time. Not really one large area, but rather three or four areas in close proximity to each other. The darkness reached out to Kevin, and within its rhythm he felt there were answers to events that had happened in his life. That his heart would be relieved of the pain he felt from past losses.

As he walked toward the sound, his body yielded to no other desire than to find the source, find that which was calling out to him. The path was clear, aloft in mid air and he began to walk faster. The sudden scent of spring gave Kevin a rush of energy and he began to run. The yearning for relief and forgiveness rose from within. Kevin had no choice but to accept this gift the darkness was willing to offer.

Deputy Stevens had seen Kevin turn to the woods to watch the moose, and was keeping an eye on him to make sure the wolves did not consider him a morning snack. He became uneasy when Kevin did not respond to verbal direction to come back to the cabin area, realized something was amiss. A fog had rolled into the grassy area from out of nowhere, along with a stench that could only be described as nearly noxious. Both deputies and Karen were coughing, their eyes stinging, as they were now yelling at Kevin to come back. Kevin showed no outward signs of being affected by the fog or odor and began running to the woods, directly at what the others were now seeing. In the edge of the woods were the floating dark forms Robert described seeing when Michael was killed!

Deputy Stevens hit full speed within three steps of his rush at Kevin. His effort and determination bordered on the fanatic as he battled the smell and fog, but he knew he had to stop Kevin before he reached the woods. Five seconds later, and with a full body tackle reminiscent of his college playing days, the deputy intercepted Kevin just in time.

Wham!

What is happening to me? Kevin's thoughts raced. He was face down, dirt and grass from the meadow lodging in his mouth and nose. His head hurt. "Ooooh, gawd, I caaaaan't breeeeth" he was able to say, but just barely. Both men lay on the ground, coughing, eyes burning. Deputy Stevens rose and began carrying Kevin back to the cabin, as the others ran out to help.

"Kevin, Kevin, can you hear me?" Karen asked.

Kevin, now laying near the fire pit, could not reply but knew he was a mess; eyes stinging, throat bone dry and ears ringing. His head was aching, his breathing was labored and he had no idea what in the world was going on. On top of everything, he was about to throw up!

"Kevin, say something," Karen was desperate for Kevin to speak.

"Raaaaaalllppphhhhhh" and with a convulsive movement that jerked his whole body, Kevin tossed his cookies directly onto Axel's boots.

"I'll bet he feels better now" deadpanned Nick. "He must be ten pounds lighter."

"And he'll never want to eat pastries for breakfast again," added Thomas.

"And my boots look ten years older, and smell like, oh jeez! Good thing these boots are all rubber, I've gotta clean them off before this stuff eats through to my feet." Axel headed off to the outdoor faucet as the others, awakened by the early morning episode, stayed put around Kevin.

"Let's take him inside," said Marcus "We'll put him in the main room by the fireplace and make sure he's warm and dry. Once he feels better we'll get some food and fluids in him and find out what in the heck he was seeing and hearing!"

It was nearly an hour before Kevin was able to sit up and recall his version of what happened. "I was looking at the moose when the wolves appeared. They looked so majestic, just running free and strong through the woods. It was like a scene from a nature show!"

"What about the dark forms?" asked Sam, eagerly.

"The dark forms? Do you mean the dark part of the woods?"

"Karen and the deputies said the dark forms appeared in the woods. That you were running right at them, into the woods," answered Sam.

"What? No way! I remember there was a darkness in the woods, but it was, I don't know, it was like this dark, beautiful area. I felt like it was calling me. It felt safe and I wanted to find out where the drumming was coming from. But I wasn't running!"

"Kevin, do you remember being tackled?" asked Karen.

"Tackled? Like in football? No," he replied. "Is that why I feel so bad?"

"Yes, you were tackled," said Karen, "by Deputy Stevens. You were running to the woods, right at those dark forms. If he hadn't stopped you, you'd have been in the woods and into those dark forms in no time. Only God knows what would have happened next."

"I don't remember it that way at all, but now that you mention being tackled, I do recall suddenly coming to, almost like waking up out of a deep sleep and hurting badly. Not being able to breath, man, it sucked. Like I was hit by a truck with no warning."

"No warning!" exclaimed Karen, visibly upset. "We were screaming our lungs out for you to stop, but you just ran faster! Thank goodness Deputy Stevens was a former football player, he was our only hope of stopping you."

Kevin looked around at his friends. Karen was so serious, and looked as if she had been crying. Would he be able to remember everything as it really happened? "Let's go through what happened and I'll see what stirs up my point of view. Sound okay?"

"I'm good with that," agreed Karen. "But first, somebody will have to ask the deputies to come in to verify my account of what happened. Oh, and the sheriff, Robert and Norma wanted to come in when Kevin was ready. Thomas, can you let them know he's awake and ready to go over everything?"

It only took a few minutes and the cabin was filled with everyone on the premises. Deputy Owens began the review and told everyone how Karen and Kevin had brought some coffee out to the deputies, and what had happened up until they heard the first loud noises in the woods. "The four of us relaxed when we realized that it was just a moose running in the woods. Kevin, though, was very intrigued with the wildlife scene playing out in front of us, walking forward to get a better view of the moose. Once it went out of view he was walking back when we were suddenly aware of an entirely new collection of wild animals; wolves. Kevin stopped in his tracks, standing very still. He was staring at the wolves as they ran through the woods right in front of us, just inside the grassy edge. About this time the sheriff pulled up with Robert and Norma in the car. Norma had felt something was wrong at the cabin, and called Sheriff Anderson to see if he could take her out there. Robert was on call if anything came up, so they picked him up on the way. Sheriff, would you like to continue?"

"Sure, Deputy. As you said, Norma had a feeling there was trouble at the cabin, so the three of us drove out right away. As we pulled up, Kevin was in the middle of the grassy area by the cabin, running into the woods. It didn't take us but a few seconds to see the dark forms, so we unloaded from the Suburban ASAP." Sheriff Anderson took a sip of coffee and continued. "I unlocked my shotgun and Robert grabbed the spotlight. We had no idea if either would do a thing, but it was all we had. Norma began to pray." He smiled at Norma.

"All heck broke loose," the sheriff continued, "I ran into the field and started firing my shotgun till I ran out of shells. Then I pulled out my sidearm and unloaded that into the forms. Robert was working the PowerBeam and Norma was flashing the headlights, all in hopes of at least getting the dark forms to leave. As all this was going on, Karen and Deputy Owens were yelling as loud as possible at Kevin to try and get him to stop running. Finally, Deputy Stevens hit Kevin like the linebacker he was and laid him out. Kevin was done running and the dark forms had disappeared. It was over, just like that."

Kevin looked up at everyone, as if he was going to break down and cry his soul dry. He didn't. Instead, he let out a gut cleaning projectile of the smelliest barf anyone in the room had ever encountered. Fortunately, he had time to turn and let it fly into the fireplace.

"Well," Axel said, not one to miss an opportunity for a great line, "that oughta take the soot off of those bricks!"

It took some time to clean up the gooey mess in the fireplace. As the stench filled the room windows were quickly opened and candles lit. Axel was the first one to start cleaning, Nick and Thomas also pitched in.

"I've had to clean up some nasty stuff, but holy hazardous waste, is Kevin gonna be okay?" Nick held his shirt over his mouth and nose as he helped clean.

"We better check the grate, it might be melting to the hearth," Thomas joked.

"This looks bad, guys. We better tell Kevin to lay off the dead fish from the stream when he's up here. I think they've rotted out his stomach." Axel had placed a bandana over most of his face, but it was of little help.

Once they had it pretty well cleaned, Sam gave it a final spray with a scented cleaner and the fireplace was done. "Let's pray that doesn't happen again," she said, "I am not up for seeing, hearing or smelling another round of *Up from the Depths of Grossville.*"

Everyone else had started to pack for home, except for Roxie and Marcus. They had planned to leave later, with Axel, and were putting together the last feast of the trip. Although everyone seemed to be busy packing, not much was getting done. Their minds were racing with thoughts of what had happened this morning and concentrating on simple tasks was difficult.

"Roxie, I think I just put double the salt into the pancake batter, and it was the last ingredient. Is that going to ruin them?" asked Marcus.

They added some more sugar to the batter.

"Sam, have you seen my contact lens case? I can't find it anywhere," Jenna was in the room the girls shared.

"I can't even find my suitcase, and it's a hundred times bigger than your contact lens case. I feel like everything has been shaken and twisted around here. I'm way off balance." Sam's mind was racing with the turn of events. She had been such a skeptic the night before and having been awakened by the screaming voices and shotgun shells being fired, Sam couldn't get it together.

"How could this be happening? Aren't we just in Havenswood Valley, on our annual get together, having fun?" The tears began rolling down Jenna's cheeks as she spoke. "Kevin looks terrible, and Karen can hardly talk without starting to shake. Everyone's walking around like this happens all the time! What would we tell Kevin's parents if he had been pulled into the woods and killed like little Michael?" Jenna was in full tears and sobs mode now, and both Sam and Allison came over to console her.

"No one knows what's going on, Jen. We're just trying to push through this moment, get home and then try to figure out what happened here." Sam knew her friend needed guidance to get out of the cabin, be on her way home, and get confirmation that everything would be all right. "Kevin's going to be fine, and so is Karen. They're freaked out right now, but people get scared by things they don't understand all the time. Don't you ever watch those ghost hunter shows, or read about weird things that sound too crazy to be true? The world is full of stuff we can't explain." Sam gave Jenna a big hug, "We'll hear what the sheriff says about all this and then go home and settle down. It's going to be okay, Jen. We'll be fine." Jenna shook her head in agreement, but her heart and soul were far from being convinced.

Breakfast was soon ready, and chefs Roxie and Marcus made sure it was filling, yet simple. Plenty of pancakes from scratch; some with blueberries, some with chocolate chips, some with banana slices. There were also two large bowls of scrambled eggs with diced ham, grated cheddar cheese in a bowl for a topping, microwaved potatoes that had then been sliced and slightly pan fried, toast, juices, avocado and a big dish of salsa. Coffee cake that had somehow survived most of the weekend and a fresh pot of coffee topped off the menu.

As the last plates were being laden with warm food and the mugs were being filled with hot coffee, Sheriff Anderson was ready to address the gathering. Everyone knew he had a tough speech to make. They all needed answers but as of this morning it seemed that even a basic understanding and comprehension of what had happened would be hard to convey. He'd waited twenty-five years for this, and now Sheriff Anderson was stirring his thoughts like the creamer he had added into his coffee, trying to make a bitter taste easier to swallow, trying to mix the nightmare of this morning with the reality of his nearly life long struggle to find an answer to Michael's death.

"I'll get right to the point, then. I know you all have a fair amount of travel in front of you today, but I'll stay around as long as anyone would like. Robert and Norma have said the same. We won't have all the answers, but we can give you as much information as we have." Sheriff Anderson took a bite of coffee cake and smiled, "This has got to be the best tasting coffee cake I've ever had." The group agreed and Jenna, her recipe given another favorable review, gave a faint smile that seemed to help clear up her red and slightly puffy eyes.

"Norma called me early this morning," he continued, "and said we needed to get down here right away. She had seen a darkness in her dream around the cabin and felt you could be in danger. We picked up Robert on the way and of course when we arrived everything was already in high gear. None of us can explain what it was that pulled Kevin into the woods today. It's something we've been working on for a long time and now that we've seen it, and Robert has seen it again, I'm at an even bigger loss for an explanation. To see something so totally foreign to what I had imagined, well, my brain can only process so much and today it was taken to the limit."

Nearly everyone was holding onto frayed thoughts of what life in Havenswood Valley was supposed to be. Wasn't this just a peaceful town where excited tourists headed for a short stay and the locals, kind as they are, put up with the population influx for a few short months a year? Serious blows to a person's standard reality take a while to be absorbed. Much like ink into cloth, only so much can be sucked up at once before you must ring it out and try taking on more. This tightly knit group was struggling to find a sure-fire way back to the innocence of Havenswood Valley.

"I'm not going to stand here and say 'I told you so' to those of you that left the bonfire early last night. Heck, most people would have done the same thing. It sounded crazy, for sure. But now that we've seen it, now that one of your own has experienced the evil we have been studying, it's a whole new ballgame. Now you are all part of the 150-year-old legend of Havenswood Valley, and for the rest of your lives you'll remember how evil reared its ugly head and nearly killed Kevin. Yes, nearly killed him the same way Michael was taken." Sheriff Anderson looked directly at Kevin. "I don't have any answers for you, Kevin, about how this experience is going to affect you in the future, but I know we'll keep in touch. At least your memory of the event, for now, is one of beauty, although a dangerous one."

"Kind of like his last girlfriend," said Axel, before he could stop himself. "Sorry, just slipped out."

"No worries, Axel. But you're right." Kevin gave a small laugh, which helped everyone relax. "I do recall the beauty in the woods, but I also know that beauty can be seductive and deadly, all at the same time."

"It requires being aware of your surroundings," interjected Norma. "You may think you are simply picking up a piece of wood to put on the fire, yet a venomous snake appears and nearly kills you. Right, Nick? Or, it may be drugs that will make someone feel good for a short time, but in the long run drugs will ruin the life and may even lead to death. Even speeding along the highway is seductive to some, however we know this can cause horrible tragedies for unsuspecting drivers." Norma wanted everyone to think outside the box of regular living. "When you go home today, keep in mind that being pulled into a wrong decision does not always require the darkness of evil as we saw today. It may start in much smaller doses, but in the end the result can be the same. You have all been witness to an unexplainable event here this weekend. Now you must use this as a way to strengthen your own life. Be prepared should you be pulled in the wrong direction while traveling the road of life." She smiled. "And yes, my lecture is over, but please remember, I will be thinking of each one of you often, hoping your paths will be clear, your decisions will be wise, and your endeavors fruitful."

"I'd say we owe all of you a big thanks. Without your help we might have lost Kevin," replied Marcus. "We'll always be thankful for your help and guidance, Norma, even if some of us did get off on the wrong foot with you the first day." He elbowed Axel, and there was a mild laugh from the group.

Norma smiled. She had said what was on her mind and was ready to continue listening to the sheriff.

"Yes, thank you Norma, and thanks also to Deputies Owens and Stevens and to Robert and Karen. It took all of us to get Kevin back and whatever we did was enough to scare off the dark forms, at least for now. Sometimes being brave is doing what happens naturally, and this morning it was our natural instinct to save Kevin and make sure the dark form knew we meant business. I doubt we did it any damage, but at least we accomplished what we needed to."

"For those of us here in Havenswood Valley," the sheriff continued, "we'll get together, go over everything that happened, and explore the woods to see what we can find. I imagine we'll find the carcass of that unlucky moose, and who knows what else. As far as an official report, well, I'm going to need more time to think about it. If anyone wants to file a report, I'll do it, I'm just not sure today is the best time. You can contact me later if you have questions."

"What about Kevin or Karen, in case they need to talk with someone or see a doctor?" asked Roxie. "Do you think they'll need a sheriff's report?"

"Hey, if I need to see a doctor I'm just going to say I've got the flu. If I tell a doctor I'm sick because I tried to chase an evil spirit I might end up in the psych ward," said Kevin.

"Might not be a bad approach, Kevin," said the sheriff. "But I will have paperwork done up and available for any of you that would like a copy. Karen, how are you doing?"

"I'm doing much better, now, but I think it's going to be a while before I feel like talking to a professional, if ever." Karen was a strong young woman, but even she knew this something that could bother her for a while. "I consider myself very resilient, but this was a pretty scary day, even for me. I'll keep in touch with Kevin and the two of us can compare notes."

"Sure you will," said Sam, "I'm betting you'll be keeping in very close touch with Kevin!"

"Oh, Sam," added Roxie, "you know it's purely scientific between these two. Lots of research in store for Kevin and

Karen. Probably in some romantic spot in Scottsdale, right Karen?"

Before Karen could defend herself, Jenna had a second outburst. "This isn't a joke or some Halloween prank, you guys!" She was still shaken up and felt everyone else was taking this too lightly. "Kevin was almost killed by something no one can explain. Maybe it's the spirit of a thousand dead souls all put into one evil monster. Maybe it's the devil looking for living souls to steal. I'm never coming back to this place again. In fact I'm going to church tonight and lighting prayer candles for all of us. You were right, Sheriff Anderson, I'll remember this for the rest of my life, not only as the day Kevin almost died, but as the day evil came forth from hell. God is where I'll find my answers, and that's how I'm going to deal with all this." Jenna turned and headed to the kitchen.

"I'm thinking now is a good time for me to say something," Robert came forward as everyone else was trying to digest Jenna's words. "I've already had to deal with seeing the dark evil, and I did lose someone to the seduction of what Kevin describes as a dark beauty." The group turned their attention to Robert, his voice holding their attention even more than it did the night before.

"Some of you will put this out of your memory very quickly. You'll get back home, back to work, back to your daily routines. It will fade in effect after telling the story a few times, the same as a visit to a haunted cemetery or old historic building might sound to you. For others, you'll go to church more often, search for answers in the words of the Bible, and reach into your inner self for an understanding of what has occurred. You'll eventually feel satisfied, but never truly one hundred percent fulfilled. Then there may be one or two of you that will have your entire life turned upside down. This weekend will become a passion and your direction in life will change. You will become engrossed in trying to find answers, similar happenings, anything that relates to the events of this weekend." Robert took a sip of coffee, adjusted his wide brimmed hat and walked a few paces to gather his thoughts.

"I went through each of these emotions, and I was each of those people over the last twenty-five years. It was like a twelve step program for me, and the stages were a way for me to handle the loss of Michael. I really didn't expect to see this evil again, or to get an eyewitness explanation like the one Kevin was able to provide. For me, this is taking it beyond the next level and into the next dimension. You'll need time to deal with this, and I'm sure you'll each find the best way to process the weekend. But at this moment, I'm full of energy and ready to get after it. I have seen the enemy, we have pushed it aside, for now, but I want to draw it back and do everything I can to make sure it dies off forever."

"I'll be right there with you Robert," added the sheriff. "But now we need to help get these fine young men and women on their way home. I'm sure Robert would be willing to talk with any of you if you have questions or just need someone that understands the situation." Robert nodded in agreement. "We'll make sure you have our numbers before you leave today. Anyone else have any more questions before we wrap this up? Jenna, everything good with you?"

"Yes, I'll be fine, and I'll make sure I add some prayers for all of you, especially Kevin, Karen and Robert." Jenna had poured herself a cup of milk to calm down, but everyone felt she was going to have some difficulty dealing with the event and would be struggling with it for months.

"Aren't you going to do more than just look around?" asked Allison. She, too, was pretty upset. "What about calling in some help, getting on the news about this and letting people know what happened? It's like the beaches after a shark attack. Are you going to keep them open until enough people get eaten and then let everyone know there's a shark in the water? You guys have something out there that might not even be able to be killed!"

Allison's remarks re-opened the topic Sheriff Anderson had hoped was already cleared up. He let them vent their fears and frustrations, with Robert and Norma answering questions as well. In the end, the cabin group had as complete an understanding of not only how the sheriff was going to proceed, but also an uncut history lesson on the evil happenings in and around Havenswood Valley. The more they were able to talk and ask questions, the more confident they were in the sheriff's plans.

"I'm satisfied, Sheriff," said Marcus, "that you have a handle, and some great help. Instead of getting too excited and too emotionally charged up, we need to let you guys get started and then listen to what you want us to help with." Although he was speaking to Sheriff Anderson and the other locals, the message was directed at his friends.

"Thank you, Marcus," said the sheriff. "Everyone else good, then?" They were, and in fact it was unanimous. The entire group, including Jenna and Allison, were in agreement with the direction and abilities of Sheriff Anderson's approach and investigation plans. It was a brand new experience and they were running on fear, anxiety and a desire to have the entire world know what happened. They knew, of course, that no one in their right mind would believe a word of it.

The cabin was a rush of activity as the last of the suitcases and gear bags were being repacked with clothing, books, hairdryers, games, photo albums and shoes. Boxes of leftover food were being distributed and carried to the cars and trucks. Bottled water, beer, and wine was carefully packed for the trip home and about all that was left were paper goods, trash bags and some lawn chairs that were brought up to the cabin. Oh, and Axels' hammock.

"Did we really bring all this stuff?" asked Thomas. "You'd think we were going to be here for a week, not just a weekend."

"Yeah, it never seems like that much until we all get here" replied Allison. "Then it's like we packed for a food festival."

"At least we had plenty of room for everything. It's nice that we're not on top of each other all weekend," said Thomas. "Uh, I mean, not crowding each other."

Allison laughed, "I know what you mean. Having enough space is nice, but I don't mind a little closeness once in a while." She smiled at Thomas and he reached out to hold her hand, then pulled her close for an embrace.

"Me either," he said.

With the packing nearly done, Sheriff Anderson and the others said one last goodbye to the visitors and wished them well.

Anxious to get out and see what they might find in the way of clues, especially in the area of the woods where the dark forms had been, Sheriff Anderson and the others took off on an exploratory walk. They were joined by Deputy Owens and Steve Reynolds, a local wildlife biologist from the State Wildlife Management Department. Reynolds had been in on some of the meetings about Michael and the dark history of Havenswood Valley with Sheriff Anderson. He was a great resource and kept things close to the vest. Deputy Stevens stayed back and walked the area around the cabin.

Sheriff Anderson posed the first question about five minutes into the trek, as they approached the South Bridge. "So, then, Robert, how are you doing? That was a heck of a show this morning. Can't say I was ready for it like I had hoped I would be. More run'n gun and flying by the seat of our pants than I like, but we did get rid of the dark forms, whatever they are."

"I really tried to see what they were, Glen. I looked hard, but the darkness was so deep, so pure. Maybe I was looking for Michael in there, or some kind of answer to what had happened to him." Robert was looking straight ahead, not done with his thoughts, but not sure the sheriff would understand. "If I hadn't been so focused on working the high beam, I swear, I might have walked right into it with Kevin." He stopped, turned, and looked right at Sheriff Anderson, "I felt it, Glen. I felt the pull of the darkness and I thank God it disappeared so quickly. I'm a grown man with a pretty damn good ability to fight and I felt it. How in Heaven's name was a little boy like Michael supposed to stay away? He never had a chance." Robert turned away.

Robert was not angry, not overly emotional, yet not for one minute would he be willing to succumb to thinking any further about what Michael had gone through. He knew going down that road would only lead to a guilt he could never overcome. And so he focused on the evil, this dark evil that took his son Michael and many others throughout the history of this area. There was no guarantee their lives would have been long, or easy, but certainly they would have reached a different outcome. Robert would renew his commitment to finding a way to destroy the powerful force that stole his son.

"This must have really tore him up today, Glen," said Norma. She had been just outside of earshot and didn't want to interrupt their conversation, but of course she knew Robert was troubled. "Poor man just wants to be left alone, but his heart is empty and he thinks an answer to what happened to Michael might let him heal. He's strong, but even strong men break down."

"More than a little shaken up, Norma. Said he felt the pull of the darkness, that he now knows Michael never had a chance to fight it. Holy hell, life is supposed to be simple in a place like this. Nobody wants complications, they just want to work hard, enjoy their family and get to church most Sundays. And a little fun now and then wouldn't hurt. But my gosh, how is a man supposed to deal with all this?" Sheriff Anderson had known Robert for many years, and this was one of the few times he had seen him let his guard down. Never had he talked about Michael in such a way, connecting with the realization that his son had been taken by an evil far beyond anyone's understanding, and nearly crumbling under the weight of his own paternal guilt.

"Sheriff, Sheriff Anderson! I found something over here you'll want to take a look at." Just off the main trail Reynolds had found the remains of the moose that had been seen fleeing the wolves. Even for a trained biologist it was startling. For the others it was on the brink of freakish.

"Wow, is that clean! Don't think I've ever seen a moose carcass finished off so quickly." Deputy Owens was an avid hunter and had seen many a kill in the wild. This one, from an animal so large, surprised him with the speed at which it was picked nearly clean in just a few hours.

"Really unusual. You'd figure this kill would last at least a day or two in the wild, even having been taken down by wolves. They usually pick at it, protect it, keep it around for the rest of the pack to catch up and share." Reynolds was an expert in many species, and in this part of the woods wolves were abundant so he made sure he knew as much as possible. "Most of the skeletal remains are here, but I can't believe the hide, meat and organs have been eaten and taken so cleanly off the bone. These were some very hungry wolves." Paw prints of wolves surrounded what was left of the moose, showing a frenzy of activity after the kill. Nothing else, though. No other predators or scavengers that had come afterwards to pick the bones clean.

"What else can take the meat off so quickly, Steve? We had a pretty weird morning, I'm open to any suggestions you'd have," said the sheriff, "including that you just don't know. Wouldn't be the first time something around here couldn't be explained."

"I've got something that can't be explained," said Norma, interrupting with a sidebar to lighten the mood. "My artwork! I make it, I price it and I put it in my store and it sells! Some lovely tourists come in, take a look around and just can't help themselves. They buy my artwork, and I can't explain why!"

"You keep hypnotizing them and they'll buy everything in the store." Robert winked at Norma. "Heck, I came home with one of your paintings, and I don't even remember going into the store. I think you caught me on the sidewalk!" The laughter broke up the mood that had gotten serious over the moose. Robert and Norma walked a few steps over to the South Bridge and leaned against the stones that formed the guard rail while the sheriff and Reynolds examined the moose, or rather what was left of it.

Reynolds returned to the discussion on the moose. "Take a look at the paw prints around the carcass. Back here," Reynolds was about twenty feet away, "you can see how they began to drag the moose down from each side and behind." He had by this time walked up to the sheriff. "Then the feast. But you'll notice the wolf tracks don't head off anywhere. Where'd they go? If they were part of the darkness, I'm willing to say they were pulled away right after they fed. And when I say pulled away, I'm talking lifted up by the darkness, which somehow, I think, also took part in cleaning the carcass."

"These wolves, they could be an extension of the darkness, a way to navigate this world, this dimension," offered Norma. "We should not be held back by our normal beliefs. We need to push beyond our limits of what is acceptable to our way of thinking."

The others nodded their heads. It was an incredible concept to think of the darkness as an entity that could create an extension of itself in the form of wolves on the hunt, but after this morning it was not unbelievable.

As they walked over the bridge, a few more explanations were discussed, but none that would fit into a report without getting flagged by the state headquarters, which the sheriff didn't want. Moose carcass cleaned instantly by wolves and evil spirit? Not the best wording on a sheriff's report. They'd leave it for now and move on, however Reynolds did fill a few small plastic bags with samples to review later.

Once across the South Bridge they passed around the rocky ledge near the stream. From there it was a short walk to where the woods began on the west side of the stream. Sheriff Anderson and Deputy Owens shouldered shotguns and carried side arms, Robert had a .306 rifle. There was a feeling of slight apprehension as they approached the first line of trees.

"Is it just me, or is anyone else getting a slight smell of what filled the air this morning?" said Deputy Owens. "Maybe I just haven't cleared everything out of my sinuses yet."

"I haven't not smelled that since it happened," replied Sheriff Anderson. "But I do agree that a blow of it is coming downwind from the trees. Reynolds, I'd like you to stay close to us, in fact let's all group up here, me in front, Owens in back." The group pulled together, then began walking again. It was easy to see ahead since they were on a fairly wide trail, keeping the scare factor to a minimum.

They walked cautiously through the woods, listening for the snarl of a wolf, looking for a deep darkness, bending down to get a closer look at something on the ground. Everyone's senses were on overdrive. It had taken about twenty five minutes to make their way along the trail that cut through the woods, and they were nearly out and into the meadow near the North Bridge when Sheriff Anderson stopped.

"I know I smell it now," he said. "It's more than just left over from this morning." Sheriff Anderson halted and held his arm up for the others to stop. Looking around he wondered to himself why he had decided that waiting a day or so was a bad idea. Seems the only bad idea was heading out into the woods right after they had seen the darkness!

"Not sure what you all smelled this morning, but I sure sense something out of the norm here. Smells like a rotted animal, mixed with skunk juice. Only worse." Reynolds knew his animal and plant smells and was getting specific. "A little decomposing wood thrown in for good measure, and a handful or two of some kind of fungi."

"Robert, Norma, Steve, how are you three feeling?" Sheriff Anderson wanted an update on their condition. "No holding back, now, I need an honest answer here."

Robert and Steve said to push on. Norma felt something was in the air; that they were in the presence of a force much bigger than imagined. Nothing was eminent, she felt, but they had better stay alert and focused.

"Okay, so let's make a note right here, at the edge of the woods, that we felt and smelled something." Sheriff Anderson continued, "Same as we smelled this morning, but without the dark forms or fog. No feeling of being pulled in, but certainly some kind of force nearby. Are we all on the same page?"

They were.

"Deputy Owens, let's tag this tree," ordered the sheriff. "We'll come back and have a starting point where we can head deeper into the woods and see if we can discover the origin of the smell." Owens tagged the tree, and the group headed back to the cabin. "Reynolds, are we in danger of seeing the wolves again when we come back?"

"Not those wolves, if that's what they really were," Reynolds replied. "To take down that moose, they'd have to be in great shape. Too good of shape for your standard northern Minnesota wolf pack."

"Or," added Norma, "if it is an extension of the darkness, next time we might see something else completely. Who's to say it won't take on a human form?"

"She's right. Who knows what it will produce, or possibly even establish, in our midst." Robert had many thoughts on the power of the darkness, and yet he had not considered this new option. "It has become stronger over the past twenty-five years, so I doubt it was out of commission. I'm thinking it has cycled back here from somewhere else."

"Most living things do have a certain range, some very local, some rather extensive. Wolves may stake out an area that covers miles, but mostly it comes down to what food source is available and the path of travel." Reynolds said in response to Robert. "Migratory patterns are incredibly long and may take days and weeks to travel, but I don't think that's what we have here. As Norma said, we have to think differently. Twenty-five years may seem like a long cycle, or migration, but to the darkness, it may be the blink of an eye. We have no idea how to relate twenty-five years to its lifespan, so this could be a cycle back as you say, Robert, or a migration from somewhere else."

"I'm thinking that somewhere else must be a pretty nasty place, and I, for one, wish it would have stayed there." Sheriff Anderson was beginning to feel the darkness had become a very real thing, and he was not comfortable with its new level of prominence. "So, Reynolds, was that it for the next twenty-five years? Will this thing head out of town for a couple decades again?"

"He can't answer that, Glen," said Robert. "None of us can. We need to come back and take a few hikes into the woods to see what we can find. Any trace of this weekends activities we'll need to find right away. Maybe with a few clues we'll be able to make a decent guess. In the meantime, I may as well spend a few nights and keep an eye on things."

"I'd rather not have anyone staying in the cabin alone, especially you, Robert. I appreciate your need to track this thing down, but you said yourself the pull of the darkness is a strong one," the sheriff continued, "and I sure as heck don't want you missing come morning. Let's nail down a couple days when we can get a few of us out here together. And I agree, the sooner the better."

Thomas looked around the group of friends as they gathered by their vehicles. "Just a quick double check just so we don't leave anyone behind or mix up the gear. Marcus, Roxie and Axel are heading home in Axel's truck. Karen will take Kevin and Jenna in her rental car. Sam's got Nick, and Allison will ride with me."

"Perfect, Thomas, thanks. We always miss something, so I'm sure when everyone gets home you'll find somebody else's whatever in your car. Text your ransom note and don't ask for too much." Marcus had enjoyed the weekend, but was already thinking about how he could get back to Havenswood Valley and begin researching the darkness that nearly killed Kevin. Helping his friends get on their way back home was the first step. "Make sure you all stop for gas and coffee in town, remember the next decent stop is over ninety miles away. Plus, it's good to support the locals of Havenswood Valley with one last purchase."

Final goodbye hugs and promises to keep in better touch were shared. Sam, Nick, Thomas and Allison were going to meet for an early dinner. Kevin assured the entire group he was fine, but would let everyone know if he suddenly had an urge to dress up like Darth Vader. Jenna had thought about staying behind with Axel, but the events of the weekend had put a wall between what may have been the start of a romantic relationship. Their core beliefs had surfaced with different views, so having Jenna driving back with Karen and Kevin gave them each a handy excuse to say goodbye, for now.

It was just past one o'clock in the afternoon, and as the cars and trucks disappeared down the driveway, a light dust kicked up from the tires and filled the air. Marcus, Roxie and Axel smiled as they waved goodbye to their friends, yet the three remaining campers couldn't help but feel unsettled. It wasn't the same as other trips to the cabin, something had invaded their family and ruined the tranquility of this formerly peaceful setting. They felt the loss of innocence, but in its place had gained insight into a world more captivating than they had ever expected.

"Then there will be a few of you," Robert had said, "that will have your entire life turned upside down." Truer words could not be spoken about these three friends.

"Let's make sure the deposit money is here for the realtor, and the keys, too. I'd hate to lose this cabin next year, that is if we all agree to come back, just because we didn't reserve it or forgot a key in a jacket pocket." Marcus wanted to keep everything in order at the cabin. He'd grown to love this place, and it would be a shame not to be able to come back, even after the crazy weekend they had just spent. In fact, it should be even more exciting next time!

"Marcus, everybody's gone but us three and Deputy Stevens. The realtor comes in the morning, just like every year, so let's put the deposit and keys into the cookie jar and head home." Roxie was set to go.

"Truck's all loaded, we just need to do a last look around." Axel loved driving, and heading back with his two best friends would make this a very enjoyable ride.

"You folks about ready to leave?" asked Deputy Stevens. He was standing on the porch, not wanting to invade their cabin space.

"Almost," said Marcus. "Just waiting for the realtor to swing by. If she doesn't get here by 2:00 pm, we'll leave the keys inside."

"I can wait for her if you like," offered the Deputy. "It's no trouble."

"You know, we usually stay and enjoy the last of our vacation. If we feel like going sooner, we'll take you up on your offer," replied Marcus.

"Sounds fine with me," answered the Deputy. "I'll be in the squad car catching up on some paperwork. Windows will be up, so just knock if you need something. By the way, Sheriff Anderson should be back anytime now. He called and said they were heading in."

"Cool, thanks," said Marcus, as the deputy walked back to his car.

"Marcus," said Roxie, "what's going on? I thought we were leaving now?"

"I'm not sure. We can leave if you want, but I feel like I need to really soak this all in before we head home." He also wondered why he had told the deputy they were going to stay. He didn't have a good answer. "Can we go inside for a while?"

"Sure, that's fine. We've always trusted your instincts," replied Roxie. "You just caught me off guard with your comments to the deputy about staying longer."

"Me, too," said Axel. "I'm good to go now, but if you want to hang here for a while, that's cool. We can see if the sheriff found anything and then head home."

"Thanks, guys. Anyway, I'm sure we left some food in the fridge, and probably some gear in the cabin." Marcus somehow knew there was something left to do, a legitimate reason to stay.

"Yeah, I'm starved already" said Axel.

Roxie and Marcus rolled their eyes at Axel. He was always hungry!

The three friends were glad they had decided to come back into the cabin and relax before the drive home. It had been a much busier weekend than they had planned, and resting in the comfortable chairs and couches of the cabin was very peaceful. Robert had the cabin rebuilt, making it an improved replica of the original homestead. The exterior of the cabin kept its authentic look with a number of features, including locally harvested logs that interlocked at the corners. He added the green colored metal roof, which was one of the first in the area, and had the trim around the triple-paned windows painted red to match the extra wide front door. Naturally aged cedar planks stretched the length of the porch, edged by a hand-turned railing and six inch by six inch rough sawn pillars. River rock was grouted three feet up the base of the pillars, matching the stones used on the chimney.

"I love these books," announced Roxie. She had found a paperback of stereograms under the glass table in the great room. "I have no idea how they do it, but getting the 3D picture from what looks like a bunch of blotchy colors is so cool!"

"We used to get these in the Sunday comics," said Marcus. "It was one of my favorite parts of the paper. I read that seeing the hidden elements has something to do with not focusing on the actual picture, and then the offset patterns allow your vision to pull out the image." They enjoyed passing around the book and taking turns trying to see what would pop off the pages. It was a nice diversion, but the fun eventually took its toll.

"Okay, this has been fun but looking at these pictures for so long is making my head hurt. The designs look as mixed up as the pattern on the dining room table," winced Axel.

"What do you mean, pattern?" asked Roxie.

"I don't know, haven't you guys noticed it?" Axel asked. "It isn't like a repeating pattern, more like, I don't know, a map of some kind."

"A map?" came in stereo from Marcus and Roxie, who at this time were positioned at his sides. They walked over and cleared off the centerpiece on the table, which opened up the entire design.

"Take a look, and you don't really have to be cross eyed," said Axel.

Marcus and Roxie studied the center of the table in silence. It hadn't been totally cleared off the entire weekend, and someone had made sure the centerpiece was in place during final clean up. The trio was not sure if what they were looking at was a map, or an artistic touch to the table. They focused on the multi colored center of the table.

"Maybe it's the standard design for the company that made this table," Roxie offered. "Wouldn't it be an easy way to promote the place where this table was made?"

"Maybe, but I doubt many people would want a logo in the middle of a dinner table." Marcus was ready to let his idea come to light. "By the looks of this table, I doubt they were thinking of branding. I'd say it's a design with some meaning for the owner of the table, either the person who made it, or whoever it was made for. Just because it's new to the cabin doesn't mean it's a new table. It could be pretty old."

"I was kinda kidding about the company logo. With no markings or a way to identify this piece, it was most likely a custom piece made by a single craftsman, not factory built. Those are different kinds of wood used in the center to give it the color variance. That's a lot of detailed work," Roxie continued, "but I do agree it was probably based on a request. Maybe Robert could explain it to us."

Axel had been thinking, which normally was about camping, rock climbing, kayaking or anything else out of doors. He loved the cabin trip and being around friends, but he would also be just as comfortable in a tent out on his own. "Maybe Robert knows, but I think it's a map of this area. I can recognize a few of the landmarks like the rocky edge that's out by the stream, shown here. And this hillside is the one that borders the cabin area."

Roxie was nearly convinced that it was a map. Her skills as a CAD engineer came in handy with this, she was used to thinking in flat, then 3D, then back to flat. She spent most of her days deeply concentrated on making written details turn into finished three-dimensional products. "Yes, I see them, too!" Roxie was getting into it now. "And I think this line of thin wood within the design is a key, a connector of some sort to pull all the pieces together. Look, it runs from the hillside, to the rocks, bounces off the stream and then heads back to this mangled area."

"I know what that mangled mess is, I think." Marcus was also now convinced the items were not just a design. "There's a tree I've noticed on one of the trails. It's off the path, but it looks kind of like that. I'd have to see it from another angle, but it's a pretty close match. I noticed it when I stopped to tighten the laces on my running shoes. I looked up and I thought it was a perfect tree for a haunted forest."

"Scaaaaarrrrrreeeee treeeee..." in a squeaky voice, was a perfect response from Axel.

"Hey, you're seeing patterns in a dinning room table, I can see trees in the forest!" and as soon as Marcus had said this, they all looked at each other and busted out laughing. It was a really goofy thing to say and Marcus knew it.

"We can squeeze in some time looking around before we have to head home. Let's see what we can figure out." Roxie was in her element and ready to take the lead on this mystery. "All right! First thing we have to do is draw this out on a big piece of paper. Then we'll add in the landmarks we know of to get a clear picture of what the woodworker had in mind."

"How will our picture be any different than the table?" asked Axel.

"The table isn't to scale," stated Marcus, still lost in the design.

"Very good answer, Cartography Man." Roxie continued, "It's like the product parts I design. At stage one they look out of place, but once you see the finished product it takes on a whole new dimension. We'll lay this out, put in the landmarks and step back. Maybe if we look at it cross eyed we'll see a secret image."

A knock on the door startled the three undercover detectives.

"Don't mean to butt in, but the sheriff wanted me to let you know they are headed back to town. He said he hopes you enjoy the last part of your stay, and when he has his report done he will call you." Deputy Stevens had come up the stairs and none of the three had heard him, nor had they heard the sheriff's car leave.

"Thanks, Deputy," answered Roxie. "None of us have any time constraints, so we're going to hang out for a while longer."

"Fine by me," he answered. He turned to go back to his car and added, "I'm on duty all day, and this is as nice a place to be as anywhere. Be sure to let me know when you leave."

"Wow, that was close. I suddenly felt like we had something to hide," said Marcus. "Let's get this drawing started and see what we come up with."

"I'm cool with that. Let's rock!" replied Axel.

And with that enthusiastic response, they began to work together converting the design on the table into a scale drawing of the area surrounding the cabin. Since they had stayed numerous times, and had hiked, biked, ran and swam just about everywhere nearby, they put the table design elements in place rather easily. Drawing them in was done by Roxie, and Axel used his orienteering skills to finalize distances. Marcus was working on a legend and any keys they could place on the map. He was also working on the concept as if he were the head detective trying to solve a new case.

"So this guy puts a map on a table, not telling a soul, that we know of. Otherwise, I think anyone that would have discovered this would have left a note about it. I know I couldn't see it and not say something."

"Uh huh," replied Roxie, not really listening too closely.

Marcus took that as a clue to continue, "He puts a map on a table, in a remote cabin where there are no TV's, no radio, and limited cell phone reception. He's thinking that you should be outdoors enjoying nature, but if you are stuck inside, here's a game you can play. I have no idea what the rules are, but maybe after we go visit these landmarks we'll have a better understanding of his intentions."

"Or maybe it's just a drawing of his favorite things in the area." And with that comment Axel took the wind out of everyone's sail, even his own. "Oh, sorry."

"Wow, that's a real mood killer. Here I thought we were on to something," Roxie put down her pencils. "Are we just too tired and ready to go home? Why did we think this was a map?"

"The connector, is what I think you called it. The line that ran from landmark to landmark. Hey, I still believe it's a map, and I'm in for checking these things out before we leave. It isn't too late and we've pretty much got our scaled map done." Marcus had wanted to stay an extra day, so leaving late was not a problem.

"Okay, then, let's take a look." Axel put his pencils down and the three stood in front of their map.

It did look very different from the table design. Everything spaced as it would be in real life, not crunched together, not out of scale and on top of each other as it appeared on the table design. Off to the left was the rocky edge, a gathering of large boulders that had somehow come together in one place and overlooked a small drop off. Maybe pushed by a glacier 10,000 years ago, they were due west of the cabin, about a quarter of a mile. The stream, which was crossed over by using the South Foot Bridge, cut between the rocks and the cabin. It ran north to south and was about fifteen feet wide on average. Clear and deep, smallmouth bass, catfish and an occasional dogfish or pike were the usual catch by the local anglers. Nick and Axel did the most fishing on the cabin trips, and they had decent luck each time. Not enough for a full meal, but a nice side dish everyone would enjoy.

The hiking path led around the rocks and to the north, headed into the woods where pines, birch, oak and maple grew thick and full. It was the last strand on the cabin owner's land that held such a number of trees, and the guests were always glad to see them upon their return. Most of the area near the cabin had been cleared out, but a beautiful meadow now stretched across the previously empty land, and was a haven to birds, animals and wind-replanted wild grasses.

Inside the wooded area is where Marcus had seen the mixture of knotted wood he felt was in the design on the table. Maybe half a mile from the rocks, and halfway between the South Foot Bridge and the North Foot Bridge. It was near a loop they had traveled many times on walks or runs, but if Marcus had not stopped one day to tie his shoes, he may have never noticed the tree.

From there it was over the North Foot Bridge a quarter mile to the meadow then about three quarters of a mile to the cabin.

The hillside was a natural earthen boundary on the east side of the cabin, and helped guide travelers back. In total, about a two and a half mile loop. A nice walk in the morning or evening, as well as a nice warm up run for those who had brought their running gear.

"I'm all set!" Axel had his shoes and jacket on, ready to head out.

"Zippin' up the jacket, boss," bantered Marcus.

"Let's do this!" was the final word from Roxie.

Heading outside, they informed the deputy one last run was a must before they left Havenswood Valley and set off a quick pace before he could think twice about it. Since it wasn't dark, and they were only going two miles, he felt it was fine for the three to loosen up before the ride home. Especially since the sheriff had come back and said it was all clear. "What could happen in two miles?" thought the deputy.

It was the golden time of day now, the hour just between late afternoon and early evening. A beautiful hue of gold bathed everything in sight. Marcus, Roxie and Axel cruised along the path to the rocky ledge, excited to be acting on their hunch! "Adventure with a purpose," is what Axel had said. His description was right on target. Once they made it to the rocks, the quickly setting sun reminded them their recon time was limited. They could have spent hours looking over the formation, but gave it only five minutes. A few uninspired notes taken, they headed off at a nice pace along the path through the woods.

"I think it's right...about...here it is!" With that declaration Marcus left the path and navigated about ten yards in.

"That, my friends, is where ugly sticks come from," Axel was in awe. "By far the most horrid tree, if you can call it a tree, I have ever laid eyes on. It puts the ugh in ugly!"

"Axel, I do believe your assessment is correct. However, I would add creepy in there somewhere. And the smell, oh my gosh, it really does stink. I noticed it from back on the path." Roxie pinched her nostrils closed to keep out the stench.

"Might be this marshy ground around here that's producing the stink. I haven't noticed it anywhere else, but it's really mushy footing, and jeez, every time you step in it, the stink gas erupts. It's like fishing for bass in shallow water and stirring up the bottom." Marcus carefully made his way to the tree. They had brought flashlights, and with his turned on he started to look over the trunk. This was the tree from the table, no doubt. Pretty good depiction of it, he thought. A circumference of about six feet, and a diameter of about three feet. Looked like it had been an oak, but not really. Height was around thirty feet, with the few branches that remained totally knotted and burned in some places. Leafless this time of year, and probably all year, the top of the trunk was half open from what looked like a lightning strike. The bottom half looked carved out but could have come from a lightning strike or a fire long ago. Marcus leaned into the trunk to get a better look up and inside, "Man, it's dank in here, like it's humid." He stepped out and shivered in the cold, "It's as if someone had just put out a fire, the trunk felt warm, the air is thick and of course that lovely stench."

"My turn," Axel maneuvered over and nudged his way into the trunk. "Helloooo in there. Can anybody hear me?" He started to turn away but something caught his eye and he quickly turned back to the trunk. "What was that? Did you see that, Marcus?"

"See what?"

"I don't know if it was the eyeball of an animal or reflection off your flashlight, but it gave me the creeps. Like someone was watching through the trunk."

"Rhooaarrr!" Roxie jumped from around the tree and scared the crap out of both Axel and Marcus.

"Haaaaayyy, what the, oh jeez Roxie, what the heck!" Marcus and Axel mixed a bunch of words together at the same time, both relieved and embarrassed.

"It was just me peeking through the trunk. Thought you knew it was me but when you freaked out to Marcus, I knew it was time to put a scare on you two." Roxie, smiling, began to laugh.

"Well, it worked. My heart's racing and I'm not sure my pants are dry." Marcus faked a wet pant leg.

"I am totally freaked! Let's get out of here guys." Axel loved the outdoors, but did not enjoy pranks, especially scary ones at dusk.

"Sorry, guys," said Roxie. "I didn't mean to do such a good job on this. I think we've got enough notes on this gnarly tree. We can stop by the stone wall for a quick look and then be back in no time."

They took off running, did a fast and uneventful walk around the stone wall and then ran back to the cabin. Deputy Stevens was still in his squad car when he saw the three running back to the cabin, jumped out and asked if everything was alright. They assured him it was, they had just wanted to run back faster because it was getting late. Once back on cabin property they relaxed and realized the tree scare by Roxie would be a very funny story to tell people. Eventually. The deputy informed them that Sheriff Anderson had called and there was nothing new to report, but he had wanted an update and was upset that the three guests had taken off on their own. The deputy would stay until the visitors left and requested they either stay in the cabin or begin their trip home.

"No worries," said Roxie. "We'll be ready to go soon. Don't want to keep you here all night."

"No problem. I've been able to get most of my paperwork from this weekend done so I'll have everything ready for Sheriff Anderson on Monday morning." He was calm, no pressure from the deputy to leave sooner than they wanted to. He actually enjoyed being needed and was hoping the cabin events would turn into something big.

"Guess the realtor isn't going to make it by today," he added.

"Doesn't look like it," answered Roxie. "Thanks again for sticking around. We'll get our things together and be on our way."

Once inside they started to discuss the table, the map and their excursion when Marcus came up with a question. "So, like I said earlier, this guy makes a table, puts a map on it..."

"We think he puts a map on it," interjected Axel.

Marcus finishes, "Right, we think he puts a map on it. We then check out the landmarks and find nothing out of the ordinary."

"So, let's look at the design again," suggests Roxie.

They agree to one last look at the design and head over to the table. They admire the workmanship, and begin to review the oval shape in the center of the table; it was a darker wood than the rest of the pine table, maybe cherry. Inlaid so it's as smooth as the rest of the surface. Same results as before, at first you don't notice the landmarks, but then, after a few minutes you can't not see them. They jump out at you, just like a Stereogram.

It was then that Marcus noticed a slight change in the pine, a very thin line of some sort that started at about ten o'clock on the oval, and led to the corner of the table. He looked at another corner and saw the same line, hitting the oval at about two o'clock. "Hey, look at this!" He pointed out the lines and Roxie and Axel also saw the four lines, one from each corner, connecting with the oval.

"A connector line," said Roxie. "Same as the one in the oval. It's pulling the four corners into the oval. Or are they emanating from the center to the corners?"

"Depends on the legend, which we don't have," Axel continued. "Sometimes a map will show a landmark, but there's a key or guide to confirm with. We haven't found a thing to show what any of this means."

Marcus did some figuring on the fly. "The oval represents the landmarks, the lines represent a path of some sort. They lead, or have led, to. Wait...four landmarks, four lines, four legs..."

"Four score and seven years ago, yes, every table has four legs," said Axel.

"How 'bout four-tee-niners? My favorite football team!" Roxie loved word play.

"Come on, I'm losing my train of thought here, what does this table represent? The whole thing, I mean?" Marcus was thinking fast.

"Food!" Axel suggested.

"Family time," added Roxie. "A place for everyone to meet, eat, play cards, drink wine."

"Exactly!" Marcus liked her answer. Axel and Roxie were now very interested in finding out where Marcus was going. "Family, food, games, wine, reading the paper, having talks, having a birthday cake. All the things you would do in a home, this table represents the cabin!"

"You're right, a well built and safe cabin at that," Axel added.

"Yes, it's a very safe place!" Marcus exclaimed. "Holy landmarks, Axel, I think you've cracked the code! Dude, grab that corner of the table."

"What?" replied Axel.

"The corner, grab it! We're going to turn this cabin table upside down. If it is a safe, there must be a door, a latch, some kind of key or code to open something up" Marcus was pumped up and two steps ahead of Roxie and Axel.

"I said it was a safe place, not a safe! Oh, what the heck, just let me get a good grip!" Axel grabbed his end but they would need Roxie to help with the maneuver so as not to damage the grand piece of wood work.

The three worked together and somewhat gently turned the table on its back. It looked like a giant, Galapagos, wooden legged turtle stuck in time, frozen stiff. They stared at the flipped table, looking for clues, wood work details, anything out of the ordinary.

"Looks pretty boring to me, I thought we were on to something here. I really liked the way it was headed, I got pretty excited." Roxie was bummed.

"We'll find something, I know it," Marcus was convinced the table was the key.

"It's all pine, no inlays, and no weird patterns. Just looks like a pole barn without a roof." Axel was perplexed. He, too thought something was going to come of the table.

"What about these? The floor guards, I bet the table maker didn't put them on. Let's pull them off." Marcus was looking for anything now.

"Marcus, come on. They're on to keep the floor from getting banged up. You're losing focus," Roxie was bringing Marcus back to Earth. "Let's put this table up and think about heading home. We'll have lots to talk about on the drive."

"You're right, I was just feeling that somehow this table was more than just a bunch of wood," Marcus was cooled down on the table idea. "Let's put it back, grab our gear and do a walk around the inside before we go."

They righted the table, put the decorations on top and then went to get their stuff. One load out to the truck, then another and they had just a few more things to toss in. They were making their way around the house when Axel found Kevin's metal detector behind the door of one of the bedrooms.

"Found something!" Axel yelled. "Kev forgot his fortune-finding metal detector. Has he ever found anything, anywhere with this beeping thing?"

"Don't think so," replied Roxie. "He always hopes to find a treasure of some sort, that's why he brings it. I think it's just a way for Kevin to get some time alone and relax. I don't know if he even turns the thing on."

"Really. Hmmm. Maybe I'll find a treasure in here somewhere. How does this thing work? Oh, here it is!" Axel flipped the on switch and did a great Kevin impression; the slow walk he does around the outside of the cabin, stopping, digging into the dirt, and finally tossing whatever he had dug up into the air.

"Looks just like Kevin, I'm sure he'd be amused," Roxie was getting a kick out of this.

"Now, if I could just find the meteor that I saw last night," Axel was now doing a full on Kevin impression when Marcus walked in with the last of his gear and had a front row seat to the entertainment. "It fell at about eighty-five degrees latitude, and about fourteen degrees longitude at a rate of about five million miles per second, right through the earth's atmosphere. If my calculations are correct, and they usually are, that would put the meteor right about here!"

Axel plopped the metal detector on the table, right next to the center oval, the very object they had been working on for the last few hours.

"Very funny," said Marcus.

It seemed funny, until the metal detector started to make noise…beep, beep, beep, beep.

"Really, very funny Axel. I get it, our map is the big find. Hope you enjoyed yourself." Marcus was done with the oval joke.

"But I'm not doing anything, I don't even know how to work this thing." He pulled it away form the oval and rested it on the floor. Now it really started to make noise, BEEP, BEEP, BEEP.

"Come on, Axel. Turn it off and let's go," Roxie was also ready to go and was becoming miffed at Axel making fun of the investigating they did on the table design.

But Axel was not hearing them. He was lifting the metal detector back up to the oval and noticed the noise would subside. It was there, just softer. When Axel placed it on the floor, it was louder. Moving it around the table, suddenly Marcus got loud!

"Stop, right there! By the leg, it's stronger. When you move away from the leg, it goes silent. Try the leg, try the leg!"

Marcus' eyes were wide with excitement, he couldn't believe what this metal detector was doing.

"Guys, it's the floor guards! Relax." Roxie was not so excited.

"Metal floor guards?" Marcus said. "I have never seen metal floor guards. Axel, try the legs."

Holding the metal detector next to the leg caused the loudest signal. He then did what anyone would do next, he ran the metal detector up the leg, like scanning a leg for a break. Everyone jumped when the detectors noise level rose in volume.

"That's why it's so heavy, the leg is made of metal," Axel surmised.

"I don't think so, I think it's hollow and there's something metal inside!" Roxie was suddenly immersed in this exercise.

"We've got to flip the table over again, we've got to take off those floor guards!" Marcus was giving direction but Roxie and Axel were already thinking the same thing. The table was flipped again and they stared at the legs. Axel ran the metal detector along the other three legs, with the same results; a loud beeping noise that was the same as the first one. Marcus pulled at the floor guard on the first leg and found a flat head nail tucked under the heavy fabric that guarded the floor from scratches. Axel grabbed a small, flathead screwdriver from a drawer in the kitchen.

"Hey, it's just a flat head nail. Let's see how they do if we pry them off." Axel, pretty adept with tools, felt this would go smoothly. He was right, as the soft pine wood let the nail pull free with a simple prying motion.

"Look at that, it's a plug." Axel said. "Right in the center of the leg, like it's filling in for a hollowed out leg."

"It is hollow, remember, with metal inside?" Marcus wanted to move to step two.

"Pull the plug already," commanded Roxie.

"You want me to pull the plug?" Axel smiled. Marcus took a deep breath and cracked a slight grin.

"Yes, please, pull the plug, thank you." Marcus found himself relaxed, but ready for anything.

"Stick in a sharp object with a little barb on the end and viola, here's your cork plug. And let's see what it's hiding in there." Roxie handed Axel a flashlight.

"Looks like a metal tube, hope it's safe." Axel was having fun, but was not fully confident in this maneuver. He had never found a hidden treasure and wanted to make sure he didn't ruin the item or cause harm to anyone.

"Wait! You're right. Let's take a step back for a minute. We've been at this for some time, and as crazy as it seems, we really did find something. Obviously Robert didn't know it was here, the table just showed up in the last year, and we certainly don't know who it came from. Are they connected? And why the landmarks? There are so many different things in this area that could have been used, why those four?" Marcus was taking stock of the day, the place, the treasure they had found, and needed to go through the steps with Roxie and Axel. They needed to put this puzzle together before they went any further.

"I can't believe we found this either," added Roxie. "It's blowing my mind, really. It's not like we're super sleuths out on case number 112. We're just normal people on a weekend trip with friends. This kind of stuff happens to other people, not us. And now, I'm ready to pull that tube out and see what's in it. Maybe we need to do it at a distance, and maybe we need to open it from behind a tree, but I can't wait to see what is inside. The trouble someone took to put it there, maybe it's gold, maybe it's a will, maybe it's drugs. But let's get it open and then decide what to do."

"So we all agree, to open it, that's great," said Marcus. "I'm going to run out and tell the deputy we will be ready to go in about ten minutes. I don't want him coming in right now." Marcus was back in two minutes, and the trio was ready to continue.

"Alright, I'll go McGroover and pull it up with some string. No, really, it'll work. Then I'll stand behind that truss support log in the den and open the tube up." Axel was ready for action, and Marcus and Roxie agreed.

Once the string was in place, Axel stood back with the line pulled over a beam near the ceiling. This seemed like overkill, but better safe than sorry. The tube came out easily, and was gently lowered to the floor.

"Hard to tell if it's old or new," said Roxie, "but the simple engraving looks like it was done by hand."

Axel picked it up. "Yeah," replied Axel, "looks like a weird serial number or ID code." He carried it to the den and wrapped his arms around the log. One end was solid, the other had a cap that screwed off. Axel opened the tube and, nothing happened. "Well, let's look inside and see...a....um, looks like a rolled up piece of paper." Axel held it out for Roxie and Marcus to look in.

"Let's see if it will slide out," suggested Roxie.

It did. Axel tilted the tube, which was about three inches across and about fifteen inches long. The contents poured out and on the floor lay a waxy looking parchment, tan in color, with text in black ink. Roxie gently unrolled the parchment, it was very pliable, and they all looked at their treasure. "Uh, can either of you read any foreign languages?" asked Axel.

"Looks like some Euro language. I would guess it's maybe Norwegian or Finnish, something Scandinavian," said Marcus. "It looks brand new, but I'm thinking the waxy layer has kept the parchment in good condition."

"Oh my gosh! It has the stone wall on it, look, at the bottom of the parchment." Roxie was surprised by her discovery.

"Yeah, and the whole thing looks tense, I don't know the language, but I'm pretty sure this isn't a love letter." Marcus was examining this like one of his client's projects. "And it's dated 1897, heck, this thing is over one hundred years old. If it's been passed down a few generations, why was it hidden?"

"Maybe the table maker was the last of his clan. He left the clues for someone to figure out, someone that would value the find." Axel had a formula to announce. "I'll bet the table maker was the last of his family and the only one who knew about this parchment, and if the other legs hold something, what they all mean. For some reason he had to keep this information secret until just the right person would find it. We are now the keepers of the parchment!"

"Get a hold of yourself, Axel." Roxie wasn't going to buy into this so easily. "Maybe it's just his land holdings. Sure at first I freaked, but think about it, maybe these four landmarks are truly that, his landmarks."

"Then why the need to be hidden?" asked Marcus. "He'd only need to publicly lay out his claim. Let's open the other legs and talk about this on the way home. It's getting late, even for me, and I don't know about you guys but this has made me jumpy."

Axel began to pry the other floor guards off. "These cork plugs will be off in a minute. Marcus, you fish the tubes out and I'll hammer the guards back on." Axel was done in no time. They flipped the table back over and finally left the cabin, waving goodbye to Deputy Stevens with as innocent a smile as they could each muster. They now had four tubes in their possession, and had no idea what the other three held inside.

"Did we just steal these?" asked Roxie.

"I don't think so. Well, maybe, I don't know. It started out as a mystery we made up, and now we've got real documents that might be a hundred years old!" Marcus was excited with their discovery.

"What about the three items that we bought at Tres Azure?" Roxie said.

"Those were paid for, not stolen. Besides," continued Marcus, "they're at the cabin."

"About that…" replied Roxie.

"Roxie, you didn't!" Marcus couldn't hold back the smile that was spreading across his face. "I was thinking the same thing, but just forgot about them when we got into the table."

"I put them in my bag last night," she said. "I really wanted to see if I could find out more about them once we got home. They weren't going to do anyone any good sitting in the cabin, and maybe there would be some kind of connection between what happened and the three items."

"You know," started Marcus.

"Hey, talk about a coincidence," interrupted Axel, "isn't that Norma?"

As they were driving at just under the twenty-five miles per hour downtown speed limit through Havenswood Valley, there indeed was Norma Brookings. She was standing on the sidewalk in front of the post office, as if she had been waiting for them to drive by. Not really smiling at them, but giving a look that froze their conversation until they had passed her by.

Axel adjusted the rear view mirror and broke the silence. "She's still standing there."

"That was so weird," Roxie had turned around and was looking back through the truck window. "What are the chances of us seeing her just as we are talking about her? Marcus? Are you with us?"

Marcus was the last to speak, and had not turned around for a second look at Norma. Instead, he was staring straight ahead, eyes focused in concentration on his thoughts. "Yeah, I'm here. But when we were talking about the three items, I was going to say something before Axel saw Norma. And now, now I'm really even more messed up about what I was thinking."

"Sorry, bro, didn't mean to jump in but it freaked me out when I saw her," answered Axel.

"No, it's not that. I would have done the same thing. It's just that here we are, the three of us that ended up being the last ones to leave, the ones that noticed the table design, the ones that kept at it and ended up finding the tubes in the legs." Marcus was still looking ahead, pulling his thoughts together as he spoke. "So, I was thinking, again, before we saw Norma, about the three items and what if they were meant for us? What if Norma knew we were going to find something and the three items were going to help us? And then at that exact minute, there's Norma!"

"Marcus, that is so totally possible! Norma knows stuff before it happens, it makes total sense! And we know you have the same ability. I can think of, I don't know, maybe three times you knew something was up but couldn't really explain it this weekend alone." Axel was sold on Marcus's idea, and was starting to believe Marcus might somehow be more connected to the situation then they all realized.

"So, we're thinking Norma had us pegged before even we knew what was going on, and somehow she knows about Marcus and his ability to sense things." Roxie, who at this point was also open to the idea that Norma had planted the items for this exact reason, was feeling it might be possible. But, she had to ask the question everyone was thinking. "Why us? Why would the three of us be the ones to end up with the items, and the tubes? Of course Marcus having insight into weird stuff isn't new to us. We've always thought he had ESP, but we just called it good timing."

"I doubt she knew it was going to be us, exactly." Marcus was getting his thoughts in line now. "I'm thinking she knew it would be three people, and somehow it worked out that the three of us were the ones that ended up really getting into this. Maybe it's just fate. And as far as my ESP, you guys have always given me a hard time about stuff like knowing when to do something because I felt it. What was it you called it, Extra Stupid Power? So I guess I'm not too freaked out about some of the things that happened this weekend."

"Before this trip, I would have said fate was a pretty weak argument." Roxie had been transformed this weekend from someone that lived in a black and white world needing detail and science to support claims, to a person that was now willing to grasp at theories she could not fully understand. "Now, I'm open to much more. There's no way to explain some of the events that happened, and I'm cool with that. I believe Norma has the ability to see things even she can't comprehend, but she has faith. She works with a different view of the world, and I can accept that, too."

"You two are way ahead of me," said Axel. "I just believe Norma can see stuff in the world that we have no chance of seeing. I'm a simpleton, but I get where you guys are going, and I'm with you. Something is going on, and I'm up for the adventure."

They were well beyond Havenswood Valley now, and in a short while they would stop for dinner. Marcus would suggest when, and of course it turned out that they would meet up with Sam, Nick, Allison and Thomas. A flat tire had delayed them for nearly two hours, and they were just leaving when the trio showed up. It was a short exchange, and not a word was spoken about the table, the tubes or seeing Norma.

Once inside the restaurant, Axel spoke up. "So, we don't plan on saying anything to the others?"

"I wasn't sure what to say, it just didn't seem like the right time to bring it up," answered Roxie.

"There's a lot the three of us need to talk about first," Marcus said. "We don't really see the others very often, so we have to figure out how much to tell them, if anything. And once we get the nerve to tell the sheriff what we found, well, no doubt we'll have to come back and meet with him, Robert and Norma."

They agreed to keep everything just between the three of them, no discussions with other friends, family or co-workers. They'd meet up soon after getting home and start their review and research. Something had been going on in Havenswood Valley for nearly two hundred years, and they were now a part of it. Dinner was fast, and soon the highway was again under the tires of Axel's truck. The mood inside the cab was full of excitement and expectations, and plenty of coffee for the driver!

"This weekend, and especially this day, has been so cool. I can't believe Kevin left his metal detector." Axel was smiling as he drove. "I can't wait to find out what's written on that parchment and see what's in the other tubes!"

"Whatever happens, whatever we find, you're right, Axel, this really was an awesome trip. I've never experienced anything like it, and, for sure, have never found something as old as these parchments. Did I say how awesome it's been?" Roxie was feeling more free, more open to new things than she'd been in many years.

"The three of us, sharing this together, that's what makes it so great. For as long as we've known each other, this is something way beyond anything we've done." Marcus was in a very good space. "We'll see what comes next, but even I don't need my ESP to know we've got tons of excitement ahead."

The Havenswood Valley Supper Club. Just hearing the name makes you feel warm inside. Located in one of the city's original homes of Main Street, this classic three story Victorian had been renovated in the 1970's with additional rooms on the main level and remodeling work throughout the house. It's a very homey restaurant everyone can rely on for good food and such friendly customer service that you felt guilty not helping to pick up the dishes at the end of your dinner. It's kind of like going over to your relatives' home to enjoy a meal. If you've enjoyed your meal, or more precisely your beverages, too much, you can have a free ride home in their vintage Chevy Nomad HVSC Taxi. The holidays at the supper club are especially busy, as owners James and Ellen Landy go all out with decorations and themed days. The basement, a small wine bar, and the second level, normally reserved for those looking for a more secluded part of the restaurant, are used for the overflow of people wanting to experience the famous holiday meals at the Havenswood Valley Supper Club.

Tonight the restaurant is nearly full. It's Friday evening and the locals have saved up for the weekend and are treating themselves to an enjoyable dinner out. With Thanksgiving approaching, the decorations of fall colors and holiday knick-knacks that Ellen has collected, and received as donations, over the years are everywhere. Ellen loves the fall, as it means a change in the menu to include heartier meals, and of course the Christmas holiday season would soon be here.

On this evening, in the upstairs level, there sat three locals at a small oak table, its natural wood grain surface covered with large plates of food that had hardly been touched. Wine, on the other hand, had flowed freely and led to deeper and deeper conversation among the trio of Glen, Robert and Norma. For all the research done over the past two plus decades, this past weekend's events were more intense then everything else combined. What they experienced at the cabin brought to light that the answers to their quest had out maneuvered them for over twenty-five years.

"It was all just a story before I saw it on the night Michael disappeared, a tale about as believable as Big Foot. And then my life changed. I walked out the doorway of my kitchen to the yard and there was a world unknown to me. Evil, death in the sky, a darkness that pulled my son to his death, and in turn sucked the life out of me." Robert had been speaking in a controlled manner, but yearned to unwind. "Excuse me, Andrea," he said to their server, "can you please bring me a rum and cola when you get a minute? Thanks." He wanted to talk and was now feeling very comfortable with his friends. Robert's guard was down and his craving for a stronger drink was up. "There's nothing in this entire world that can heal the pain I have from losing Michael. It would be one thing if it had been an accident, or a disease, you know, something normal. But this, I can't even begin to understand the enemy, the power it has or the reason it exists. What did we find out this week that's going to help us? What in God's name is going to happen next?"

Glen knew Robert was hurting deeply tonight, and Norma was also well aware of Robert's fragile condition. Seeing and feeling the darkness in the woods brought everything surrounding Michael's death crashing back full force like it had happened just yesterday. They were all feeling the effects, and Sheriff Anderson knew he had to pull the three of them together with his ideas on how to move forward. He'd been working on it for two months and knew it was a long shot.

"God save us all, Robert, because he's the only one that would stand a chance against this. I know this week has been extremely hard on you. You're feeling upset and lost right now, but we have to stay strong in our convictions. You both know that's the only way we can survive and the bare knuckle truth is that we have to strike against this enemy now. We can't waiver." Sheriff Anderson had that steely look in his grey blue eyes, a deep, penetrating stare deep into the hearts of Robert and Norma that at once gave them comfort and trepidation. "We are going to do something, and then we're going to do something else, and something else after that. I don't know exactly what each step is going to be, but I'll tell you right here and now, I will not rest until we figure out how to keep that damn evil out of our valley!"

"Glen, we know it won't be easy. My mother died wondering how, in this beautiful world, a force so dark, so evil, can exist." Norma had been brought to tears this evening while talking and remembering Michael and Kevin and their experiences. How the pull of the darkness had lied to them, tricked them into thinking they were being called to explore a wonderful mystery deep in the woods. Poor, young, Michael not having a chance to fight it once he realized what was happening. And Kevin; saved by those around him, or he, too, would have been a victim, lost by his friends forever.

"However, since it does exist, that gives us a chance to uncover something about it, a clue that, perhaps, will lead us to another step." Norma continued with a look on her face that said it all. "My life here in Havenswood Valley is enriched by the people around us. Look at this place, full of life, of love, of people moving freely about and enjoying a wonderfully social night. Imagine this same place, our whole town in fact, under an expanded threat of the darkness we witnessed, or worse yet, under the rule of this evil. It could happen, the darkness attacking in the city, and these fine people would never know what was going on. The randomness would have them guessing for decades. I agree with you Glen, we need to act now. I'm ready. My senses have been overactive for a few weeks and I don't feel them letting down anytime soon. I think the timing to do something is right now."

"Other than a few more of these rum and colas tonight, nothing could make me feel better than knowing we stopped it." Robert was now very melancholy. "Let's destroy this thing. Even if it takes years, I'd be happy just knowing we're pissin' it off along the way."

They laughed at the thought of evil being mad at them, which allowed Sheriff Anderson an opening to begin discussing his plan. "All right then, now that we've all committed to doing this, here's what I have in mind. Just like I do with any in-depth investigation, we need to put together a profile on the victims to see if we can find common threads. It took some extra time the past two months, but I've chosen ten names of past victims, which we'll divide between us, to dig into and set up profiles on, plus we'll need to do one on Michael, which I'll do, and Kevin, which Norma will do."

"Why ten? How did you choose them?" asked Robert.

"Part of it was seeing a show last summer on TV, and it listed the top ten most wanted by the FBI. I thought if they only knew what was going on over the years around here, and then it hit me. Let's figure out our own top ten victims. I went through our lists, and began sorting them, classifying them, same things I do with a case. By the time I got through everything, there were ten names that really stood out and covered every nuance of what's been going on." Sheriff Anderson continued, "Plus, I felt we needed to add Michael and Kevin. We know more about them than any of the other victims."

"Just let me know what you want me to do, Glen, I'm ready," said Norma.

"Well, Norma, there is one thing I'd like to ask before we get started. Your store, actually underneath your shop, is where I'd like to set up an office for this endeavor. I know you don't use it, in fact you've mentioned on several occasions it's gotten creepy down there, so now we have an excuse to clean it up, put in more lighting and turn it into our research and meeting room. Are you open to that?"

"You guys can knock yourselves out if you want to, but I'm not setting a foot in that dungeon until it's as clean, as bright and as comfortable as any room in my home. Creepy doesn't begin to explain how I feel about that downstairs trap. I'll be doing my research topside until you two have it ready for my inspection."

"Don't worry, Norma," said Robert, "I'll have that space set up in no time. I've been looking for a project to do and this is a great way to keep me busy. Granted, you'll have to decorate it once I've finished, but I'll make sure you are as cozy down there as you are in your home."

"Hey, I swing a pretty good hammer and I also run a fairly straight saw, so I'm not going to let you have all the fun, Robert." Glen had known the store basement was going to be the only venue for a private meeting place, somewhere they could leave work in progress without anyone seeing their secret files, notes and plans. "We'll get a layout together, buy some materials and have this completed before your customers even realize what's going on."

"My customers are pretty sharp, so you best figure out a plan for what you'll say when they ask if I'm adding new space to the store," replied Norma.

"I'll tell them we're building you a first class private office that will be locked at all times and off limits to customers. Same as most of the other downtown businesses," said Sheriff Anderson.

"That sounds just fine," answered Norma.

"I don't know exactly what we'll be doing a month from now," said Robert, "but I'm sure as heck going to work my tail off to make sure we're ready for anything."

"Thanks, Robert, for your support, and thanks Norma, for agreeing to let us set up an office in your basement. I have a feeling there are going to be new challenges every day, my friends. All I ask is that we make sure to keep in touch daily for a while." He looked at Norma, and then at Robert, "Starting tomorrow, we begin our journey anew. Any one of us could easily get in over our head and, well, that usually ends up pretty ugly. I've seen it before and if I think it's too much for any of us, I'll call it off. For now let's finish our drinks and enjoy some lighter conversation. We'll ask Andrea to warm up our dinners, I'm finally hungry."

"I can't believe you're really here! This week seemed so long, but now, here you are." Karen had a wonderful way of being able to talk and smile at the same time. Meeting Kevin at the airport baggage claim was like finding a four-leaf clover, and she let him know how good she felt as they embraced. "I'm so glad we set this up."

"I was thinking the same thing, Karen." Now that Kevin was actually standing with Karen, it hit him how hard he was falling for her. When he looked into her eyes he felt a need to protect her, to provide for her. Classic male stuff, and although Karen was doing just fine on her own, he already knew he wanted to be a big part of her life. Their first hug was warm, strongly knit and finished with a lingering kiss. "I don't think I could have waited another week, I would have gone stir crazy. Thanks for inviting me out, Karen. It's going to be a great week."

It was a typical fall evening in the desert; clear skies, light winds and once out of the city of Phoenix the stars above began to appear more readily to the human eye. Kevin and Karen couldn't have asked for a more perfect start to their time together. By the time they arrived at the restaurant she had picked out, their appetite was for much more than dinner.

It was on the drive home when Kevin asked about the openness of the desert and the foothills nearby. "There is such a different feel here than anywhere I've ever been. What's it like out here at night, in the open desert?"

"Well, let's find a spot and I can show you first hand," Karen replied with a smile. "My home isn't far and I come out here fairly often, though not this late by myself, to enjoy a walk. I'll pull over up ahead and we'll take one of my routes."

Nothing seemed out of the ordinary for Kevin and Karen as they began their short trek, in fact a few other late night walkers and hikers were also out enjoying the evening. In the area were local fauna, namely owls, bats, lizards cutting from rock to rock and not seen but certainly close by, snakes of various species.

"Seems pretty natural being out here together," said Karen.

"I know, I'm so comfortable with you. But if you need some space this week, just let me know. I can take a day to sightsee or just head out for a while."

"Oh, I don't think we'll be getting in each other's way. In fact, I'm pretty sure we'll want to see as much of each other as possible," Karen smiled.

"You're on, then. You may have to load me into your car to get me to the airport in a couple of weeks, and I'll be kicking and screaming the whole way," Kevin said.

The path Karen had chosen was a well traveled trail, and easy to maneuver along as the two talked about the scenery, constellations and how everything still radiated heat from soaking up the intense desert sun rays. They hadn't been out more that a half hour when Kevin said he was beginning to feel lightheaded.

"I think it's just the travel and trying to adapt to the heat too quickly. Maybe just a short stop here and then we can head back to your car." Kevin felt clammy, he told Karen, and maybe a little dehydrated.

Neither one thought much of it, as it seemed very plausible that Kevin was done for the day. Nothing a good night's sleep wouldn't cure. But just as they stood up from the rocks they had rested on, Kevin caught sight of something moving among the cacti nearby. "Hey, did you see that, Karen?"

"See what?" she answered.

"Over there, by those tall cactus trees, uh, plants, uh, bushes?"

"We get that question a lot," Karen laughed. She was straining to see anything moving where Kevin had indicated. "Those are saguaro cacti, they're succulents. And, no, I don't see anything. You'll get used to the night the more we come out. It can be a strange place sometimes, even for the locals. Those saguaro can look like all sorts of things."

Kevin felt embarrassed thinking he saw something, even though Karen understood it was his first night out in the desert. "Thanks for saying that, but I feel like such a rookie out here, you'll just have to...whoa! Now that's something!" Kevin yelled.

Karen turned to look in the direction Kevin was pointing, and by the time she looked and was ready to speak, she realized Kevin had grabbed her left arm and was nearly dragging her back down the path.

"Ke, Kevin, is it... is it coming after us?" Karen asked. She didn't want to turn around and look at it again. Her heart was racing and she was moving as fast as she could. Kevin was able to run down the path pulling Karen and still keep an eye behind them.

"I don't know, Karen! Keep running! I don't see it, but who knows where..."

"KEVIN!" Karen shouted, and she tried to dig in and stop the two of them from moving one more inch down the path. "STOP!"

It was all she could do or say, her eyes popped open as wide as they could, her heart missed beats and her brain just couldn't put everything she was seeing into one thought process. Kevin turned just in time to see the tall, dark shape that was blocking their way, and he felt it sense the two of them were stopped by fear. Kevin and Karen were stuck between screaming for help and trying to decipher what was going on when the form dissipated in an instant and the air was filled with the sound of dirt bikes. Rounding the corner with their single headlights spearing the night, four stud tired, bone rattling, dust raising bikes tore up the path. It had been enough to disperse the threat of the dark form but now the two hikers had to jump to the side and avoid a collision with the two wheeled desert racers headed their way.

"Hey, we're really sorry you had to jump off the trail, it was so dark out here we didn't think anyone was around." The bikers had stopped as soon as they saw Kevin and Karen. The one on the white and green bike continued the apology for his group, "We must have turned off the riverbed early, thinking we were already around this spot. It looked empty, just like the desert trail does and then all of a sudden, bam! It was like we broke through a wall and there you guys were, jumpin' off the trail."

"Actually, you guys came at a really good time. We were kind of turned around trying to find our car, but once you showed up we could see the car from the trail," Kevin replied. "So, thanks and have a good ride."

"Ok, cool. Just didn't want you to get the wrong impression of the dirt bikers around here. We just want to ride and not bother anyone. Later."

Kevin and Karen ran the fifty yards to the car and couldn't stop talking as they drove back to Karen's house. Once inside, they fired up Kevin's laptop and began going over what had happened. They knew once the experience was written down they would have to call Marcus and find out how he'd get the information to Sheriff Anderson. This was very important to everyone, so the two desert explorers spent the next hour discussing and detailing the events of their night hike. By the time they were done it was nearly 2:00 am where Marcus lived, so they'd have to wait and call him the next day. Sending an email was not the way they wanted to break this news.

It was going to be a tough night to get a restful sleep, so they decided to roll out some blankets in front of the TV and fall asleep watching a late night movie. The movie didn't keep their attention, and recurring thoughts about what they had seen and if it was really related to the cabin kept their minds too active for sleep.

"It's hard not to keep rehashing this, Kevin. Do you really think it was the same thing we saw at the cabin?" asked Karen.

"Well, like we talked about earlier, Karen, the more I think about it I'm wondering why the guys on the dirt bikes said it was like a wall. Maybe it was some kind of desert weather phenomenon. What kind of weird weather do you have out here?"

"We have dust devils, you know, a kind of little dirt tornado. They can raise up a lot of dirt, causing visibility problems for a short time. They come and go really quick, too."

"Could be something to think about, it would be tough to see through one at night. I have to say, Karen, that deep inside I believe there's no way that what we think we saw could be related to the cabin. It's impossible. So what's left? I'm thinking we might have exaggerated the whole experience, we were pretty excited today. Maybe between being more than a little distracted, we overreacted tonight. I'm a practical guy, so for me it's going to be tough to wake up tomorrow and think tonight's event was anything other than the two of us feeding off each others emotional reactions."

"I know I felt something tonight, almost more than seeing it. Maybe it was my emotions rising up faster than reality. It's only been a week since the cabin, we should be allowed to overreact. I don't think we're being stalked by some evil force from Havenswood Valley, but then again if there was something out there tonight, I sure wouldn't be able to explain it." Karen smiled and said, "I'd rather say it was us getting swept up in the moment."

"Now that's the kind of talk I've been waiting to hear from you, getting swept up in the moment is a great idea. Karen, I'm really happy about being here with you, and even with a wild end to the day I know the next two weeks are going to be even more exciting. Let's get some sleep and tomorrow we can take a look at this with a fresh view before we think about calling Marcus."

Karen looked deeply into Kevin's eyes and replied with a big smile, "Sleep?"

CHAPTER
16

Throughout his life, Marcus had experienced life-defining challenges most people only see in movies. Some were inner battles fought for a few fleeting moments. Other struggles lasted for weeks, or even years. His insight was a blessing, mostly. It seemed a curse at times early on, but he and his parents grew stronger in dealing with the events and emotions Marcus would go through. He never gave up. They knew their son would eventually discover his true calling, and each building block of his life journey would better prepare him for what lay ahead.

There were visions that would appear without notice, causing Marcus to explode forward, looking for a resolution to a sudden occurrence. Once, as a teen, he had been with a group of friends near a lake when he saw a full grown brown bear chasing a moose. Both were headed right at him and his friends. It was pandemonium as Marcus screamed, "Run! Run for your lives! There's a bear and moose charging right at us!" He was pushing his friends to move, which some of them did, but others were not convinced and wanted to see this dangerous duo for themselves.

No one remembers for sure, but as some kids were running to hide behind a few large boulders nearby, the sound they all heard began as a creak and instantly turned into thunder. Crashing thunder! A sixty foot tall oak came thrashing through the trees as it fell to the forest floor, crushing everything beneath it and bursting apart like a Halloween pumpkin thrown onto the street.

It was talked about for weeks at school and throughout the whole city, how Marcus had warned everyone to run moments before they would have been killed by the tree. It didn't matter that it was a tree and not the wild animals. From then on his visions, episodes and premonitions were respected by nearly everyone. Of course there were a few detractors, some parents that gossiped and a couple kids that would make fun of Marcus, though not to his face. He had grown into a strong, skilled and intelligent young man that rarely backed down. As time went on Marcus became more comfortable with his gift and learned to understand and handle each incident with growing maturity and confidence.

All these past experiences paled in comparison to what had happened at the cabin the weekend before. Sitting at home with his parents, Marcus needed their feedback once again, before he headed out to spend a few days with Roxie and Axel. He had filled them in on what had happened at the cabin, now it was time to hear what they had termed over the years as 'The Breakdown' discussion. It was a play on words that at first dealt with the family having a breakdown due to the highly emotional effects some of the episodes would bring upon the trio. Later, the breakdown discussion had more to do with the analysis of the event and how they would interpret and deal with it. Normally they allowed a few days for everyone to hash it out on their own before the breakdown, and this week was no exception. They were all ready to talk, and Marcus led the way.

"Well, Mom, Dad, being able to see the activity at the cabin has made this possibly the most impactful week of my life. It's opened up a whole new world to me, literally! But, thanks to you two always supporting me after everything I've gone through growing up, well, I was able to handle the situation pretty well. In fact, I'm really looking forward to working on this with Roxie and Axel. We're going to spend the weekend together and see what we can come up with. I don't know where it will lead us to, but I feel a very strong connection to what happened and I know I'm supposed to keep involved. And, we have the sheriff, Norma and Robert to work with as they ramp up their work on this. So, what are you two thinking?"

There followed a long conversation between Marcus, his mother, Anna and his father, Troy. The three of them had been through many events during Marcus' life, but none like this. Nothing came close to presenting such an opportunity, a challenge in fact, to work on a true mystery. Something that has been around for so many decades, and may continue for who knows how many more. Marcus was entering a new phase of dealing with extraordinary events and circumstances. He was ready to go full-steam ahead, but his parents were feeling very nervous. However, once Marcus let his views be known, they stated that before their breakdown conversation, the two of them knew Marcus had to continue on with the research. His life had trained him for it and he was the most suitable person they knew to be in this situation. Marcus would be able to provide the sheriff with a level of help no one else could, with the exception of Norma. They felt her psychic powers would lend specific help in solving this mystery, too.

"Marcus, we agree with you. It is time for you to move ahead to the next step in your life. With this event, and all that comes with it, you have an exceptional opportunity for personal and spiritual growth," Troy said. "We support you one hundred percent. Even though we're going to worry about you pretty much all day, every day, we know this is something you need to do. We, too, believe this is a purpose you were meant to fulfill."

"It's scary for us, Marcus," Anna added, "you going off to track down this evil force is a huge undertaking, even with the team that is coming together. Please, son, watch yourself as much as you protect your friends. Life is a series of many short challenges and you must be ready for each and every one. Remember how much we love you, and that we'll always be thinking of you."

"Thanks, Mom. Thanks Dad. I guess you've been preparing for this day more than I realized. Knowing my future before I was mature enough to see it, you've been guiding me to become confident enough to accept this endeavor as a natural progression of my life. I love you both and I can't thank you enough for everything you've done for me. But now, well, now it's my turn to take the lead and I'm ready for it. I'm a little scared, but in a good way, the kind of scared that keeps you on your toes and your senses alert. With all the good people that are around me I'm sure we're going to figure this thing out."

"Marcus, we know you'll do fine, but like your father said, we will worry about you, it's only natural." Anna reached out and held Marcus' hand, "Just promise us that if you do get in over your head, you'll reach out to us. We're your biggest fans and we'll do whatever is needed to help." She kept her gaze, looking straight into his eyes until he answered.

"Yes, Mom, I promise. I'll never leave without saying goodbye, and if I ever get into a bind, you and Dad will be the first ones I call. I imagine there will be some periods without contact, but I'll be thinking about you and Dad, too."

"Thanks, Marcus," said Troy. "It really helps knowing you feel so confident and sure about doing this. We can see it in your eyes, in the way you talk, even in the way you have been moving about the house this week. You're focused on the task at hand and when you're on target you rarely miss. I can't wait to hear how this ends! All I can add is, good luck and may God be with you."

"Thanks, Dad, I am ready. And I've said a few extra prayers lately, especially last weekend. If this truly is a battle of good versus evil, then I know we'll triumph. It's just a matter of time. Besides, don't the good guys always win?"

Troy looked at Anna, and then at Marcus, "Good does triumph, Marcus. Sometimes the cost is higher than planned for, you just need to believe in yourself and persevere like a warrior in battle. Work with your friends and teach them what you can about being aware of their own premonitions. A band of warriors on alert will always see more, hear more and be able to defend themselves better than a single warrior."

CHAPTER 17

At this particular moment, as he sat in the car with Roxie and Axel, it was tough for Marcus to imagine himself and his two closest friends, just some average kids from Andover Glen, Minnesota, preparing to fight evil. They were just now hitting their stride in life and heading into this unknown territory was going to seriously send them off track. Who knows where they'd end up and how they'll feel about each other, especially if things got even more dangerous. He loved them both, and if anything happened he'd certainly blame himself. For now he'd sit and relax, taking time to enjoy their banter and try not to think too hard about the meeting they had arraigned with the Prairie Falls librarian.

"How many times a week do you eat out for lunch, Axel?" asked Roxie. They had finished up their lunch in a grassy area near the parking lot of the Prairie Falls Library and were now waiting in Marcus's car until it was time for their appointment.

"Probably three times a week, on average. Usually a sandwich shop. Why do you ask?"

"Personal survey," said Roxie. "My parents said when they grew up the fast food places were mainly burgers and fries. Now we have so many more options, and most of them are healthier for us, which I think is an overall lifestyle improvement for our generation. I like to track things that are better now than during the last generation or two, and I'd have to say at least the eating part of our daily existence is better."

"Or worse," added Marcus, "there are so many more choices now. We must have passed a couple hundred places on the way to the library. We might be trying to eat better, but with so many temptations, it's easy to break down for a burger once too often."

"True," replied Roxie, "the world is filled with much more temptation, good and bad. Guess it's the circle of life weeding out the weak."

"You know," replied Axel, "it's not really a circle of life. A merry-go-round is a circle, and you get a bunch of chances to grab the brass ring. Life is more like a long march forward, and once you die, there's no more reaching out for the brass ring. It's over, for humans, at least, since we don't need to feed off of each other like animals do. Once dead, always dead."

"So you don't believe in heaven, or ghosts, or any kind of afterlife?" questioned Roxie as they headed to Marcus' car to retrieve their items.

"Sure I do, I believe in it all. There's no way all the thousands of weird or odd stories and experiences throughout history can be explained with common sense or science or religion. So, yes, I think anything is possible. Look at what we just went through!" answered Axel. He tossed the lunch trash into a recycling bin.

"If that's true, then what we saw was definitely the bad side of life, or death. And if what we know as the 'modern world' is trying to protect itself, who's to say the dark side isn't also trying to gain control?" Marcus looked at his friends and continued, "I've been thinking about this all week. Even though my life has been lived feeling most people are good at heart, I now have to confess, with the emergence of such darkness and evil right before my eyes, there really is another force here on Earth also trying to shape the world. Only it wants one that is a terrible, dark, cold and evil place."

"What a great way to sink into total depression mode," said Roxie. "Are you saying it really is as simple as good versus evil at the center of our universe? That's it? Good guys versus bad guys?"

"I think Marcus has had too much time to think and has taken a mental trip too far from home base," Axel chuckled.

"Listen, I'm just saying that once we get these four parchments translated, we might have a better idea of what we are up against. But, in the meantime," Marcus looked at his friends, "Start thinking, really thinking, about good versus evil, man versus beast, God versus Satan. I think you'll find we might be on to something a whole lot more that just a few dark shapes in the forest."

Marcus opened the car door and was headed to the trunk of the car before Roxie or Axel could respond. They had lunched near the library and were now set to meet with Mrs. Eleanor

Hamsteen, an interpreter of a few different languages and the one person they felt would give them a chance at finding out what was written on the parchments. The ploy was to say these pieces were found in Roxie's parent's home and they were writings from a long lost great-great aunt that loved to tell stories. They would be pretending to hope that these stories would be the basis for a book. If the librarian bought into it, they would swear her to secrecy as to not let the story idea out. And, of course, to keep a lid on any unusual comments that may come up. It was a gamble, but one they were willing to take.

The three budding sleuths walked into the Prairie Falls Public Library, the largest one in the county. The early twentieth century building was an engineering masterpiece of decades old features up front and a 1970's addition that tripled it's size. The front included cement columns standing guard near the entry, an ornately carved fascia just under the roof line, and a granite apron of twelve steps up from the sidewalk. Sandstone blocks made the outside walls look warm all year long, and the large clock at the tip of the front façade was as reliable a timekeeper as any electronic billboard in town. Inside, the internet wired library housed plenty of books and resource material, second only to the state university library in its depth of subject matter. The connection of old and new buildings was nearly seamless. In fact the county had won a few architectural awards over the years; some for design, some for function, and one community spirit award called 'Awesomeness', just for the concept alone. After a brief stop at the information counter they were directed to the Reference Room of the library, recognizing Mrs. Hamsteen from the staff photo on-line. Sorting through a stack of language books, she sensed the group and looked up just as they approached her desk.

"Well hello, such a nice group to meet with. I was expecting your parents when you explained the situation on the phone." Mrs. Hamsteen loved young people, and at age sixty-seven, most everyone she dealt with was young. She had been working in libraries for nearly thirty-five years, and loved to help people research, gain wisdom and discover new things. This, she had thought, would be another great adventure for her.

"Thank you, Mrs. Hamsteen," said Roxie "We really appreciate your time. My great-great aunt was said to have been quite a story teller. We have some written history about her in our family genealogy research book, and finding these will surely add another colorful chapter to her life story."

"I am so pleased to be able to help you with this, Roxanne, and it would be a pleasure to read about her some day. Come by any time and you can show me your family book."

Roxie was now feeling slightly guilty. Why did it have to be her great-great aunt? Axel would have probably blown the ruse, but Marcus could have pulled this off. Oh well, it's just a little white lie and it really is for a good cause.

"Mrs. Hamsteen, thank you for helping us, but we do need to remind you this story can't be told to anyone else. We tried to translate this on our own, but it just didn't make sense. We needed an expert, one we could trust. That's why we're here meeting with you," said Marcus. "Can we count on your confidentiality? That you won't tell anyone what we find on these parchments?"

"Well, unless it's a confession to murder, yes, I will keep my word and not tell a soul. Heaven knows the only people I could tell wouldn't remember it anyway!" Mrs. Hamsteen laughed a quiet librarian laugh, and everyone felt at ease.

Sequestered in a back room in the basement of the library, the group settled at the large table in the center. The library had been kept remarkably up to date through local business sponsorships. Successful companies knew that a strong and vibrant learning system was essential to a productive society and smart future employees. The library had everything it needed to access information from around the world, and Mrs. Hamsteen was the one person who knew the most about sourcing details. She would prove to be a very important ally.

The door shut, the lights dimmed, Marcus pulled the four metal tubes from his backpack. Laid upon the table, they seemed to vibrate excitement into the room. How the three friends wished they could share with Mrs. Hamsteen the tale of how these parchments were discovered, how they had stumbled upon this find and were now desperate to see them fit into the puzzle of evil that has fed upon Havenswood Valley. Their lives had been altered during a weekend outing with friends, and now they were on the edge of a discovery that would change the course of their lives forever.

"Robert! Robert, wake up!" Norma yelled as she ran to the sink, grabbed a dishtowel and wet it with cool water. As quickly as possible she returned to Robert as he lay on the floor. Face ashen, body limp, breath just a resemblance of a living person. "Robert, you foolish old man, wake up! Now!" She again yelled upstairs for help but nobody replied. The old door, along with the solid framework of the original building, kept noises out from above, and muffled any trace of vibration even thinking about drifting up the stairs and through the door to the sales floor of Tres Azure.

"Hello?"

"Glen! It's Norma! Robert's passed out here and I can't wake him! I need help. Where are you?"

"Four blocks away, I'll make a u-turn and be there in two minutes. Damn, why does he always have to push himself so hard!"

"He's much worse than the last time and I can't get into the cabinet. I don't know what happened down here, but this place is a real mess. Hurry, Glen!"

It was a blur that lasted just a few minutes, and then the door leading to the downstairs basement of Tres Azure flew open. The stairs were cleared in record time by Sheriff Glen Anderson, hardly touching a step on his way down.

"Glen, I forgot my key! Can you get the bottle?" Norma had been cleaning her jewelry the night before, and had decided to rearrange the keys on her charm bracelet as well. She hadn't finished and left it for later, not thinking she would need the locker key so soon.

"Key's already in the lock, here we go!" In a top cabinet, around a corner and out of sight from nearly any angle in the room was a medium sized storage cabinet with an antique lock. Inside were a few select research articles, some photos, a couple of physical pieces of what they loosely termed as evidence; cash, a satellite phone, passports, contact lists, keys, two handguns, and the bottle.

Over the past few years Robert had been dealing with a health issue no one could resolve. Doctors said it could be anything from age to allergies. After a while he quit going back for tests. 'Useless' was the term he fondly repeated when asked about his latest doctor visit. They eliminated most every kind of disease and ailment, but couldn't come up with an answer as to why he would, on occasion, pass out.

Robert would say, "I'm just overtired and need rest, not as young as I used to be but I sure as heck won't admit I have to slow down!" But it was more than being tired, more than getting old. Something was attacking his system, and what was once an annual episode now struck Robert on a more frequent basis. This was a challenge to his physical and mental health, and it was apparent that the effects were becoming more damaging.

Glen forced Robert's lips apart and slowly poured the elixir into his mouth, just a trickle to get things started. The fluid would seep quickly into Roberts's system this way, and the aroma would double the effect as it filled his nostrils. Norma's Great Aunt Eloise had been visiting during one of Robert's spells, and the very next morning had mixed together a liquid that she still sends to Norma every so often. Norma knew better than to ask for the recipe, "It's more than what's in it, it's how what's in it, gets in it," was Great Aunt Eloise's standard reply.

"It's taking too long, we need to call an ambulance, Glen!"

"He's coming 'round, Norma, look at his skin, already filling with blood and flushing out the grey. And his breathing is getting stronger, lungs are filling up. He'll be with us in a few seconds."

"Just, like, old, times," Robert mumbled. He had come to and gave a weary smile with his announcement. Glen and Norma, while relieved, knew they would all have a long discussion about this latest incident, and Robert would be tougher than usual to deal with. It seemed the harder the impact these were on his system, the meaner he got about beating it back into submission. Robert hated to lose control, it reminded him too much about his wife and son and their losing battles against death. His outcome would be different he would say, he'd go on his own terms when he was good and ready!

"No, Robert, this is not like old times, this is much more serious. I'm telling you right now, you are not going to leave my sight until we figure out what is wrong with you. I don't care if we have to see every doctor in the state, we are going to find out what in the world you have going on inside that string bean body of yours!" And with that, Norma walked over to the sink and splashed her face with cool water, not wanting to show the tears that were now flowing down her cheeks. She loved her friends, and these debilitating episodes affected her deeply, especially when she thought about the possibility of Robert not coming back to full consciousness, falling so deep under the spell of this sickness that he would, in fact, die in her arms.

Glen knew Norma was upset, and as he helped Robert to a comfortable seat on the couch he spoke directly to the issue at hand. "She's right. You've had three big spells in the last four months, and this one was the worst yet, nothing like the ones you've had over the years. Something's going on, Robert. If Norma's aunt hadn't come up with that juice we use to revive you, you'd be sitting in some kind of rest home, trying to remember your name. I'll be calling your doctor on Monday, and starting next week we are getting to the bottom of this!"

"Fine, fine. Just let me get some rest tonight and I'll be ready to go." Robert wasn't feeling defeated, he just knew rest was a great friend on the road to recovery. They were right, this was the worst episode he'd had, but they had no idea of the internal battles he was dealing with, they just saw the after effect. Robert had been battling demons since the day his son disappeared. It had taken him years to figure out, and then he never felt comfortable telling anyone, too proud to admit something was happening. Fearing he'd be called crazy or that he was going insane at the loss of his son and wife. Too much for a man to take, they would say. Robert hated pity and so he kept it all inside, fighting against the powerful draw to walk into the forest alone, but today he realized that he was now being chased, stalked, by the darkness that had taken his son. He was getting on in years and now the forces of evil were getting stronger in Havenswood Valley. Today was the moment of truth and he had lived through it. His closest friends were about to get an explanation of the truth that while not totally out of left field, the reality of it would surely hit them hard. It was time to come clean, and time to ask for help. After being helped home by his two friends, Robert freshened up and took a short nap while Sheriff Anderson and Norma prepared dinner. They ate quickly and with little conversation, allowing Robert the courtesy to begin whenever he was ready.

Sitting in the living room while Robert had walked back to his bedroom, Norma and Glen talked about how to manage Robert for the next few weeks. The three had gone full steam working on what had happened at the cabin and this latest spell seemed to sneak up on Robert. How could they not have paid better attention to him? It had happened before, recently in fact, and they felt guilty thinking they had let Robert falter.

"Norma, I've got a weird feeling about these episodes of Robert's. What if it isn't old age or a rare disease? Last weekend he said he felt the darkness calling out to him, trying to get him into the woods." Glen looked at Norma, "Do you think it could be some kind of dementia that's taken hold? He's had a very tough life, and maybe his body and mind are just shutting down when he's under too much stress."

"I've thought about it, but today was the first day I would say he went over the edge," she replied. "My God, I thought he'd never recover. I don't know what triggers it, but if we can find out we have a chance to help him. It's time I get Aunt Eloise back here, she's got to come clean on what's in that bottle! Maybe Doc Jenstone can figure something out if he knows what ingredients are bringing him back."

"I'll tell you what triggers it, it's those damn tourists that keep asking for directions. Heck, this town isn't big enough to get lost in, why don't they just look around once in a while?" Robert had walked into the room and caught the last part of the conversation taking place between Glen and Norma. He looked very serious, and then the grin quickly began to spread across his face. "Aw, you know I love talking to visitors, they're kind'a funny most of the time, and always real polite. Just wanted to see the look on your faces thinking I'd gone crazy."

"You are crazy, Robert," said Norma, "it's when you get serious I've got to worry. Or sick, and I'm rather bored finding you passed out on the floor looking like you're ready to be put six feet under." She was upset, but had a purpose to her impromptu lecture. "If there's something else going on, I, well, we, would like to know what it is. Cancer? Do you have cancer, Robert? Or heart disease? I can handle the truth, Robert, but I can't handle not knowing how to help or comfort you. Be honest, is there something else the doctors have found that you're not telling us about?"

"Robert, before you answer that, let's take a few minutes to unwind. Wine anyone?" Glen had opened a bottle of Merlot and began pouring a glass for each of them. It gave everyone a chance to settle into the comfortable furniture in Robert's living room and relax. The fireplace, the centerpiece of the room, was river stone from floor to ceiling, and the hickory timber mantle held photos of his wife, son, family and friends. Robert had wanted to stay in the country, but when he finally moved to town he turned a worn out house into a friendly home where every guest felt welcomed.

"Okay, so we all know that it's time for Robert to take another round with the doctors," started Sheriff Anderson. "So let's see about setting up a list, other than your regular visits with Doctor Emling. Let's start with Doc Jenstone here in town. You've known him all your life, but I don't think you've ever seen him for anything medical, have you?"

"Well, no, I haven't, and by the way, nobody has told me I have cancer, or heart disease, Norma. They all say I'm in great shape for a man my age. Even Doc Jenstone, in passing, has said I look healthy as a horse, even though he's heard about my spells. Fact is, he's a great doctor and I would have seen him first but it was a family thing. Emling was married to my cousin. But, say, before we get too far down the road on this doctor list, I'd really like to talk with you two about something that's been on my mind for a very long time." Robert got up and walked to the refrigerator and pulled out some cheese, then went to the pantry and grabbed a sleeve of crackers. "You know, ever since we started this wine thing I've always made sure to have plenty of cheese and crackers around. Nothing special, but I can't believe wine and cheese really goes together so well."

"Maybe we should head to France some time, I hear they know a thing or two about wine and cheese." Norma winked at Glen.

"Sure, but we'll have to make some side trips. I'm still a beer and whiskey man at heart. I think there are a few countries we could travel to that would make it worthwhile!" Glen really did want to travel to Europe and see some historic sights, and yes, sample some adult beverages, but they were getting off track. "Robert, before we start thinking about flight reservations, you said you had something on your mind you wanted to talk about."

Sitting together, relaxed after a long afternoon and evening, the three friends knew this was the right place to be, collecting their thoughts on what had happened, and what still lay ahead. So much had transpired the past week, it was time to take it all in and make sure they were headed down the right road. Finally committed to presenting his inner struggles to his friends, Robert began the only way he could.

"It's been a long day, and I'd like to again thank you both for taking care of me, for saving my life." Robert was very humbled by what his friends had done for him, for today would be remembered as the day he had finally fallen in battle. Thank God his friends were there to pull him back to safety. "This past year, especially, I've had a tough go of it. You've both been witness to how I've struggled. Hell, it's been a long life of struggles, some pretty sad times, but friends like you two have kept me going, kept me on course for living a life with meaning."

"Robert, you've given so many people in town inspiration, helping out so many with your generosity. People look up to you. It's you that have kept them on course." Norma smiled at Robert.

"Thanks, Norma, that's nice of you to say. I guess I have tried to do my best when I can, nothing that other folks wouldn't do for a friend or neighbor. That's why I love this town so much, never wanted to move away like some suggested, thinking if I got away maybe the bad memories would fade sooner. Well, that's a load of junk. Never run from the truth, face it and deal with it. With your support, that's what I'm doing tonight, facing the truth."

Glen and Norma exchanged surprised looks and waited for Robert to continue.

"Today, well today it looked like I had bought the farm alright, passed out and looking pretty grim I'm sure. To you two it must have looked like a bad heart attack Maybe a blood clot or one of those brain hemorrhages. I wish it could be explained that easily. So, let me go back a few years, to when I first started feeling these spells. It was about twice a year when I'd start to feel it, not the flu, but more than headaches and ragweed. It would last about two weeks and then I'd get to feeling fine again. I noticed these sick days came at a certain time of year. Three years in a row, early spring and late fall, like clockwork. And what was I doing that time of year? Yep, spending my time out at the farm, working on trees, clearing brush, taking care of the buildings. Just regular stuff. But last year, that was the year I got scared. Not scared from being sick, but scared thinking I was getting sick from being around the farm, being around where my son had been killed. My mind was playing some pretty mean tricks on me and I was beginning to believe it. Odd noises, dark shadows, strange visions, it all made me jumpy." Robert looked uncomfortable as he continued. "And then this last spring it showed itself in a real physical form, which I thought was a hallucination, until today. Now I'm convinced I met the enemy face to face."

"What showed itself, Robert? What exactly are you talking about?" asked Sheriff Anderson.

Robert locked eyes with the sheriff. "I'm talking about the evil that took my son, Glen. It's more than some kind of dark energy that pulled Michael into the woods and murdered him, more than a mystifying force that drew in Kevin. Last spring, I thought I saw someone spying on me from inside the woods, saw him so clear I gave chase. For a good fifteen minutes I sought that image like a wolf on the trail of a wounded deer. Yelling, firing warning shots with my 12-gauge, I was leaving nothing to chance. A couple of glimpses were all I got before I headed back to the cabin. I hadn't realized how full of anger and hate I was, but afterwards I began shaking so hard I could barely sit down. The next day I woke up thinking, what in God's name was I doing out there? Seeing ghosts? Chasing my own personal nightmare? I swore to myself I wouldn't let my inner thoughts torment and beat me up like that again. I locked it down and never thought too much of it again, until last weekend. I've been trying to find the right time to tell you both, and today my hand was forced open. I've been fighting this evil in my head and on my land for years and I've never really known the enemy. Now it, or them, whatever it is, it's growing stronger. It's definitely after me, and I think after anyone else it can reach," he answered.

"Oh my God, Robert! I don't know what to say right now." Norma was surprised at Roberts passion, she had not expected to hear this from her good friend. "I have to be honest with you, this sounds..."

"Like I'm out of my mind?" he finished her sentence.

"To an outsider, sure it does. But, no, Robert, it's not that. Years ago I had helped my mother with some people that had very strong dealings with what she said was 'the devil at work'. It sounds like a cliché, but her conviction to beating back evil can be traced back to events she read about in the Bible. Things that have been explained simply as good versus evil in written form since civilizations began painting on walls and sketching in stone."

"So, you don't think I'm crazy?"

"Of course not! Our planet has so many unexplained happenings, events, places, history, and every day something new is discovered. Most are good, but there is evil, too, and we can't deny it." Norma continued, "Why shouldn't you be one of the good people that have a personal battle with evil on their hands? Thank God you're such a strong person. I'm glad someone like you is in the war that has been waging since time began. Crazy? I think you're more sane than the rest of us, if only because you have seen the true enemy of mankind."

Sheriff Anderson needed to stand up and walk around the room. He looked out the large window overlooking Third Street and took a drink from his glass. "This is real, isn't it? All this darkness, this evil hanging over us, it's happening now. We've seen it in action, it's deadly forms rolling through Havenswood Valley." He turned to stare into the fire, unable to hold back his innermost thoughts. "Growing up, this kind of adventure was something you'd read about in books, or see at the movies. Ghost stories and tales of horror were for getting scared and then heading home to safety. I always gave reason to tales of wizards, dark magic, voodoo, paganism, all the non-traditional worship, as fantasy and ignorance. Thinking those followers would eventually give up their superstitious ways and realize their error in judgment. Now who's the ignorant one? My world stops about fifty miles outside of town and I'm the one calling centuries of other people's philosophy wrong? Funny how humble we can become when the curtain is raised and we are shown a view we never knew existed." Glen poured himself another glass of wine and sat down near the fire. "Robert, I don't have a clue as to what is out there in the woods, but I'm damn sure it ain't no Big Foot that you chased. And if you say it's coming after you, I believe you, but it scares the hell out of me. Seeing the power it had over Kevin last week, and knowing it was attempting to try something with a cabin full of people, I'm sure it's grown stronger since Michael died. And stronger means hungrier, more aggressive, more daring and less concerned about consequences, just like the criminals I've tracked for years. For whatever reason, you are a target and whether you've been infected at the cabin or picked out because of Michael, it doesn't matter. First, we have to see to it that you're with someone at all times. Now that you've got Norma and me as shaken up as we could be, I have to put on my sheriff hat and question you about how it came to be that Norma found you half dead in the basement of Tres Azure."

Robert began to explain exactly what had happened, and while it sounded like a sci-fi story, Glen and Norma accepted it without hesitation. There was no reason for Robert to lie or exaggerate any aspects of his experiences, and his heartfelt telling was proof enough for the two listeners.

"Maybe I felt that Michael was somehow tied into this resurgence of the darkness, and that if I kept an eye on things I might catch a glimpse of him. I prayed that maybe he had been kidnapped, taken somewhere out of our sight and if only I had the chance to get into their world I'd be able to rescue him. Not until today did I really give up hope that I'd ever see him again, and that really hurt. Hurt so bad I didn't want to fight back after a while, I just let him win." Robert looked like he'd just lost his son all over again.

"Robert, you say 'him' like it was someone in the store with you," the sheriff questioned.

"There was someone. He came over to me as if he had appeared out of thin air."

"Explain exactly what you saw, and in the order it happened, Robert. Take your time, I don't want any mistakes on this." Sheriff Anderson was writing this all down on his notepad.

"I unlocked the door to the basement, turned on the light, stepped down and then turned back and locked the door. Same as

I usually do. Got to the bottom of the steps and walked over to my table and sat down, same as I usually do. I remember I pulled out a blue pen, new one I had bought is why I remember so easily, and just as I was reaching for the newspaper I smelled it. Then a chill ran up my spine and I got goose bumps just thinking about last weekend at the cabin." Robert gave a shudder as he recalled his memory. "Geez, funny how something can stand out so clear in your mind and in your senses. So I'm sitting there and start to feel out of sorts and off balance. Then I get a whiff of the smell from the meadow and my head fills with thoughts about the cabin. Thinking I should get some water when all of a sudden I jump up from my chair and just about wet myself at the sight of him standing, or floating, at the bottom of the stairs. I tried to yell something like 'Who the hell are you?', but not a darn word would form. The more I yelled the dizzier I got, and then he started to step toward me. I swear I yelled, looked around for something to defend myself with, and I just got weaker at everything I tried. My God how I tried to fight it! Tried to just move, to think of a way out and all I could see was this hideous figure coming so close to me, and that terrible stench! It filled my nose and nearly knocked me out."

"My goodness, Robert, this is incredible! I can't imagine being in your position," said Norma.

"Let me tell you two something, it happened so quick I had no idea what to do. Couldn't talk, couldn't move, felt like a cat in a dog fight. He came up to me and I was nearly out, my mouth dry as dust, head spinning like crazy, gasping for air. I thought it couldn't get any worse and then, and then he smiled at me. A nasty, mean spirited 'I've got you now' look in his eyes that said my time in this world was up."

"Guess he didn't think to ask what kind of manners we expect in Havenswood Valley, did he?" asked the sheriff.

"Reckon not, Glen. I began to think about my wife, my son, and everything that meant anything to me and at that moment I was not about to let some son of a bitch from the dark side take me down without one last punch. Don't know how I did it but I kicked myself over and grabbed the nearest thing I could, which happened to be the fire extinguisher. I somehow got it to spray and when that dry foam came out dusty and cold, quick as he came in I saw him disappear into a cloud of salt and pepper and blow out through the basement window. I would have let out a cheer, but I was overcome with exhaustion and the last thing I remember is thinking to myself, 'Well, at least if I die he won't be here to gloat over me.' That's when I must have passed out."

"Robert," asked Norma, "you didn't say anything about this person talking. So he didn't say a thing?"

"No, as a matter of fact not a word, not a noise, just a nasty look in his eyes and that nasty smile."

"Well, not so strange I guess. We have no idea where this thing comes from, and the fact it can appear instantly, in the shape and mannerisms of a human, and then disappear in a puff of smoke makes me think that while it may be of this planet, it is certainly not of this time." Norma was trying to piece the puzzle together. "Who's to say we don't have a time traveler on our hands?"

"That's a good option, Norma. I think we've thought about that over the years as a way for the darkness to be in so many different places so quickly," said Sheriff Anderson. "I'm just asking, but how odd is it that here we are calmly talking about all of this? We don't bat an eye thinking we're dealing with evil, a time travelling menace or whatever it comes to be known as. I imagine if someone were to be told about all of this in one sitting they'd think we had all gone mad. So few people believe in anything close to what we're dealing with, I wouldn't blame them." Glen sat down and looked solemnly at Robert and Norma. "This is progressing so much faster now. It's been what, just over a week since the cabin and now it's strong enough and brave enough to attack one of us in downtown Havenswood Valley!" Sheriff Anderson was thinking of the effect the news would have on the town. "We'll be in a serious mess if word about this leaks."

"Word about this won't spread from any of us, Glen," said Robert. "Now, maybe some of those kids from the cabin or someone who actually encounters this life-taker, well, they might spill the beans."

"Life-taker, that's a good way to put it, Robert. That's exactly what it does. Norma, if someone does see something I'll have to ask you to be an authority on the situation. I'd have to play it as a single episode, so as not to help anyone connect the dots like we have. Once we get a jump on finding the source and evaluating options, then we can decide if we should blow the lid off all this. Or, we figure a way to end this madness by ourselves."

"That's fine with me, Glen. I don't have a problem with taking this one step at a time and keeping a few things under our hats. No need to throw too much light on it without proper preparation," said Norma.

"And if by some chance a reporter or researcher comes my way," added Robert, "I'll just play my gruff self and keep my door and mouth shut."

"Thank you Norma. Robert, well, you've shared a lot with us tonight, and we're glad everything worked out today. If Norma hadn't gotten to you in time, it might have been a different story. It's a different time here in Havenswood Valley. Something is out there, something we can't prove, or talk about. If we hadn't seen the event of last weekend, it would be tougher to grasp what you went through today. Maybe it's seasonal, maybe it's self survival of a species. No matter what, until we get a handle on this situation, let's continue to keep in very close contact with each other." Sheriff Anderson was already thinking about follow up details. "Well, I think it's time to wrap this evening up. If you don't mind, Robert, I'll stay here tonight, and then tomorrow we'll start fresh."

"Sure, Glen. And thanks, Norma. You know you're welcome to stay, too. Plenty of room."

"You know, that sounds like a good idea. I'll just get my bag from the car and I'll be right back in."

"You mean we'll be right back in," said Glen as he and Robert stood up to walk out with Norma. The three smiled at each other, knowing that whatever was to come their way they'd be in it together.

Marcus was the strongest of the three friends in body, mind and spirit. His tenacity and his inner cognitive power had earned him many different life experiences, so it was only natural for him to be here today. Flanked by Roxie and Axel, it was a comforting feeling that filled his heart. Gone was the tension from what-ifs and second guessing decisions. This was a natural stop along the path to his destiny. He had felt tranquility in bits and pieces throughout his life, and today he was fully engaged with his true self, and it felt good, very good. This brought forth a strong aura of confidence and leadership to his friends and they were all beneficiaries of the life-changing journey now poised before them. Right at this time, right at this place.

The three had chosen to bring the parchments to light under the eyes of a trusting interpreter, local research librarian Mrs. Hamsteen, and held no reservations on this decision. Lucky is how they described it; a great opportunity to discover the contents in a setting that seemed as safe and secure as any other situation. Should the librarian feel she needed to spill the beans publicly, the trio had already agreed, as much as they would not like to, that they would deny the story and paint the librarian as a kindly person that had somehow mistaken their story for someone else's. If they had to cover their tracks, a replacement story had already been written by Roxie, and would be presented to the press, should it go that far.

Roxie picked up the first tube off the table and slowly twisted the end until the cap was removed. Roxie thought to herself, such a simple device for storing vital information. She turned the open end back to the table, which had been draped with a soft cotton sheet. She gently coaxed the first parchment from the container that had held its secret contents for who knows how long. Still slightly curled, it would take just a few minutes and the parchment would lie nearly flat. The waxy covering that kept the fabric supple gave a slight yellow tinge to the piece of sand colored parchment. It looked like a treasure map you'd see in a movie, penned in black ink, with a few designs placed throughout the document. For it was a true document, one that looked as serious as any current day certificate, letter or legal filing. Whoever had scribed this was surely intent on passing along their thoughts in what appeared to be a very dramatic fashion.

"My, that is a very interesting letter, uh, parchment. We shall see what it really is once we start to look at it more closely and learn about the story your great aunt wrote," said Mrs. Hamsteen. Her eyes would not leave the document as she spoke. Marcus and Axel were as fixed on her responses, verbal and physical, as Mrs. Hamsteen was on the document. They glanced at each other as if to say 'Have we made the wrong choice here? Is she going to think we are pulling a fast one on her?' Roxie began to open the second tube.

"Here's another one. We really didn't mark them in any kind of order since we weren't able to read them. We just go by the etchings on the tubes," she said. She unfurled more of the trio's thin white lie, along with the second parchment. "We know them by some of the drawings on the different pieces." Mrs. Hamsteen's eyes were now transfixed on the second document as Roxie spoke.

As Mrs. Hamsteen's demeanor continued to change, Axel felt their interpreter was trying to memorize the information for making her own notes later. "Mrs. Hamsteen, have you ever seen anything like these before?" Axel asked, trying to get her to verbalize her thoughts.

"No, uh, no I have not," she stammered. "Very different from anything I have ever seen."

"Well, we have two more to lay out on the table for you," added Marcus. At first he was thinking Mrs. Hamsteen was not the least bit interested, that she was going to politely examine the parchments and give herself a way out of this situation. But she now appeared to be looking at the documents so intently they might burst into flames.

"Yes, two more, that will be very interesting," she said, almost to herself. It was more of a reflex than a reply.

As Roxie was about to open the third tube, Mrs. Hamsteen spoke up. "I'm just going to sit down for a minute," and she abruptly turned around to sit down on a small couch that was positioned along a nearby wall in the room. "I just need a few minutes to clear my thoughts."

"Mrs. Hamsteen," asked Marcus, "are you feeling ok?"

"Can I get you some water?" asked Axel.

"Oh, yes, thank you, I would like a glass of water." She smiled but there was a vacancy behind her eyes. Mrs. Hamsteen's thoughts seemed far away at the moment.

"If this isn't a good time we can come back another day," suggested Roxie. She didn't really mean it, nor did Marcus or Axel want the translation delayed. They knew, however, that it would be best if Mrs. Hamsteen was truly on her game when she began to read the parchments. Any missed words or inferences could make a major difference, and they could ill afford starting off in the wrong direction.

"I'm sorry, I just, well. Oh, thank you, Axel." She drank nearly the entire glass of water and then sat silently, looking ahead as if staring out at the ocean from a beach chair.

"Is there someone we can call for you? Someone here at the library?" asked Roxie.

"No, thank you, dear. Oh my, here, let me walk around the room. Get a deep breath or two and I'll feel better." Mrs. Hamsteen walked around the room taking in deep breaths, letting her arms loosen up with a twist here and a swing there. She looked as if she had inhaled the breath of life and seemed renewed. Cheeks flushed to a rosy pink, eyes clear and focused, spirit high and then she suddenly walked straight to the parchments on the table. "Okay, much better. Well, let's get straight to the point. First, from the few lines I can read I don't think this story would make a very good children's book. Second, if we're going to do research together I need complete honesty and open communication between us. Third, I can understand your need for secrecy before you get to know me, but I'm not going any further until we clear the air on where these parchments really came from. Sorry to be so forward but I have a very personal interest in knowing your involvement and participation in anything to do with these documents." She looked the three friends over to see if they would hold together or unravel. "I'm not going to share this with anyone, so please don't worry about me breaking your trust." Her mood softened, "I certainly want to help you, I just need you to fill in the missing pieces about these parchments."

As Marcus exchanged looks with his two friends, he began to tell Mrs. Hamsteen their story. "We appreciate you being direct with us. We had no idea who we were getting involved with but I'm sure I speak for us all when I say you appear to be a perfect fit!"

"I'll second that!" added Axel.

"As far as how we came to discover these parchments, well, it's a surprise even to us!" Marcus continued on, with some pieces still left missing, and with the help of Roxie and Axel they told Mrs. Hamsteen of their recent discovery. However only the discovery of the parchments, nothing about the dangerous events of the weekend cabin trip. At this point it seemed to Mrs. Hamsteen like an unlikely happenstance of how the friends came into possession of the parchments. Not the whole truth, but not a lie, either.

"Thank you for the background," Mrs. Hamsteen said, feeling better about the situation. "Okay, let's continue on and we'll cross any new bridges as they appear in front of us." She drew a fresh full breath and began her own background story. The trio was not prepared for what they were about to hear!

"Now it may be your turn to sit down, as what I'm about to say may sound like the words of an old, lonely, slightly crazed librarian who's read way too many books on, sure, let's get it out in the open then, evil!"

The three sat down in unison on the couch as if on cue. The look on their faces was as easy to read as a children's board book. If Mrs. Hamsteen was going for a dramatic impact, she succeeded with flying colors, since none of the three could bring themselves to talk. They sat with mouths gaping, dazed by her words. It was Axel who first tried to speak.

"E, e, evil?" coughed Axel.

"Oh yes, you are correct Axel. Evil as the day is long." Mrs. Hamsteen walked away from the table, sat down in a very comfortable, overstuffed chair, and gathered her thoughts before continuing. "Five years ago I began researching missing children for a close relative in Ohio. She has a friend whose child had disappeared, and she contacted me since I had ready access to so much information. While doing the research, I came upon a case in a town north of here that caught my interest. I noted this particular case in one of my personal files and after the missing child research was handed over to my cousin, I began to delve into it. I feel very strongly these parchments will have some kind of connection to the case north of here."

"Was it the first missing child case you worked on?" asked Roxie.

"Yes, Roxie, it was, and although my cousin knew that, she contacted me anyway. She's pushy, but I love her dearly. Nearly all of my research has been historical, mainly on events and people, but I have, on occasion, done some medical, legal and other data mining. Excuse me, Axel, may I have some more water, please? Here I am talking on and on, it's no wonder I'm thirsty."

"We're all ears, Mrs. Hamsteen," said Marcus. "Please continue."

"Well, I don't want to get too far off track, but I just can't believe what I saw on the parchments you have. Of course I've just glanced at them, but having no one to talk with about my research for years and suddenly, here are three strangers rolling out a roadmap that may bind us together in a mystery that I have no idea how to deal with. Had I told any of my friends what I was doing, they would have though me a nutcase!"

"Believe me, Mrs. Hamsteen, what the three of us saw recently would have us all labeled lunatics!" said Marcus.

"So, you began to investigate a case. What case was it?" asked Roxie.

"The case involved the death of a young boy and it dealt with a family that had a surname I recalled from my childhood. I worked at it slowly, but the more I dug in the more frustrated I got. Nothing was available for me to research in the public files. It was as if they had closed the case without a true resolution and no one cared. Well, I did, and I began my computer workaround with a decision to research this town's history, and that's when it really took a twist. In the five years I've been working on this, I've discovered that over the past one hundred and forty years this town has had many unexplained instances of disappearing people, strange events and even deaths. Although they have been

142

spread apart between many decades, my research is telling me they are connected in some way. However, since the fury of citizen outcry dies down between one event to the next, no one has ever tried to bind them into one research project."

"Until you did," interjected Axel.

"But have I? Some days I look at my research and think it's nonsense. That I'm so thick into this I believe it's just due to the fact I've written about it so many times. Repetition builds belief, they say, and I've talked to myself for years on the subject."

"The surname, Mrs. Hamsteen, what is it?" inquired Roxie. She had been dancing around subjects with softball questions, but Roxie wanted to get this point nailed down.

"You know, it's interesting you should ask."

Roxie, as well as Marcus and Axel, each let out a sigh that caught Mrs. Hamsteen's attention.

"Did I say something wrong?" she asked.

"Oh no, not at all," Marcus spoke up. He knew the apparent frustration they exposed in her delay to directly answer Roxie's question caught Mrs. Hamsteen off guard. "We've been working on this so much lately, any new clue is another step forward. We're just anxious, so please excuse us for being impatient about the surname."

"I'm sorry, I'm not used to verbalizing this topic. Five years is a long time to work on a secret project, I'll communicate better, I promise."

"You're doing fine, Mrs. Hamsteen, take your time and explain anything you like. In the long run we'll understand more completely the research you've gathered," added Roxie.

"You are such fine, kind, people. I am so glad it was you three that came to me with the parchments. Some days I feel like a robot processing things for people that don't appreciate a fine research project. Roxie, the surname of the family from Havenswood Valley I researched is Washburn, and the young boy's name was..."

"Michael!" the trio said in unison.

"You know about Havenswood Valley?" asked Marcus.

"How, what made you, our Havenswood Valley?" mumbled Roxie.

"This is not happening," said Axel to no one in particular.

"Yes, Marcus, I am very familiar with Havenswood Valley. Roxie, it started when I was doing the research on missing children. And, Axel," Mrs. Hamsteen paused, "this is most certainly happening!"

Suddenly, it was time to talk before they went any further with the parchments. The three parchment bearers had been blindsided by Mrs. Hamsteen and her admission that she was somewhat of an expert about certain goings on in Havenswood Valley.

"Mrs. Hamsteen, although we've visited Havenswood Valley for many years, your insight into a connection of dark events from so long ago is something that will be very useful, in regards to the parchments. We do know about Michael. We met his father last weekend." Marcus continued and again with input from Roxie and Axel they filled in the missing pieces of their weekend at the cabin for Mrs. Hamsteen. She was in awe of their first person experience and became more and more intrigued with the possibility of being a part of their mission.

"Oh my word!" Mrs. Hamsteen sighed, "This is so much more than even I had imagined. Incredible that we've met, it must be fate. Alright, then, how can I help? And I mean really help you three with this mystery."

"Can we start at the beginning? Can you take us back 140 years and allow us to take notes on the events you've studied?" asked Marcus.

"I'll do better than that. Let me know what evening works for you three and I'll have you over for supper. We can review my research without a time limit or fear of being interrupted. Once we work through that, I feel it would then be the proper time to open up all the parchments."

"I think that's a great idea," said Roxie.

"Me too, I'm always open to a home cooked meal," added Axel.

"Well, it's unanimous. How about Wednesday?" asked Marcus.

They agreed on Wednesday and all were in a very good mood, looking forward to discovering more about Havenswood Valley and the secret parchments.

As the three left the library, Marcus asked a simple question, "I wonder what the sheriff, Robert and Norma are working on?"

144

That gave way to a longer discussion than they had planned, but it did provide resolution for their current predicament of dealing with the parchments.

"I'm betting we'll be headed back to Havenswood Valley later this week," said Axel. "Sheriff Anderson is going to want the parchments in his office ASAP."

"It was probably a poor decision on our part not to show the sheriff right away, but then we wouldn't have found Mrs. Hamsteen," answered Roxie. "I don't know if I'd do it the same way again, but I also believe in fate and if having us bring the parchments home led to Mrs. Hamsteen, I'm good with that."

"I don't think Sheriff Anderson will rush to judgment on us. He seems like a fair man and will understand why we reacted the way we did with the parchments," said Marcus. "And I agree with you, Roxie. Finding Mrs. Hamsteen will help everyone, including the sheriff. She's going to be a great asset to the team."

"Team?" asked Axel.

"Sure," answered Marcus. "Between the sheriff and the others in Havenswood Valley, the three of us and now Mrs. Hamsteen, I'd say we're a team. Maybe not officially, yet, but once we get back to meet with the sheriff there's no way we won't all be working on this together!"

"What if he doesn't see a need for us to be involved? What if he takes the parchments, says thanks and tells us to head home?" replied Axel. "We really don't know him, Marcus. He may go into total sheriff mode and lock us out of the investigation. And we haven't even opened up the third and fourth tubes yet!"

"Look, we have to call him, but it won't do us any good until we meet with Mrs. Hamsteen," replied Marcus. "We'll take some heat about not telling the sheriff sooner, but that's okay, we can handle it. Let's focus on making sure we get all the information we can on Wednesday. Then we'll figure out how to tell him. If he wants the parchments, we'll just have to give them to him."

"Then we better prepare ourselves before we call," said Roxie. "One of our good friends was attacked and could have been killed, so we'll always be a part of this. He can tell us to go home and wait until he has something new to share, but we should have a back up plan of our own. Once we open up the other tubes we can take all the parchments to a printer and use their blueprint machine to make copies. Right now those are our trump cards and each of us should have a copy in case something were to happen to the originals. But, we shouldn't get too far ahead of ourselves with planning until we meet with Mrs. Hamsteen. Who knows what we'll find out and what direction we'll need to go with her, our friends and our family." Roxie smiled at Marcus. "Then we'll see who's going to be on this team."

"Great ideas, Roxie. We did get pulled into this, and I've never felt a stronger tie to an event than I did at the cabin. Something about this tells me we're onto something more than just the history of Havenswood Valley." Marcus looked up to the night sky as he spoke. "I can hardly wait for us to meet with Mrs. Hamsteen. I'm pretty sure the parchments will give us fresh answers, but I'm afraid they may also give us much bigger things to worry about."

Winter was approaching the upper Midwest and the first flakes of snow would soon be falling. Daytime temps were maxing out in the upper fifties, and sub freezing nights were becoming more and more common. Thanksgiving snow was a treat for the heartier folks living in Prairie Falls, even for those traveling to family gatherings. It pushed the holiday spirit into overdrive as Christmas decorations would be brought up from basements, trees trimmed and outside lights could now be turned on each evening without the homeowner coming across as too anxious. The out of doors turned over activities to deer hunting, and soon to follow would be snowmobile riding, cross country skiing and of course anything that could be done on a frozen lake. Hockey, broomball, and ice fishing were just a few of the options available once the ice was thick enough. It's a great season to experience in Minnesota, as long as you get outside and play! Kids are easy to get outdoors; snow forts, snowboarding, sledding and the occasional snow football game. It's tougher to coax adults out the door when it's twenty-two degrees and the wind is kicking up, but you figure out a few ways to enjoy the beauty of winter!

Driving together to Mrs. Hamsteen's home, Marcus, Roxie and Axel kept their minds busy talking about fall and winter traditions their families kept. It was an easy conversation, and their mood was friendly and festive, mixed in with a dash of anxiety and a pinch of nervousness.

Finally, Marcus brought up their impending meeting. "So, we'll be there in about fifteen minutes. Are we all set with our plan?"

"Roger that, Captain," answered Axel. "She talks, we listen, and then we ask for a break to figure out how much we want to let her in on. And if she spills the beans about our secret we call in the big dogs."

"The big dogs?" asked Roxie.

"Uh, yeah," said Axel. "We'll ask my uncle George to pop over to the library to spill a few books on the floor, or try to check out a reference book. I'm sure he still has a library card."

They all laughed and felt more relaxed, Marcus had to break the ice on their mission and this helped them remember that being low key would be the best way to keep their minds open and ready to make good decisions quickly.

"Well, you're right, Axel," said Marcus. "Not about old man Hubbard, but yes, let's listen to what her research shows. If she's been as thorough as we think she has, then it should lead us right up to our weekend encounter. And I can't wait to hear what she considers evil."

"I've been thinking about what she said the other day, too," continued Roxie. "Is it evil as in a person that may have kidnapped and killed someone from Havenswood Valley? Or does she think there is evil in the town itself?"

"Five years of research with her resources, I'm thinking she's tied evil to people," said Axel. "Sitting in the library she's got no clue about the actual surroundings. She's only reading reports and stories from people, most of it second hand, I'd guess."

"Axel, you deal with technology all day long, too," countered Marcus. "You see how quickly things progress. Maybe she's got a program that has helped her connect the dots to every event over the past one hundred forty years and helped her put together a pattern, or a geographical map. She might have answers to questions we haven't even thought of yet."

"Which wouldn't be too hard to do," said Roxie, "since we've only been at this for a couple of weeks."

"Technology is useful, but the application has to be field tested, and each use is unique. You can only get so close in the model, then we get on site and that's where we put our skills to work and fine tune everything." Axel was a pro at getting the most out of a system. When he installed lighting with a home theater, it glowed like a room full of miniature moons. When he set up the sound it put the homeowners in audio heaven. He felt that Mrs. Hamsteen was a fact-based researcher, no gray areas. "I'd bet my big screen, and you guys know it's a really big screen, that our potential teammate is going to need some help from us. Sorry to be so blunt, but she's from the black and white

TV generation, guys, I bet our phones do more than every piece of technology she owns."

"You might be right on the money, but having another viewpoint is going to help us immensely," said Roxie. "At the library, when she was having trouble dealing with the parchments, I saw that as real life. Maybe she does think there are people out there causing all these deaths over the years, but she's had time to think that maybe there's something in the water, so to speak. Certain regions around the world stand out for particular reasons, and she may have researched those places and come to the conclusion that Havenswood Valley should be on the list. I'll take your bet, because I'm hoping Mrs. Hamsteen is a pretty sharp woman and she's going to blow us away with what she knows."

"I'll agree she'll have a lot to say, but you'll be the one that will have to revive her again when we tell her there really is a boogie man in the forests of Havenswood Valley," said Axel. "When she finds out that it's not some crazy, lunatic cult out there that has been passing down secret handshakes for generations, we'll be looking for her nitroglycerin tablets."

"I'm right down the middle on this one, guys," Marcus said. "I'll bet we surprise each other. She was pretty passionate about what she saw on the parchments. Part of it may have been that we caught her so off guard, but part of it would be due to all her time and energy spent working on past wrong doings that she felt were never put right. She's making up for lost time and lost souls, and that's a pretty heavy commitment. At times I'm sure she was ready to give up but she kept at it, all on her own, with no one to share her work or her questions. Seeing the parchments brought a mystery to life for her."

"True, Marcus, all true. She's done so much on her own but I don't think it would have kept my interest. Too much like homework, researching people I had no connection with." Axel was always open to ideas, but once he decided on the final set up, he was on his way to the finish line full tilt. "I'm just being my usual self, looking at the information and drawing my own conclusion."

"Your own black and white conclusion?" teased Roxie.

"Very funny, Roxie, but sure, my mechanical engineering mind tells me here's the data, thus, here is what the answer will be. That is, until I get to the implementation part and fortunately I was blessed with right side, creative brain power. Not a ton, mind you, but enough to get the most out of a situation. So, I'll be open and flexible to Mrs. Hamsteen. Same as I'd expect someone to be with me, even when I go off on a tangent."

"No problem here," replied Roxie. "I know how you tick, Axel, and I love seeing you work through things. It's one of your best qualities."

"I second that emotion," added Marcus. "This will be a great night, I'm sure of it, and as long as we keep discussing things and keep an open mind, or three, we'll be fine. Besides, I'm pretty hungry so let's hope Mrs. Hamsteen has read plenty of cook books."

"Looking at the size of her house," observed Axel, "I'll bet there is going to be plenty of food to go around!"

"You have arrived" announced the GPS.

"Why thank you," answered Roxie. "I love my GPS, I'd be lost without it!" she laughed.

Roxie receive a dual "Ugh!" from Marcus and Axel for that comment. But it was true, they had arrived at Mrs. Hamsteen's and it was time to take the next step.

"Welcome, welcome to Hamsteen Manor!" Mrs. Hamsteen was all smiles and as much aglow with excitement as her home was with Christmas decorations. The holidays came early for Mrs. Hamsteen. Living alone she did what she wanted, when she wanted to, and Christmas decorations never truly disappeared completely from view in her home. There was always a Santa on a bookcase or a snowman on a mantel, and snow angels tucked high on a shelf for those that looked close enough.

"Thank you for inviting us to dinner, Mrs. Hamsteen. It was very generous of you to open up your beautiful home," said Roxie. "Oh, and the guys promised me they'd bring their good manners with them."

"Of course, dear, you are all welcome. I just hope you didn't get the wrong impression of me at the library the other day. I don't usually fall to pieces so easily. Just too much to process so unexpectedly." Mrs. Hamsteen smiled. Her comment was an ice breaker for the trio and it worked perfectly. Everyone felt at ease.

"You were awesome, Mrs. Hamsteen. I think we were the ones knocked back when you told us about your research," replied Axel. "I never would have thought you'd know so much about the history of Havenswood Valley."

"Well, Axel, you should never put too much stock into what you think you know. After all," she continued and with a wry smile looked directly at Axel, "sometimes even the best laid plans have to be redrawn midstream." She finished putting their coats away and had a pair of slippers for each of them to wear after they had taken their shoes off. "Come now, let's move into the great room and have a seat by the fire. Dinner isn't ready, so we have some time to visit."

The house was located just a few blocks from the historic, downtown section of Prairie Falls. The area had been founded in the heyday of logging and the home had been built by a successful lumber baron and used by his family as a second residence. When her husband passed away some twenty years ago, Mrs. Hamsteen had opened her home to friends and family that were in need of a room or two to rent. With plenty of space still left for her three children to visit, it was nice to have people in the home all year. A portion of the rent money was used to pay for a part-time housekeeper and cook, Katrina, who ended up spending many nights at the home, too. She started with Mrs. Hamsteen nearly fifteen years ago, and when Katrina's husband passed away seven years ago, she and Mrs. Hamsteen were linked by a common bond.

"Appetizers are ready, Eleanor," announced Katrina as she came from the kitchen. She held an armful of plates and began setting them onto the large oak table.

"Thank you, Katrina," answered Eleanor. There was a beautiful hutch, made of quarter sawn oak, built into a wall in the great room, and on it's countertop of granite sat an urn of fresh coffee, hot water for tea and cocoa and a collection of liquors and wine. "Would anyone care for something to drink before dinner? I'm going to mix some Hailey's Irish cream into some hot chocolate."

"You know, that sounds great, Mrs. Hamsteen" said Roxie.

"Please, call me Eleanor. Mrs. Hamsteen sounds so formal and already I feel like we're friends."

Roxie smiled, "Of course, Eleanor, thank you."

"Marcus, it's my night for designated driver so go ahead and help yourself," Axel offered. "I'll do just fine with some tea for now."

"Thanks, Axel. Maybe I'll have a glass of wine," and Marcus was on his way to the hutch.

"Next time I'll make sure to have you picked up. That way you can all enjoy a glass of wine with dinner," said Eleanor. "And dropped off, too, wouldn't make you walk all the way home, don't you know." She smiled.

They settled back with their drinks and appetizers. A modest fire glowed in the oversized, stoned wall fireplace, warming the entire dining room. An Italian opera played in the background, transporting the three to a time when life didn't move so fast; phone calls were made by dialing, and televisions weren't the main attraction in such a room. It was a comfortable setting and a pleasurable diversion from the hectic mental state they had been in for the past few weeks.

There was just enough time for Eleanor to provide a quick background on her life to her guests before dinner. How a young couple with three children seemed to be in the right place at the right time for so many opportunities, from career choices to stock investments and finally to their purchase of this home, where they raised their children.

"We were so blessed, Joe and I, and our life together was never taken for granted. Sometimes we'd ask ourselves how did we get so lucky? Joe was very successful with his career as an investment advisor, so I was able to volunteer at the library. Once our children left home it became a career for me, along with turning the manor into a Bed and Breakfast. While my Joe was taken too soon, he lost a quick battle with cancer, our time together was probably better than most marriages that last years longer. Thankfully our three children live fairly close, so I get lots of visits and babysitting time to spend with my four grandchildren."

"And your house guests, they must provide a nice flow of daily activity to your spacious home?" commented Roxie.

"Oh yes, it's wonderful to have an extended family living here. Katrina does a fabulous job in the kitchen, Erica comes in twice a week to tidy up, and Mr. Ellering keeps everything working and the landscaping in order." Eleanor looked around the room and smiled. "I really can't imagine not living here, and since our children all have homes of their own, this is a perfect setting to share with others. I have the resources so I think of it as another way to give back for the joys we were blessed with."

"Dinner is ready!" Katrina smiled at the group. She could tell everyone was relaxed and enjoying their glimpse of how life worked here at Hamsteen Manor.

"Well, that was a quick preparation. Let's see what Katrina has in store for us, shall we?" Eleanor led them to the table and once the group was seated, Katrina pulled out the main entry pocket doors to close off the dining area from the rest of the home, providing a private atmosphere for their meal and discussion. A side entry door that led to the kitchen allowed Katrina and her staff access for serving the meal.

After dinner had been served and a few more tidbits of Eleanor's family history were revealed , Marcus took the lead, as the three had planned, and broached the topic that had brought them all together.

"Eleanor, this evening is one of the most pleasant I've had in a long time. I'm sure I speak for all of us when I say your hospitality is way more than we expected!"

"Thank you, Marcus, that's kind of you to say. It's not every day I get to entertain three such talented adventurers." She looked at each of them.

"I guess we'll soon find out how adventurous we really are, once you read the parchments. I'm not sure how much talent we have in this arena, but we're willing to do what we can," Marcus answered.

"Not much talent?" Eleanor questioned. "The three of you discovered very rare documents all on your own! That's pulling history into current time, a very stellar feat in my book! Axel, you must have seen something that didn't look right. Every engineer recognizes structural clues, be it a hidden compartment or a community project needing guidance." Axel looked up, puzzled at Eleanor's last comment.

"Roxie, your experience with three dimensional work must have been a good asset during your discovery of the parchments. Someone with as much expertise as you have in CAD work would add fresh perspective to any discovery phase."

Roxie had the same look Axel was wearing, somewhat blank with a splash of thanks.

"I assume Marcus had you all working overtime on this, that somehow he knew there was more, more of something but he wouldn't know for sure until you found it." Eleanor sat quietly for a few seconds while her guests digested her comments.

"You must realize, that not all senior citizens sit around and play bingo," she continued, "I've been in the business of research for many years, and nowadays finding out a little about each of you started with a simple internet fact-finding search from my den. But I see by the looks on your faces that I've surprised you somewhat with my due diligence. I hope you're not offended."

"Eleanor," said Roxie, "I think it was a wise decision to check up on us. You really had no idea who we were. Besides, being able to find us on the 'net at your leisure was probably a pretty easy process."

"Yes, Roxie, it was. We had the house set up for wireless a few years ago." Eleanor continued, "It was such a frustration to come home and have the computer react so slowly, so I ordered faster connection service and now we can log on from anywhere near our complex."

"Wireless is such a great advancement," Roxie said with a teasing look that was meant for Axel. "My new TV has wireless internet and is so big I'm not sure where to put it. Axel, when you bring it over, we might need to try it in a few different places before I decide exactly which is best."

"I wouldn't count your channels too soon, Roxie. The reception's good, but I still don't know if all the channels work." Axel wasn't about to give up his big screen so easy, and although he doubted Roxie would call him on his earlier bet, he still wanted to see how much information Eleanor was going to provide this evening.

"Roxie!" Marcus jumped to his feet and was totally focus faced, "where's the gear bag with the parchments!"

Stunned, Roxie answered without thinking, "By the fireplace, between a couple of couches."

BOOM!

It was as if thunder had singled out Hamsteen Manor and gave a special appearance right outside the windows!

Marcus was already up and sliding the pocket doors open, he was shouting orders as he went to retrieve the backpack that held the maps to their next steps, and maybe their future. "Get everyone under the table, and make sure there isn't any glassware around! Axel, find Katrina and get her in there with you! Roxie, make sure the houseguests stay in their rooms!" He slammed the doors shut as he left the room.

Axel was into the kitchen in a flash, grabbed a jaw dropped Katrina and had her under the table in what seemed like mere seconds.

"Roxie, there's a large yellow button on your left as you enter the kitchen. Push it once and everyone will know to stay in their rooms." Eleanor looked at Roxie in a direct, but somewhat relaxed manner. "Go now, it will only take a moment."

She was there and back in less than ten seconds. "Red, yellow and green, you drive cars in here Eleanor?" Roxie laughed nervously, not expecting an answer.

BOOM!

The house shook and rattled again, but it would take more than these blasts to damage this home.

"Marcus!" shouted Axel. "What are you doing? Get in here!"

The thunderous noise was one thing, but the horrendous wind storm that seemed to materialize instantly from within the home no doubt brought a whole new level of survival awareness to everyone. It came from every direction, through the kitchen doors, and from under the door leading to the hallway. The pocket doors were being pushed back into their interior walls.

"Axel! Axel can you hear me!" It was Marcus, he sounded so far away yet they knew he was right in the other room.

"Marcus, hold on, I'm coming!" Axel pushed himself against the wind and fought to get through the doorway into the great room. Roxie, Eleanor and Katrina held onto each other and the sturdy legs of the table as the wind whipped through the room.

"Oh my God! Marcus, hold on!" Axel had made his way into the great room, only to see Marcus being pulled up to a high window that had been busted out. His legs looked as if they were tied at the ankles, no shoes on, in fact no socks either! His left arm wrapped through the straps of the gear bag, his right arm locked around a piece of the ceiling beams. He looked tired, but nowhere near giving up.

"Mrs. Hamsteen! I need a gun! A big one! Fast! And call 911! Tell them the place is on fire!"

"Roxie, tell Axel there's a gun in the closet by the door, I'll go press the red button." Before Roxie could head to the closet, Eleanor and Katrina were on their way to the kitchen, and Roxie moved as fast as she could against the wind.

"Marcus! Axel, do something!" Roxie yelled as she tried to open the closet door. "Axel, help me! It's stuck!"

They worked together and pulled it open. Axel found the 12-gauge shotgun, whipped around and fired both barrels through the busted out window and into the night sky.

Axel then found himself on the floor, shotgun thrown across the room and well out of reach. Roxie was blown back into the dining room and into the arms of Eleanor and Katrina, headed back from the kitchen.

"Axel! Once more, from outside! Go outside and fire again!" Marcus was holding strong, but he was getting tired. The gear bag was beginning to tear at the seams, and he knew something was going to give.

"I'm there, Marcus, just a few seconds and I'll be outside!" Axel crawled against the wind, now full of dust and leaves, found the shotgun and crammed two more shells into their chambers. He felt like a running back, getting knocked back by every linebacker on the defense, as he made his way out the front door and around to the side of the house.

Over the chimney, a mass of deep darkness was moving and breathing, like a giant leech sucking the life out of the house. It wasn't the wind blowing in, it was the air being pulled out! Axel stood there, in awe of this form, this life that was at once a miracle and also the menace that had tried to kill Kevin and was now on it's way to disposing of Marcus and the parchments.

He didn't hear the screams from the bystanders, who at first figured this must be some kind of Halloween stunt, or the sirens of help on the way. The intense look on his face showed a ferocity that allowed none of the neighbors or the firemen that had gathered outside a chance to reason with the man with a gun. As fast as Axel could, he ran to the side of the house, held the shotgun to the sky and unloaded not one, but three rounds of double barrel loads into the sky. When he began screaming that he had 'kicked it's ass' everyone was already huddled together behind cars, well clear of this psycho. The police were arriving, as was an ambulance, and surely they would be able to handle the crazy situation that had erupted on this normally uneventful street. None had noticed the darkness that had tried to suck the life from those inside the Hamsteen home. Their everyday lives had little option but to see only that which they knew. Seeing the evil took a much higher level of awareness than any of the sidewalk gawkers could muster.

In a matter of three minutes, Eleanor Hamsteen had assembled her guests and Katrina, and had made sure everyone, including Marcus, would be able to manage a short review by the local authorities, and then gave the speech of her life.

"Now, I don't know what in heavens name that was, but I do know there isn't a soul in Prairie Falls that would believe a word we'd say about trying to connect this event to Havenswood Valley. So this is what we'll do. It's my house, so it's my word. I've paid plenty to every charity in this town, to the politicians and the police and fire crews. If I say we had a party that got out of hand, the chief may shake his head at me, but if none of you say anything to the contrary, I guarantee they will be on their way. Is it a mess in here? Windows busted, the house a disaster, guns fired into the house and into the sky? Yes, yes, yes. But I'm old and rich, and I get some leeway around here, so tonight I'm going to ask for a big helping of it. And once they leave, you can bet we'll be spending some time talking about what the heck you all saw up in Havenswood Valley, and why in God's name it's so mad at you!"

"Well, we've been driving for nearly an hour and a half, add twenty-five minutes for our stop at Fire Tower Bakery, that's almost two hours on the road. What's your best guess for arriving in Prairie Falls, Glen?" asked Norma.

"Usually less time than getting to the bakery from Havenswood Valley. Clear night, full moon and the roads are in great shape. Should be knocking on Mrs. Hamsteen's front door about midnight" was Sheriff Anderson's reply.

After taking a lengthy phone call the previous day from Marcus, Sheriff Anderson, Robert and Norma were now headed south to Prairie Falls. Although the three adventurers had planned to call the sheriff soon, and wondered how upset he might be at them for taking the parchments, the call was made easier considering everything that had happened earlier in the evening at Hamsteen Manor. They needed help and they needed it now, no matter the consequences.

"Say, Norma, do you want a maple or chocolate Long John, or a cinnamon roll, strawberry and crème filled croissant, Old Fashioned, er, probably not that one, or one of these caramel covered chocolate bars?" asked Robert. He had a box full of Fire Tower Bakery goods on his lap, a steaming cup of hot coffee in a center section cup holder and a look of great anticipation in his eyes. Robert loved sweets and from the time he was young, every trip from his home in the north to the big cities in the south always included a stop at the Fire Tower Bakery. What started as a small bakery soon grew to a full restaurant and was now a famous stop for most travelers. You could pop in for a quick box of goodies or sit down and enjoy a well cooked meal any time of day, along with a side of the most friendly customer service you could ask for.

"There will be something left for our hostess and the other guests when we arrive, won't there, Robert?" questioned Sheriff

Anderson. "I'd hate to hand Mrs. Hamsteen a box with two donuts and a bunch of crumbs!" he laughed.

"You might want to pull out those handcuffs, Glen, I'm not sure if Robert can help himself. But yes, I would like an Old Fashioned donut, if you can spare one." She smiled at Robert, knowing full well he'd wanted the Old Fashioned for himself. "Oh, changed my mind, I'd like a caramel chocolate bar instead!" and laughed as his face changed from mild disappointment to understanding her humor.

"Very funny, Norma, but I've already taken care of the bakery goods. While you and Glen were talking with your friends Barb and Steve, I ordered another box along with some bread. We'll have plenty of pastries for breakfast and breads for lunch tomorrow!"

"Glad to hear that, Robert, I knew you had everything under control," said Sheriff Anderson. "So, then, how about we spend some time discussing what we all expect to hear once we get to Prairie Falls? For once in my long journey of working on all these cases it sounds like we've finally got something that could tie them all together."

"If what Marcus said was true," said Norma as she stared out the truck window, "then we are in for one big turning point in all this mystery, and a much larger impact on our lives."

"Well it's about time," added Robert. "I'm not sure how much longer I've got in this world, but I'd sure like to get some answers, and maybe some revenge, sorry Lord, before I head to heaven."

"Ok, then, let's talk," said Sheriff Anderson, "about the fact that we've had the same kind of attack, only in a much more populated area, with many more people involved, and a focused plan, if you will, of this evil trying to retrieve something. Something we think is tied to the deaths in the area of Havenswood Valley and whoever or whatever is responsible. And," he continued, "another event all the way out in Arizona with Kevin and Karen. I know we all want to jump right into the parchments ASAP, but I'm hopeful that having them stored in one of Mrs. Hamsteen's well insulated safes will keep our enemy away. Tomorrow morning we can take time to discuss all the events that have taken place so far and set up a plan of action. A little breathing room for everyone will clear our heads and make for much better decisions. Somehow this evil is tracking certain people from the weekend at the cabin and we've got to figure out what in the heck is going on before anyone gets hurt. Pronto!"

"Don't hold back on my account, Glen. You were going to say killed," Robert said. "I've been through enough and I'm ready for anything that comes my way. I just hope this lady that says she can read the parchments is the real deal."

"It's going to take all of us working together. Each of us may have certain ties to it, and not even know how. We know your involvement, Robert, but for Glen and I there will be much to learn." Norma's comments were right on target with Glen and Robert. They all knew what was at stake for themselves and the others who were now involved.

"For whatever reason, this thing has chosen to come back like it has over the many decades we've read about. It's showing no fear regarding when or where it wants to make a move. Other than everything happening at night, we really don't have too much to put into the mix about how it operates," said the sheriff.

"And up until now," replied Robert, "most of the victims had a real weak spot. They were young, or lost, or had a tragedy that left them vulnerable. That's why I could feel it the night it tried to get Kevin. I wallowed in self pity over Michael and it got to me, trying to pull me into the woods right in front of everyone. Damn, I don't need that."

"Robert, it's after all of us now so you won't have time for any more self pity. I know you'll be more concerned with protecting me and the others," said Norma, "now won't you?" she smiled.

"As long as you can outrun me, you'll always be safe, Norma!" Robert joked.

"Sorry to interrupt, but I'm getting a little worried about my transmission, feels like it's slipping. Robert, you hear any noises under the truck bed back there?" Sheriff Anderson asked.

"I don't hear like I used to, but far as I can tell nothing's broke back here, Sheriff." Robert turned his auto repair senses up and became very serious. He loved working on cars and trucks and was a master at figuring out what the cause of trouble was.

"Dang truck feels like it's hydroplaning every once in a while. This hasn't happened before. There, there it is again! Feels like I've got zero power in the back end."

160

"Try putting it in neutral, then into a lower gear, then back into your driving gear," suggested Robert. "Might want to slow down first."

"Sure," answered the sheriff. "Ok, slowing down, sliding into neutral, oh geez, I'm losing traction, it ain't workin' Robert! Hold on you two, this trucks got a mind of it's own tonight and I don't like what she's thinking!" Sheriff Anderson wrestled with the steering wheel like a cowboy hauling in a roped steer. Norma and Robert held on tightly to the hand holds.

"Keep at it, Glen, something's got to give! Brake it harder!" said Robert.

"Working on it, working on it! It's driving me off the road like a plow pushin' snow. I'm braking, shifting down, and this thing is still pushing me off." Sheriff Anderson was fighting a force he didn't understand. "I don't want to turn the engine off, them I'm dead in the water. Robert, any other ideas?" yelled the sheriff.

"Holy Mary, Mother of God!" screamed Norma. "Oh my dear God pray for us! Did you see that Robert!"

"Only thing I saw was a giant man-bird swoop past us like it was on the hunt for three trapped mice! Glen, you got control of this rig yet?" Robert yelled.

"Not a chance! This truck is a beast that's not about to listen."

"Glen, don't fight the push, looks like the party started early. I can see out the back window that it's the same dark shape we saw in the forest. Find an open spot to aim for and then put it into four-wheel, floor it and drive like heck," directed Robert. "Maybe you can pull away from it and we can see what's going on back there!"

"I'll try anything," he replied.

"Look out!" yelled Norma.

"You're freakin' kidding me!" was all Sheriff Anderson could say before he let off the brakes, set the truck into four wheel and pressed hard on the gas pedal. Imbedded in his mind was an image the bright moon had shone upon for mere seconds as it sped by the truck. A giant raven, with a glossy upper torso shaped like that of a man, yet with wings instead of arms. Ugly, nearly transparent wings and drifting at the rear of this man-bird creature, just below it's feathery tail and rump, were talons the size of pitchforks. The most striking thing he glimpsed was the head of the flying creature. A man, but not a man. It was a mutation with large eyes, tufts of skin for ears, a long crest and a sharp beak. Glen Anderson was startled beyond measure. His training of over twenty years gave him the skill to identify an object with just a few seconds of looking and yet his brain was telling him that what he was seeing could not be true, could not be happening!

"Robert, what do you see?" yelled Sheriff Anderson. "I've only got a little more room before I have to turn this truck around!"

"Get us out of here Glen! Please!" screamed Norma.

"It's right behind us, Glen. You got loose, but it's still coming at us!" yelled Robert.

"Robert, grab the shotgun behind you, it's already loaded. Push open the back window or bust it out if you have to and let's get a few rounds into it!" ordered Glen. "Norma, turn on the spotlights and sound we hooked up! Let me know when you're ready!"

"Glen, on your left! Watch out!" yelled Norma.

There was a split second for reacting, and Sheriff Anderson took it. He swung the truck around in the soft dirt, allowing the rack system over the bed of the truck to swat the giant bird like a baseball player hitting a line drive to the outfield. It was a sweet spot smack that sent the creature tumbling across the field where it lay motionless. Most likely not dead, but it sure wasn't moving any time soon.

"Yes!" shouted the sheriff. "All those days of four wheeling in the dirt finally paid off!"

"Great move, Glen, but we've still got that dark shape on our tail," said Robert, "I'm ready to fire. Counting down on three, two, one, now!"

Instantly the air in the desolate field was filled with bright, blinding light, deep, pulsating bass sounds and the crack of a 12-gauge shotgun. The external sound system, set within the square steel racking system that had sent the attacking bird rolling across the field, was worth every penny Glen spent!

"What's going on, Robert? What do you see back there?" yelled the sheriff.

"I don't see a thing!" he screamed, trying to be heard over the noise. "It's gone!"

Sheriff Anderson had slowed the Chevy Silverado down and was turning to where the giant bird had been, but it was gone. He maneuvered the truck slowly in a couple of circles within the large field as everyone's eyes were busy scanning the area, looking for something they couldn't believe had been there just a few minutes ago.

Maybe it was true, that the enemy was gone and they could collect their thoughts. Sheriff Anderson stopped the truck, clicked off the lights, killed the engine and stepped out of his rig. Norma and Robert joined him in front of the truck, Robert holding the shotgun at the ready.

"Funny how life seems simple, sometimes boring," Sheriff Anderson mused. "Then one day your whole concept of life, death, history, everything you think you know something about, it shifts a hundred and eighty degrees. You may as well just toss aside all that you've ever learned and start from scratch because somewhere along the line they left out this part. I'm usually pretty good with sorting through things, but this, well, I'm not even going to try and explain what just happened here."

"I don't think we can explain it, Glen," said Norma. "I don't think anyone can. We do know it's evil, smart evil at that. My senses tell me this power has been around a long time, ages maybe, and now it's on a new mission. The parchments have been found and moved, and fortunately we've been able to turn the evil back a few times. My world's always been a little different, with my mother being a seer I was brought up with uncommon happenings as a way of life. Now that I've grown into my own clairvoyant skin, something like this gives me reason to work even harder and with more courage against the turmoil evil causes." Norma looked up at the full moon, shining brightly upon the field. "We think we understand things, all our scientists, religious deities and philosophers. We don't know squat!"

"We do know survival, Norma, and that was about the best driving I've ever seen, Glen! You handled that like a pro, just wish I could have enjoyed the ride more," Robert laughed, trying to bring the mood up. "The hit you put on that oversized bird, well that was something any game hunter would be proud of. Too bad we weren't able to retrieve it and hang it on the wall of the courthouse!"

"Oh yeah, that would go over real well. I'm sure our Chamber of Commerce could come up with a great way to promote the giant bird man of Havenswood Valley," the sheriff replied sarcastically.

"So where did it go? Once it was hit, I never looked back at it, I was too busy watching the attack on the back of the truck," Norma brought them back to the moment. "And by the way, are we done here? Not only am I getting cold standing here, I'm thinking this would be a good time to get back on the road to Prairie Falls."

"That's a good idea, Norma. Why don't you hop inside the cab and Robert and I will take a quick look around the truck, make sure it's good to go."

"Uh, Glen, looks like we've got company." Robert saw a Ford Bronco pulling off the road and heading their way. It would turn out to be a local sheriff responding to a couple of calls about a truck tearing up a field, probably a drunk driver. After a short conversation between the two sheriffs the three were safely back on their way.

"I told him we were on our way to the cities for a meeting on crowd control and driving tactics for rural areas, that I found this field and wanted to do a final test before we tried it in front of the big brass. Just to make sure everything was working okay," Sheriff Anderson told the two others. "He wished us luck and said he'd like to know more about it once we get it approved. Hey, maybe we're onto something!"

"Oh," said Norma, "we're onto something, but I don't think he wants to know anything about it!"

CHAPTER
22

As the travelers made their way through town, conversation was sparse. Their unbelievable encounter had sucked the energy right out of them, and they were looking forward to a good nights sleep. The comforting sights that greeted them along the well lit streets of downtown Prairie Falls began to lighten the mood. Over the past thirty years the river city had revitalized its downtown section while homeowners and businesses kept pace by remodeling and rebuilding, all with the same goal in mind; making Prairie Falls a great place to live, work and play. With so much to offer residents and visitors, there was never a doubt the investment wouldn't pay off with more jobs and a better standard of living. It did, of course, and thus giving back to the community with parades, seasonal decorations and numerous events became a standard, and then a mission, for the City Council, Chamber of Commerce and the many organizations with charters in a city so firmly dedicated to its populace. It was a historic city that never looked tarnished, yet under the well kept veneer Prairie Falls was as normal, and as fragile, a city as any in small town USA.

"My mother used to spend a fair amount of time in Prairie Falls," offered Norma. "She would come down for extended periods, working with people from here and the surrounding area who were deeply troubled by personal demons. It's hard to imagine living around here and stressing out about anything."

"Well, look at my life in Havenswood Valley. Could sound pretty boring and stress-free, unless you knew about the trials I went through with my wife and son. I manage getting along by having good friends around me for support and a wide open outdoor environment for my therapy," Robert answered.

"And then you've got people living in big cities that never seem to have a care in the world," continued Norma, not ignoring Robert, but still focused on her own train of thought.

"People that are blessed with a lack of violence, free from poverty in their lives, getting along just fine and, hopefully, once in a while helping those less fortunate. It's a delicate balance, isn't it?"

"Yes, it is, Norma," replied Sheriff Anderson, "and sometimes I think it's a miracle humanity has been able to survive for so many years. Especially if there are many more of those flying man-birds around. "

Norma was ready to get off the road. It had been an exhausting evening and her head hurt. "Maybe if we had kept in better harmony with the earth we wouldn't have so many man made challenges. Maybe one day our species will realize our environment is really a living organism, not a resource to be used up. We can be parasites or we can live in paradise, but not both."

"Sounds good to me," said Robert. "We sure don't need to be everywhere on the planet. It's like overfishing a lake and having to wait decades for the fish to come back to strength, if ever. I agree with you, Norma, we do need to leave some breathing room."

"Speaking of breathing room," Sheriff Anderson said, "we're just about to the Hamsteen home. Either of you want to explain to the others about tonight, or do we wait until morning?"

"It's pretty late. I'm fine with getting in and hitting the sack, don't really expect too many of them to still be awake anyhow," answered Robert.

"Me, too" said Norma. "Besides, we called and let them know we were running late and they shouldn't wait up for us."

"Okay, then we'll say our hellos and goodnights and present our story in the morning," said the sheriff.

"Thanks, Glen, I feel better already," said Norma.

"And I feel asleep already, are we there yet?" asked Robert.

"As a matter of fact, you can pull on your one piece, Robert. Looks like the Hamsteen castle is dead ahead," replied Sheriff Anderson.

"Oh, my," Norma said. "I remember this house, it's such a beautiful turn of the century home. Magnificent. I've always wanted to see what it looked like on the inside!"

"Norma, I don't recall you ever being so taken aback by a house before. What's got you so excited about this place?" asked Sheriff Anderson.

"I don't know, Glen." Norma looked around the neighborhood. "There's something about this place that's special and I can feel it holds something of interest for all of us. This is going to be a remarkable week!"

"Norma, every week with you is remarkable," said Robert. "You're just so used to this kind of stuff happening all around you it's hard to see the forest for the trees. When you do notice, it scares the heck out of us."

"Sorry, Robert. I guess I'm just overloaded from what happened tonight, and now I've got memories stirring things up even more." Norma was settling back into her calmer self. "Don't mind me, it's just how we emotional seers act when we're tired. Let's get in there and get some sleep." Norma smiled at Glen and Robert and the three grabbed their belongings from the truck. They were making their way to the front door when a large greeting party welcomed them with smiles, hugs and cheers.

"You're all awake?" questioned Sheriff Anderson.

"The heat's out!" exclaimed Axel.

"Once we figured out the furnace wouldn't be working overnight we lit a fire in the great room," Marcus added. "Everyone ended up coming in to ask about the heat so we decided to stay up until you arrived. Welcome!"

"Sure you've got room for us?" asked Robert.

"Come on in, everyone. It's cold outside and we have plenty of food and drink left." The group headed inside for drinks, desserts, and conversation. As much as the newly arrived trio had wanted to head off to sleep, a lively party was in motion with too much momentum to slow it down. Still, even as they relaxed and enjoyed the impromptu celebration, none of the three let slip about what had happened on their way down to Prairie Falls. That topic would have to wait until morning, as this late hour was not the time to open up the discussion of a third attack.

CHAPTER
23

When her home is filled to capacity with a mixture of family, friends, tenants and guests, Eleanor Hamsteen feels as if she is in heaven. With such an increase in activity throughout the grounds and within her home, Mrs. Hamsteen supports her staff with extra help. Katrina's expanded workload includes three or four additional staff that arrive at the home well before most, if not all, of the guests are awake. She also enlists extra help for Mr. Ellering, as he will be running from outside to inside and end to end with multiple duties. Everything from making sure the hot water stays hot to keeping every part of the homes interior, garage and grounds in top condition.

Today, Edgar Ellering arrived extra early, first to fix the heat, second to stabilize the previous night's damage, especially the broken window, and take stock of what would be needed to repair the home. He found no trace of the evil, but had discovered a strange substance on some of the wood trim from around the window. He carefully placed the broken oak window casing into a paper bag for Mrs. Hamsteen. She had informed Edgar of the young people she recently met and of their impending visit, and after hearing what had happened to cause the damage he was very careful to make sure any clues were kept safe.

As she often does, Mrs. Hamsteen was up early and walking through most of the estate with Edgar. Checking this and that, knowing full well her staff is not only highly efficient, but that they pride themselves in making sure the property is in top shape. This morning the two are walking with only one discussion topic on their minds; the attack of the previous night.

"I don't know how else to explain it, Eleanor, other than a dark substance, like a glue, on the window casing. I was careful not to touch it, and I'm sure once you've had some discussions with the group you'll want to see it. Just let me know and I'll bring it to you."

"Thank you, Edgar. I'm looking forward to going over it with the others. And by the way, I hope this attack has made you realize how much I appreciate your work here," said Eleanor.

"It has. I couldn't get here fast enough." Edgar stopped and said, "I was worried something might have happened to you or one of the other staff members. It would have been terrible if someone had gotten hurt!"

"Yes, it would have, and I'm glad everyone is alright." As Edgar headed to the workshop, Eleanor walked into the kitchen. Moments later Marcus came in.

"Good morning, Marcus," said Mrs. Hamsteen. "Up early today, are we? It's not even seven o'clock yet."

"Good morning, and yes, I am. Thought I would be able to sleep in after a late night but the body clock kicked in and so I thought I'd head out for an early run." Marcus helped himself to a glass and filled it half full with tap water.

"Ah, a runner in our midst. You know, Prairie Falls hosts four running events each year. You should think about entering one and come back to visit our fair city. I know of a nice place you could stay while you are here."

"Sounds like a great idea," Marcus said, "and depending on the dates, I could probably get Axel and Roxie to join me. For this morning, can you direct me to a park or trail in the area?"

"One that's flat, or even downhill would be best." Axel had a wide grin as he stood in the doorway, also dressed for a run.

"Maybe with a view of the river," Roxie said. All geared up for a run, she walked past Axel to the coffee pot. "Thanks for asking, Marcus. Oh, and Happy Halloween!"

"I'll stay with you till the sidewalk, and then you're on your own." It was Robert, ready for his morning walk. He pulled a coffee cup from the open cabinet and made his way to the freshly brewed elixir.

"You know, Robert," said Norma, now coming into the kitchen, "you're not the only one around here needing a morning walk. How about some company with that coffee?"

"Doesn't anyone sleep in anymore?" asked Sheriff Anderson with a smile. "I know we have a full day ahead of us, but did it have to start this early?" Glen helped lower the tank on the coffee urn with a generous pour of the morning blend.

"Well, Katrina, looks like we might be starting our breakfast earlier than we had planned," stated Mrs. Hamsteen. "With so much exercising going on we'll need to make sure there is plenty of everything! If you run down some of the side streets you'll see some great Halloween yard decorations. How long will you be out for your runs and walks?"

"Depends on how many stretch stops Axel needs, but I'd say about an hour, nothing too long today," answered Marcus.

"I'll need a couple of stops to stretch, and yes, catch my breath," Axel said with a smile, "I really haven't been running too much lately, but you and Roxie never seem to mind a break now and then."

"True," said Roxie, "we just enjoy it more when you're the one that's out of shape!"

"Forty minutes sounds about right to me," added Robert, "Norma, Glen?"

"Perfect" answered Norma.

"I think I'll be able to make it to the front porch and then work on this cup of coffee," said Glen. "Mornings are my favorite part of the day and I'd hate to spoil this one by breaking into a sweat," he said with a smile.

The group embellished the sheriff's humor with a few good-natured retorts, and then with a 'good luck' from the sheriff and Mrs. Hamsteen, the walkers and runners were on their way, leaving the kitchen staff, under the direction of Katrina, to increase the food portions they were preparing for breakfast.

"That's a dedicated group you have assembled, Sheriff," said Eleanor as she walked through the doorway and onto the front porch. Sheriff Anderson looked up from the morning paper. "A wonderful mix of people and personalities that should help tremendously in our effort to find out what's been going on in Havenswood Valley over the past decades."

"You know, I'd been working on the one case for so long, Robert's son that is, and when it seemed to have led to other deaths I didn't know what to do at first. But over the years I received help and guidance from others and it enabled me to keep chipping away at it." Sheriff Anderson took a drink of his coffee and continued, "But what's happened lately is a whole new dimension. Seeing the evil, seeing people affected by it firsthand, it's more than I ever expected to encounter and yet the people I'm surrounded by now are fully ready to fight against this sinister energy like it's their own personal battle. You're right, Mrs. Hamsteen, it is a fantastic group, one I'd dare say is capable of heroic efforts."

"Sheriff, you called it a sinister energy just now and a thought just came to me. Being involved with words all day, nearly every day, I'd like to coin a word for you. Sinergy."

"Synergy? Isn't that already a word?"

"Sin-ergy, Sheriff. S-i-n-e-r-g-y, with an emphasis on the word sin." Mrs. Hamsteen thought out loud, "It really is a sin, what's been going on, and the best description I can give to the dark mass we saw two nights ago is an energy, albeit evil, of some sort."

"Hmmm, I see that as a real possibility for a profile name. Sinful and sinister do describe how I feel about the evil, and it certainly does posses an organized energy, so the play on words really works. Let's try it out today and see if it strikes a cord with the others. Thank you, Mrs. Hamsteen. You've just provided us with a workable name for our enemy, and once we have an ID, we usually get our culprit."

"You are very welcome, and please, call me Eleanor, Sheriff."

"Okay, Eleanor, as long as you return the favor and call me Glen."

"It's a deal unless, of course, I need you as the heavy hitter, then it's Sheriff Anderson in front of the guests."

"Wouldn't want it any other way, thanks."

Sheriff Anderson then asked Mrs. Hamsteen about the property she lived on, which led to a very educational discussion on the home, the city and some Prairie Falls history. For nearly forty minutes more the two talked, and when Robert and Norma began approaching the manor, both Sheriff Anderson and Mrs. Hamsteen were surprised at how quickly the time had passed.

"Welcome back!" Mrs. Hamsteen exclaimed. "How was your walk?"

"Fantastic!" exclaimed Norma, "This is such a beautiful area. I told Robert I'm going to start looking around town to see if I can find a location to expand my business and have two stores, the one in Havenswood Valley, and one here, in Prairie Falls."

"She thinks she's busy now, just wait until she has two stores going," said Robert. "It's plenty more than twice as busy, and although I know Norma will do just fine, I told her I had to be the one setting up her new location. No sense in spending all that money on something I can do just fine. Besides, I kind of like it here, too."

"So you're saying I'll have to run for Sheriff of Prairie Falls if I want to see you two?" asked Sheriff Anderson.

"That might be a tough vote, Glen. Our sheriff is liked here as much as you are in Havenswood Valley," said Mrs. Hamsteen.

"Then that settles it, I'll just have to get used to seeing Robert and Norma a lot less." He smiled and added, "That should take me about a day or two to adjust."

"First round of breakfast is ready!" announced Katrina. She had pushed open the front door and caught the group by surprise, "Fresh pot of coffee and plenty of Fire Tower Bakery pastries to get your appetites started." She smiled and went back into the house.

"That's about the best way to start the day, and I sure don't need to be asked twice," said Robert. As he headed inside the kitchen, the others began to follow.

Mrs. Hamsteen and the sheriff were still seated on the porch when she commented, "With such an early breakfast I'm sure we'll be able to get to the parchments sooner than we had all expected, Glen. Maybe everyone was just too anxious to sleep in today."

"Or their heads were too full of nightmares," said Sheriff Anderson. "The past couple of nights have been beyond anything I could have expected, and I for one couldn't clear my mind well enough for a good night's sleep."

"Past couple of nights, Sheriff?" asked Mrs. Hamsteen. "Our excitement was two nights ago, but nothing last night, and tonight is Halloween. Is there something the rest of us don't know about?"

"You don't miss a thing, now do you Eleanor?" he replied. "Yes. Robert, Norma and I have news to bring to everyone. We decided to wait until morning before we would talk about it, but we will present it right after breakfast, before we get into the parchments."

"I get the feeling ours wasn't the only sighting of the Sinergy lately, am I on the right track?" asked Eleanor.

"You're in the fast lane and ready for a green light." Sheriff Anderson looked around after hearing voices and saw that Marcus, Axel and Roxie were a few houses away and walking up the sidewalk to the Hamsteen home. They were on their cool down walk and looked as fresh as when they had left. "I will tell you this," he said so only Eleanor could hear, "the Sinergy is getting stronger and more aggressive and yet, for some reason we are its only targets. I've been searching every county, and spoken to a few contacts I have throughout the state, but not a thing has shown up on any sheriff's report to suggest violent attacks like we've experienced. Something we've done, or taken, if it's about the parchments, has really set it hot on our trail. Today we may find some clues, but I think even more importantly we'll need to start thinking about how we're going to protect ourselves."

"I've been praying for answers and guidance, Glen, more than I ever have. I agree that this is a very dangerous enemy and while I fear for these fine young people, I do feel they hold the key to something that's instrumental in solving this mystery." Eleanor smiled and rose from her chair as the running trio walked up the porch steps. Sheriff Anderson did the same and as he and Eleanor greeted the runners, Glen wanted to tell her that while these three may play a part, he knew everyone involved was important to the success of discovering the mystery of the Sinergy, and that someday soon its answers would unfold on their own terms.

"You all look so refreshed!" Mrs. Hamsteen gave them a wry smile, "Did you really go for a run?"

"Thanks, Mrs. Hamsteen, and yes," Marcus laughed, "we did go for a run, but an easy one so Axel could keep up!"

"Hey, I didn't even need a stretch break today!" Axel said in his defense. "And Mrs. Hamsteen, you were right about the Halloween decorations. I haven't been through here in years but the neighborhoods have really gone crazy with the displays!"

"They were really creative, and gory! But, the city park is beautiful, and the dirt paths are a treat to run on," added Roxie.

"Can't wait to head out again tomorrow, this is really an awesome running area," said Marcus.

"Well, now that you are all back we can sit down for breakfast as soon as you are ready," said Mrs. Hamsteen.

"Give us fifteen minutes and we'll be at the table, fresh and famished," replied Roxie as the trio headed inside.

"Glen," said Mrs. Hamsteen, "before we go in, there is something else I need to speak to you about. My property, Hamsteen Manor. Well, it's been around for some time and for this area at least, it is unique."

"I would agree with that. It's beautiful, and the grounds are extensive. Plenty of room for a home in a city."

"Yes, thank you. My husband and I fell in love with it right away and we worked very hard to get it in livable condition. You see, it was in terrible shape when we discovered it. The grounds had overgrown the buildings, most of the windows were broken, and the interior, oh my word, it was a disaster, even for the low selling price. After the three years it took to clean up the home and grounds to a decent and livable condition, well, that was when we accidentally came upon the secret access ways and hidden rooms and we really began to worry about why it sat vacant so long, and why the price was so reasonable," Mrs. Hamsteen looked at Sheriff Anderson with a mild fright in her eyes. "But eventually, we wrote it off as Prohibition era building designs. The original owners were wealthy and entertained constantly. We thought they needed those things for safety and security against the police raids and FBI." Eleanor grabbed Glen's forearm with a firm grasp and said in a near whisper, "Thank goodness we haven't found any dead bodies!"

Roxie sat at the base of the stairs, each tread a beautiful plank of quarter sawn oak, her stocking feet waiting to be placed inside a new pair of Sportrock shoes. Leaning against the stocky newel post, she was daydreaming as the din of voices began to thicken inside the kitchen and escape like pinballs and bounce from wall to wall of the nearby rooms and foyer. Hamsteen Manor was full of guests feeling excited and nervous. Roxie was right there with them, and the morning run, while a mild sedative, provided only temporary comfort and confidence for what lay ahead. She had always felt so good and so safe around Marcus, and his confrontation with the evil just two nights ago strengthened her faith that he would continue to be her rock. Emotionally, Roxie was more attracted to Marcus than ever before, but she wasn't sure when or how to talk with him about it. Not just yet though, her feelings had surfaced so quickly she hadn't made time to come to terms with them. She wanted to show him how strong she was and to let him know that he could count on her when things got tough. Giving away your heart is easy, she knew, it's having it returned without use that's so hard. Years ago they had tried a relationship, and it was fine, just not the best of timing. She promised herself a talk with Marcus soon, get this out in the open and deal with it. Enough with the daydreaming, Roxie shook herself back to the present time and rose from the stairs. Ready for the day, ready for the challenges and most certainly ready for breakfast!

"Wow, it would be like totally amazing to be able to eat here every day," Axel announced.

"We'd gain too much weight," joked Marcus.

"It would be worth adding more miles to my training!" Axel laughed.

By now the kitchen was the busiest room in the house. A few of the regular Hamsteen Manor guests had wandered in for their breakfast and were expertly choosing which offerings to eat, it all looked so good! These tenants, not trying to seem offended by the newcomers, knew the event of two nights ago would be addressed by Mrs. Hamsteen, however they wanted nothing to do with whatever caused the terror and destruction. They weren't mad at the newcomers, but they were upset about not being forewarned of the circumstances, even though no one could have predicted the attack. Hamsteen Manor was their safe haven from the rest of the world, and the sooner these newcomers figured a way to keep the evil away, or leave and take the threat of a return event, would be a true blessing for all.

After filling their plates with a wonderful array of food, the new guests began to gather in the dining room, allowing themselves a semi-private breakfast conversation. The built in cherry hutch had coffee, tea, juice and water placed on the granite countertop, providing the group with plenty of choices for drinks while they ate and talked. A beautiful day, the sun shone through the tall, south facing window, illuminating the room with rays of optimism.

As they were getting situated at the table, and a few minutes from saying grace, Marcus's text alert sounded. He looked at his phone and then asked the group, "Can you please excuse me for a minute? We have two more guests that have just arrived for breakfast. I'll go help them unload and we'll be right in." He got up from the table and was on his way to the front door before anyone in the surprised group could utter a word.

"Marcus got a text late last night from Kevin," Roxie said. "He told us about it this morning on our run. Kevin just got back into town and Marcus felt it was important he be here today."

"Kevin?" asked Mrs. Hamsteen.

"Kevin was also at the cabin," interjected the sheriff. "Actually, Eleanor, he was the one person that nearly succumbed to the," he paused briefly, "to the Sinergy."

"Synergy?" echoed the group to the sheriff, nearly in unison.

"Everyone," broke in Marcus, and with a big smile on his face said, "I'm pleased to introduce the newly engaged couple, Kevin Stover and Karen Brach!"

The entire group stood up and cheered, and the moment turned into a hug-fest. Even Mrs. Hamsteen, who had never met either Kevin or Karen, seemed overcome with emotion at the announcement. Upon hearing the good news, a few of the tenants and kitchen staff came into the room and shared their congratulations to the couple.

It was nearly ten minutes later when the group sat down to eat. Just enough time for the superb staff to reset the table to fit the additional guests in, and to have dished up a warm helping of food. Eleanor noticed how her dear friend, Katrina, and the staff, had moved so quickly behind this scene of excitement. She would remember this and make sure to send a note and small gift to each one as an acknowledgement of their efforts for the day.

"I'd like to make a toast," Marcus stood and raised his glass of orange juice. "To Kevin and Karen, great friends to all, best friends to each other. May your wedding be joyous, your marriage blessed by God and your life together one that is filled with happiness and enduring love."

"Thank you, Marcus," said Kevin. "I know this seems sudden to you all, but Karen and I are very sure about what we are doing. Thank you for your good wishes."

"You might be asking yourselves if we're crazy. Maybe a little," smiled Karen. "That's what we love about each other, I'm so glad that Kevin and I are engaged. I'm happier than I've ever been."

Robert then said a prayer of thanks for the group, asking for guidance and support of their efforts, and that the newly engaged couple be blessed with the Holy Spirit and be open and accepting of all the love the Lord offers to them. A loud amen by all followed and breakfast was finally under way.

The sheriff took the floor a few minutes later and turned to the topic at hand. "Well, then, I guess this is a good time to set up our schedule for the day, and our goals for the weekend." He looked around the table. Robert on his left, then Norma and Eleanor. Karen, Kevin, Axel, Roxie and finally Marcus to his immediate right. This is a solid group of individuals, he thought to himself. And they make a team that is committed to finding out exactly what had been going on in Havenswood Valley over so many years, and how the current activity is related to past events.

"Let's make this morning a session," Sheriff Anderson said, "to put the main events on the table. We have a few to discuss and it will clear the air for all of us to be on the same page. After that, we'll break and come back for the parchments, which should take most of the afternoon. The dinner session, for which Eleanor has planned a meal, will be a time for each of us to give input on the situation. How you see it and what your suggestions will be for any part of this task. Which, by the way, is something else we need to identify and pinpoint."

"Do you mean we need to pinpoint what in the world we are doing here?" Axel said, half jokingly.

"Yes, Axel, I do. We've been reacting to what's been going on around us, and now it's clear that we'll have to go on the offensive at some point." Sheriff Anderson looked around the table, "This is our reality check meeting, folks. From here on out we'll need to depend on each other more than we have on anyone else, ever. And it will get tougher day by day until we figure out exactly what we are dealing with. If at any time you don't think this is right for you, any of you, just let me know. No one will think any less of you, in fact you may be the most sane of the group. So, then, that being said, let's talk about the events we've experienced."

"Sheriff," asked Roxie, "just before Kevin and Karen arrived you used the word Synergy to describe the evil. What did you mean by that?"

"Actually, Eleanor coined that word. She spelled it S-i-n-e-r-g-y, a coupling of sinful or sinister, and energy. Which I agree with, as this is a sinful energy we are fighting and Sinergy was a good description. We thought we'd test it out and get everyone's feedback."

"I like it," said Kevin, "very descriptive."

"It works," added Norma, "on a couple of levels. I can see why you are so good at your job, Eleanor. Excellent word usage."

"Thank you, Norma. Funny how things come out of nowhere sometimes."

"Okay, like I said to Eleanor this morning, let's try it out the rest of this weekend and if it sticks, we've got a name for our enemy," said the sheriff. "Now, who'd like to start our discussion on the main events?"

"What about us?" said Axel, "Who are we? What do we call our group?"

"That's actually a good point, Axel. We've created a group with no name," stated Roxie.

"Did we create it, or were we all called to it," asked Norma. "I think we answered a need and everyone fit together."

"I think so, too," answered Marcus. "I've felt it my entire life, a calling to do something more. I feel right at home, here at Hamsteen Manor, making plans to battle the enemy. At times in my past I was out of place and out of step, but now it all makes sense to me and I'm all in for what I feel are exactly the right reasons."

"Eleanor came up with a name for the bad guys," said Axel. "Maybe she can come up with one for us good guys."

"I think it's more than just being the good guys," said Kevin. "Who knows what lies ahead of us."

"Very true," replied Mrs. Hamsteen. "We're heading into uncharted waters."

"I know, The Navigators!" Karen said excitedly.

"That's good, but how about something more Minnesotan?" suggested Robert. "How about The Voyageurs! Those early trappers and traders were always heading down uncharted paths!"

"Like Norma said before," Kevin added, "excellent word usage."

"It feels like the perfect name to me," added Marcus. "As a group or as an individual, we can be The Voyageurs."

"I like it, too," said Sheriff Anderson, "for our group of adventurous members."

They started their discussion as The Voyageurs and it quickly became apparent each member would be taking on certain duties and responsibilities. Mrs. Hamsteen, with her skills at the keyboard and her command of the English language, was asked to be Scribe of The Voyageurs. She began taking notes as Robert and Sheriff Anderson relayed their experiences with Michael's death, but was hard pressed to keep focused on her duty. She wanted to ask so many questions, but knew their goal was strictly about laying out the events. There would be plenty of time for questions later on.

"I know this may be obvious to everyone, but I'd like to move that we ask Sheriff Anderson to be our lead person of The Voyageurs, our first point of contact that everything will run through." Marcus was saying out loud a view everyone felt; that Sheriff Anderson was the person they needed as the leader of this group. Not only due to the history of what he had gone through, but also his experience as a sheriff. Everyone already looked up to him as the person in charge. A group vote would make it official.

"Good suggestion, Marcus, I second the motion," said Norma.

"That's fine with me but I'd like you all to know that Robert will be my right hand person on everything. We've worked together on this for years and he's close when I need help," replied the sheriff. "Okay, then, now that we have some structure set up, let's continue on with our discussion of the past events."

They went on to review the next event on their time line, the weekend at the cabin. It was here that Mrs. Hamsteen benefitted from hearing all about what had happened; the strange sounds and movements of the first night, Norma's secret trick to get the objects from her shop to the group, Kevin nearly being captured by the Sinergy, and how the trio had found the parchments that had been hidden inside the table.

"Since we still have so much to do, and I don't want to get into it now, but some time this weekend we'll need to set up protocols for discovery of information. I understand how the three of you felt when you discovered the parchments, I've felt that way with information on a case," Sheriff Anderson said to the group. "But every bit of information is important and sharing it among all of us will be the best way to see if each discovery is a lead or a dead end. Let's make sure we're all working to build a safe and trusting partnership for the group that allows for full disclosure. Once we gain the full confidence of one another we will undoubtedly move forward at a much faster pace."

"That being said, I'd like to present an event that happened soon after the weekend at the cabin. It led the three of us, me, Robert and Norma, into a long evening discussion about Robert," said the sheriff. "Full disclosure means just that, and although it may stir up a painful memory for Robert, you need to know everything we know about the Sinergy and all of its activity."

The three went on to talk about the attack at Tres Azure on Robert, and his explanation of why he was struggling with what his friends thought was a periodic sickness over many years, but turned out to be the Sinergy coming after him. This took the

Sinergy, in the minds of the others, to a whole new level of darkness, yet in some ways bridged the gap between the cabin and other events. It showed progression and intent, which they hoped would be clues to work on when they met later to plan their strategies.

The group continued on down their list and talked next of the attack at Hamsteen Manor. It was still very fresh in the minds of those in attendance and was a very memorable event to share. It was easy to put together how the evening progressed, how the attack happened and was a fairly quick discussion topic.

"If it's all right, Karen and I would like to tell you about the recent experience we had," said Kevin, and instantly regretted his choice of words.

"Whoa, Kevin, it's too early in the morning for this kind of talk. We're happy for you two, but now is not the time to brag about your romance. Maybe later, over some beers," joked Axel.

A newly engaged couple is ripe for digs and off-the-cuff remarks, and Kevin's line continued to be an easy target for a few minutes, providing some relief from the tension that had been building.

Once the good natured comments ended, Kevin and Karen told the group about the night they saw the image in the desert. Although they had planned to contact Marcus right away, the more they talked about what they had seen the more they convinced themselves there was no way it could have been real. They decided that it must have been due to weather, and the fact they were overtired and overly sensitive from what had happened recently at the cabin. Now they felt differently.

After hearing their story first hand, there were now more questions that begged to be asked, and the lightness that was in the air just moments ago was replaced with a another heavy dose of anxiety. While the notion of being followed, like Robert was, or tracked from Havenswood Valley to Prairie Falls to be attacked, as happened just two nights earlier, it was still amazingly hard to digest the possibility of being found in Arizona. It was absolutely unimaginable.

Roxie looked at Karen and said, "I'm so glad you and Kevin were able to be here and talk about this in person."

"Thankfully we had each other that night, and, well, danger and adventure are great ways to discover the true nature of another person," she looked at Kevin. "Even though we got caught up in the moment, I always felt safe with Kevin there."

"Speaking of nights, as in last night, is it time to share your encounter with us Sheriff?" asked Mrs. Hamsteen.

"Yes, Eleanor. We do have one other event to add to the list," replied Sheriff Anderson. He, along with Robert and Norma, took another turn and explained the attack they dealt with on their drive down to Prairie Falls. The drama of the story was not lost on this group, as they could sense the intensity of each moment that unfolded, much as they did when attacked at Hamsteen Manor.

"I realize we're going to talk about all of these events in more depth later, but it occurs to me, especially after hearing about your encounter, Sheriff, that the attacks are happening in a more overt manner. In my research," explained Mrs. Hamsteen, "most of the deaths in the Havenswood Valley area were one person at a time, with no witnesses. Our recent encounters are taking place with groups of people present and little regard by the Sinergy to hide itself. We should all be very aware how rapidly the aggression is increasing."

"I never thought of it that way," Axel said. "We've only known about it since the cabin and so to us, it's been aggressive from the start. Kind of like finding a trapped animal in the woods, it growls and bares its teeth as soon as you get close. You'd never know it has a less confrontational disposition."

"That's a good comparison, Axel," replied the sheriff. "Whenever a criminal is trapped or found, their first instinct is to lash out. It might just be that the parchments have the Sinergy feeling very vulnerable, so it's moved past living in the shadows of the woods and is now doing what comes naturally, fighting for what has been taken from it."

"Or discovered," said Marcus. "It's possible the Sinergy had no idea where the parchments had been hidden for who knows how long, and now that they have been brought to light the Sinergy is deadly intent on gaining possession of them."

"But the Sinergy isn't of this world and the parchments are. How can they know of them? What's the connection between some kind of dark force and a physical item?" asked Kevin.

"Kevin, within the last few months of my research I have discovered some connections that I had no idea could be possible," said Mrs. Hamsteen. "This home, in fact, held some very dark secrets for many decades, and I bet there are more I have not uncovered. Robert has seen it first hand, how the Sinergy has been able to appear in human form, so I'm sure it knows what's on the parchments."

"My mother," said Norma, "would always remind me there are things in this world that are passed down over millennia of time. It's hard to fathom that kind of time span, but if the Sinergy is an ages old force, we must assume it has developed far beyond what we are thinking."

"Wait a minute," said Roxie. "Are we going to assume this evil is centuries old? I don't think I'm ready to go there."

"I don't think we have a choice, Roxie," replied Robert. "Mother Nature isn't always about beauty, it's about survival, about life and death on a daily basis." He stood up from the table and looked out the window. "If there is balance in the world, then we are dealing with the dark side of time that has been here from the beginning."

"*El Diablo*," said Karen.

"No way!" Axel exclaimed.

"Oh, there is certainly a way, Axel, a very real way," answered Norma. "Yin and Yang, positive and negative, whatever Karma you'd like to choose. Our world has known evil since the Garden of Eden. Believe it!"

"Okay, now, I think we are heading into a long discussion without direction," interjected the sheriff. "I understand we all have some deep beliefs that will be challenged, but I would prefer we table those topics for now. Let's break until three o'clock at which time we'll get to the main course, the parchments. Until then, please make time to prepare your thoughts on the situation, and how you would like to be involved. Remember, there's no formal duty to sign up for. You can be as active in this investigation as you like. That means it could be from nothing at all to a life changing passion. It's your choice, and no one will be judged either way."

"I'd like to add something, Sheriff," Robert addressed the group. "Your decision is going to take some gut checking and soul searching, so I don't think you should decide everything today. I can attest it will take over your life if you're not careful, which is okay for me. With all that we've learned in the last couple of weeks, the future of this challenge is a heck of a lot more dangerous than anything I've been through. Make your decision with your head, not your heart."

"My head says yes, but I'm bringing my whole heart into it, too," said Roxie.

"I'm ready now," added Marcus. "I've been waiting for this my whole life."

"Well, I'm not leaving you two on your own. You're stuck with me, too," said Axel.

"So," said Robert, "you didn't hear a word I said about waiting to make your decisions?"

"Oh, we heard you, Robert," answered Marcus. "But we made our minds up last week that we're in this for the long haul. Even after this morning's updates, we're still all in."

"Karen and I decided before we flew out here," said Kevin. "She'll be moving here as soon as she finds a job and sells her home. We're in, all the way!"

"Well, then, that's moved things up on our agenda," said Sheriff Anderson. "Obviously Robert, Norma and I will work on this from Havenswood Valley, and so that leaves Mrs. Hamsteen as our only undecided member to declare. Somehow I have the feeling I know your answer," he smiled.

"Well, every organization needs a headquarters, and I think Hamsteen Manor would be a perfect location. Welcome, Voyageurs!"

The group rose in unison, hands clapping and cheers shouted. They congratulated each other on their pledges to The Voyageurs. They felt the beginnings of a bond that would grow stronger each day, through each experience and challenge. In a meeting filled with dangerous news and belief shaking realizations, The Voyageurs now had confirmed members and a place to call home. It was a very exciting and productive morning.

"Well, Sheriff, this has been a morning we should all be proud of, and I'm looking forward to our afternoon together. Would you mind if we met at two o'clock?" asked Mrs. Hamsteen. "I've made dinner arrangements for us at 6:00 pm and I have the feeling a three o'clock meeting might cut our time too close. We'll be eating at a wonderful restaurant downtown. Katrina and her staff will be preparing for an after dinner get together here, with a little Halloween theme. I've invited some friends and guests to join us, I thought it would be a nice diversion from all the work we've got ahead of us."

"Now, Glen, I know you like to get to the bottom of things when you're on a case," Robert piped in, "but I suggest you follow Eleanor's lead here and take the two o'clock time slot so we'll be sure to get things wrapped up in time for dinner. I know it's a tough call, but I'm sure you can make it."

"What a thoughtful idea, Mrs. Hamsteen," added Karen.

"This is going to be a great night!" said Axel.

Norma was also intrigued. "I think dinner downtown will give us a chance to see more of Prairie Falls!"

"Okay, this is an easy one. Two o'clock it is, and we'll get right to it. Everyone okay with the change?" asked Sheriff Anderson. There was a chorus of yes throughout the room.

"Hate to be a downer here, but before we take our break, I'd like to pose a question for this afternoon's meeting," Marcus said. He was standing next to the fireplace and knelt down to place a couple of logs on the fire, taking care not to disrupt the hot coals already warming the room.

Marcus was taking his time with the fire, so Axel prodded him by asking, "Did you say your question was for this afternoon, or when it was afternoon?"

"Yes," Marcus said, turning his attention back to The Voyageurs. "Sorry about that, lost in the fire for a second."

"Go ahead, Marcus, take your time," said Mrs. Hamsteen.

Marcus took a breath, and then took their breath away. "If the Sinergy had gotten my backpack the other night, where would the parchments be right now?"

"Anderson, here. Oh, hello, Stevens, what can I do for you? Uh, huh, yep. No, I don't think so. Yes, I've got time, go ahead and explain the situation." Sheriff Anderson held the cell phone to his ear and pulled his notepad out to take notes. "Wait a minute, you're telling me the entire road is without power?" He continued to listen, write and ask questions for nearly five minutes. "Yep, I'm sure he did say that. Well, tell the mayor I'll be there in a few hours and we can sort this out. I don't see any reason to go overboard, but I sure as heck don't want anything of importance hidden from the public. I'll give you a call when I'm on my way. And thanks for calling so quickly, Deputy." He put down the phone, looked over his notes and walked directly to Robert's open door.

"Robert, can we talk for a few minutes?" asked the sheriff.

"Sure, Glen, what's going on?"

"Just took a call from Havenswood Valley. Deputy Stevens called about a mess with the power in town. Says Fourth Street lost all power about twenty minutes ago and the power company can't figure out what's causing the problem. Mayor Turner is in a heck of an uproar about it, wants me there as soon as possible."

"Figures. That man is a piece of work. I have no idea how he keeps getting re-elected. Okay, then, Fourth Street is down? Well, that's not good if it means the hospital is using reserve power. I'm not sure how long that will last."

"I am, and it isn't very long," answered the sheriff. "Not to mention the nursing home down the block."

"No idea what caused it, eh?"

"Not a clue yet, Robert, but the power company feels they should be able to isolate it once they get started."

"So why do you look so worried, Glen? What did he say that has gotten you so fired up?"

"Anything that happens, first thing I think about is the Sinergy, are they behind it?" he replied. "Havenswood Valley is known for Brackett's Bluff and the Passage River and I don't want our heritage to be changed by some sinister force that happened to land in our town."

"I would have to agree with you, Glen, but this power outage, there could be dozens of reasons for it."

"You're right, but whatever it is I'm uncomfortable. If the mayor is going to be on the phone every five minutes I need to be in my town doing what I can to help the situation."

"Okay, I'll get my things packed and be ready in five minutes," said Robert.

"No need, I'll be going solo on this trip. I need you here, Robert. In fact everyone needs you here. Once they start looking at the parchments you'll be the one most connected to the area and what's been going on. I've already thought this through so there's no use arguing."

"And what if it is the Sinergy, Glen? You don't think it's going to find you on your drive back, do you?"

"I'll be up there in no time, well before dark. Hopefully back early tomorrow. Sure, I'd like to have someone with me, but it doesn't make sense for anyone to ride along. The group needs to be here going over the parchments. I'll see if Reynolds will want to join us and he can drive back with me tomorrow."

"I don't like this, Glen, it's not safe to go alone." Robert wasn't used to being told what he could or could not do.

"You're right, but who would you choose to go with me? Norma? One of the trio?" Glen suggested. "No, it's better if they stay here. If there is trouble, I'll do whatever I have to and make it safely back to Havenswood Valley. Besides, I'm pretty sure this is going to end up being a problem with our city power system. You know how old some of that stuff is. We should have done the overhaul three years ago when the city had it planned. Probably why the mayor is so hot on this, he knows it was his vote that stopped it from being passed, all because he didn't want the streets being worked on and disrupting his business anniversary celebration."

"Dang straight about that. He's going to be questioned big time! Okay, you get yourself up there ASAP and give me a call once you get into town. Keep your cell phone charged and your

GPS on, just in case." Robert relinquished the fact Sheriff Anderson was going on alone. "I'll keep things on track here and give you any updates once we get started on the parchments. I still don't like this, but there really isn't a better option. Good luck, Glen."

"Thanks, Robert. I'll be on the road in ten minutes. Good luck with the group today. I'll start back as soon as I can tomorrow." Sheriff Anderson grabbed his gear from the room he had stayed in and headed downstairs to give a quick explanation and say goodbye to Mrs. Hamsteen. As he walked out to his truck, he felt uncommonly nervous. He pulled away from the manor knowing deep down that something was not right in Havenswood Valley, and that he may not get back to the group for a few days. It was game on, the battle for the parchments had begun. Whatever secrets they held, he wanted to find out before the Sinergy could cause any real damage.

Robert looked at his watch, almost noon, time to get ready for lunch and the tour. He would let everyone know right away why Sheriff Anderson had left, and how he asked that they continue on with lunch, the tour and then jump right into the parchments. Robert would let them know he would be keeping the sheriff updated on their progress. Sounded simple enough, he just hoped they would all react with the positive spirit that had brought them all together. He was sure they would.

"Axel, surprised to see you here early for lunch," Kevin was kidding, of course. "I figured you would be taking a nap or something."

"Well, you're half right. I did sleep some, and then the sound of lunch being made woke me up," Axel replied. "I started dreaming of hot sandwiches and when I woke up, I could smell whatever it is they're baking in the kitchen."

"Me too," added Roxie. "I didn't sleep, but this place seems to always have something being baked or cooked in the kitchen and I couldn't wait to get down here. Must be the run this morning kicking in for some more calories."

"Hey, where did the sheriff go?" asked Kevin. "I saw him take off about fifteen minutes ago with his gear bag. Will he be here for the tour?"

"What?" asked Norma as she walked into the dining area. "Sheriff Anderson's gone?"

"Are you sure, Kevin?" asked Karen.

"You know me, I don't miss a detail. Had his gear bag, seemed serious and never looked back." Kevin said.

"Dumped us like a bad date," Axel added.

"I'm sure it was some official business, didn't look like he was running away, as you might leave a date, Axel," Kevin joked. "He just looked like he was going somewhere important, fast," said Kevin.

"Well, it is important. Maybe not as important as what we're doing today, but since being sheriff requires 'round the clock service, he was called into action on account of something going on in Havenswood Valley," said Robert. He had joined the group in the dining area and had heard a couple of the comments. He would give a full explanation once everyone was there.

"What happened?" asked Roxie.

"How about if we wait until everyone is here, then I'll explain. It's pretty simple, won't take but a couple of minutes and it's not something we need to be concerned about." Robert replied. "Let's see if we can help with lunch for now."

By noon everyone was seated. Marcus, Axel, Roxie, Kevin, Karen, Norma, Robert and Mrs. Hamsteen. Edgar had also joined the group for lunch.

"I asked Edgar to join us for lunch today," announced Mrs. Hamsteen, "and I've informed him of the situation at hand with the Sinergy. He's been invaluable to us here at the manor, keeping it running and in perfect condition over the years and he would like to help in any way he can."

"Not sure what I can do, exactly," Edgar offered, "but if it needs building or fixing I'm the man for the job. Anything I can do to help out here I'm ready, any time."

"Looks like we've got ourselves an on-site jack of all trades," answered Robert. "As someone that has lived in a place where doing things yourself was vital, I think having Edgar as part of our team is a very good decision."

"I do too," agreed Axel. "I bet I could learn a lot from you, Edgar. Just give me a holler if you need an extra hand."

"I motion that we add Edgar Ellering as a new member!" said Norma.

It was unanimous and as everyone welcomed Edgar, he in turn thanked them for allowing him into their newly formed group. Robert then explained the sheriff's quick departure.

"I'll get right to it, then," Robert stated, with the Minnesotan quirk of an extra 'then' added to a sentence. "Sheriff Anderson received a call from Deputy Stevens at the Havenswood Valley station. Seems that the power to Fourth Street has gone out, with no apparent source of the problem. We've seen power shut offs before, but usually from a storm, or a car accident or a worker cutting through a line somewhere. It's early, but so far there wasn't anything reported that could be connected to the Sinergy. And, Fourth Street has our hospital and a nursing home on its part of the grid." Robert looked around the room and could see some of them begin to put two and two together. "Don't worry, they both have back ups, and the other businesses on Fourth are going to be fine. Some of this is political, the mayor stopped the city from updating the lines a few years ago and now that there's a problem, well, he'll be the one everyone blames for anything that may happen!"

"Does Sheriff Anderson think the Sinergy has anything to do with this?" asked Marcus.

"No, not at this time. As old as our system is, and the fact it should have been replaced three years ago. That tells us it was just a matter of time before it broke down." Robert sounded believable. "Anything is possible, Marcus, but we can't overreact to every event like it's part of the Sinergy."

"I would have to agree with Robert," said Edgar. "We've done a lot of repairs to our city and it would be a miracle if we went even one year without a major problem popping up. Things wear out and just stop working. I'm sure the power company will get everyone back on line soon."

"Let's hope Sheriff Anderson can get everyone calmed down and return to Hamsteen Manor soon," added Kevin.

"Okay, enough said." Robert looked around at the group and thought to himself that maybe the sheriff had made too quick a decision to head back to Havenswood Valley. Still, one had to stay aware in every situation and being ready for action was never a waste of time.

"Well, then, let's grab our box lunches and begin our tour of Hamsteen Manor!" directed Mrs. Hamsteen.

The group headed to the oversized, rustic oak picnic tables on the west side of the home. An extended fall season pallet of beautiful, earth-toned colors splashed from boundary to boundary of Hamsteen Manor. Leaves floating down to the still green grass and rushing edge over edge in any direction the wind cared to blow. Gathered in sections throughout the entire grounds were a variety of fall season bundles; dried corn stalks, mounds of bright orange pumpkins and collections of squash mixed with prairie grasses and flowers. A very traditional autumn feel to the yard, with a few touches of Halloween ghouls and goblins hidden in plain sight.

Mrs. Hamsteen began her tour with some background information of the property. She waited until everyone was seated and had their lunch boxes opened. Eleanor explained how Hamsteen Manor, established in 1893, was as splendid now as it had ever been, thanks to the detailed records kept on the home. She and her husband, Joe, were able to read about construction materials, architectural designs, manufacturers and more. It gave them a great heading to follow in their quest to rebuild the home to it's 1893 standards. Originally constructed during the golden age of the Minnesota lumber industry, it was placed on the Historic Homes of Minnesota list in 1997, and is open a number of days throughout the year for events and gatherings. The entire remodeling and restoration project was planned by Mr. and Mrs. Hamsteen, with the guidance of local architects and historians. The Hamsteens invested their own money, bypassing rebuilding grants they felt could be better used on other, less well funded projects. Their work was a labor of love, times two. First and foremost their main reason was to revive the overall structure, function and appearance of the residence, inside and out. Second, with each improvement and refinement on the home, the relationship between the Hamsteens grew stronger. Their work together brought them great joy and a satisfying sense of accomplishment that they continued to share until Joe Hamsteen's passing.

As the talk ended, everyone had finished most of their lunch. It was now time to leave the tables and walk the rest of the grounds. Mrs. Hamsteen was able to add in bits of historic information to the tour, including dates of what was going on when certain families owned the home, dramatic weather events, holiday programs and even the celebrated and famous guests that had stayed at the residence. Some had come specifically for the experience of the manor. Others had requested a room while in town for a variety of reasons, from political to entertainment to health. The latter being a request for family members to stay while a loved one was receiving care at the renowned Westchester Hospital.

Even in the cool months of fall, the grounds were beautiful. Mature trees edged the property line on the west side, with apple and maple trees mixed throughout the inner section. A brick paver walkway was laid around the entire home, which the guests followed behind Mrs. Hamsteen. From the table area they crossed the crushed limestone driveway, passed through a large flower garden and made their way to a beautiful pond. Next up was a large fire pit, and behind this section was a half acre of space buffering the northern property line. Most first time visitors to the manor drove up to what is actually the back side of the home, mainly because the front entry was on a well-traveled street and the back had plenty of parking and provided a grand entrance to the home. There was a traditional styled, columned portico that covered a full length porch at the drop zone. It was a wonderful way to enter the home. Cars would pull up, guests could unload and not worry about the weather, and the driver then followed the oval shaped driveway around the central courtyard and parked. There was a walkway from the parking area that crossed the courtyard and went past the three layer, eight foot tall water fountain, directly to the front door. It made for a busy stage on an event night at the manor. With an exceptional lighting system throughout the grounds, every walkway, garden, courtyard and of course the manor itself, looked magical. Visitors felt they were in a very special place.

The east side of the manor held a large, four stall parking garage. From tools to toys, a workshop, shower and bathroom, this garage was a homeowner's dream come true. Above the garage, and well insulated from the sounds, sights and smells below, was a set of guest rooms. With an exterior side access exit at the end of the hallway, and an inner walkway to the main building, the guest quarters were a favorite area of the home for travelers to stay, and were usually sold out during holiday vacation times. These upper rooms were spacious and offered a nice glimpse of Prairie Falls. Connected to the main house via a middle section of the residence that was added in 1922, it turned the stand alone garage into a part of the manor and at times whole families stayed in this upper level portion of the home.

The southeast side was little more than a few trees, some prairie grasses, a garden shed and greenhouse. Both were smaller than expected for a property of this size, but large enough to accommodate a sufficient assortment of gardening tools, supplies and tables for flats of flowers and vegetables that could be watered throughout the growing season.

From a birds-eye view the manor was an insulated island, edged by trees, and well trimmed hedgerows, a grass buffer and more trees, and flower gardens. Over the years the manor had seen parties, gatherings, weddings and wakes. It had a solid history, but it also held secrets that had been covered up, literally, for years. Once the outside tour was over, Mrs. Hamsteen led the group through the interior quarters of the home; upstairs, main floor and the foundation level. The guests had seen most of the home, but she made sure everyone walked the entire house with her. This was part tour, part defensive education, in case anyone needed to get somewhere within the home quickly, or out of the home in an emergency.

"Now that we have seen the grounds and the inside tour has been conducted," Mrs. Hamsteen said, "I'd like to take a short break. It's nearly two o'clock, and that would be our time to begin working on the parchments. As you saw in the basement, there is a large safe in there, however this is not the safe with the parchments. Now, I'd like to ask that each of you keep what I am about to tell you very confidential. It's nothing personal, but it does impact the house, our guests and possibly the future of our group. Can I get your agreement on this next point?"

Each member gave a verbal yes to Eleanor, feeling Mrs. Hamsteen would never ask for more than someone would agree to.

"Well, then, I'll get right to it. When my husband Joe and I were remodeling this home, we unexpectedly discovered a secret door in the basement that led to a hallway and four rooms."

"Wow, that is so cool! Any treasures?" exclaimed Axel.

"Were there any papers or photos?" asked Karen.

"Good questions, both of them, and I'm sure you will have more. Let's take a short break, and then we'll head to the secret door and to the safe area where the parchments are stored. I spoke with the sheriff and we decided the best place to read the parchments will be in one of the secret rooms." Mrs. Hamsteen added, "They're secure and insulated from the rest of the house, and we will be well protected from any unwanted visitors."

"Just say the word, I'm ready!" said Kevin.

"As long as we are not trapped. I can get claustrophobic." posed Roxie.

"Well, there is only one way out," replied Mrs. Hamsteen. "So I guess we'll have to keep an eye on you. Marcus, can you manage that?" Mrs. Hamsteen smiled at him. "Really, though, nothing to be afraid of as the secret rooms are the safest place in the home. Okay, let's all meet back here in fifteen minutes, agreed?"

Everyone agreed, and in an instant Mrs. Hamsteen was off, leaving the group excited, yet somewhat apprehensive about the secret rooms.

"Eleanor is pretty sharp, Marcus. Make sure you don't let her down watching over Roxie," Karen said.

"Roxie knows I'm here for her, Karen. I think Mrs. Hamsteen might be seeing more to the situation than there is." He looked at Roxie, who returned his glance with a questioning look as if to ask for more of an explanation. "At least at the moment," and he smiled knowingly at Roxie.

"Okay, I just wanted to make sure," replied Karen.

"And what am I?" asked Axel. "Chopped liver? Oh, snap, back to being the third wheel. No worries, you two are my favorites and I wouldn't have it any other way."

"Seems everyone has our life planned out for us, Marcus," Roxie said. "So, Kevin, Mr. Speed Dater, when's our wedding?"

"At the rate you two are going, how about in five years?" Kevin answered.

His answer gave everyone a chance to laugh and relax before Mrs. Hamsteen returned. As the others left to freshen up, only Marcus and Robert remained.

"I wonder why Eleanor or the sheriff didn't mention the rooms earlier?" asked Marcus.

"I don't think the sheriff knew until this morning," replied Robert. "He was under the impression the safe holding the parchments was in the basement. He told me very briefly when he was leaving this morning that the parchments were in a secret room Mrs. Hamsteen had just told him about, and that they had agreed to let everyone know during the tour."

"What about our vow to keep all information out in the open?" asked Marcus.

"I thought about that too. Eleanor is opening up and I'm going to give her some slack on this one," said Robert. "Besides, I believe that we're supposed to let the sheriff know first, which she did, and then he has our approval to make decisions. If we aren't clear on that, we should discuss it when he returns."

"You're right, Robert, that was how we framed it up this morning," Marcus continued. "Wow, was it just this morning? Still, I do think we should make sure we're all on the same page, because I'd like to know what's going on, when it's going on."

"Fair enough, but there will never be enough time to get every bit of information out to everyone as things are happening." Robert looked at Marcus with the classic fatherly concern. "I appreciate your need to know, Marcus, I'm right there with you. But, we did agree to have Glen be our leader, and you will come to realize he's a great manager of situations. He's had some tough decisions to make in his career, and he's gotten better at it than nearly anyone before him as sheriff of Havenswood Valley. Your confidence in him will grow quickly, I can assure you of that. Fact is, I see a lot of the same qualities in you, Marcus. You're about the same age as Glen was when I first met him and I think you've got what it takes to become a great leader, too. It's part of why he's let you and your friends into this investigation so quickly."

"Thanks, Robert. I just hope we can hold up our end of the challenge." Said Marcus.

"You already have, Marcus, you just don't realize it."

CHAPTER 27

"Ah, everyone is here and ready to start, I see." Eleanor Hamsteen walked gracefully into the main foyer of her home, glad to see the group was ready to proceed. "Sorry to have rushed off so quickly. Truth be told I noticed one of our communication lights was suddenly glowing orange and I had to see what was needed in the kitchen. Nothing too drastic, it seems we need a plumber is all, and I think Katrina may have overreacted!"

"Communication lights?" asked Kevin.

"Yes, during one of our remodeling phases we added a system that allows a visual alert to be issued without bothering our guests, as you just experienced. It's subtle but works exceedingly well for our staff." Mrs. Hamsteen continued, "I'll have Edgar present the color codes tomorrow, along with our alarm system and any other programs he feels you may need to operate."

"Can we include a driving lesson for the Studebaker in the garage?" asked Axel.

"Hmmm, I think you'll need to discuss that personally with Edgar," replied Mrs. Hamsteen. "He's had that car for many years and drives it only on special occasions."

"Before you ask, Axel," interjected Roxie, "the answer is no!"

"Aw, c'mon, Roxie, you've seen how I drive!"

"I rest my case!" she laughed.

"Shall we, then?" asked Mrs. Hamsteen.

She led them down to the foundation level of the manor and into the basement they had seen during the tour. It was a well-appointed portion of the house, and although it was not a full underlayment of the ground floor, it was a large room none-theless. The small basement windows prevented natural light from completely filling the entire room, however during the remodeling phase there was plenty of lighting installed that could bring the room to life at the touch of a few switches.

The stairs emptied out in the middle of the room, at the far end, away from the main attraction. Once the bottom of the scalloped staircase was cleared, each visitor could be seen by those that were already in the room. Eleanor and Joe figured it was most likely a defensive design from the days of prohibition. Rounding the stairs you entered another era, updated 1920's turned 1960's. You'd expect the Rat Pack to be hanging out at the bar, which had been perfectly restored. The cherry wood was aged as fine as the wine in the custom lattice cabinet. Its rich patina gave the room an air of refinement without feeling pretentious. Leather couches, a few high backed chairs and a matching collection of very comfortable bar chairs, perfect for long stints at the bar rail, provided each guest a variety of choices for seating.

Decorating the basement walls and bar area were historic photographs of the Hamsteen Manor, guests of the home and local events with the very same people involved. It seems that those living at the manor were always active around the town of Prairie Falls, and anything that happened outside the city limits was someone else's concern. Once seated at the bar, however, it was all modern times. Appliances, electronics, food and beverage makers, glassware, gadgets and games, all in perfect working order. One was not left wanting for anything in the basement, it was a place for serious fun!

Mrs. Hamsteen asked the guests to wait on the stairs before they were fully into the basement. She stopped at the bottom, turned, and put up her hand. "If you wouldn't mind holding for just one minute, I'll be just a moment."

Within seconds, a hissing sound could be heard from the other side of the room, causing most in the group to jump as if startled by a snake!

"Thank you for waiting," Eleanor said as she came back into view. "And now I'd like to request your presence in the basement, please watch your step!" said Mrs. Hamsteen. "Oh, Edgar, you made it!" Edgar was at the back of the group as they came down the stairs and into the room.

"Just in the nick of time! Didn't want to miss the first trip for this group!" he said. Edgar and Eleanor had spoken privately about his part in The Voyageurs. While at first he was hesitant about the need for him to be involved, the more they discussed what was taking place, the more apparent it became that he would be crucial to The Voyageurs becoming connected with Hamsteen Manor. No one knew the manor like Edgar, and in a tense or emergency situation it would be Edgar at the top of the list for help.

The Voyageurs poured down the stairs and into the manor's most infamous room, wanting to know what had caused the sound they had all heard. As they walked around the stairs and into the main area, their eyes widened and their hearts almost stopped.

"The secret rooms!" said Norma.

"I can't believe it," added Kevin. "This is so like a movie."

"Dang," said Axel, "I've always dreamed about stuff like this, but I never thought I'd really be in a room like this."

"Yeah, and you never thought the boogie man was real, either," replied Marcus.

"Oh I thought he was real, alright. I just never thought I'd see him," said Axel.

"How did you find the key to opening up the wall, Mrs. Hamsteen? It's incredible!" asked Roxie.

"Like many discoveries, it was really an accident," she answered. "Joe and I were down here on our own, as usual, and we were cleaning the bar area for about the third day in a row. He noticed a loose piece of the decorative base trim woodwork and decided to pull the baseboard up in hopes of repairing it to its original condition. As Joe pulled on it we both heard a soft click, as if something had moved into place behind the wainscoting on the wall. We took turns maneuvering it around, handling it as if we were trying to open a safe by touch rather than a numbered sequence."

"We were sure it was a way to open a small part of the wooden bar, maybe a place to hide money, drugs or jewelry," Mrs. Hamsteen continued.

"Or guns!" added Axel.

"Or bodies!" said Kevin, sarcastically.

"Thankfully it was neither. We kept working on it for the next two weeks."

"Two weeks!" interrupted Axel.

"Geez, Axel, how about some more caffeine?" asked Karen.

"Oh, that's fine, Karen," said Mrs. Hamsteen. "I know Axel's wound up, but so were we. Hardly any sleep those two weeks and we wouldn't let any of the contractors, architects or carpenters down here."

"Didn't they get suspicious?" asked Norma.

"Yes, at first they did!" Mrs. Hamsteen laughed. "They didn't think we were up to the task, and both Joe and I felt we may have gotten in deeper than we should have. Bit off more than we could chew, so to speak. We finally convinced them we wanted to do this area on our own, especially since there really wasn't any construction - more of just cleaning up and making small repairs. Of all the rooms, this one was in the best shape."

"So, two weeks and then it just happened?" asked Marcus.

"Yes, and by accident. Joe had figured out two moves of the wooden parts. He had left them up and when we returned from lunch that day he backed into one of the ends."

"Ouch!" said Roxie.

"Hurt him like the dickens, but it was worth it," said Mrs. Hamsteen. "It seems as if the one piece he bumped was stuck and the force of his leg pushed it more than he was willing to do by hand for fear of snapping it off. It was then we first heard the whoosh of the air exchange and the doorway opened. It was magical."

"Wow, that must have been awesome!" Axel said.

"At the moment of the first opening, there was a rather foul stench that filled the room. It was somewhat scary taking the first steps into the five rooms. We were surprised to find each room completely clean. No treasures, no trash. Clear and swept as if they were ready for a military inspection."

"Bummer!" Kevin said.

"Yes, it was pretty disappointing, really. Although we figured there would only be a small hidden cabinet connected to the loose piece of wood, once the doorway opened our hopes ran high. For what, we didn't know, but not finding anything seemed to make it even more of a mystery. Then we decided we should do something in each room and make it our own personal safe house. Fortunately for us there was already plumbing in for a sink and toilet as well as electrical wiring and some ventilation. We realized they needed repair and since neither Joe nor I could do the work we contacted the one person we felt comfortable enough to allow in. One of my uncles was the main contractor for the rest of the remodeling and he was as trustful as he was capable. He did the work on the secret side of the door and then tied it all into the main basement improvements. Just as a precaution, he also made sure the foundation of the house that covers the secret basement still looks like it has nothing under it at all. Whoever added the secret rooms did a nice job initially to cover it up, but Uncle Jordan updated it just the same. Come, into the hallway and I'll show you the rooms."

The hallway was fairly wide, well lit with a smooth cement floor, tan colored stucco walls, and doorways to five rooms. Two on the left, one on the right and two at the end of the hallway. The knotty pine doors looked almost new, and the six panel design gave the hallway a feel right out of the 1950's. As they passed the first door on the left Mrs. Hamsteen reached the doorknob and pushed it open. "A very compact bathroom. The plumbing backs up to the bar on the other side of the wall, so we have hot and cold water as well. Just enough to stay clean and healthy." She pulled the door to close it and took a few steps further into the hallway. On the right was a set of double doors. "This is the largest room, so we made it comfortable for spending the most time in. Three sets of bunk beds and two fold down couches make room for ten. The books and magazines were all hand picked by Joe and I, now that was a fun time!" Eleanor laughed gently as she recalled the memory of her and Joe working on the room. "There are some folding tables along the wall we can use for the parchments," she added, then turned around and took just one step across the hallway to the other side.

"This room on the left is our connection with the outside world." Eleanor opened the single passage door and walked in. "It's a good sized room and we stuffed it with a fantastic collection of computers, cameras, and all the extras. The computer is tied into our main system upstairs, so we can see everything our security cameras see. On occasion I've come down here to do some research. It's lonely but very quiet compared to a house full of guests. And there's plenty of room for books, papers and storing research."

"Wow," Kevin exclaimed, "Mrs. Hamsteen, this is one fantastic set up."

"Why thank you, Kevin. It's a real passion of mine to have everything I need close by when I work. Nothing more frustrating than having to go upstairs to look for information or print out a document when I have the world at my fingertips down here."

"When did you add in all the furnishings?" asked Karen.

"Even though there isn't too much down here, we did have to wait a while, and even then it was tricky. We just made sure when we purchased the larger items we did it ourselves, or had Uncle Jordan help out," answered Eleanor. "Along the way, and more so once Joe passed, I have let others in on the secret room. You know, it's more fun when you can share something like this with close friends, and now that you all know, well, I've more than doubled the number of people that know about it now!"

"Thanks for your trust, Eleanor," said Robert. "It means a lot to us. We know you could just as easily have met with us anywhere in your home."

"Yeah, this is so cool it makes me want to give up my day job and work on this full time!" added Axel.

"Well, maybe we can discuss that once we read the parchments, Axel." Mrs. Hamsteen gave him a look that showed she had ideas of her own for the future of this group, and the resources to make it happen. "For now, as you can see, the rooms are set up with the basics for people to be able to spend a few weeks down here. Which leads us to the fourth room. Well, it's more storage than a room."

Eleanor opened the last door on the right and stepped into a walk-in pantry. "As you can see from the doorway, this is where we put a variety of foods, fluids and whatever else we think we would need for a stay, survivor-wise. It was tough to figure out what to put in here since we don't plan on having to stay long, and we didn't want things to spoil. There is still plenty of room to add food and supplies if we think we'll be using the basement on a regular basis."

"I could definitely live down here!" said Axel.

"This is nicer than your apartment, Axel. It would be a real upgrade," replied Marcus.

"That is definitely true," said Axel. "I could turn my music up a lot louder at night and not have to worry about neighbors complaining!"

"I bet your screeching guitar would be something Mrs. Hamsteen would hear all the way upstairs," Roxie said. "That sound you create would probably shake the walls loose down here."

"Hmmm," Mrs. Hamsteen said, "I might need to reconsider my plans for you, Axel. Your friends have just provided some insight into what life with Axel in the house might be like," she laughed. "Not to worry, I'm sure your music has its moments."

"Yes, it does, Mrs. Hamsteen," replied Marcus, "right when he unplugs the amplifier!" The group had a good laugh, but truth be told Axel really was a talented musician.

"One day I'll bring my guitar in for a short concert for you, Mrs. Hamsteen," Axel countered. "You can be the judge of my talent. I'm sure you'll be much kinder than my close friends here." He smiled at the good-natured ribbing.

"I'm looking forward to it already, Axel. Now, for the last room on the left." Mrs. Hamsteen turned and took a short step across the hallway and opened the fifth door. "In here we have non-food supplies, some tools, a few things like batteries and flashlights, that sort of thing." She looked into the far corner of the angled room, "And in this corner we have two file cabinets and a fire-proof safe. Not too many files stored, nor too many items in the safe. In fact, right now we just have a few old things sitting in here, waiting to be opened." She smiled at the group, opened the safe and there were the parchment tubes. "We don't usually set the combination to the safe, not too many visitors down here on their own. Marcus, would you care to bring these into the large room?" Eleanor asked.

"Of course!" he replied. As the group made their way to the room, Marcus grabbed two of the tubes and handed them to Axel, then took the last two himself. By the time they walked into the large room, the four tables were set up and made ready to view the parchments.

"I can't believe it's really happening," said Roxie. "Weren't we just at the cabin?"

"And didn't we all just meet each other a few days ago?" asked Norma. "I haven't been this excited since my mother and I helped find the Robinson child in the state park."

The mood had turned from wonderment to nervous energy in a matter of moments. Each member of The Voyageurs was moving into high mental gear for the unveiling of the parchments, they wanted to be in top form and contribute in any way they could.

Suddenly, Edgar was yelling, "Red, Eleanor, it's just turned to red!" Edgar was looking down the hallway. "I'll be right back, don't anyone move!" He bolted down the hallway, through the still open secret door and was nearly up the stairs when Mrs. Hamsteen spoke.

"It's the light system I told you about earlier. Edgar will report back to us as soon as he finds out what has happened. Marcus, follow me, quickly now," directed Mrs. Hamsteen as she walked briskly down the hallway to the secret door.

"What's going on, Eleanor?" Marcus asked.

"Marcus, right here, and I mean exactly right here and here only. This is the one way to shut this secret door from the inside without locking yourself in for good." She looked directly at him, staring into his eyes with confidence that he would understand everything she was about to show him. She went through the process of shifting pieces and pushing back the door to its closed position, hearing the click that ensured it was completely locked. "Now this part is the most important. There are two metal bars on the back side of the doors. Twist them like so, and now you've got a double reinforced wall of wood and steel that will take an army to bring down. If they get through, odds are you've done something bad enough to deserve what ever it is they bring."

"Oh yeah, this I can do." Marcus was in full-blown alert mode and totally in tune with the call of duty as directed by Mrs. Hamsteen. "How will we know when the coast is clear?"

"Great question, Marcus. There are always the security cameras, but if the electricity and back up power are out, we have another way to check. Took us a while to find this, but there is a viewer through the door. Lift here, and then the mirror and glass pieces in the door will provide a full view into the room. It's all built into the trim so no one will ever notice when you are looking. Believe me, we've tried to see and have yet to detect anyone looking through."

"Seems like they thought of everything when they put this together. Anything else?" asked Marcus.

"Yes. You're sworn to secrecy on how all this works, but if you need help you can show the process to whoever is helping you. Just remember to trust your instincts."

"Thanks, Mrs. Hamsteen," Marcus said. "I appreciate your faith in me."

"Okay, I'll take a look and see if Edgar is back yet. Please let the others know we are secure," she said.

Marcus went back to the room and had just let everyone know they were still waiting for Edgar when Eleanor called him to come back.

"Marcus, I want you to open this up, please. I'd like to see how you do."

"No problem. First, I need to make sure it's Edgar on the other side. No use opening up for the wrong person, right?" asked Marcus.

"You get an A plus, Marcus." Mrs. Hamsteen smiled, knowing she had made a good choice in choosing to help Marcus and his friends. "Yes, make sure it's the right person and then go ahead and open up." Once open, Edgar burst though the doorway with a look of grave concern on his face.

"Sheriff Anderson," Edgar exclaimed, "he's in the hospital!"

CHAPTER
28

"Eleanor, if you would please gather everyone in the front room," said Robert, "I'll pass along the information Deputy Stevens and the mayor gave me over the phone." Robert had spent the last fifteen minutes on the phone with Havenswood Valley Mayor Evan Turner and Deputy Sheriff Stevens, talking about Sheriff Anderson and the reason he was in the hospital.

"Of course," she replied, "it will only take a minute and we'll be ready."

"I'll go check on Kevin," Edgar said to Eleanor, "he's the only one not here. I'll be right back."

"Thank you, Edgar," Eleanor replied. Mrs. Hamsteen was correct in her time estimate to Robert, as Edgar was able to retrieve Kevin quickly. Now everyone was present and ready for Robert to explain the sheriff's situation. Robert was the person Deputy Stevens had asked for, and once he rushed upstairs from the basement to get to the phone, Mrs. Hamsteen felt it best that everyone in the basement should make their way back up to the main level of Hamsteen Manor.

"I am so ready to see the parchments," announced Marcus. "I can barely concentrate on anything else, and now the sheriff is in trouble. If the Sinergy is involved we are in for a long battle."

"I hope Robert got all the details," Norma said. "My senses are very active and it gives me the feeling the Sinergy is going to try and shake us down again."

"We need to know why the Sinergy wants those parchments, and soon," Roxie said.

"Don't we already know they want them?" asked Karen.

"We know they want them, but why? What makes them so important?" Roxie looked at Kevin and continued, "Kevin, we know you want to marry Karen, but we don't know every single reason why. Sure, there are the obvious ones; that you two are soul mates and want to be together and explore the world, build a home, maybe start a family. But there are so many more reasons why two people get married, and only those two individuals understand them all completely. With the Sinergy, we don't even know the basics as to why they want the parchments. Even after we look at the parchments, we may still be at a loss."

"You're right, Roxie. We're miles away from having a clue as to what is going on, and until we read the parchments we can only guess at why the Sinergy is so cranked up about taking possession of them," answered Marcus.

"What did I miss?" asked Kevin as he walked back into the room with Edgar.

"It's all over. The sheriff is dead," announced Axel to Kevin.

"Holy crap, are you serious?" Kevin asked with a look mixed with fright and disbelief.

"Axel!" interjected Norma, "Don't you dare say such a thing! The sheriff is fine, I'm sure, Kevin. Robert is coming in to let us know what he heard from the mayor and deputy." Norma looked back at Axel with a glare that would melt the North Pole.

"Sorry, just wanted to freak Kevin out," Axel said with an undertone of regret.

"Well, it worked," replied Kevin, "scared the heck out of me!"

"What's next, Axel, are you going to tell us one of the guests fell off the roof and broke their neck?" asked Roxie.

"Sorry. Really sorry guys, that was over the top." Axel was truly sincere about his verbal gaff. "It came out before I could think. I'll work on filtering my jokes."

Norma was steamed. "How about using your brain first and your mouth second."

"Axel has a way of making comments that can sound abrasive at first, but he's never intending to offend anyone." Marcus wanted to cool the tone down with Norma, "We're all on edge so let's take a second and relax some. Robert will fill us in and then we can decide what our next steps are going to be. It's important we keep focused and not let our emotions pull us off our plan."

"You're right, Marcus." It was Robert. He could feel the tension in the room between Axel and Norma. "We do need to stay focused. Norma, I know you're close to Glen but Axel deals with stress by keeping things light, and we're going to need that to keep us all feeling relaxed. Axel, I did hear your remark to

Kevin, and I'm sure his reaction might have looked like a cartoon, jaw-dropping moment, but now you've found another line that can't be crossed." Robert looked around the room at the others. "Okay, enough said about all that, let's move on to the sheriff."

"Understood, Robert," replied Axel. "Sorry, Norma, I didn't mean to upset you."

"And I'm sorry for my quick temper. Thank you," replied Norma. "I'm feeling overwhelmed and that caught me off guard. No hard feelings, Axel."

"All right, then, here we go," started Robert. "We all knew there was a chance Sheriff Anderson would run into trouble on his way back to Havenswood Valley, but it was a risk he was willing to take. Let's start with the good news first. Sheriff Anderson is alert, nothing broken and appears to have all his wit and wisdom in working order."

"Thank God," sighed Norma. Everyone felt relief at Robert's initial bit of good news.

"Deputy Stevens assured me Glen's ready for release, but the doctors want him to stay until tomorrow morning, just to be on the safe side. Seems his truck somehow blew two tires and sent him off the road and into the trees. Truck is pretty trashed, but as I said, Glen seems to be a-ok."

"Isn't Sheriff Anderson a pretty good driver, Robert?" asked Marcus.

"Glen is one of the best drivers I know and that's part of the reason I was on the phone so long with Deputy Stevens and the mayor. I've seen Glen perform some outlandish maneuvers so I tried to ask questions without tipping my hand I was searching for clues about the Sinergy. As far as the reason Glen was on his way back to Havenswood Valley, the energy company says it was a hard-to-find transformer gone bad. The mayor is back in the hot seat again about not repairing that area three years ago, but power to the customers is almost fully restored."

"Still seems weird it happened, like it was almost a lure to get the sheriff back to Havenswood Valley," suggested Roxie.

"I agree, and I bet we find out from the sheriff it wasn't just the blown tires that made him crash," added Axel. "If he's that good a driver it would take a lot more to make him leave the road and end up in the trees."

"Who found him?" asked Karen.

"He radioed for help as soon as he crashed," answered Robert. "Glen was only fifteen miles from town when it happened. Lucky for him there was a squad car only five minutes away and an ambulance trailing right behind. We'll get the details from Glen, but Deputy Stevens told me the first responders said he was standing next to his truck with his shotgun at the ready. They told the deputy that Sheriff Anderson looked like he was expecting trouble."

"If they only knew!" said Mrs. Hamsteen. "I'd say there's no doubt Sheriff Anderson had more than tire trouble on his trip! Robert, I know you're already thinking this, but as soon as you can get a private conversation with Glen it would be very helpful to understand exactly what transpired."

"Of course, Eleanor," Robert answered, "I'll try later and see when I can get a direct line to Glen. In the meantime it's up to us to move forward and be aware of any signs the Sinergy may be near." Robert continued, "So, there really isn't any bad news about Glen, other than he will be delayed getting back here. He's going to bring Deputy Stevens and Wildlife Biologist Steve Reynolds. He's with the Department of Natural Resources, something that was planned before the three of us came down on Friday. We'd like to get both of them down here ASAP and up to speed on what we know so far for two reasons; first, Sheriff Anderson will need someone he can trust in the department and second, not only is Reynolds a good fit for us, he's been begging to get more involved since we called him out to the cabin."

"More recruits, I love it," replied Karen.

"I'm glad they're coming, too," said Marcus, "but from here on out let's make sure we get group approval for any new members of The Voyageurs."

"One hundred percent with you, Marcus," said Robert. "Like I said, these two were planned before we officially put our group together, but if anyone wants to suggest otherwise, let's talk about it right now."

"As a newcomer," it was Edgar speaking to the group, "I would say it sounds very logical to have the two join in. They both have special skills that would serve the group well, and, of course, they come highly recommended from the sheriff. Plus, we know there is strength in numbers. I'll just have to make sure the water heaters are set for more guests!"

Everyone agreed with Edgar, bringing two key members into The Voyageurs was a smart move forward. Eleanor added their names and basic personal information to the ledger she was keeping for The Voyageurs. She would complete their profile once they arrived.

Robert gave one more directive to the group, "Any more questions?" Not wanting to delay their mission, no one said a word. "Okay! Let's try it again and head downstairs to pull out those darn parchments!"

Eleanor Hamsteen had entombed the parchments in the one place she could trust such valuable and sought-after relics; the secret rooms in the basement. Although everyone had been told the parchments were stored safely away after the attack, they now understood why Eleanor was so calm when asked about them over the past couple of days. Not only were the parchments protected, but whatever vibrations or Sinergy attractant resonated from the documents was somehow tempered by being secured so deep within the earthen walled basement of Hamsteen Manor.

Prior to the sheriff's departure for Havenswood Valley, Eleanor had discreetly made efforts to clear her home of extended guests for the next month. Only a few visitors had been staying recently at the manor and most had left after the attack. Mr. Pearson, a local writer who loved to spend time at the manor, was the last to leave. Hoping he would be able to return soon, Stanley Pearson was happy to oblige Mrs. Hamsteen's request and left before the group had their first tour of the basement. No one had noticed the manor was empty of guests until Karen suddenly realized she hadn't seen anyone all day.

Just after Robert had gone over the update regarding Sheriff Anderson, Karen asked Mrs. Hamsteen a question. "Eleanor, why is it so quiet here today? Where are all the guests?"

"I thought it would be best if we had the manor to ourselves for a while. You may not have noticed before today, but most of them left late in the morning the day after the attack. Only Mr. Pearson remained and he had no problem with leaving," answered Eleanor. "With things getting more serious I knew we needed our privacy, and I certainly didn't need any guests getting in the way, or worse, getting hurt."

Nobody wanted to talk about the possibility of death, but it weighed heavily on their minds after the sheriff's crash and internment at the hospital.

"Well, then, let's just make sure everyone has each others back at all times," said Robert. "We know this won't be an easy road, and at times it will be downright dangerous, but we agreed to go all in." Robert looked around the room. "Now would be a good time to double-check your commitment to The Voyageurs, before we head downstairs to the basement. Anyone want out?"

There were no takers to the offer, but there was a knock at the door that startled most everyone gathered in the front room. Katrina came from the kitchen to answer the door but was stopped by Marcus.

"Hold on, Katrina, I'll get the door for you," Marcus said. "For some reason I have the feeling this isn't someone we've been expecting. Kevin, will you join me?"

"Right with you, Marcus." The two of them went to the door, looked through the narrow, etched windows on either side of the door and gave each other the thumbs up sign to open the door.

"It's one of your guests, Eleanor," announced Marcus.

Stanley Pearson stepped into the foyer and was taken aback by the greeting he was receiving. "Oh, excuse me, Mrs. Hamsteen, very sorry to interrupt you all." Stanley had no idea what was going on, but he felt the pressure of everyone's eyes upon him. "In my rush to leave I left behind a few research books. Would you mind if I went up to my room and retrieved them?"

"Everyone, this is Stanley Pearson, a wonderful writer and a regular guest of ours here at Hamsteen Manor. He's written half a dozen books of history based fiction and they are selling very well," said Eleanor. "We are always glad to have Stanley here, and we can usually coerce him to share some of his latest work."

"Exciting," said Roxie. "What are you writing now, Mr. Pearson?"

"Currently, and again, sorry to interrupt your meeting, but right now I'm working on a project that has more to do with my doctorate studies at the university. As you can tell, I'm a late bloomer as a student, and I'm foregoing fiction for a while."

Axel asked the question that was hanging in the air, "And that project would be?"

"Right, obvious question, thank you for the cue. Well, my Masters is in European Society during the Dark Ages, and my doctorate thesis explores the link between religion and the printing press." There were some blank stares among the group as they were trying to process Stanley's information. "Yes, I know, it's odd sounding to most everyone, but actually very interesting once you dive in. I learned so much about how religious cultures broadcast their views and how populations and countries dealt with the proliferation of the printed word. I'm not only educated on the religions, but also on things that began as lore and were passed along through the centuries. Pretty amazing when you begin to put timelines together and, oh, listen to me go on and on! Eleanor, I'll just be a minute to collect my books, do you mind?"

"Of course not, Stanley, take your time," she replied. As Stanley began to make his way upstairs Eleanor turned to the group. "Robert?"

"Eleanor?"

"Is anyone thinking what I'm thinking?" Norma queried.

"How weird is this?" asked Kevin.

"I don't think it's weird at all," said Roxie. "Think of how things have been happening to us and for us. This is just one of the good things."

"Huh?" asked Axel.

"I'm in," said Marcus. "Let's see how crazy he thinks we are."

"Does he know anything, Eleanor?" asked Robert.

"Some. He and I talked after the attack and now that I understand what he's working on his inquiries make more sense." Eleanor continued, "He asked some very penetrating questions, like he already knew what was going on. I think he could be a valuable asset."

The light bulb finally went on for Axel, "Oh, I get it, we want Stanley to join our group! Cool!"

"That's okay, Axel," added Karen. "Things turn on a dime around here and I was standing at the last corner with you on this one." She smiled at Axel, "If Stanley wants in, I think he could really help us with the parchments. I would agree with asking him to join us."

"All right, then. Let's discuss this with Stanley when he comes down," said Robert.

"Discuss what?" asked Stanley.

"Back already?" answered Eleanor. "We were just discussing your expertise in the Dark Ages and religion and how it might fit into the project we are working on. You know, the one we talked about after the incident here the other night."

"Yes, the attack. You gave me the feeling that it was a taboo subject," Stanley replied.

"Oh, it's taboo alright," said Axel. "And voodoo and a little doo doo, too!"

"I see," said Stanley. "Everything that goes bump in the night, eh?"

"Stanley," Robert said with a great deal of conviction, "we're deadly serious here, and I do mean deadly. There is a set of possible clues to something that has been going on for many decades, and now it's go time. From what you've said about your background, you just might be able to help us understand the information we have recently discovered, making it much easier to decipher." Robert took a breath, looked Stanley straight in the eyes and said, "Stanley, listen to me. We've had some deaths related to this information, and, as you saw, some very close calls. Sheriff Anderson is in the hospital right now due to what we feel is the enemy, not a random auto accident. I don't know what your situation is, if you're married, got a family or whatever, but before you answer our request you need to realize that at any time there could be another attack, another death. They've already come after me and Kevin. Next time it could be you. Any place, any time." Robert stepped back and relaxed his demeanor. "Okay, Stanley, talk to us."

Stanley looked about the room and asked, "You're all in this, together?"

"One hundred percent," answered Marcus.

"And this enemy you're fighting, how would you describe it?" Stanley asked.

"My mother would say it was the dark force of evil," said Norma. "Something you feel right through to your soul. Nothing of our world, nothing we can truly understand."

"It's merciless," added Kevin. "First, it will rob you of your thoughts. Then it will try and rob you of your life."

"Stanley, this evil took the life of my young son and left me without purpose for years. Finally I was able to muster the strength and courage to start fighting back, thanks to Sheriff

Anderson." Robert took in the strength of the group as he said, "Now we have a team working together and I know we're going to make a difference. I know we're going to discover what in the world has been going on for the last hundred plus years around here. If you want in on this, now may be the only time we'll ask."

"It's a lot to consider. Other than Eleanor, I really don't know any of you. And this entity you're fighting, well, it certainly took the guests here at the manor by surprise. However," Stanley paused, "while researching in Europe for some of my books I did more than just visit libraries and museums. Part of my time was spent investigating and digging for information behind the scenes, in locations most citizens would never travel to. You're right. I would likely be able to help your team, and enjoy it, too!"

"That sounds pretty close to a yes to me," cheered Karen.

"But, before I commit myself as a member," Stanley started.

"Dang!" interrupted Axel. "I knew there would be a catch."

"No catch, it's just that I'd like to get to know you better, work with you on this project for a few days and see if we are a good fit for each other. It would give you a chance to see if you still want me involved." Stanley finished his comments by adding, "I would be honored to join your ranks and since I am a widower with no pressing matters, especially book or family wise, now is as good a day as any to begin."

"Excellent, Stanley," said Eleanor. "We know our invitation is on very short notice but we've had to get used to things happening rather quickly. Fate has reared its ugly head at us more than once already, and it's nice to have some positivity come our way now and again."

"Anyone else have a question for Stanley before we make this official?" asked Robert.

"Just one," replied Norma. "Stanley, in regards to your research so far, has it had an impact on your personal religious views?"

"I was raised Catholic and spent many hours at mass while I was growing up," he answered. "However I must admit I may have said more prayers during my research time in Europe than I did all those mornings in the pew, combined! I'm still Catholic and after everything I went through abroad I feel even stronger in my convictions that there must be a wise and generous supreme being that not only created the universe but also oversees it. I firmly believe there is good and there is evil in the world, so unfortunately when I say I believe in a supreme being, I will also have to admit I believe there is a very powerful counterpart." Stanley added, "Far from me to hypothesize about something I've just learned, but the force you are fighting, yes, whatever it was that came crashing into Hamsteen Manor the other evening, it's much stronger and more dangerous than anything I came in contact with in Europe. I'm hoping you are all confident in your own personal relationship with God, whichever one you believe in, because I can attest from personal experience you are definitely going to need Him on your side."

"Do you ever wonder if you might have been overreacting to your encounters because you were in unfamiliar surroundings?" asked Kevin.

"At first I did, certainly. As much as I knew from the studies I had undertaken beforehand, you might say I was in great shape for such a journey." Stanley sat down in one of the oversized chairs and continued. "While exploring the hidden places I found in Europe, I spent a solid two weeks of that time talking to myself and trying to figure out what I was seeing, hearing and experiencing. I thought I was going crazy! Not until I opened up to a stranger and spoke about the events did I realize my mind was fully engaged in what I would call supernatural events. It was just the happenings going on around me were rather insane compared to my regular daily life. Thankfully I had met exactly the right person at exactly the right time and he helped me gain the strength I needed to continue my work for the following ten weeks. It was a Godsend, so to speak."

"What was it that you saw, Mr. Pearson?" asked Marcus, "and who did you meet."

"My battle was more faith-based, Marcus. From deep within I felt the world was twisting and turning right before my eyes," answered Stanley. "Yes, I had studied hard and knew many things, but it was from a classroom setting and once in the field it became a more challenging endeavor. I was outmaneuvered by a force that I was unable to deal with. I had flunked my first field tests and was at the point of failure when I met a man by chance at a local brewhaus. At least I thought it was by chance but the more we talked, the more I realized he had found me flailing in a desperate attempt to uncover clues to the way people acted hundreds of years ago."

"That's how I felt, in the field at the cabin," interjected Kevin. "I questioned everything after that day, my world was never the same and it's only because Karen helped me pull things together that I made it back here. I knew this was where I needed to be if I was ever going to come to terms with what happened."

"You may never come to terms with it, Kevin," said Robert, "and I know it's only going to get harder for us. I don't know who you met, Stanley, but I'm glad he was able to keep you on track. Can you tell us what exactly he did that helped you to deal with the stress?"

"Let me take a try at this," said Norma as everyone turned to her, surprised at her challenge. "I'll say he told you the answer would be discovered from within, that all you had to do was look inside your soul instead of trying to see what was beating at your wings of faith. Only when you understand your strengths and weaknesses will you be able to fight a force that is invisible, yet unstoppable. Once you are able to see your true self, the enemy will appear in full view and your horror of the unknown will be replaced with the knowledge that there really is an eternal battle our souls here on Earth must endure, and you must make a decision to join the battle, or ignore the war."

"That was deep, Norma!" said Axel, as everyone was waiting for Stanley's reply.

"Norma, that was very moving," said Karen.

"Just a little something my mother used to say," Norma smiled. "Change a few words around and you can use that speech for just about anything. Right, Stanley?"

"Spot on, Norma," replied Stanley. "I never saw the man again, but his little speech of words very similar to your mother's cut through all the clutter and I was able to keep straight on course throughout the rest of my research. Funny thing was, I really never experienced the same level of activity among the places I visited from that day on. By the time I came home I was convinced I had been caught up in the trip and let my imagination get the best of me. That was until this week when my feelings of dealing with the supernatural reappeared here at Hamsteen Manor. Norma, how did you know?"

"My mother was an amazing woman and prepared me for many things," said Norma. "One of her greatest gifts was to help me understand the nature of people, especially someone that is struggling with a personal challenge. You were ripe for the meeting of the mystery man. I would like to know what his angle was, especially since you never saw him again. Most times people like him set you up with an epiphany and then hit you for a donation of some sort or try to get you as a regular client. This guy just walked away after giving you a great big key to your inner self. I just wonder why he chose you."

"I think after I opened up to him about my project he pictured me as struggling and used me as a way to find out where I was going, what I was doing and see for himself what was happening. Truth be told I was in way over my head and if he hadn't stepped into my life who knows where I'd be today," said Stanley. "Faith, luck, karma. Whatever it was that drew us together I'm forever grateful. And now these same cosmic energies have put me here with all of you and again I'm grateful, and even more than that I'm excited about the potential of finally doing some good for the world, even if it's just a small contribution."

"By the time we get done with this, I think we're all going to feel we've done some good, Stanley," said Robert. "Small contributions add up to big sums, and right now I'll take every penny of effort we can get! Okay, Eleanor, let's make sure Edgar and Katrina have secured everything on the main and second levels and then we're ready to head downstairs. Everyone, clear your heads and open your minds, it's parchment time!"

So it began. The Voyageurs were finally ready to unroll the parchments and fully dedicate their time and effort to figuring out how the parchments connect with the Sinergy. However, so far no one had verbalized the unthinkable truth, that maybe the parchments held nothing at all for the Sinergy, that this newly formed group of friends-by-accident was actually targeted by the evil force strictly because of their chance encounter at the cabin. . If that was the case, then the parchments were nothing but a distraction from the very real evil now on the prowl for them, not the inanimate objects they held in their possession. This was a terrifying option each of them had considered at one time or another but had not yet discussed as a group. It's one thing to be chased for something you've stolen, it's terrifying to be hunted down just because you happened to be in the wrong place at the wrong time!

The group stepped down the stairway to the basement floor, past the beautiful cherry wood bar and through the secret passage. Eleanor and Axel closed and locked the big door once everyone was through. The Voyageurs were now locked in a space that was built many decades earlier and honestly felt as if they had stepped back in time.

From the time the manor was built, its various owners had crafted the property's historical record to mimic the moods and temperament of early twentieth century America. After the city plots were developed, the original owner, a lumber baron, built the massive home under direction of the leading contractors and architects in the region. Next in the ownership parade was a Prohibition era alcohol supplier and suspected gangster. After World War II ended, the home was purchased by it's third owner, a very successful banker, who was believed to be laundering the residence from it's checkered past, since the gin runner and banker were secretly funding each other's business.

The house was remodeled by the banker over a period of about two years and sold to a local business owner and his beautiful bride. During the next fifteen years the home was filled with children (the couple had four), parties for nearly any occasion and holiday, and all sorts of celebratory events. It was a time that saw the manor flourish, but finally ended when the husband was discovered by his wife with another woman in their bedroom. There was no separation, however, there was an agreement reached through the efforts of more than a few lawyers. The social activity was curtailed, rendering the perennially festive home much quieter and a few degrees colder. Once the last of the four children had married, the final part of the agreement fell into place. The businessman, who's company continued to be very successful, on the side but rather discreetly socially active, finally moved out. At this time a divorce settlement provided his wife with a large sum of cash and monthly payments that could have supported a lavish lifestyle, but she chose instead to live discreetly, spending nearly every free moment with her children and grandchildren. She put most of her money into investments while letting the home fall into disrepair, knowing full well none of her children would ever want to live in the home where they were raised. When she finally passed away, her profits, worth a very tidy amount, were divided among the four children. The businessman passed on a few years later, and his younger wife would inherit the company after a generous payout to the children. The house, years after the loving couple had moved in and now in total disrepair, was to be sold immediately upon the death of the businessman, with the proceeds being divided up among the four children. It took time, and a number of price reductions, before the Hamsteen's agreed to the purchase agreement for the home.

Once they discovered the secret rooms, Eleanor began researching the home's history and was able to trace ownership details back to when the home was constructed. Even with an eccentric and crazy history, and knowing some of the locals talked of only the gossip stories surrounding the house, buying what would become Hamsteen Manor was a decision Eleanor and Joe, as well as the city of Prairie Falls, would never regret.

Inside the large room of the secret area, the four tables had been covered with sky blue covers made of a thick cotton weave, providing insulation from the hard surface of the tables and not allowing the parchments to slide around. Enough chairs were available for everyone to sit, however in the anticipated excitement of reviewing the parchments it was expected that most of the group would be too anxious to relax, so the chairs were left lined up against a side wall of the room. There were two easels displayed on tripods and a rolling cart with snacks and drinks that Katrina had brought in.

"When Joe and I discovered this area of the house, I never dreamed we'd have a need for this level of secrecy or security," Mrs. Hamsteen offered. "I can't imagine what it was like back in the days of Prohibition, but I'm sure there were many nights when the secret door was closed with someone notorious hiding back here behind it!"

"I still can't believe you didn't find anything in these rooms," said Karen. "You would think something would have been left behind or forgotten."

"There must have been some valuable stuff kept here," added Kevin. "Worth the effort to take it with them and clean up any trace of it ever being here."

"Maybe it was more than physical possessions," said Norma. "Maybe some bad things happened down here and they had to scrub down the rooms, top to bottom." Norma gave a shudder as if the room were freezing, and sent a cold chill through the entire group.

"Oh great," complained Axel, "now all I'm going to think about is how bad guys must have killed people down here. Ugh, what a way to go and no way to escape or be heard, thanks for the visual, Norma."

"I'm not saying anything like that did happen, just that this is a place it could have occurred, and that would explain why everything was moved out and cleaned up." Norma looked at Axel. "Sorry. I didn't mean to upset you."

"Oh, that's okay," Axel replied. "My imagination gets carried away too easily."

"Well," inserted Mrs. Hamsteen, "the rooms are very clean and safe so please don't worry about anything at all while you are down here Axel, and that goes for the rest of you, too. This has to be about the safest place in town, so let's all relax and get started with the parchments."

"All right, then, let's go over our plan," said Robert. "Marcus, would you mind?"

"Not at all." Marcus gathered his thoughts and went through the process they had discussed earlier. "Since this will be the first time we've laid these parchments out together, our goal is to do an initial visual inspection and take notes of our own thoughts and observations. Once we have all had a chance to review the four parchments, we'll each read our notes to the group. The group will just listen, no discussions and only short questions for clarity on the notes. When everyone has read their notes we'll see where we are. If we need a break we'll take one at that time."

"As slow as Axel writes, I know I'll need a break," laughed Roxie, nervously.

"Is there a limit on our notes?" asked Stanley. "How detailed should we get?"

"That's a really good question, Stanley" answered Marcus. "Robert, what are your thoughts on how much we should write for our notes on the visual review?"

"I'd suggest taking notes for as long as you have something to say that's relevant to the parchment." Robert said to Stanley, and then he turned his attention to the others. "Stanley may see some things only he would understand due to his extensive training and research. But I would ask that each of you write to your heart's content about what you see and what you feel from these papers. Sometimes clues lie dormant for years, even decades, before the right person sees the clues for what they really are, a simple way to solve a puzzle. Eleanor, you've had a glimpse of one parchment that basically set this whole review in process, so I know you in particular will have a lot to write about on at least one of the parchments."

"And for the rest of us, even though we've all had some terrible moments thanks to the Sinergy, they've actually helped us all gain different experiences," said Marcus. "Each of us may pick up on something different due to what we've gone through."

"That's a very positive and helpful insight, Marcus," said Norma. "Physical experiences have a way of imprinting our brain with more than what we think we saw, especially when it's in a frantic state of anxiety, danger or emotional distress."

"Wow, then I must have a ton of stored up imprints I need to sort through!" joked Axel. The group relaxed with Axel's humor, and then Marcus got the ball back on track.

"Okay, we've got notepads, pens, pencils and a couple of cameras. Please don't use your cell phones as cameras," Marcus directed. "At this point there shouldn't be any photos of the documents floating around on phones or the internet. That being said, Karen, I'd like you and Kevin to be in charge of photographing the parchments at some point today while we are down here. Since we need to store the parchments in the safe, having digital images to review on a computer will be a big help."

Marcus finished by saying, "Once we get through our visual review, I'm sure there will be many questions and a ton of research to do, so we'll set up a system to get everything covered. For now, let's see what we can come up with from the documents. Any questions?"

"What about Sheriff Anderson?" asked Roxie. "Isn't it weird that he isn't going to be here when we look at these?"

"Well," replied Robert, "Glen is pretty upset he can't be here with us. He's put more time into this than anyone, and if the parchments are related to the history of Havenswood Valley I'd wager he'd be able to pick out more clues than the rest of us. Let's hope he gets out of the hospital soon and makes his way down here ASAP."

"As a reminder," said Eleanor, "Edgar and Katrina will both be our lifelines to the outside world, Katrina on the inside and Edgar outside. They are both able to work our light code if they need to contact us with any news from Glen, or any news at all, while we are down here. There is also a light code for asking us to use the communications room, and that gives us real time audio and visual on both ends. We can talk with them directly from that room. Oh, and we can't rely on cell phones down here, very weak connections."

"That's fine by me," said Karen. "It will be nice to be out of range for a while."

"Okay, let's get started. The tubes are pretty easy to handle but let's be careful, just the same. Roxie, can you please grab the tube we wrote number one on and set it on the table on the far left?" asked Marcus.

"Sure," she replied.

"Axel, number two for the table to the right of number one?" Marcus asked.

"Got it, chief!" he answered.

"Robert, number three for the front right table?" Marcus continued.

"On it!" he said.

"And Norma, number four on the front left table, please." Marcus directed.

"Certainly, Marcus." Norma put the tube on the last open table.

Everyone was obviously very anxious at this point. Only two of the tube's contents had been laid out before, and only for a brief time. Marcus, Roxie and Axel had held true to their word of not opening up the other tubes until there was a formal time when everyone could gather. Once things were established with Eleanor it was determined that they would hold off until this very moment.

"For the unveilings, let's do this in the same order as we just set out the tubes," said Marcus. "Roxie, if you and Karen will please open up tube number one, it's the first one we opened and showed to Mrs. Hamsteen, and lay it on the table. We'll watch each opening together and then we'll start with our reviews. Go ahead, ladies."

"You make it sound so easy!" said Karen. "I'm a nervous wreck!"

"Take your time, Karen," said Roxie, "no rush at this point."

Karen slowly opened the tube, set the open end on the table and let gravity draw the parchment out. She moved the tube slowly from left to right at a slight angle and the parchment appeared as if it were being birthed from the cylinder, with only a little help from Roxie to pull it clear of the tube. Although it had been rolled up for who knows how many years, as soon as it was clear of the tube it unfurled easily and lay flat on the table, it's yellowish color a perfect compliment to the blue tablecloth.

"It's beautiful," Karen said in a tone of wonderment.

"Now that's a parchment!" added Stanley, excitedly. "I've seen a few, but never one that's in as good a shape as this one. It's so thick, I think that's one reason it's still in such pristine condition."

"Just as I remember it," smiled Eleanor. "Only this time you don't have to worry about me nearly fainting at the sight of it!"

"Axel," Marcus's tone brought everyone's eyes up from the first parchment. "Will you and Norma please open up the tube we marked as the second one?"

"Yes, sir!" Axel was at the ready. "Since Karen did such a great job I'm going to follow her lead and let this one out the same way."

Axel's steady hands opened the tube and just as Karen had, he moved the angled tube from left to right and the second parchment slid out as if on cue. Norma pulled it clear and parchment number two unfurled in the very same manner as the first.

"Consistent buggers," said Stanley. "Same look, same texture and the same action of the parchment as the first one."

"Definitely not the same story," said Norma. "Just a glance will tell you this one has a lot more to say than the first one. I just can't believe what wonderful shape they are in. They look as if they were just made yesterday."

"And now that we've had a glance and it's safely on the table," asked Marcus, "Robert, will you do the honors for number three?"

"If you don't mind my interrupting," said Stanley, "is there any particular reason the tubes are numbered?"

"Partly the way we found them," answered Axel. "Put them in the order we pulled them from the table legs, like parts from a car. We even numbered the legs in case we needed to go back and look at the table. Plus they do have a small area with some markings that we'll have to decipher."

"I see. Nice and logical and a good way to treat a find," said Stanley. "Many times it's much harder to replace something correctly than it is to, well, borrow it."

"Ready, Robert?" asked Marcus.

Robert nodded yes and opened the third tube. This was the first time tube three had been opened and it let out a gasp, as if needing air, when the seal was broken. "Guess it needed to breathe," joked Robert. In the same manner as the previous two, Robert tilted the tube, but nothing happened. Robert gave the tube a gentle side to side shake, mimicking the movement used on the first two tubes, yet still nothing even peeked from the opening. "Well, then, this one seems to be stuck," he surmised. Robert turned the tube around to look inside. "There's something like stuffed paper in the end here," he said. He held out the open end and displayed it so everyone could get a look inside.

"That looks like old wrapping paper," Eleanor suggested. "The type you would see in an old western movie when the shop owner would wrap the customers package and tie it up with string."

"We just figured they all held the same thing," said Roxie. "They weighed about the same, felt the same, and none of them made any noise like there was anything other than rolled up parchments in them."

"Eleanor, can we grab a couple of flashlights from the storage room?" asked Marcus.

"Yes, of course," she answered, and in less than a minute Marcus held one in his hand. "You know," Mrs. Hamsteen continued, "it seems as if our time down here will take longer than we expected. Would anyone mind if we dined here tonight instead of in town? I can call Katrina and let her know, if you are all fine with that." Of course they agreed, no one wanted to leave the house now! Mrs. Hamsteen made the call and in addition had Katrina cancel the after dinner party. There would be plenty of excitement without the addition of a few more guests!

"Stanley," said Marcus, "will you please grab the end and help Robert with the tube? Once you pull the paper out, go ahead and take a look inside the tube with the flashlight."

Robert held the open end of the tube up so it was horizontal with Stanley's line of vision. This made it easy for Stanley to reach inside and gently pull out the paper.

"Funny, the paper feels waxy, I expected it to be dry and brittle," noted Stanley. "It's needing a tug to pull it out, yes, here it comes with some tension against the sides of the tube. Must be from the paper being crushed in place when it was sealed. Ah, here it is. Norma, will you unwrap this paper and make sure there isn't anything inside?" Stanley handed the paper to Norma and she unwrapped it quickly and announced, as everyone could plainly see, that it was empty. "Alright, let's have a look inside this kaleidoscope now."

Stanley clicked on the flashlight and as he lifted it to the open end of the tube he felt the anxiety in the room. He also felt as if he had stepped into someone else's party. Stanley put the flashlight down. "Robert, I'd feel much better if it were you looking inside here. I know what it's like being the first one on a discovery, and if anyone deserves to be first to see something, it's you." Stanley stepped around to the side of the tube and put his hands up to replace Robert's.

Holding the tube for a few seconds with Stanley, Robert smiled and said "Well, then, that's a good thought. Don't mind if I do, thank you, Stanley."

"You're a class act, Stanley," said Kevin.

Robert held up the flashlight and pointed the light beam into the tube, and as he looked inside he smiled and chuckled. "Well, thanks anyway, but all I see is a piece of wood wedged into the tube. There's what looks like a leather strip that if we hold the open end down more I should be able to reach it." Stanley lifted the closed end up. "Give it a shake and some more angle, Stanley. Yep, a little more, okay, that's good." Robert easily reached the strip of leather as it had drifted nearly to the end of the tube. He pulled the slack out of it and it extended about six inches past the tube opening. "Any suggestions?"

"There could be anything under that wedge," said Marcus, "and we don't want anyone to get hurt trying to dislodge the wood. Let's figure a way to pull it up without anyone's hands or face taking the brunt of a spring loaded trap."

"I say we wrap the leather around something that goes across the opening and have two people lift up, that way no one is directly over the tube when the wood piece comes uncorked," said Axel.

"You are quick with the mechanical options, aren't you, Axel," said Norma.

"That's me!" he replied. "Here, let's use my belt." Axel removed his belt.

Robert tied the leather strip from the tube to the middle of Axel's belt. Stanley held the tube and Robert and Axel each held one side of the belt, their hands about eight inches away from the opening of the tube.

"Okay, let's lift slowly and see how it goes, ready?" asked Robert.

"Yep, let's do this," answered Axel. They inched the belt up. "How's the tension feel for you, Robert?" asked Axel.

"Not bad, let's keep it even and see if this thing comes straight up," Robert replied. "I think it's moving, can you feel anything?"

"Yeah, it's coming up. I can hear it scraping against the side," Axel said.

They continued to lift the belt up with the wedged piece of wood sliding against the metal tube. It was a steady slide, then a loud pop and whoosh emerged from the tube at the same time the belt loosened. Instinctively they both stopped lifting.

"Is it loose?" asked Roxie.

"Oh yeah, it's loose like a bad lug nut," answered Axel.

"Continue?" Robert asked of Axel.

"Can't stop now," he replied.

The two men easily raised the belt with just a slight bump of the wood against the inside of the tube. It was only a few seconds until a one inch thick wood plug came into view. As Robert and Axel held the belt slightly higher, another wad of crushed wax paper appeared and was somehow attached to the underside of the wood. The paper held the shape of the tube even after it was set carefully down on the table. This time the paper appeared to be more than stuffing. It was shaped as if it were wrapped around an object, protecting it from being rattled around or damaged while inside the tube. Its length was consistent with what it would take to fill the tube from the wood plug down.

"Not what we expected," stated Marcus.

"I love surprises," said Karen.

"I hate surprises," countered Robert, only slightly kidding. He held the flashlight up to the open end of the tube and peered inside, looking to see if anything else was ready to be extracted. "That's all she wrote for this tube. She's empty as a gin bottle at half past midnight."

"This is how it goes, sometimes," said Stanley. "We plan, we prepare, and yet we are still caught off-guard. Expecting one outcome and something completely different happens."

"True, Stanley, very true," said Norma. "But I love presents and it looks like we have one to open here. I say let's unwrap this one and see what we have on our hands."

"Robert, will you do the honors?" asked Eleanor.

Robert set down the flashlight and Axel pulled his leather belt out of the way. They left the leather string tied to the belt, for now, and the wood plug was on its edge, held up by the wax paper bunched below its underside. It did look like the paper was wrapped around something that was somehow tied or nailed to the wood plug. The paper wadding was about twelve inches long, and as Robert began to carefully peel it back, the room grew very quiet. Each member of The Voyageurs was totally focused on the simple paper before them, trying to guess what lies within.

"I can see the edge of something," said Robert. He lifted back a layer of the crumpled paper and there, nestled in the aged wax paper was an odd shaped envelope tied at one end to the underside of the wooden plug. "Well I'll be," said Robert, "there is something attached to the plug."

"It looks like it's made from the same paper as the parchments!" Karen proclaimed.

"I think so, too!" agreed Kevin. "And I'm not just saying that because Karen is my fiancé!" he added with a smile.

"You two are right, though," said Marcus. "It looks like they used the parchment material to wrap around something, and then tied it up with string. Norma, your comparison to a package being wrapped was perfect, that's exactly what this is!"

"Well, I do have a sixth sense about me," Norma said, and she winked at Marcus.

"Stanley," asked Robert, "anything special we need to do before we unwrap it?"

"Eleanor," Stanley said, "let's use one of the cameras you have down here and I'll take a couple of photographs of what we have so far. Then we'll unwrap it and see what's inside." Stanley took a dozen photos of the contents from the tube, making sure to document how each piece was positioned as it was when pulled out. "Okay, Robert, it's all yours," said Stanley.

"Wow, this must be what it's like opening some ancient Egyptian treasure!" said Axel.

"Not exactly a great tomb, but, yes, Axel, opening a relic of any kind is always exciting," answered Stanley.

"So, then, I'll just start to unwrap it," said Robert. "Here we go."

Understandably anxious, Robert slowly untied the string that kept the wrapping snug around the object. It was actually very easy to do, even with his large and usually uncooperative fingers. As he pushed back and smoothed out the paper that had nestled the object for who knows how many years, there was a nearly simultaneous gasp from The Voyageurs.

"Oh, my," said Eleanor.

"Awesome!" exclaimed Axel.

"It's gorgeous," Karen, could barely breathe the words.

Before them lay a magnificent specimen of what appeared to be a large precious jewel.

"Never in a hundred years would I have guessed this," said Norma. "I said I love presents, but I did not expect something so incredible. Do you think that's gold around the edges?"

"I'm no expert," answered Robert, "but I'd say yes, that sure looks like gold."

"I thought I was an expert," said Stanley, "however this artifact is going to take a lot of research to figure out both where it came from, and where it rightfully should be."

"Should be?" asked Kevin.

"I believe what Stanley means," interjected Norma, "is that this piece was not destined for a rich princess in some exotic land. It was made to be functional, not fashionable."

Stanley looked up at Kevin, "Norma is correct, at least in my humble estimation."

"You're the closest we have to an expert, Stanley. Why don't you give this thing the once over before we move on to the next tube."

"That's a good idea," said Norma.

"Alright, I'll do a short review. But remember," Stanley warned, "this is totally off the cuff. I'm sure we'll find out much more over the next few days. Agreed?"

"Agreed!" they echoed.

Stanley reached out and lifted their new find from the paper, flipped it over and laid it back down on the tablecloth. Although a fast maneuver, it provided him with a tentative weight estimate of about eight ounces, and the knowledge that the object was nearly identical in appearance from either side or end. Stanley then visually scanned the object and noted the size; about seven inches long, two inches wide and one inch thick. The overall shape was oblong, yet blunt on each end. The color was a rich, emerald green, both clear and a possibly milky center at the same time. On first glance the clarity was amazing, but upon a closer inspection which was, for this exercise, hasty at best, Stanley saw the variance in the center and he would spend more time on it later.

"Stanley," asked Roxie, "have you ever seen anything like this in your travels?"

"Not exactly," he replied, still staring at the emerald colored object. "However, many relics are similar in nature, just slightly different in their final application. I'm betting the parchments will help us figure out what this is and how it may be used."

"Well, no matter how it's supposed to be used, I am totally blown away by this," said Karen. "I know we're going to wait to make our comments, but this presents a whole new set of questions that I can't begin to think about. I know I'm rambling right now, but really, I'm speechless."

"You're right, Karen," responded Norma. "The introduction of an item like this object - whether it turns out to be glass, a jewel or a precious stone, - is going to give us many things to ponder. Earth objects are extremely powerful and very important in the spiritual world. This will not be easy."

"Stanley," Eleanor said, "any initial thoughts on the object?"

"Again, this is strictly blind guesswork," Stanley looked up and around at the members standing in front of him, waiting patiently for his feedback. "As Norma said, objects that are born from or directly made with naturally occurring elements are commonly used as a tool of some sort. First, I would label this object a jewel until we study it further. Second, the fact it has been trimmed with what appears to be gold tells me there is a use for this jewel that involves some kind of conductivity. Gold is only a precious metal because we say it is, however as a practical element it's very useful in a variety of applications. Third and fourth, the weight and clarity will need to be studied. It's so light for it's size and there appears to be a movement or variance within the body of the jewel, two factors we definitely need to look into. Other than that," Stanley finished with a wry remark, "it looks very pretty."

Stanley's last comment provided some well needed humor.

Robert addressed the group, "As Stanley said, the parchments will most likely give us some answers on this object, uh, this jewel, so, as pretty as it is we shouldn't get too deep into trying to figure it out just yet. I'd like to suggest we move on to the next tube."

232

"I second your motion," Marcus answered, "that is, if no one objects."

There were no objections to be made, and the only sound in the room was that of The Voyageurs standing anxiously at the ready. Knowing full well another unchartered chapter in their adventure was about to open up, they became like moths to a light, and instinctively circled the table where the final tube lay.

"Eleanor," Karen's clear voice cut through the small talk taking place as the group was about to open the fourth tube, "I think the phone light is on!"

"Yes, Karen," Eleanor replied, trying to sound calm, "Let's step into the communications room and see who's calling. Maybe Katrina has an early supper planned for us." She smiled and began moving to the room across the hall. Although they could not all fit into the room, everyone followed. Robert, Marcus and Roxie stood directly behind Eleanor as she sat at the keyboard, preparing to reply to the light signal.

"Looks like Katrina wants to talk with us," she said to the group. Eleanor was all set, and had turned the speakers on for everyone to hear. "Katrina, it's Eleanor. We saw the light, what do you have for us?"

"Eleanor, Sheriff Anderson is on the phone. He wants to talk with Robert!" she announced with some anxiousness in her voice. The images were crystal clear on the monitor, Katrina was standing at the end of the kitchen nearest the passage to the dining room. In the background was a clear view of the back door and rear entry hallway into the kitchen. Although Katrina was not yet enthralled by the new guests staying at Hamsteen Manor, she was willing to do everything she could to make them feel welcome.

"Robert's right here, Katrina. Go ahead and put the sheriff on hold and I'll pick it up down here. Thank you, Kat. By the way, we'll be staying in for supper, just something light, and will you please cancel our dinner reservations?" She turned to Robert after she saw Katrina nod yes, and then place the call on hold. "Robert, do you want to take this call privately?"

"Nope, I'll just let Glen know we're all listening. If he has anything private to talk about he can let me know. I'm thinking at this point anything he has to say he can say to all of us."

"Okay, here he is!" Eleanor pressed a few keys on the keyboard and then greeted the sheriff. "Hello, Sheriff Anderson. This is Eleanor."

"Well, hello right back at you, Eleanor, nice to hear your voice."

"We're all together down in the basement communications room, and I've placed you on speakerphone so everyone can hear. Robert's right next to me, ready to answer any questions you may have."

"Hi, Robert!"

"Hey, Glen," Robert replied. "How you doing?"

"Couldn't be better," said the sheriff, "especially now that I'm out of that darn hospital!"

"Did you escape?" Robert asked. The group gave a nervous laugh.

"Not exactly. They knew I was ready to go and most of the paperwork was done. Told them I had some friends waiting for me and if I didn't get out the party would be over before I even showed up!"

"You're pretty close on that one," Robert said. "We did get started and can't wait to show you what we've got here. You're not going to believe what we found in one of the tubes."

"Well, then, guess we'll have to keep the pedal to the metal and hope we don't get stopped by any of our fellow peace officers," replied the sheriff.

"We?" Axel asked, as if by reflex.

"Hey, Axel, how are you? Yes, I did say we. Deputy Stevens and Biologist Reynolds are both with me. We should be at Hamsteen Manor in less than twenty minutes. Tried Robert and Norma's cell phones a couple of times but it kept going to voice mail. Finally decided I should at least give a heads up to the staff that we would be arriving soon."

"Glen," asked Norma, "any unwanted guests show up on your drive?"

"Well, as you all may have guessed, I did have some company on my way back to Havenswood Valley. I'll fill you in on the details once I arrive. All I will say for now is to please make sure you are always aware of your surroundings. I was nearly caught off guard, it happened so quickly. Oh, and don't go anywhere alone. Especially now that the tubes are open, who knows what may happen next."

"At least you won't have to worry about being dragged away by the Sinergy with Deputy Stevens on board," interjected Kevin. "He's the best tackling deputy in the state. Can you tell him all the bruises have finally healed?"

"You just did," replied Sheriff Anderson. "We're on speakerphone, too."

"Hey, Kevin," said Deputy Stevens, "glad to hear you're safe and sound."

"He's safe," joked Marcus, "but I don't know how sound he is."

"Actually, we're all doing well, Glen." Robert steered the conversation back to the basement activity. "Really looking forward to having you back here with us so we can get started on the parchments. Might have to adjust our research plans based on what we find in the last tube."

"Sheriff," it was Steve Reynolds, the state biologist, "remember to let them know about our thoughts on the sound defense."

"Right. Say, Robert?"

"Yeah, Glen, I'm here."

"Remember all that firepower and lighting we unloaded on the Sinergy the night Kevin was almost taken?" asked Sheriff Anderson. "Reynolds and I have been working on a theory that there is a combination of sound waves and physical vibrations that mess with their system. We still need to narrow it down, but at least we have a path to follow."

"Is there anything we have now to generate the waves and vibrations?" asked Robert.

"It's pretty early in our research," replied Reynolds, "but for instance the pellets in the shotguns had no impact. It was the actual percussion from the blast, creating the low level vibration that wreaked havoc on them. At least that's our theory."

"What about the sound waves?" asked Roxie.

"Unfortunately that's a much bigger challenge," answered Reynolds. "It could be anything from a silent dog whistle to a few notes on the music scale, or some off the wall pitch created by an action that has nothing to do with either man-made music or naturally occurring sounds. For now, we do think higher pitch sound waves and lower scale vibrations will be more successful. Not rocket science, but as Sheriff Anderson said, at least we have a course of action."

"Sounds like a survival defense effect," Stanley said, more to himself, but the microphone picked up his comment.

"You might be right, whoever said that," Reynolds replied. "It sounds gender biased, but as humans will generally do, women scream in a high pitch to ward off attackers, and men yell out in a deep guttural voice to defend their turf, in both cases causing the attacker to stop if not retreat. If this evil is earth-based then it might fall right into the category of having a basic survival defense mechanism we can try to mimic."

"Gee," Karen said sarcastically, "that sounds so modern, so 1950's! I'm sorry but are you seriously thinking that if Roxie and I scream loud enough at a high pitch this 'non-human' evil is going to run home to mommy? Why didn't I think of that when Kevin was being pulled into the forest!"

"Hey, listen everyone, this is all in the early stages of discussion," replied Sheriff Anderson. "Let's not read too much into it before we can all sit down together and go over the research. No need to push back too hard just yet, we're all in this together and together we'll figure it out. Karen, everybody, are we okay?"

"I'm okay, Sheriff," answered Karen. "I just want to know what we should do, not what might work. Things have gotten more serious. You'll see when you get here."

"Karen's right, Sheriff, but we're good," said Marcus. "The situation is hitting us pretty hard, but we'll take a break and bring you up to date on the tubes, and our newest member, Stanley. We know you have a lot to talk about, too."

"Excellent thoughts, Marcus. And don't worry too much, Karen. We'll be there very soon and make sure you have all the direction you need," said the sheriff. "Save us a seat for supper, we're getting pretty hungry!"

Eleanor clicked off the phone system after everyone had said goodbye and spoke directly to Katrina. "Kat, are you there?"

As Eleanor began to speak with Katrina, the group loosened up and began to drift back into the large room. Upstairs, Katrina had been standing nearby and now walked to the phone, "Yes, Eleanor, right here."

"Sheriff Anderson and two more guests, Mr. Stevens and Mr. Reynolds, will be here shortly. They will be joining us for supper and staying on at the manor. Can you please make sure they are added to our list?"

"Certainly, Eleanor. I'll have the staff attend to their rooms and I will include them for our supper. I've already canceled the dinner reservations. Should I also cancel the after dinner party?" Katrina looked around the kitchen, then back to the monitor. She seemed to be ready to ask a question, but her mouth would not cooperate and her eyes suddenly looked vacant. The clarity of the monitor left nothing to the imagination.

Eleanor instinctively turned off the audio to the intercom system, her eyes glued to the monitor.

"Is she okay?" asked Norma, she had stayed in the room with Eleanor. "She looks pale."

"I was thinking the same thing," added Eleanor. "I've never known Katrina to be at a loss for words. She just seemed to go blank."

"Should we go up there?" asked Roxie. Hearing the discussion continuing, the group started to gather again back in the communications room.

"Everything alright?" asked Marcus. The group was now back into position, looking at Katrina standing awkwardly in the kitchen.

"Katrina!" Eleanor had turned the audio back on, "Katrina are you alright, dear?"

"Me? Alright?" she answered. "Oh, yes, I'm fine, just lost my train of thought for a minute. Worried about everyone down in the basement, that's all."

"Whoa! What was that!" cried Roxie.

"I saw it, too," Norma was keenly focused on the monitor. "Robert, did you see it?"

"What are you all talking about?" asked Kevin.

"No, I wasn't watching. What was it?" Robert asked.

Eleanor took a breath, "It was a dark shape, went from left to right across the back door. Am I right?"

"It wasn't just a shape. It was your Sinergy making a house call before the sheriff gets here," said Stanley.

"Holy crap! Does this thing have a rewind button? That just totally gave me the chills!" added Axel.

"We installed the system for monitoring, not recording, but the computer RAM stores a few minutes of information, I only need to press a few keys and we can see if it will show up," said Eleanor. "Everyone please watch the monitor, this is what we just saw, pay close attention to the back door window."

Eleanor ran the computer and the replay came up for the group to review. The air in the communications room thickened with anticipation and time seemed to crawl by as the shape of darkness slid across the back door of the Hamsteen Manor.

"While it's still in the computer memory, can you show it one more time? Then we'll head upstairs for the staff and Edgar," directed Robert. "This time, slow it down as the shape comes into view."

As The Voyageurs held their collective breath, the Sinergy entity came into view once again. This time the slow motion option showed a shape just beyond the kitchen door that clearly replicated a man dressed in oversized clothing, baggy, almost flowing like a cape. It was there for only a split second, just a slight hesitation as if to look down the hallway and into the kitchen, and then it was off the screen.

"Quickly, Eleanor," directed Robert, "back to Katrina in the kitchen!"

Eleanor obliged and instantly the monitor showed the kitchen, with the back door wide open, but no Katrina.

"Katrina!" screamed Eleanor. "Katrina, where are you!"

There was no reply.

"Katrina!" she tried again.

Suddenly, Katrina appeared, running into the hallway from the back door.

"I'm here, Eleanor, I'm here! Is everything okay?" She looked startled and out of breath.

"Where were you?" asked Eleanor.

"Where was I?" she replied, looking into the monitor. "I was in the herb garden getting some basil for supper. I came running when I heard you yell my name on the intercom! Are you alright?"

The group in the basement relaxed momentarily after hearing Katrina's explanation, but they realized basil for supper may have turned into a deadly seasoning choice for Katrina. Time was suddenly moving extremely fast, and The Voyageurs were very aware the tubes were an open invitation for the Sinergy to visit, they just didn't think the RSVP would come so quickly!

"We're fine, Katrina," answered Eleanor. "Now, close and lock the back door. Quickly! Some of us will be up in just a minute. Call the staff in at once and for heaven's sake, if you see Edgar, call him indoors, too. Do you understand?"

"Yes, Eleanor, I understand. Are we under attack again?" asked Katrina.

"We are, Kat. Be careful!" Eleanor hadn't had time to consider exactly what was going on. "Please, lock the back door! We'll be right up."

Robert spoke first, "I see it this way, we send some of us upstairs, and everyone else stays down here with the parchments and jewel."

"I'm heading upstairs with Robert and Kevin" said Marcus. "Try and see how you can help us by using the communications room. Call Sheriff Anderson, watch the grounds and keep us posted. We'll do the same from the kitchen."

"Let's go!" said Kevin.

"Wait! You can't just run up there without a plan!" pleaded Roxie.

"No time to waste, Roxie," said Karen. "Decision made. Now let's move on and stop holding up progress. You guys get up there and we'll figure out how to help from down here. Now go!"

"Axel, come and lock the door behind us!" commanded Marcus.

The three men made a hasty exit from the basement and were in the kitchen in no time, nearly running head-on into Katrina and the other two staff on duty.

"Katrina!" Marcus said. "You and the staff can head downstairs into the basement, Roxie and Karen will show you where to go. Quickly!"

"Wait, where's Edgar?" asked Robert.

"I don't know!" answered Katrina. "We haven't seen him for a few hours."

"Okay. Go ahead and make your way to the basement," said Robert.

"Eleanor, can you see me? Hear me?" asked Marcus. He was in the kitchen working the monitor and intercom. "The staff is on their way down to the basement."

"Loud and clear, Marcus" she replied. "We'll let the staff in. Any sign of Edgar?"

"Not yet. Katrina hasn't seen him for a few hours. I think we'll have to go outside," Marcus said. "Can you scan the grounds and look for him?"

"Yes, wait inside until you hear from me!" Eleanor said.

"Marcus, let Eleanor know I'm calling Glen with my cell phone," said Robert.

"Got that, Robert," answered Eleanor. "Thanks for saving us a call!"

It was controlled chaos at Hamsteen Manor. Downstairs the group was hunkered behind the secret door, but connected to the outside world like they were a major cable company! Upstairs, the men were looking for signs of the Sinergy, Edgar and the sheriff, not knowing who they would see first.

"We need a plan, Robert. We can't just rush around and wait. Plus, it's almost dark and we'll be at a huge disadvantage." Marcus was glad he had come upstairs, but now they needed a course of action.

"Yeah, we sure do. Okay, first, find Edgar and get him inside, then downstairs. Then we'll have Axel come up here. Next, the sheriff and our two new recruits arrive and the six of us will stay up here." Robert continued, "Now comes the tricky part. If it happens in that order, we're okay because we'll all be here and ready for them. If the Sinergy gets here before the sheriff, well, it's time for the guns and noises show again!"

"Robert! Marcus! I found Edgar!" It was Eleanor on the intercom. "Can you hear me?"

"Eleanor, where is he!" answered Robert.

"He's by the pond, across the big parking lot, on the other side of the main entry road," she cried. "I think he's working on the dock. Hurry, he's all alone out there!"

"We're on our way!" yelled Marcus.

There was something else on its way to Edgar, too, and it had a head start. Although the single entity of the Sinergy had unknowingly been seen through the back door of the kitchen, it felt camouflaged as it moved to the unused hay loft in the barn out back, right next to the pond.

"Marcus!" huffed Kevin as they ran to the pond. "Do you see Edgar?"

"Not yet. The trees are blocking the view. Let's take the path by the road - the one we took on the tour!" Marcus was moving with ease across the grounds. His nearly daily runs kept him in great shape and he quickly left Robert, and then Kevin, behind.

It had spotted the lone human standing thigh-deep in a pond that was surrounded by trees and large brush. The Sinergy drifted down and kept low to the ground, a shadow unseen as it flowed over the dock.

"There's the path!" yelled Marcus.

It came silently, like fog rolling into a low valley, enveloping everything in its way. You don't hear it, you don't smell it, yet suddenly it's there, right on top of you! In his haste Marcus had taken the long path to the pond area, giving Kevin time to catch him as the dock came into view.

"Is that Edgar? There, standing in the water by the dock!" suggested Marcus.

"Sure is, but what's happening? He's falling into the pond! Edgar! Edgar!" screamed Kevin.

Darkness falls quickly. We turn around and before we know it, our day is over, our time is up. There is no control in our lives over nature, over powers we cannot foresee. The darkness that ends our lives comes unannounced, unwelcome and yet in the end we can do nothing but succumb to its power.

"Edgar! Get out of the water!" Marcus was in a full sprint, Kevin flailing behind, Robert now just yards behind Kevin. "Edgar! Oh my God, Edgar!"

As Marcus approached, splashing wildly into the water, the darkness that had flowed over Edgar and weighed him down below the surface rose quickly from the pond and disappeared into the trees beyond Hamsteen Manor.

"You son of a bitch!" Marcus screamed. He dove to the spot he had seen Edgar fall, it wasn't too deep and he rammed right into Edgar's lifeless body. He began to pull Edgar to shore when

Kevin came crashing into the water, grabbing for Edgar's arms so he, too, could help pull him to the edge of the pond.

"CPR, Robert! We can do CPR!"

"Sure, sure we can, Marcus." He replied knowing full well the life had been pushed from Edgar by the same evil that had claimed the life of his son. There was no chance Edgar was going to be revived, but he let Marcus and Kevin try. The sirens in the distance gave false hope to a lost cause.

"Here comes Axel!" said Robert. "And I hear an ambulance, too."

"Guys! They saw the whole thing from the basement!" yelled Axel as he approached. "There's an ambulance on the way and Sheriff Anderson is right around the corner! Oh, God, Eleanor saw it happen! She's collapsed in the basement!"

The ambulance pulled in right behind Sheriff Anderson's SUV. They had turned off their Code 3 lights and siren upon entering the property. The EMT's acted quickly, yet methodically, to assess the situation. They hauled their emergency gear as Sheriff Anderson and Deputy Stevens grabbed the gurney to bring down to Edgar's side. One of the EMT's took over from Marcus and continued CPR while the other hooked up an oxygen mask over Edgar's nose and mouth. Robert grabbed the warming blanket that had been set next to Edgar and placed it over Edgar's legs and lower torso. Questions, reactions, adjustments, more questions. The EMT's had seen this situation too many times before, and while they may have felt reviving this victim was a long shot, their efforts to bring Edgar back were, nevertheless, heroic. The emergency responders multi-tasked so effortlessly that in a matter of minutes Edgar's lifeless body, unresponsive to the portable defibrillator, had been loaded onto the gurney for transport to the local hospital.

As the ambulance started to pull onto the city road, the trip to the hospital was downgraded to Code 2; lights and siren only, no speeding to the hospital. The decision had been made. Edgar had passed and it would be made official at the hospital. Watching the ambulance hug a turn and disappear around the corner, Marcus let out a long, emotion-releasing sigh.

"Yeah," said Robert. "Son of a bitch."

By now, some of the neighbors had made their way over, and the sidewalk held court to a number of passersby and early trick-

or-treaters that had seen the commotion. Sheriff Anderson's presence helped keep the onlookers from getting too close, and once enough of the local police arrived, order was restored and the neighbors and gawkers were asked to move on.

No one from the manor had come out after Axel did, and the men from The Voyageurs were all thinking the same thing. It was tough being at Edgar's side, seeing him pass, but it was going to be much tougher to face those inside. The men were sure it was pandemonium and that Roxie, Karen, Norma, and Stanley had their hands full consoling Eleanor, Katrina and the other two staff members. Edgar had no close family to speak of, but he did have many friends in town. There would be people to call, arrangements to make and tears to be shed, many by Eleanor. The pain of seeing poor Edgar killed would haunt her for years, and as an extra burden she would have to hold the cold, dark truth of his death within the circle of The Voyageurs.

There was a quick shift in the chain of command at Hamsteen Manor. Eleanor was upstairs in bed, Katrina and Norma at her side. The kitchen was busy with Roxie, Karen and the two part-time staff members, Abby and Cassidy, preparing supper and more. Axel and Kevin were downstairs, making sure the parchments were safe. The house would be full with The Voyageurs staying over, and even though meals would pour in from neighbors and friends, with so many at the manor it would be a challenge keeping meals ready to heat and eat.

Outside, Sheriff Anderson, Marcus and Robert, the latter two wrapped in blankets from the sheriff's SUV, were meeting with the Prairie Falls Chief of Police since he had assigned himself to file the report on Edgar. Chief Benson had known Eleanor and Joe Hamsteen for many years, and had met Edgar six years ago. He felt it was his obligation out of respect to the Hamsteens and Edgar, even though this looked like a simple case of a heart attack, to handle the paperwork.

"Well, thank you men for what you tried to do for Edgar. You never know when it's going to be your time. If the good Lord calls your number there isn't anything you can do about it," said Chief Benson. "I just hope Eleanor will be able to get through this okay. She's pretty tough, but she considers all her staff as family."

"Wish we could have done something more," said Marcus. "Seemed like we never had a chance."

"Probably not, heart attacks strike hard and fast. Guess it's better that way," answered the Chief, oblivious to the actual event that killed Edgar. "For now, I've got everything I need to file for the death certificate. Please let whoever is handling the funeral arrangements know that the body will be sent to the Prairie Falls Mortuary on Third Street. They need to call by tomorrow to get things rolling. Are you going to be around town for a while? Not that I need to ask more questions of anyone, just want to know if Eleanor will have some extra company."

"I'm in town for a few days, maybe longer now for the funeral," answered Sheriff Anderson. "Then I'm heading back to Havenswood Valley. Once Reynolds can get his meetings finished we're free to go. No offense, but I prefer a slower paced community."

"No offense taken, Sheriff, I completely understand." Chief Benson let his guard down and said, "I'd be up north in a second if the wife would agree. Seems she likes the city more than relaxing on a lake. Oh well, she's the best thing that ever happened to me, makes it easy to hang around. Gotta go men. Busy night ahead keeping the Halloween crowd under control. Thanks again and please take good care of Eleanor."

The chief headed to his squad car and was off the grounds in no time. The men looked at each other with relief. The questioning had gone much smoother than they had anticipated. Chief Benson went through the standard questions like a husband running down his to-do list on a Saturday morning.

"I think we did a good job answering his questions," offered Marcus.

"I do, too. We gave him truthful replies and told him exactly what happened," said Robert. "That Edgar went under while we were trying to find him, and that we did all we could to revive him. He believed it when we said our guess was a heart attack, and since no-one was around to see the Sinergy attack him, he has no reason to believe otherwise."

"I don't like having to bend the truth," said Sheriff Anderson. "I know, I've had to do it before. Sometimes you have to squeeze by a situation to make it through to the final battle. That's what we did today, because there's no way anyone would believe what really happened."

"You're right, Glen. It would sound insane to the common person and yet we know the Sinergy is real," said Robert. "I sure hope things settle down quickly around here. We've got work to do!"

"Well, if Edgar's funeral follows standard protocol, there should be visitors showing up over the next few days," Sheriff Anderson said. "That could help us move within the manor without too much notice that the house is full of strangers."

"So, how are we going to convince people we're here for reasons other than opening up long lost relics?" said Marcus.

"Good question. I think we better go talk with Eleanor and see how she's doing," Sheriff Anderson said. "A lot of this may depend on how she's feeling."

"Okay, so let's have someone talk with Eleanor and see what she wants to do," said Marcus. "I know it's tough, but the sooner the better."

"Marcus!" called Roxie from the back entry doorway. "You guys ready to come in?"

"Be right there!" he replied.

As the three men walked back to the house, Robert asked, "Was it just because he was an easy target? Is that why it was Edgar?"

"I think so," answered Sheriff Anderson. "They wanted to make a statement and Edgar was a sitting duck out there."

As soon as the men walked into the house they knew bread was baking, and whatever was being cooked on the stove smelled delicious! The kitchen was set up for a buffet, with plenty of beverages in the dining room. It seemed amazing that so much had been done in what seemed like such a short time to the men. Had they been outside for that long? Marcus asked Karen if she wouldn't mind going upstairs to ask Norma to come down and talk with Sheriff Anderson, and then staying with Eleanor and Katrina until Norma came back.

"No problem," Karen replied, and she headed upstairs. Kevin and Robert followed as far as the upper level hallway, and then headed to their respective rooms to get some fresh clothes and grab a shower.

"Glen, Karen said you wanted to speak to me," said Norma. "What's on your mind?"

Sheriff Anderson was sitting in the dining room, he turned more serious than the relaxed form he had held when Norma entered the room. "Norma, thanks for helping Eleanor," said the sheriff. "How is she?"

"She's strong, really strong," replied Norma. "And now she's even more focused on finding out what's in the last tube. She said it's time we get down to the work of solving this mystery. I think she wants the Sinergy to pay dearly for taking Edgar from the lives of his friends."

"Awesome!" said Axel. "I was worried about her but it sounds like she's already making plans to strike back." He had come into the room just as Norma began speaking.

"Yes, that is great news. I'm glad to hear Eleanor is doing well but we have to act fast on a couple of key issues. Has she said anything about us leaving?" asked the sheriff. "We have to quickly figure out what we're going to say to people when they stop by and ask about us. We really are strangers to this town, and certainly to this home. It could cause some suspicion if we're not careful. Oh, and Axel, how's the situation down stairs?"

"Just as we left it. Not a thing was stirred or shaken!" he replied. "I'm going back down if you don't need me up here."

"That's fine. Thanks," said the sheriff. "So, then, Norma, any thoughts on us staying here?"

"Well," Norma began, "Edgar dying is going to bring extra attention to the manor for a few days, and we're all trying to stay under the radar. I don't know what to say if someone asks why I'm staying here, or how I know Eleanor. I'll go up right now with Katrina and we'll speak with her. "

"Thanks, Norma," Sheriff Anderson said. "We need a pulse on how she feels about all of this, ASAP. Also, ask her when she'll want to meet as a group."

"I've been in a similar situation," said Stanley. He was sitting at the dining room table, munching on some kind of deep fried drop of deliciousness the housekeeping staff had prepared while handing out candy to the steady stream of trick-or-treaters. "We may be over thinking this, Sheriff. Logically we can say that you are here on business with Robert, the deputy and the biologist. Norma is visiting a town she came to often as a child, and Roxie, Marcus and Axel are here working with Eleanor on a research project. Kevin and Karen simply stopped by to share the news of their engagement. I think that covers everyone."

"Well played, Stanley," said Kevin. "I was thinking the same thing. Let's just keep it simple." He caught the conversation on his way to the kitchen.

"Alright, then, let's do just that. Keep it simple!" added the sheriff. "But first we need to make sure Eleanor is still on board with this; otherwise it's back to the drawing board. Let's wait for Norma to return and then we can have a group session. The house is clear of visitors, at least for a while."

As soon as he said it, of course, the wave began. The doorbell rang and there stood the local news channel, looking for a sound bite and some video footage. Once it was announced by Stanley that the media had arrived, Sheriff Anderson jumped to action and was able to expertly rid the manor of the camera crew and reporter. He gave them a statement that in the end they were so bored with, the video never showed up on TV. The only mention was Edgar's obituary in the local paper that appeared almost a week later.

After the reporter left, there was a mixed collection of visitors stopping by, mainly neighbors and friends that had heard the news about Edgar. There was a flurry of activity which included a visit from one of Eleanor's children, Paul. He had heard the news from Katrina and came by after work. It would be a short stay, but he would be back the next day with his siblings to help their mother.

It was understood that people who knew Edgar, and friends of Eleanor, would need to reach out and offer their condolences. It wasn't long until Eleanor herself was in the living room, greeting friends and looking better by the hour. She had stayed in her room for just under two hours, and suddenly sat up for one last cry. She then brushed back her hair, went into her bathroom, washed her face, put on a touch of make up and headed downstairs. Not surprised by her quick bounce back, the house staff and The Voyageurs welcomed her with warm hugs. They knew she would help to lead the charge of getting back on track with their mission.

It was nearly 9:00 pm when the parade of costumed kids had ended and the house was suddenly void of visitors. The members were asked to move downstairs to quickly gather for a short meeting. A few more visitors would straggle by, they were sure of it, so they had to take advantage of this time with Eleanor. Katrina and the other two house staff, Abby and Cassidy, remained upstairs.

"Death be damned!" Eleanor began once the group was in place. "We are going to get to the bottom of this and make sure no one else is ever hurt again!"

"We all feel the same way, Eleanor," said Robert. "You deserve to be angry, so go ahead and be angry for a while. We'll watch out for you and keep things under control. When you're ready to move ahead, that's when we'll continue."

"I'm ready now, Robert." Eleanor stood up and addressed The Voyageurs. "I've been through some tough times in my life. Not too many these past twenty years, but I know how to get back up after being knocked down. Don't let this little old lady body fool you, I've got a nasty side that's just been primed for some action." Eleanor walked over to Roxie, sat down by her side and took her right hand. "Roxie, my kids are about your age, you know. Oh, I guess a few years older - you seem so mature for your age. Paul was intimidated by the whole thing tonight, but you'll meet them properly tomorrow. The thing is, I'd fight to my death for them, as I would for you," and then she looked around the room, "and for all of you. You are my new family, the ones I will be with for what may be many years of battle against an enemy I have unknowingly been researching for some time. The past few hours I've been thinking about so many aspects of my life and I finally realized, we are in a war and even though we just lost a soldier I cared about deeply, the battle continues."

"Oh, Eleanor," Roxie said to her, "I'm so sorry for you, for Edgar." She wiped the tears from her cheeks as Eleanor began speaking again.

"Thank you, dear. I know you all feel terrible about Edgar, but we can't let his death slow us down. And so, I'm going to say to each of you, stay! Stay here as long as you can," Eleanor offered. "We are tied together by a bond that transcends normal life, and I feel blessed that you have come into my life. I'll grieve for Edgar, of course, but I will not let the Sinergy gain any advantage whatsoever because of it. Together we will find a way to beat back the evil that is the Sinergy!"

"Eleanor, you are amazing!" said Stanley. "I believe you, and I'm right with you!"

"What about your family?" asked Norma. "What kind of questions are they going to be asking about us?"

"Well, now, we do need a plan, and I am going to leave that up to you to figure out," she replied. "Provide me with an outline so when my children will check up on me I'll be able to manage them."

"That should help get the focus off Hamsteen Manor rather quickly," suggested Stanley.

"The focus will be on Eleanor," said Karen. "She's the one person most affected by Edgar's death. Not to sound too detached, but if she can deflect questions and move the process along this should blow over pretty quickly. Not that you and the staff can't take more time to grieve, Eleanor. Wow, does that sound as emotionless to hear as it did to say?"

"You've got yourself a real Florence Nightingale, there, Kevin," joked Axel.

"Oh, come now, she's right," Eleanor came to Karen's defense. "As soon as we pay our respects to Edgar I can get back to helping with our investigation. I don't plan on taking a back seat for too long. I now see a much bigger picture of my life and of my purpose for being here. Edgar was a very special blessing in our lives, but I have many things that call me to action, and I must answer each one with as much vitality and passion as I possibly can."

"If I hear you right, Eleanor, then we have the green light to continue our work here?" asked the sheriff.

"Yes, of course," she replied. "Once Edgar has been laid to rest I'll be back, full-time."

"Until then," added Robert, "we lay low and keep out of sight as much as possible. I have a feeling our work downstairs will keep us occupied for some time. Anything we need to do will most likely take us off the property, so around here we should try to be invisible."

"It's getting pretty late, and it's been a long day. I think some of us should get back upstairs," suggested Marcus. "Axel and I can show Sheriff Anderson, Deputy Stevens and Reynolds what we have uncovered so far. Once we secure downstairs we'll come up and then we should have a planning session, maybe in one of the large bedrooms, so we can hit the day hard from the start tomorrow."

"You always did like the late nights, Marcus," said Kevin.

"Yeah, but he's a bear the next morning," offered Roxie.

"Oh really?" asked Karen. "And pray tell how you would know that?"

Roxie just blushed and Marcus didn't say a word. Thankfully Sheriff Anderson came to their aid.

"Well, then, let's take Marcus' suggestion and send everyone back upstairs. We don't want Katrina and the staff alone too long. We can take care of things down here, as Marcus said, while everyone gets a bite to eat. Eleanor, any suggestion on the best room to use for a group meeting?"

"Yes, actually, the last room over the garage is pretty large," Eleanor answered.

"Fine by me," replied the sheriff. "Okay, we'll meet in the last room over the garage in, what, forty-five minutes? Norma, if you can be our angel watching over Eleanor for tonight, please stay with her if someone comes to visit at our meeting time. Best that she has one of our members with her at all times."

"My pleasure, Glen," answered Norma.

"One last thing," said the sheriff. "Tomorrow I'll fill you all in on what happened on my way back to Havenswood Valley. As you can tell, the Sinergy has stepped up their game. We need to think about keeping everyone safe, so when we meet tonight let's discuss how Hamsteen Manor will function as our headquarters. The attack last week that kept them on the perimeter and the fact the Sinergy only looked inside the house today tells me there is something about this great home that keeps them from entering the structure. For now, I feel safe here, but part of our discussion will need to center on protecting this building, and each other. Be forewarned, if any one of you go off alone and get yourself killed, I'm going to be awfully mad at you!"

CHAPTER
34

"Eleanor is talking with her last visitor of the night," reported Roxie. "She and Norma will be up in a few minutes, and then Katrina will tell anyone else that calls or stops by that Eleanor is resting and will try her best to greet them tomorrow afternoon."

"Thank you, Roxie," Sheriff Anderson said. "Okay, then, let's get started. Robert, I'd like you to make sure Norma and Eleanor are updated on anything we go over tonight. Now, for everyone, as the first step in our buddy system, I have already asked Norma to stay with Eleanor. Not only for Eleanor's sake, but also to make sure someone is near Norma. From here on out, any time we are outside the manor we need to travel in pairs, at the very least. Inside the manor, well, it seems from the two times we've had incidents that we have some kind of protection from the Sinergy, but we shouldn't take it for granted. Let someone know where you are at all times, and don't feel bad about knocking on a bathroom or bedroom door to ask if everything's okay. As with any situation that involves a potential attack, we want to error on the side of caution."

"Sheriff," asked Karen, "are we going to have someone stand guard during the night?"

"That's a very good question," he replied, "and one that I will leave up to the group for discussion during our meeting. I jotted down some notes. Here's what I'd like to cover, but feel free to add or ask questions about any subject. Main topics I feel we need to talk about are the parchments, security and Eleanor. If we were to handle this like a police investigation, I would work on an overall plan of action, break the sub-topics up and assign them to individual officers."

"I don't see anything wrong with that approach," offered Marcus.

"Me either, Sheriff," agreed Robert. "Let's share the work load. I'd be willing to take on the upkeep around the place for now."

"Sorry we're late," said Norma, as she and Eleanor entered the room.

"Not to worry, ladies. I was just going over what I felt are the main topics we need to discuss. The parchments, security, sharing responsibilities, and you Eleanor. I had already talked a little about making sure you always have someone with you when venturing outside, but even indoors, it would be best to have a person with you at all times. I've asked Norma to be your shadow. Again, for everyone, please make sure someone always knows where you are, don't spend too much time alone, and don't be embarrassed to knock on a door to see how they're doing. This may seem like basic safety to some people, but if we take these precautions and turn them into habits, then we have a much better chance of everyone remaining safe and sound. Any questions on security?"

"Sheriff," said Axel. "As part of our security efforts, I'd like to offer to handle the communications room downstairs. I'm pretty good with computers and anything mechanical, so I feel I can catch on fast to the system Eleanor has set up. That is if it's okay with Eleanor."

"Good idea, Axel," he replied. "Just before you came into the room Robert offered to handle the chores around the manor. Eleanor, what do you think?"

"Yes, Sheriff, that would be a relief to me and since we are trying to stay in pairs, I think Axel should train in whoever he is paired up with. Someone will need to team up with Robert for the maintenance duties. The more we all know about how Hamsteen Manor functions, the better."

"Okay, then let's check those items off our list. Axel, you are now the security systems and communications guru and Robert, you're head groundskeeper!"

"Since Axel has offered to handle computer communications," said Karen, "I'd be glad to manage our paperwork, Secretary of The Voyageurs, if that's the way we want to word it. I'm good with keeping minutes of meetings, schedules, anything that needs to be written down that's in addition to what Eleanor notes as our scribe. I can also help

Eleanor and Norma with any follow up on arrangements that need to be made for Edgar."

"Thank you, Karen," replied the sheriff. "I was beginning to wonder how we were going to keep track of everything. Feel free to start now"

"Yes, yes, Karen can track it all!" applauded the group.

"Okay, then, about the parchments. Axel's taking care of the communications, so I'd like Marcus and Roxie to continue taking care of the tubes and their contents. Stanley, I'd like you and Reynolds to handle collaboration of the research. So, that leaves Kevin as Axel's first trainee, and since Karen is going to be managing information, the three of you can work together as a team. I'll team up with Robert for anything that has to do with the property, inside and outside. Eleanor, you and Norma will have to manage the staff and any visitors. Of course you can enlist any one of us to help at any time, especially for the next week or two. After that, it should simmer down and, depending on how many of us are able to stay around, Hamsteen Manor should be back to normal."

"What about Deputy Stevens?" asked Kevin.

"Deputy Stevens was brought down here for a quick trip to get updated on the situation; something that was never offered to me when I joined the Sheriff's Department," answered the sheriff. "I want Stevens to know as much as possible in case something happens to me or this goes on after I retire. I know he's going to be around the department a long time and he's the one deputy I want by my side when things go sour."

"Thank you, Sheriff," said the deputy. "That means a lot to me. I just want you all to know I'll do my best to make sure Sheriff Anderson gets everything he needs from the department when he's down here, and when he's back in Havenswood Valley I'll be right there with him to fight this enemy. I've seen it first hand, and like Mrs. Hamsteen said, I want to make sure it doesn't harm anyone else."

"That brings up another good point," said the sheriff. "Each of us will have our own schedules we can keep in regards to The Voyageurs, so let's do our best to make every hour we have together as productive as possible. Deputy Stevens and I will be driving back to Havenswood Valley day after tomorrow, and I know the rest of you are trying to figure out how you're going to squeeze The Voyageurs into your real life."

"Sheriff," Eleanor interrupted. "That's a very important point, I mean in regards to how each of us will be able to manage the role we have taken on as members of The Voyageurs. If you don't mind, I'd like to ask a favor before you begin to fill in your calendars. Tomorrow, after we have opened the final tube and had lunch, my favorite meal of the day, by the way, let's discuss how each of you, in detail, would like to be involved with The Voyageurs. More than a duty within the group, I would like to hear how each of you would imagine your involvement if you were unencumbered from any obligations outside of our project."

"You mean like not having to go to my job?" asked Axel.

"Not only your job, Axel, but anything you are regularly required to do," Eleanor replied.

"You're not asking us to cut off our friends and family, are you?" asked Roxie.

"Quite the opposite, Roxie," Eleanor answered. "I would imagine it more like having the freedom to come and go as you please. Visit whoever you want, whenever you want."

"I'm not sure I understand," said Karen. "Can you be more specific?"

"I hadn't planned on bringing this up yet, but Glen has a good point. Our time together is so valuable, and today's terrible attack on Edgar reinforces that it's all the more important that I take time to at least broach the subject with you," said Eleanor.

"Only if you are ready, Eleanor," said Robert. "If you've got something on your mind that you're not ready to discuss, then we can all wait until tomorrow. Don't worry about us, we're fine."

"Oh, my, I've misspoken and I bet you all think I've gone off the deep end tonight." Eleanor let out a nervous laugh, "Roxie, you must think I'm trying to start a cult here at Hamsteen Manor! It's been a long day, and I am feeling tired and out of sorts, so let me just say a little about my request, and then I'll have to ask Norma if she'll help me get settled into bed for the night."

"Are you sure, Eleanor?" asked Sheriff Anderson.

"Yes, I'm fine. Well, as I may have said while giving you all the tour," Eleanor began, "Joe and I were blessed with many fine years of his career doing well and our investments producing very high returns. What I'm trying to say here tonight is that if

Hamsteen Manor was able to provide each member of The Voyageurs with a place to stay and a stipend for your work on our project, would that be of interest to anyone? The details would have to be worked out, but as I've had the pleasure to get to know you all during a very remarkable situation, I'm confident, even on such short notice, that we were meant to see this through to the end, together."

"So what you're saying, if I understand correctly," said Kevin, "is that you would hire each of us to work on the project?"

"Not exactly hire, Kevin, it's more like sponsor," Eleanor replied. "Room and board, too. I'd like to speak with you individually tomorrow in regards to final details."

"That's very generous, Eleanor," said Stanley.

"Generous, I would agree, but since I do have the funding it's really about finding the best way to fight against the evil we now call the Sinergy." Eleanor continued, "I've been researching this subject for nearly five years, and now that we have a team assembled I'm going to be selfish and see if I can keep you all on board. If we work on this part-time from different locations, I'm afraid our efforts would be watered down and not as productive. This is the best way to make the most progress and may also be our safest option."

"Wow," said Marcus. "I know Roxie and Axel and I will want to get together and talk about it before we can answer. What do you think, guys," Marcus directed his question to Roxie and Axel, "get up for an early run and yak about this?"

"For sure, Marcus," said Axel. "I'm interested."

"Yeah," agreed Roxie. "I'm in."

"Well," said the sheriff, "thank you for the offers. Let's check with Karen to schedule your meetings with Eleanor about her proposal to sponsor the project. I say we call it a night and get an early start tomorrow morning. Meet for breakfast in the dining room around 8:00 am?"

Everyone agreed, and Sheriff Anderson then announced Deputy Stevens would be taking the night shift for guard duty. Nothing too serious, but just having someone up and awake throughout the night would help everyone rest easier. Reynolds offered to wake up at 3:00 am to check on Stevens, and the sheriff assured the deputy he would be up by 5:00 am to take over for a couple of hours.

"Try not to worry about sleeping, we'll always have someone awake for the next couple of nights," Sheriff Anderson said. "If no one else has any questions, let's adjourn and say goodnight. Thanks again, Eleanor."

"Just so you know, there is no time limit on my offer," Eleanor smiled.

"Okay, then, see you all in the morning," the sheriff said.

"Before we head to our rooms, I'd like to say something," said Robert. "Sorry, I know it's late and you're all ready for some sleep, but if you can wait just a couple more minutes I'd appreciate it."

"Of course, Robert," answered Eleanor. "What's on your mind?"

"Trying to figure out what exactly it was that took my son has been a long road, but there was always something that kept me moving forward. Hope. It's an amazing thing, hope is, and right now I can't believe how lucky I am to have all of you so darn interested in helping to find the answer. Sheriff Anderson and I have put in years of work on this, and well, I'm humbled to be a part of this group."

"We're humbled, too, Robert," interjected Marcus. "You've shown us strength by keeping the faith. You've never given up."

"That's true, Marcus, it's been a real battle and not once did I or Sheriff Anderson ever think of quitting. I guess what I'm trying to say is that I believe in all of you, in us, in The Voyageurs. I hope you will all seriously consider Eleanor's offer. It's going to be one heck of a journey, and I'm sure you'll never get another chance like this in your life."

Roxie plopped down in the soft, overstuffed chair that filled the bay window cubby as if it was made for her. The room Marcus and Axel were sharing at Hamsteen Manor was rather large, with plenty of room for the chair she was in, but it would be considered an extravagance of furniture in a normal sized bedroom. The hour was late and although Roxie was tired, the announcement from Eleanor had the three friends much too excited to sleep. They had talked previously about finding ways to spend more time working on the tubes and the mystery of Havenswood Valley, but Eleanor's opportunity had never entered their conversations. Roxie picked up the merino wool blanket that had been draped over the left arm of the chair and placed it on top her now curled up body. She was cozy, and ready to talk.

"Guys, are your heads spinning as much as mine?" she asked.

"This is so weird," replied Axel. "I know we talked about trying to find a way to work on this, but man, I can't believe Eleanor just put it out there like that."

"It's an amazing offer, a really amazing offer." Marcus was sitting against the headboard of the four-poster bed, pillows stacked behind him. It had been a long day, one he would never forget, but right now his future was forming and the three of them had to hash out a plan. "When I left my parents' home, they knew I was ready for whatever came at us, that I could be gone for a while. If we stay here The Voyageurs have a headquarters to operate from all day, every day."

"For me, I'd need to know Eleanor's terms and how long she would want us to work on this together," said Roxie. "I think she's very serious, and even though we've just recently met her, she's earned my trust. You two probably feel the same way, like we've know her forever, as if she were a member of our family.

If we all agree with her guidelines, let's do this. My apartment, my job, I can find new ones after this is over, no sweat."

"Give me time to put my stuff in storage and I'm ready," confirmed Axel. "This is a perfect time in my life to do this, and besides, I wouldn't want to be on my own until this evil is stopped. I'd be too freaked out to be alone anyway!"

"Okay," said Marcus. "I'm in, too."

Kevin and Karen had the room next to Roxie, and had seen her walk past her door to follow Marcus and Axel into their room after the meeting had broken up. They thought about joining them, but felt it better to discuss the offer on their own. Their recent engagement had their heads already filled with plans, and Eleanor's offer was enough to cause an overload. Karen was readying herself for bed, taking a few minutes in the quaint bathroom off of their bedroom to freshen up, while Kevin was lighting a small fire in the stone fireplace. It was a perfect bed and breakfast room, very intimate and perfect for the two lovebirds.

"Kevin, I know you're thinking about Eleanor's comments," said Karen. "What do you think we should do?"

"Well, I think it's mostly about you, not that I want to duck the responsibility of the decision," he answered.

"That sounds like a dodge to me," Karen laughed.

"Yeah, it does, doesn't it? Sorry. It's just that you're more set in your career than I am, and even though we talked about you moving out here, I just figured it would be me moving out to Arizona."

"Me, too. But after what happened at the cabin, and then out in the desert when you came to visit, and now Edgar. I don't know, Kevin, I'm worried about being on our own. I feel safer with the group, and I really want to help solve this mystery. I can always find a job later, but there's no chance I'd ever be able to do this again."

"That's definitely true," he replied. The fire was set, Karen was now comfortably beneath the quilts and covers, Kevin nearly ready to join her. "I'd like to figure the Sinergy out and kick its butt. I can't say I'm not scared about being pulled in again, but on the other hand, like you said, I also feel safer being with everyone else. I think we listen to Eleanor's offer and if it's reasonable, we say yes."

"Oh, I'm fine with that," Karen said. Kevin was now in bed with her and she looked into his eyes. "It's just that, well, I'm scared, Kevin. But being with you, I feel safe and I know we'll be alright if we stick together."

"We will, Karen, we'll be alright for a long, long time."

Sheriff Anderson, like all good sheriffs are wont to do, took mental notes of everyone's sleeping arrangements. The trio and Stanley were upstairs, Deputy Stevens and Reynolds ended up taking the night watch together, Katrina and Norma were bunking in with Eleanor. He and Robert had rooms next to each other. The other two house staff had already left and would return early the next morning, which really wasn't too many hours away. Feeling satisfied things were settling in, the sheriff and Robert had a few minutes to talk before they each hit the rack.

"You know, Robert," the sheriff began, "I think those kids are going to be all ears to Eleanor's plans tomorrow, but I don't know about anyone else. There's no way I can spend much more time down here. Norma, either, if she wants to keep her business going. I doubt you'll take anything Eleanor offers, other than room and board here at the manor."

"Well, you're right about me. I don't need anything from Eleanor, but like you say, if we begin to find clues and get some direction on what to do, yes, I could spend time here. Norma, she'd have to find a store manager she could trust, or move the store down here. She's already seen a few spots to check into for a second location, so she's thinking about it. As far as Marcus, Roxie and Axel, I'm just as interested in hearing their plans as I am Eleanor's. Those three are pretty sharp, I'd love to see them be able to hang around a while. Kevin and Karen, too."

"I don't know how it happened, but we make a darn good group. Can you remember how long we've been working on this? And now, it seems like things are happening so fast we can't keep up." Sheriff Anderson walked over to the large window that faced west and looked out to the city of Prairie Falls and the lights that dotted Main Street. "I really like it here, Robert. It's like an updated version of Havenswood Valley. I get a good feeling about Eleanor, our whole group, and even though that evil took a life today, I know we're going to figure a way to stop it. The momentum is on our side now. If the Sinergy is coming after us it means we've got something very valuable. Something that we desperately need to figure out how to use against it."

"True, Glen, all of what you say I agree with." Robert said. "We beat our heads against the wall for so many years, and now, in a matter of weeks we've learned more than everything else combined. It's a lot to take in, but it's also got me primed to finish this thing off. I ain't gettin' any younger, so we best be making hay while the sun shines. Let's hope this group we have is the answer to my prayers. Lord knows I've said enough of them over the years."

"Amen to that, Robert," replied Sheriff Anderson. "Amen to that!"

Stanley made his way into the kitchen, well ahead of the scheduled 8:00 am meeting time. Katrina, Cassidy and Abby had obviously been hard at work for some time. The counters were full of everything from mixing bowls scraped nearly clean of their batter to serving size cups of fresh cut fruit. The center island was loaded with the next batch of breads and muffins ready to be baked and the blenders were ready to turn out a few pitchers of smoothies. Three tall glasses, slightly filled, sat near the pitcher of filtered water. A telltale sign the runners had already been through here on their way out for an early morning run.

"Good morning, Katrina, anything I can do to help?"

She looked at Stanley and smiled, as if this were just another normal day at work, no stress, just a calm focus that gave you the confidence everything was moving along like clockwork. "Good morning to you, Stanley. Well, there might be a thing or two you can help with." She gave Stanley a wink.

He began his assignments, and as other members of The Voyageurs entered the kitchen area Katrina asked if they would help Stanley. As the tasks were finished she added new ones to the list. Katrina knew the day's schedule for The Voyageurs would soon have the group downstairs and out of touch for most of the morning, so having them available to help her get the manor in order was an opportunity she was not going to let slip by. As the senior staff member, Katrina was in the best position to delegate the daily chores. At first it seemed odd to Katrina that everyone was up so early, and then she realized these new guests all had the same idea, that it was time to pitch in and keep Hamsteen Manor as close to normal as possible. Eleanor's children and who knows how many friends would be stopping by over the next few days and the members of The Voyageurs wanted to do everything they could to help. Katrina felt a connection with them she didn't think would mesh so quickly. Brought together by a strange evil, the entire group of guests and staff appeared to have a bond that had been many years in the making. There was a natural feeling to this kinship that gave Katrina comfort knowing Eleanor was in good hands.

"Katrina, you're always in such a good mood," said Karen as she was pulling some placemats from a drawer. "It's so easy to be around you."

"That's interesting," she replied without skipping a beat, "I was just thinking the same thing about you." They laughed together as Karen headed out to the dining room table.

Slightly after 8:00 am, The Voyageurs were having breakfast. It was going to be a full day and a hearty meal first thing in the morning was a foolproof way to get started on the right foot. They talked about the previous day's event, and although there were still heavy hearts over Edgar's death they felt a renewed spark in their goal to find answers to the evil. Edgar had joined a list of who knows how many others before him that had died at the hands of this unknown killer, and The Voyageurs were inspired like any other team with a fallen member, they wanted retribution!

The phone had only rung a few times, so far, each one easily handled by Katrina. One call was from the funeral home wanting to set up an appointment, another from the church making the same request. Eleanor's son, David, had called to say he would arrive around 10:00 am. He added that he had spoken with his brother, Paul, and sister, Tessa, and they would be there late in the afternoon. Katrina relayed the information to Eleanor.

"Okay, I should be able to spend a little time with the group this morning," announced Eleanor. "I plan to be downstairs until 10:00 am or so, and then back up to the main level to attend to arrangements for the rest of the morning. I will be ready to speak with each of you after lunch, if you can break away from your research."

"Well, then, let's take ten minutes and we'll meet right back here and head to the basement," Sheriff Anderson said. "I got up a little early to give Deputy Stevens a chance to grab some sleep. I'm sure you're ready for a full day, right deputy?"

"Yes, sir," he replied. "Rested and recharged!"

"That's the spirit," said the sheriff. "Just so you all know, Deputy Stevens will be on the main level at all times today. Katrina, if you can please teach him the process of contacting us downstairs I'd appreciate it. Everyone, see you right back here in ten!"

Katrina spoke as the sheriff headed to his room. "Yes, Sheriff, of course. And please, leave everything on the table. We'll take care of the clean up," she announced. "Thank you all for your help this morning and good luck today!"

There was a round of return thank yous right back to Katrina and the staff for a wonderful meal. It was a simpler time being in Hamsteen Manor, even with evil in their midst they felt secure. Everywhere they had been there was a chance the Sinergy could strike, even as far away as Arizona. And while they did not take feeling safe for granted, especially with the first attack and then Edgar's murder, it was calming to work, eat and sleep within the walls of their new headquarters.

Eleven minutes later the group was getting ready to head downstairs to the secret room. "Picture time!" exclaimed Katrina, coming around the corner from the dining room, digital camera in her hand. "Eleanor asked me to take some group photographs this morning."

"Oh, that's right," said Eleanor, "I hope you all don't mind."

"It's a great idea!" answered Karen.

"Do we have to include Axel?" Norma joked.

"Love you too, Norma," he replied.

"C'mon, Axel, you can stand next to Sheriff Anderson," added Roxie. "You're used to getting your photo with cops, aren't you?"

"So much love in the morning," Axel said, "I can't wait until dinner."

"After a day together," said Marcus, "we'll all have plenty of love for you, buddy."

"Feel you already," Axel replied.

They moved to the stairway that led upstairs, as it would provide tiers for the group to fit into a single photo frame. Katrina, after many years of experience at the manor, was a pro at arranging group shots and began to corral The Voyageurs into place. "Well, I've done this a few times before, so let me take a quick look and then I'll ask you to take your spot on the floor, first step or second step. Won't take but a couple of minutes then you can be off to your adventure." Katrina scanned the group and began to call out names and locations.

"Sheriff Anderson, please, if you wouldn't mind starting the first row on the floor, far left. My left, thank you, your right," directed Katrina.

"Marcus, will you please stand next to Sheriff Anderson," continued Katrina, "and Axel, next to Marcus. Thank you."

"Thank you. Now let's have Robert stand next to Axel," said Katrina. "That will be our first row."

"Row two, on the first step of the stairs, from your right to left," announced Katrina. "Mr. Reynolds, then Karen and Kevin, then Deputy Stevens. That's Reynolds, Karen, Kevin, Deputy."

"Alright, almost ready. On the second step let's have Roxie on your right just behind Mr. Reynolds, then Norma, Eleanor and Stanley on your left end. Yes, that's it, Roxie, Norma, Eleanor, Stanley. You are such a cooperative group!" laughed Katrina.

"Great looking group! Nice! Ok, let's hear a bright and happy 'Hamsteen' on three!" directed Katrina. "One, two, three!"

"Hamsteeeeeeen!"

The Voyageurs were now assembled in the main room behind the secret door in the basement, patiently waiting as the fourth and final tube was about to be opened. With two parchments and a unique stone already given up by the first three tubes, they were beyond excited to find out the contents of tube number four.

"Three down, one to go," said Karen.

"Let's do this!" added Axel.

"Marcus, will you and Kevin open up the last tube?" asked Sheriff Anderson.

"Of course," answered Marcus. "Ready, Kevin?"

"Oh yeah," he replied, "I'm all set."

Standing before the fourth table, Kevin and Marcus began to work the tube open. The Voyageurs knew as soon as its contents were laid upon the blue tablecloth they were free to begin working on the parchments.

"Now that we've been surprised with the contents of the last tube we opened," Roxie said excitedly to Karen, "I hope we get something else in this one, too."

"Me, too!" said Karen.

"Any bets on what's in this one?" Robert asked of the group.

"Not another parchment!" Axel guessed.

"Okay, here we go," announced Marcus. He held up the tube at a forty-five degree angle so Kevin could remove the end.

"You mean here we go again," replied Kevin as he looked into the open end of the tube. "There's the same kind of paper stuffed into the end, here, see?" He pulled it out and it was nearly identical to the wad in the previous tube. "And I see another string attached to a wooden plug, just like the last one."

"Awesome!" exclaimed Axel.

"Lucky guess," said Norma.

"Same maneuver as with the last one?" asked Marcus to Sheriff Anderson.

"Yep, no sense in getting sloppy," he replied.

Axel strung his belt through the string that was hanging from the end of the tube, just as he had done with tube number three. He steadied the tube as Marcus and Kevin lifted the belt. In one smooth motion they heard the same gasp for air once the plug began to move up to the open end, and the same slight scraping of wood against the inside of the tube.

"Here it comes," announced Kevin.

As the wooden block appeared, everyone saw the section below the wooden plug was nearly identical to the last tube, more old paper appearing to be wrapped around something.

"Looks like we get another prize at the bottom of the tube," said Robert.

"You ever see anything like this, Stanley?" asked Sheriff Anderson.

"Never," Stanley replied. "Never so lucky to have this many items to open, and no chance I'd have a group like this to work on it with."

"Don't be shy, gentlemen," said Eleanor, encouragingly, "I'd like to see what's under the wrapping."

"You heard the lady of the house," added Sheriff Anderson, "let's move this along!"

With gentle but firm handling, Marcus reached out and began pulling the paper away from the underside of the wooden plug. The paper was crumpled into halves, and as he began to pull the sections apart he pressed the paper onto the table. He was the first to see the contents. His eyes quickly widened and his jaw became slightly unhinged at what lay upon the paper.

"What is it?" asked Roxie.

"I'm not sure," Marcus answered.

Two or three pulls with his fingers and a few smoothing moves of his palms against the paper and the final pieces of the tube were exposed for everyone to see.

"Well, now, that's interesting," Norma observed.

"Thank goodness it's not a giant spider," said a relieved Karen, "that was my first thought, a giant, dead spider!"

"First glance," commented Stanley, "can bring different reactions. Someone may see a spider, others may see a weapon."

"Is it one thing or a strand?" asked Eleanor.

"Good question," Marcus replied, "I think it's a strand of many."

"Stanley," queried the sheriff, "any special precautions before we proceed?"

"I would be cautious as far as the strength of the strands, and any connections, clips or clasps," responded Stanley. "If I can take a closer look. Eleanor, do we have anything such as a pair of tweezers available?"

"Karen, if you'll step into the storage area with me we can look through the first-aid items," said Eleanor. "I'm sure we'll find a pair or two."

"Do you think those match the stone from the other tube, Stanley?" asked Robert.

"I think so," Stanley replied. "I'd just like to see how this bundle breaks down."

"Then by all means," Eleanor said, "see if these will do the trick." She handed Stanley two very nice sets of tweezers, one a regular size you'd find in most homes, the other about half again as long.

"These should do nicely, thank you," he said as he picked the longer one. "Okay, let's start by putting more light on this. Kevin, would you mind shining that flashlight at the top of the strand for me?"

Kevin grabbed the flashlight from one of the other tables and pointed it at the end of the strand near the wooden plug. Stanley was correct, it was a bundle of strands, and at the end near the plug each of the twenty strands had a small rectangular piece of metal that a string was run through to hold them together. Each strand was approximately eighteen inches in length, made of a lightweight material that could be anything from animal hair to plastic. The middle of each strand held a small stone, similar in color and clarity to the large stone found in the third tube. Stanley cut the string holding the strands to the wooden plug and pulled up on one of the ends. A single strand easily broke away from the bundle.

"Oh my word," exclaimed Roxie, "it's a necklace!"

"Yes, but I don't think this is any ordinary necklace, Roxie," replied Stanley.

"Not in the least," added Norma. "My mother would have called that a *manteau d'armure*, a coat of armor. She felt there were things in this world that helped protect you in certain situations. The trick was in finding out what item you needed at the right time!"

"Stanley, can you lay that one down so we can all take a closer look at it?" asked biologist Steven Reynolds.

"Of course, I'll set one down at each end so we won't crowd each other." Stanley placed one strand at each end of the fourth table. "As you can see, the end that was tied to the plug has a small rectangular metal piece on one end and a small curved piece of metal at the other end. Not a classic clasp, but it would be a way to make a loop and keep this around someone's neck." Stanley picked up one of the strands and showed how this would work. "Simple yet very reliable. The strands themselves seem to be made from a natural fiber, I just can't tell if it's plant or animal based. Whatever it is, there is no smell from it and it's in excellent condition."

"Really?" asked Kevin, "it looks like black string."

"Most animal parts have been used in jewelry for centuries," said Reynolds. "It's very common. I'm sure you've seen the bones and teeth of animals used in all sorts of ways. I'd guess these are made from a tendon that has been treated and cured in a way to keep it supple. Previous generations were masters at figuring out how to use what nature had to offer. We've become so dependent on science-based products it would probably take us years to replicate the process they followed to make these strands."

"What about the stone?" asked Karen. "Is it the same as the one from the other tube?"

"Yes, Karen," Stanley answered. "I'm very sure these are the same type of stone. Reynolds, would you agree?"

"My expertise is in animals and plants," he said, "but along the way I've done my fair share of geology studies. I would agree, though, that these stones are a match to the one from the other tube."

"They certainly are as beautiful as the stone," added Eleanor. "I sure hope they were made for a good use, I'd hate for something so pretty to be used in a negative way."

"Me, too, Eleanor," added Karen.

"How do they look to you, Norma?" asked Roxie. "You've got so many different pieces in your shop. Are these fairly unique?"

"Oh, yes," Norma answered. "From the little metal pieces on the ends to the strands, whatever they are comprised of, to the stones in the center, these pieces are fantastic. And they look new, really, as if I had just ordered them from one of my suppliers."

"They may look new, but I can assure you these are very old, a hundred, maybe two hundred years, at least," Stanley said.

"Wow!" exclaimed Kevin.

"Dang!" added Axel, "this is so cool!"

"Yes, Axel, this is very cool," agreed Stanley.

"Alright, then, I think we need to talk about reviewing our plan of action." Sheriff Anderson addressed the group, "We were going to have each person take their own notes, however, with the unexpected items we've uncovered I'd like to suggest a new course for our research."

"You're the investigator, Glen, go ahead and let us know your thoughts," said Robert.

"If we can work on the two parchments together," the sheriff said, "and I mean as a focused group working on both of the actual parchments at once, I think we'll get more done, and at a faster pace."

"That's an excellent idea, Glen," said Eleanor. "Everyone, your thoughts?"

It was unanimous; a group review was the way they would proceed.

"I have a few things in the storage room I think we can use to hold up the parchments," offered Eleanor. "Axel, would you and Kevin be so kind as to rummage through the drawers on the far right side of the storage room? You should find some string and clips, I'm sure you'll figure out what would work best to display the parchments on the easels."

"On it!" said Axel as he and Kevin left the room.

The group set about rearranging the room. The two tables with the stone and necklaces were set to one side, and as Axel and Kevin returned with a collection of tapes, strings and clips, it was decided to put away two tables and use the easels to display the parchments. This allowed everyone to see each item as a group and still provide access for close inspections by individuals. When they were done it felt like a classroom ready for the professor to give a lecture. They decided Stanley should lead the review.

"I'll do my best to simulate my recent class formats," Stanley said as he walked to the parchments. "Everyone have their notepads ready? Oh, and I don't mean to write down what I say, but for your own thoughts or ideas."

"So there won't be a test afterwards?" asked Karen, to the amusement of the group.

"Not from me," Stanley chuckled, "but this whole project is one big test."

"Eleanor," said Marcus, "looks like Katrina wants to contact us, I see the green light just came on."

"So it has," she answered. "Oh my, look at the time! I bet David is here already. Axel, here I go again asking for your help. Will you and Kevin please go into the communications room and see if that's the case? In the meantime I'd like to explain my initial reaction to the parchment I first saw in the library."

"Of course, Mrs. Hamsteen," replied Axel. "I'll show Kevin how to work the system for next time."

"Thank you so much. Before I go upstairs, I know you've heard the story of how I came to join your group, and how I reacted to seeing the first parchment. Now it's true that I did recognize a few words, but only because I had been doing research for five years." Eleanor looked up at the parchment she was discussing. "Other than those few words, and mainly because they consist of words I had seen repeatedly, I don't understand anything else. I'm sorry if you felt I'd be able to do more, but we do have access to the internet down here and my suggestion would be to find a translation web site and begin plugging the words in. Unless someone happens to understand Norwegian, or whatever this language turns out to be."

"Eleanor," said Norma, "no one expected you to be able to read and translate these documents, we all figured it happened the same way you just described."

"I know I did," said Marcus. "Maybe for a few minutes I thought you had read some of it, but once we talked and you looked at it briefly again, Roxie, Axel and I knew it was going to take some time to decipher these."

"Well, if that's truly the case I'd feel much better," Eleanor replied. "I guess I put too much pressure on myself about this."

"You were right, Eleanor," exclaimed Axel as he walked back into the room. "Deputy Stevens was on the other end and said your son David is upstairs. He said to let you know it's just him, not his whole family."

"Thank you, Axel," she answered. "I'll be off, then, and I look forward to having time to talk with each of you later today. Good luck with the parchments!"

"See you soon, Eleanor!" said Karen. The others followed with good-byes of their own.

"She's upstairs and talking with David, a-ok!" said Kevin. He had stayed on the monitor with the deputy as Marcus handled the secret door duties for Eleanor's walk up to the main level.

"Okay, then, guess we need to take a vote on how to proceed with the parchments," suggested the sheriff.

"I like Eleanor's idea about using a translation web site," said Roxie.

"Me, too," added Marcus.

"Do they really work?" asked Robert.

"Let me suggest we try one," said Stanley. "The internet, as you can see, is the first means of research for our younger members. They grew up with it! For the rest of us, it's been more self discovery. It was an immense help before my trips overseas, and I did use translation sites. I think, for our initial go at this, it's a wise use of time."

"That's all the endorsement I need," said the sheriff. "Karen, let's have you and Kevin be the leads on this. I'm going to rely on you five, and Stanley, to set up a way for us all to help on this. It's old fashioned, but the more hands we have, the quicker the work gets done. You've got fifteen minutes to set it up, ready?"

"Sure, we can do that!" Karen replied.

Sheriff Anderson sat down with Norma, Robert and Stevens and let the rest of the group get started on their task. Delegating jobs to others, especially when they know more about the subject than you do, is the sign of a skilled leader. Sheriff Anderson knew they would come up with a process to streamline the research and get everyone involved. Their action plan took more time than they thought, about thirty minutes, but the sheriff knew it was going to be worth the wait. It was Kevin that announced they were ready to present their plan.

"Here's what we've come up with to translate the parchments," Kevin said. "This first stage is translation only. We won't stop to interpret these until both are done and posted on the tables. Sheriff, you, Robert and Norma will be reviewing the research of the dead and missing from our region that Eleanor has been working on. Her notebooks are down here, and since you three have been involved with this phenomenon the longest, we feel you've got the best chance of relating events to the Sinergy."

"I love research," said Norma.

"Great," replied Kevin, "and we know you three will find something that will help us. Now, regarding the translating; we've decided there are two ways to decipher the text on the parchments. First is to do as Eleanor suggested, use a translation program on-line. We just signed on for a paid program and Karen, Stanley and Reynolds will be physically typing in the text line by line and printing out the results."

"Sounds like a reasonable plan so far," said the sheriff.

"Good to hear. Now, for the second part," continued Kevin, "Axel, Marcus, Roxie and I will be working on translating the parchments using the scanner and a reader program. This may be a quicker way, but we have less opportunity to tweak the text. We'll mainly be using the scanner version as a back-up, although it might throw in a few words or sentences we will need to double-check against the typed-in version."

"Over all," interjected Karen, "we have two different data entry systems that should produce slightly different results. We will review and compare the two outcomes and if we need to we'll go back in and do another data entry round of any words or phrases we don't completely understand."

"To keep things moving along, we'd like each team to have a floater," Kevin added. "Someone to post the translations in the main room, and generally communicate with the other teams so we know each others status. Norma, Reynolds, and Marcus, if you would be your team rep?" They each nodded yes to Kevin. "Great, thanks. The three of you can relay updates and handle any requests, that way we're not interrupting entire teams. I'll work as the point person. Any questions you three can't resolve, come to me."

"For as little time as you had," said Robert, "you sure came up with a sharp plan!"

"Thank you," said Kevin. "It was a group effort."

"I agree with Robert," said Sheriff Anderson. "You've put together a well thought-out plan of action to reach our goal, congratulations! Let's move ahead under your direction and see how much we can accomplish in the next three hours. I'm sure that's enough time to make a dent before we break for lunch. Kevin, Karen, go ahead and get us started!"

"Before we get started," said Marcus, "we do have one question for Robert." Marcus took a couple of seconds before he continued, not sure how to ask, so he just went for it. "Robert, we're pretty sure you've been thinking about this since you found out about the tubes. Do you know where the table came from?"

It was a totally relevant question, and one that should have been asked as soon as the group had formed. Everyone suddenly felt like they had missed the biggest clue to the history of the tubes!

"I do hope I'm not speaking out of turn here," said Stanley, "but, really? This subject has not yet been discussed?"

"Nope, not a word," replied Robert.

"We're not trying to pry, Robert," Roxie said. "It's just something that we wondered about when we were first exploring the table, and honestly hadn't thought of it again until last night."

"It's true," added Axel. "We got so excited and caught up in everything we left the table question back at the cabin."

"I can understand that," replied the sheriff. "Our new officers often get rolling into a situation and forget the reason they got involved in the first place. Things progress and snowball."

"Well, Robert, do you want to let out the secret of the table, or should I?" asked Norma. "After the tubes were found, it's become a hot discussion topic between the three of us."

"Yep, and not too far from embarrassing if you must know," Robert said. "For us, that is, not you three."

"Sheriff, I'll keep it short, but you can fill in if I miss anything." Robert began his tale. "It was just last year and Norma and I were headed to the cabin to do some chores. Place was empty and I wanted to fix a few things and Norma wanted to come along. On the way I saw a car pulled over, looked like some city folk having engine trouble. Well, one thing led to another and we got their car running. Afterwards they stopped over at the cabin for lunch and we had a real pleasant visit."

"You made a real impression on them, Robert," added the sheriff. "I can say that because I stopped on the road for a few minutes to see if they needed help, but Robert was all they needed."

"They were a nice young couple, mid-thirties I'd say, and yes, they did like Robert," Norma recalled. "Up from the cities to visit, they said thanks and that was that. Or so we thought."

"I get a call a week later," said the sheriff, "and it's the same two people that Robert helped! Said they had something for him, but they'd like to surprise him and could I help arrange to meet at the cabin and let them in. Sure, I said, long as everything was on the up and up."

"Glen asked if I'd go along," said Norma. "Of course! I said."

"Well, you can figure the rest," Robert broke in, "I get a call from Sheriff Anderson that someone had broken in, that I needed to come out to the cabin. The couple had already left, but boy, was I in for a shock! Never had someone given me such a well crafted piece of furniture. If it had been smaller I would have taken it to my home in the city."

"Really glad you didn't," Axel said.

"So we've been trying to figure out a way to tell you all how we missed the clues on the table, and that we never took any contact information from the couple." admitted Norma.

"They not only drove away," said Sheriff Anderson, "they disappeared!"

"If we cut to the chase, then it appears these two are somehow connected to the tubes?" asked Stanley.

"No idea," Norma replied. "Yes, they certainly could be, and that would have been a very calculated undertaking. And very successful."

"Or just a couple returning the favor for the help you gave them, albeit in the form of an amazing gift," said Karen.

"Point is," said Sheriff Anderson, "we lost track of the table owners as potential help with all this. So, forgetting to ask about the table, well, we totally understand!"

"That's a lot to think about," said Marcus. "I know we'll talk more about the mystery couple, but for now I think we're all ready to move forward with the parchments!"

Marcus' direction was all they needed to get back to the job at hand. Kevin and Karen restated everyone's jobs and once they were all in place they gave a short overview of what was to be done. Each team had duties and each member was assigned a specific detail.

"We have no idea if this will take thirty minutes or the entire three hours, but the end result we want is good information. No shortcuts, no guesses," stated Kevin. "Let's dig in!"

As if they had been training to manage this workload for the past six months, the teams dove into action with the efficiency and professionalism of a world class operation. Each group flowed the information at hand through the chosen processes and, in what seemed like mere minutes, there were freshly printed documents being taped to the two stored tables, now on their ends like giant poster boards, in the main room. Having team reps was a huge key to keeping the operation running smoothly. They were busy from the start and spent most of their time running documents to the main room and checking status with the other team reps. Had there been more of anything to do, the basement area they were working in would have been too chaotic. This level of activity was perfect and everyone felt good to be working on something so important.

Roxie and Axel were in total sync as they maneuvered parchment number two through the scanner. Prints were made of the sections, and Marcus checked to make sure the entire parchment was being entered into the software program by Axel. Marcus would then take the printed paper and post it on a table, using it as a progress report for Kevin.

The scanning process was ahead of the typing process, as far as information being entered into the software program. While Karen was rolling through parchment number one as quickly as she could, it was apparent the other team would be waiting for her before they could scan the other parchment. It would remain to be seen which process was completed first since the software programs were going to run at opposite speeds. The scanning program would end up taking longer to translate than the typed-in program would, in regards to cranking out results.

Sheriff Anderson, Robert and Norma were doing their own scanning process of the notebooks Eleanor had been keeping. They found reading her information very interesting and were taking notes of their own. Every few minutes one of them would ask about a particular piece of information to see if either of the other two had heard about it. They didn't expect to get through it all in one sitting, so they had decided to scan through it fairly quickly the first time, compare notes and then after speaking with Eleanor, go through the sections they felt would most likely yield the strongest clues and connections to the Sinergy.

"Marcus, Norma, Stanley, can you all come in here for a minute?" Kevin asked. He was in the large room looking at the information that had been taped on the tables. Sheriff Anderson, Norma and Robert were sitting on the couch in the room viewing Eleanor's research.

"What's up, Kev?" asked Marcus.

"It's only been an hour and look at all the pages we've posted so far!" replied Kevin. "I think we're going to have these translations done in about a half hour."

"Me too," said Norma. "Everyone is so focused."

"Let's keep the pace up," Marcus said "As soon as we can, we'll roll right into reading what we've come up with."

"And as we discussed earlier, we'll have two readings of each one?" asked Stanley.

"Yes," answered Kevin. "We said we'd read the typed one first, then the scanned version. If the translation results follow what we think will happen, then we use the typed version as our lead document and the scanned version as the backup."

Kevin's predicted finishing time was nearly right on the mark. Forty-five minutes after he spoke with the team reps the entire group was in the main room, looking at the postings as if they were artistic displays in a museum.

"Well done, teams!" exclaimed Sheriff Anderson. "Very professional."

"Yes, indeed," agreed Stanley. "You all worked so hard, and performed so well together."

"This is awesome!" said Axel. "I'm still having a hard time believing this is all happening, but I wouldn't want to be doing anything else!"

"I wish my mother were still alive," said Norma. "She would have loved working on this. Maybe she did make a difference in some small way with some of her early research."

"I have a feeling she did," said Roxie. "Maybe we'll find out more when Eleanor goes through her research with us."

"Well, since we are all in agreement that we did a great job with the translations," said Kevin, "why don't we turn this back over to Stanley and he can lead us through the readings?"

"About time!" said Axel.

Everyone agreed with Axel, it was certainly time to read the parchments!

CHAPTER
38

"So we are all agreed," Stanley said with a focus that belied his fatigued state of being, "these are the final edits?"

"Yes!" the group answered formidably and in unison. Everyone was tired and more than a bit scrambled from the day's efforts, which in addition to all the project work included a quick lunch and a very short break. They had pushed through the initial work of translating the parchments, which turned out to be written in Danish, and began right away to tackle the grammar and structure of the text.

It was now early evening and The Voyageurs, excited, yet exhausted, had done so well they just wanted to be finished for the day. Eleanor had made her way back downstairs just a couple of hours ago and she, too, had put in a full day. After dealing with family, friends and follow up in regards to Edgar's death, she had finally returned to the group.

"As we are all agreed on the wording, with some editing due to Robert's son Michael's unfortunate experience being part of the first parchment," Stanley continued. "I'll read through the two final versions of the parchments, and we will use them, as is, to conduct our research on the Sinergy. We are also agreed that if we find a person that we feel should have an opportunity to read the parchments for reasons of improving our understanding of its contents, it will take a majority vote to allow this to happen. Agreed?"

Another unanimous decision, "Agreed!" came the reply from The Voyageurs.

"Alright, then I'll begin," said Stanley. He looked around at the people in the room and realized while they had just moments before been tired and unfocused, The Voyageurs were very alert and attentive. Everyone was ready!

Stanley turned to the parchment and began reading. "Missing children were the first signs of misfortune in the village of

Havenswood Valley. Following next came the bodies of unknown travelers, found rotting in places less frequented, such as under bridges or within a thickened patch of wild brush. A chilling hysteria crept into the valley when area residents were the next victims, numbering to five within a year and four months time. Not until near seven months had passed without a death did the valley begin to settle. Death had won numerous battles in and around this small town and the invisible scars of heartache and anguish would take years to heal," read Stanley. He took a breath to relax and then continued reading.

"By chance we learned of these horrible events that had taken the soul of a small town in northern Minnesota and torn it to shreds. A member of our family was passing through and heard one tragic tale after another, spoken between two friends as they talked with each other about the history of the town's deadly accidents. After children and then adults went missing, the accidents began. Drownings, falls, suffocations, faulty wires, so many different ways in which people were dying. Then came the tales of murder, of a dangerous force hidden in the hills and forests that was able to kill a person without using any type of weapon." Stanley stopped before he read the next line. "Evil had settled in the valley and our family knew it was time to take action."

"As travelers, our duty is one of providing a solution for the local people to discover and implement said remedy on their own terms. You have made the discovery. Now it is your time to decide upon making a difference in not only the lives of those in your community, but in your own lives, your own hearts, your own souls."

"If you should choose to accept the challenge to eradicate the danger from your locale, be forewarned it will be a matter of life versus death, good versus evil and God versus Satan. You must be of sound mind and body, virtuous in your actions and faith-filled beyond reproach. Without these qualities, and more, you will fail in your quest."

"Do not squander time in pursuit of our family, for it is not relevant to know who we are or where it is we reside. We will answer only that you are not alone in dealing with such matters and yet you will be left to your own accord in how to master that which you are about to attempt. You are now entrusted with the privilege of clearing away the deadly atmosphere that cloaks your village. You should be concerned only with each other's safety and protection. The evil of which we write seeps into the world as if it were water from a natural spring. Be pleased that you should manage to stop a tributary; do not expect to destroy the Source. Follow that which we proscribe on the parchment that accompanies this one and the outcome you seek will be within your grasp. The teachings are from generations of experience, we hope you have not taken too long to find these. We cannot confirm you will remain unscathed, but for that reason alone do not turn back! You are strong enough to claim victory! May the Lord God watch over you and grant you the belief that your faith will be strong enough, your path will be clearly marked and your aim will be true." Stanley turned to the group, "That's the end of the first parchment."

"So, we're not crazy," said Robert. "This has been going on for a long, long time."

"Whoa," sighed Karen, "things sound a lot worse than when we were putting it together a sentence at a time."

"Oh yeah," agreed Axel, "this is big! Are we going to find these people and get their help? It sounds like these parchments aren't that old."

"I'm with Axel," said Kevin. "Are we going to track down the people who wrote these?"

"Sorry to disappoint you two, but I'm voting we do as the parchment suggests and just focus on the challenge," said Sheriff Anderson. "We still have another parchment to read and I suspect it's going to hold just as much, if not more, information."

"Guys, you know we can't go looking for them, there's too much to do," added Marcus. "Like Sheriff Anderson said, let's stick with the plan they are explaining. If it works I don't care who it was written by. If we fail, maybe then we can look into it."

"Let's at least get through the second parchment," suggested Norma, "before we start making new plans."

"You're right, Norma," said Eleanor. "We need to keep our focus on the parchments. Even though we all want to know who wrote these, like Glen said, we haven't even read the second parchment yet. Let's not succumb to quick decisions."

"I'm just overly excited. Sorry," said Axel, "but I really want to know who wrote these."

"I do too, Axel," replied Sheriff Anderson. "For now let's continue with the second reading, hmmm...sounds like I'm at Sunday mass...and after that we'll open things up for discussion. There's no shame in getting excited, I've learned over the years that if you're not fired up over a case then you shouldn't be on it. Just don't get caught up in your emotions and do something you'll regret later."

"I'll second that," said Reynolds. "Let's keep reading and go over everything afterwards."

"Amen!" said Robert. "Let the preacher, I mean teacher, continue!"

"Stanley," said the sheriff, "the floor is all yours."

"Thank you, Sheriff," said Stanley. "I know for most of you this is the first time you've ever done anything like this, and I certainly understand your excitement. Like Sheriff Anderson said, if you're not feeling your hearts pump faster when we open up a tube or read the final versions of the parchments, then I'd be worried about you. So, kudos to everyone for your high spirits and let's move on to the second parchment!"

Stanley began to read parchment number two. "Upon review of these documents, in your possession should be two parchments, one of history, this one of direction, one Sealing Stone, and twelve and eight Wearing Stones. Should you not have all of these items, continue searching the exact place you came upon this parchment and locate the other pieces. There is no need to continue unless both parchments and all stones are in your possession."

"Place a Wearing Stone around your neck as soon as possible. Once placed do not remove it. Ever. Should you have extra Wearing Stones you may find a craftsman to cut these jewels and place small pieces into rings or bracelets, using only gold settings. These smaller pieces will be helpful in protection, and will also serve as a sign to others, (yes, there are others), that you are in the service of killing evil spirits of the Source. You are to seal the entry point of the evil souls to put an end to the deaths that have taken so many from your region. Task one is to find the point of entry. Search where people have been killed, not found. It will be a place hidden and unlikely, yet within an uncomfortable closeness of where humans live. You will confirm the entry point with a match of the Sealing Stone you now possess, as it will fit over the opening."

"Before you can seal the opening, all evil spirits must be within their domain. Great care needs to be taken to assure none are left on the earthly side before it is sealed. You must know the whereabouts and capabilities of each evil spirit when you are ready. The Sealing Stone and the Wearing Stones will serve you as weapons to corral them into their hellish home. If a dark or grey evil spirit, these are dangerous but less so, is left behind, that is of little consequence, as it will likely perish into nothingness or exist as a simple ghost to haunt a lowly forest. However, take no action to seal the entry point if any spirit that is capable of taking on animal or human shape has not been counted as within the realm of their evil domain. These are the most deadly of all the spirits and they will resist your efforts foremost. You will be tested mightily when trying to snare these spirits, so much so that the weakest of you may fall. Hold fast to your will to stand victorious and do not succumb, for you have the tools to succeed in your quest to defeat the evil spirits. You must persevere!"

"Place the Sealing Stone with the gem facing into the opening. It will serve as a mirroring shield they cannot penetrate. Once you seal the entry point you must then bind it closed. Do this in such a manner that prevents flora, fauna, including man, any chance of discovery. Take great pains to erase the location from detection, yet do not disrupt the area nearby as to call for attention. The Sealing Stone will keep the evil spirits back, but you must be vigilant in watching for any sign of escape in the future. Once sealed does not mean forever sealed."

"That's the end of the second parchment," announced Stanley.

There was a moment of reflection keeping the room hushed. No one said a word, but their inner thoughts were running a mile a minute!

Marcus spoke first, "In case anyone is thinking of pulling out, don't feel bad. This adventure just turned itself up a few notches on the danger scale!"

"I'm going to have to think about this, Kevin," said Karen. "I know we came here to be a part of the solution, but I had no idea what was ahead, and I still don't know what's going to be asked of us. I hope you won't be disappointed with me if I change my mind."

"I'd never be, Karen, don't worry about that," Kevin replied. "We're all shell-shocked at the moment. It's alright to give yourself some time to absorb all this. If this really is a way to get at whatever has been doing all the killing, I want in and that doesn't mean you have to stay here, babe. I want you to feel safe, not threatened."

"My mother would have loved to be here with us," said Norma. "She lived for this kind of interaction with the other side and would be fighting toe to toe against them. I hope I can live up to her toughness!"

"I have to say, I'm glad to have this opportunity," Stanley said, "but it's turning out to be more research than I've ever done. This is going to be an incredible project to include in my resume!"

"Except no one is ever going to believe you," said Axel.

"Doesn't matter," added Robert. "The world's full of real stuff people don't believe. I'm glad to be here and I'm damn ready to find their gateway. I'd like to plug those bastards up so tight they'll die out completely."

"I'm usually finding ways to help species in nature live longer," said Reynolds. "This is going to be a switch for me, but I know all about invasive species, too, and I have no intention of letting this evil infiltrate our town any longer. It goes against my training, but this is going to be a species eradication that I'm going to savor!"

"Sheriff, now I can see why it's taken so long to figure things out. This is not only a deadly but also an extremely smart enemy. I know we've been in danger from the first weekend we spent at the cabin, but after hearing the full content of the parchments it seems very real. What are we going to do now?" asked Roxie.

"You know, Roxie, I have no clear idea of our next step, yet," replied Sheriff Anderson. "I'm sure we'll figure it out, but right now everyone's first priority is making the right decision about their own situation. No one fully understood what they were getting into before tonight, so all previous commitments are off. We're starting The Voyageurs from scratch and I don't need your answers about staying involved until at least tomorrow morning, after you've had a chance to sleep on it. Eleanor, would you mind sending word to Katrina that we'll be upstairs soon and ready for supper? Let's get some food in us and maybe a beer or glass of wine. We'll all feel more relaxed at dinner and we can continue our discussion then. Sound reasonable?"

"I always think better during a meal," said Robert. "Another great idea you have there, Glen. Let's go eat!"

"Yeah, I'm starved," added Marcus, "and I enjoy a good discussion at dinner! Like talking about the fact that these parchments can't really be very old if they were written after so much had happened."

"That's a good point, Marcus," said Stanley. "Unless there have been more deaths and missing persons than we know about, even with all of the research that's been done by members of this group that would be an amazing list. The parchments and paper were made to age well in case it was a long time before they were found."

"We were surprised at the excellent condition everything was in," added Reynolds.

"Yes, and we all figured they had been prepared and stored many years ago," said Eleanor. "We must take a second look at all the evidence. Oh, we have lots of work ahead of us!"

"Let's get some dinner and see where the conversation leads," said Marcus. "Sheriff Anderson is on the right track; we're going to have to sleep on these decisions, for sure."

"You're right, Marcus," Karen replied. "I really need some time to think about everything. Don't worry, I'll still be here in the morning, I'm only a seven out of ten on the how-scared-are-you scale."

"Perfectly natural," said Norma. "You should have seen me during some of the things my mother took me to! Oh, my, those were some pretty scary days, but I made it through and I know all of us will, too."

"We certainly will," added Eleanor. "When I think about Robert's family and all the others that have had their lives taken from them, I feel we have only one answer for this challenge."

"Yes!" Axel nearly shouted in response. As everyone rose to go upstairs and eat, he continued his battle cry. "Yes, The Voyageurs are going to seal the entry point and kick some evil Sinergy butt!"

"I've got to say, Eleanor," Robert raved, "your staff has put together one of the best tasting stews I've ever had, and I've had many. Not sure what all they put in here, but it's a recipe worth a few blue ribbons."

"This dinner is another amazing Hamsteen Manor meal," added Roxie. "I can't remember having so many great homemade foods without it being a holiday!"

"The breads, are my favorite!" Axel proudly announced. "Awesome baked breads, if I had to pick one food I'd need to survive, it would be bread!"

"I was very lucky to have met Katrina years ago, by chance!" said Eleanor. "She was working in a restaurant in town and after she catered an event here I followed up with the owner of the company and asked if she'd mind if I hired Katrina for my own home. She was delighted for her and Katrina and I have since become good friends. She's hired her own staff for the manor, so please make sure to thank them for all the meals, it's really her skills and leadership that have made Hamsteen Manor famous for the food at our gatherings."

"You should sell the bread to local bakeries," suggested Kevin. "Katrina's Hamsteen Manor Baked Goods has a nice ring to it."

"Not a bad idea, Kevin," said Eleanor. "I'll have to ask Katrina about that. Since we ran out of time to meet, I'd like to follow up on my comments about supporting The Voyageurs. Today's reading opened up our eyes as to what lies ahead, and as Marcus said earlier, there's no reason to feel anything but completely at peace if you reconsider and say goodbye to The Voyageurs. However, for those staying on board, I need to know by sometime tomorrow what your overall commitment to The Voyageurs will be. During the research on the missing and dead that got me started on all this, I sometimes wondered what it would be like to have a team of investigators to work with instead of being on my own. I've imagined the situation we are now in many times before, so I feel like I'm ready to move fairly fast with my offers. First, I'd like to cover any group expenses we may incur, and if anyone has a special project for the cause I'd be glad to look at that, too. Anything that gets a majority of our groups' approval , I'm good for."

"Wow, Eleanor, that is so generous!" said Roxie.

"Thank you, Roxie," she replied. "Now for the details! I have two handfuls of envelopes with me, one envelope for each of you that want to remain with The Voyageurs. I understand that in your heart each of you would like to throw caution to the wind and come on board full time in our quest to stop the evil spirits, but I also know some of you have jobs and family that keep you from doing so. The fun part for me is that I have two options for each of you to choose from. Just let me know full time or part time and I'll hand you an envelope with my offer. Each monetary amount is exactly the same for everyone, as is the duration of my sponsorship, five years. I did try and add a personal incentive for each of you, something that in the short time I've come to know you I hope will show my intent on keeping us all connected. Thank you all for letting me indulge in my chance to share my prosperity and sincerity. I do hope this helps us succeed."

"I don't know what to say, Eleanor," Robert said in a hushed tone. "Sheriff Anderson and I have been at this for so long but now, as The Voyageurs, it seems like a fresh start. Everyone is committed to figuring out a way to defeat this deadly enemy and helping those that have lost friends and family. I'm humbled by each person here. Listening to you talk about supporting our efforts so we can fight without worry, well, I'm at a loss for words except to say thank you from the bottom of my heart."

"Me, too, Eleanor," added Marcus. "My parents have been dealing with my strange gift of being able to foresee things since I was three years old. My friends know that sometimes I've gone off the deep end in a situation, but always for reasons that are justified afterwards. The people closest to me have trusted my decisions in some pretty tight situations, and here you are doing the same thing, adding trust to a whole group of people. I am so going full-time with this, no matter what's in the envelope, because I know you'll be here for us through thick and thin. Count me in!"

"Thank you, Marcus, and Robert," replied Eleanor. "Those are very kind words. I'm honored to be a part of our new family."

"Aw, what the hay," said Axel. "I don't need to open the envelope either, I'm full-time, too. Someone's got to save Marcus once in a while."

"And what am I, chopped liver, again?" asked Roxie. "No way you two are going to lose me. I'm full-time, Eleanor. These guys would be so lost without me."

"Kevin and Karen," said Sheriff Anderson, "we soaked up a lot of information today, there's no need to rush into this. I think it's a good idea if you two wait until morning."

"Thanks, Sheriff," replied Kevin. "We think so, too. It's been a crazy week for us and there's a lot to consider."

"Stanley, same for you," added the sheriff. "I know you realize how important all of this work is and how much is yet to be done. I appreciate you taking time to figure out how much you can commit to the project."

"I would love to be a part of this for as much time as I can squeeze in between my book and school work. I'm stretched thin these days however, something like this doesn't come along but once in a lifetime. I'll just need to creatively explain my way out of a few weeks of chapter deadlines and class assignments. Shouldn't be too difficult."

"Well, then, let's look at updating our plan," said Sheriff Anderson. "Karen, would you mind keeping notes tonight?"

"Got it covered, Sheriff!" she replied, pen and paper in hand.

"Thanks. So, as we heard today," the sheriff continued, "we have a few major topics to consider and I'd like to headline them to see what areas we need to cover. Let's run them down, in no particular order, and if anyone has something to add, please jump in, this is an open forum. First, we believe the parchments are not as old as we thought. Second, the authors are part of a family that has already dealt with this type of situation."

"And they are probably still alive!" Axel interjected.

"Yes, Axel, I think we would all agree to that point, and no, we are still not going to track them down, but good try," the sheriff said with a smile. "Okay, where was I? Oh, yes, third, there are different levels of evil spirits and they are all dangerous, some more so than others. Fourth, we have some serious work ahead of us tracking and trapping the evil spirits, and fifth, people have been dying for a long time and we have no reason to expect it to stop, unless we're successful at closing the entry, whatever that turns out to be. Anyone want to add to the list?"

"How about the part that said some of us won't survive?" Karen answered dryly.

"Or that we have to find a secret hole, which is apparently about the size of a sub sandwich, somewhere in or around Havenswood Valley," said Axel.

"Actually, Axel," said Reynolds, "I'm looking forward to that search. It's going to be like trying to find a nearly extinct species, which may be easier than you think."

"I'm interested in finding out more about the stones," said Marcus. "Over the years there have been certain things or places that seem to impact my being able to pick up what is going to happen. If these stones are a way to bring out the evil spirits and even help get them back into their domain, that's a weapon I want to understand better."

"Very good points, especially the survival one, Karen," said the sheriff. "We do need to come to grips with the fact that this is an enemy that is ready to kill any place, any day, any time."

"I brought up the Wearing Stones," announced Norma. "The parchment said we should start wearing them at once, so here we go, everyone, please take one and put it on."

"I saw a few pieces like these during my last trip to Europe," said Stanley. "For centuries people have believed in the power of stones. Some call them crystals, or gems, jewels or other terms, but they are all earthly objects that are used to fight off evil or bring positive energy. I have no problem wearing one and I'm very interested to see how they work around the evil spirits."

"I'm going to put mine on a different chain," said Roxie. "That's okay, right Stanley? I remember you reading that on the second parchment."

"Yes, I do recall that," he answered.

"Sheriff," Eleanor began to ask, "can we discuss the timing of our next steps? I think it's important we outline what the next few weeks are going to look like for everyone. Personally, I don't see myself travelling, especially over the next ten days or so, but I know everyone needs to start making plans."

"You're reading my mind, Eleanor," Sheriff Anderson replied. "Since Hamsteen Manor has become our southern headquarters, this will be home for those of you not travelling to Havenswood Valley. We know Prairie Falls is well within reach of the Sinergy, so even though we'll be causing a ruckus back home, we don't know for sure how that will impact their efforts here. Already we've had one night attack and a killing in broad daylight, and while it seems the Sinergy can't get into the manor, it's still very effective anywhere on the grounds. You'll be safer here, but not completely, so you'll have to be just as vigilant as we will be up north. You'll have to be just as cautious."

"How safe, Sheriff?" asked Karen.

"That's not a question the sheriff, nor anyone else can answer, Karen," replied Stanley "We have no idea how many evil souls the Sinergy has. Once we start poking around in Havenswood Valley, that may effect what they do here. It may be they are only after the stones and whoever put them inside the tubes did so for safekeeping. We might discover that the tubes enable the Sinergy to transport the stones, even if they have an ill effect on them. If they could have taken the tubes and destroyed them it would have been one less option for a group like us to use against them. My gut tells me they won't be back once we show up in Havenswood Valley. Of course when they see us with the stones we have no idea if they will run for the hills or come at us with a vengeance."

"Oh, great," said Axel. "So you're saying we could have on a Wearing Stone necklace with the power to stop them or it ends up being something that says 'Hey! Here I am, come get me!' "

"That's one way to put it, yes," Stanley answered.

"Stanley brings up a couple of good points, but it won't change our plans. We know the dangers and risks, well, we know what we know so far, but I think our plan to have some of us stay here and the rest go back to Havenswood Valley is the right course to take."

"I'm going out on a limb here," said Robert, "but are we thinking the cabin will be our northern headquarters? It's fine with me, I'd be glad to spend more time back at the cabin, and I've got an in with the owner," he said, smiling to the group.

"Yes, Robert, that's just what I was thinking," said the sheriff, "mainly for those that don't live in Havenswood Valley. Myself, Deputy Stevens and Reynolds can stay at our own homes, but everyone else should stay at the cabin. Tomorrow, Deputy Stevens, Reynolds and I head back, although we should have left today. The mayor's on my case to get back. For the rest of you, we'll need to coordinate your travel plans and make sure everyone is travelling with at least two other members. I think we're all ready to get started, so the sooner the better for those of you heading north."

"What if we ask which members will be staying here at Hamsteen Manor?" asked Robert. "That way I can get an idea of what I need to do to prepare the cabin and clear out any rental bookings with the realtor."

"Great idea," replied Sheriff Anderson. "Just to lay out some ground rules, there is a lot of work that can be done here. Two areas I can think of, off hand, are; helping with any research needed by those in Havenswood Valley and going over in more depth Eleanor's past research for any clues that could help us locate the entry point. For anyone heading to Havenswood Valley you'll need to be ready for anything. Pack like you're going on an adventure trip, not a vacation. We might need to camp, but just bring your basic gear, we have plenty of tents and equipment. Our goals, according to the parchments, will be to search out their secret passage, locate the evil souls and try to figure out how to force them back in. We'll put together a detailed plan once everyone is settled in."

"So, find a needle in a haystack and then put a ship in a bottle?" joked Axel.

"From the description on the parchments that seems about right" laughed Marcus.

"Hey, what's a challenge without some impossibility thrown in?" asked Reynolds.

"Wouldn't want it any other way," added Stanley. "Easy is for the average person."

"Well, you're all right. One way or another, this is going to be a tough road," said the sheriff. "Okay, then, let's have a show of hands. Who will be staying at the manor?"

Karen, Kevin, Norma and, of course, Eleanor each raised a hand.

"I'm pretty sure I'll be staying on," offered Karen. "Not just because of the support from Eleanor, although I'm sure that will be a big help. Kevin and I came out here to share our experience in the desert hills, and even if I'll be nervous and scared it wouldn't feel right leaving. I want to stay and help, and when the timing is right, Kevin and I will head up to Havenswood Valley to join you."

"That's great news," said Norma. "There will be plenty for us to do here. For me, it's a blessing that I have such an experienced manager working for me so I don't have to worry about my store. I know staying here is a good decision and I'm excited about working on Eleanor's research. Who knows what we might find in all her notebooks?"

"You know, Norma, after reading the parchments, I'm going to look at my research differently," said Eleanor. "I felt so alone while I was doing all that work, it's going to be a welcome relief sharing it with The Voyageurs."

"For now, staying here is the best choice for us. But, like Karen said, I'm sure we'll head up north to join you soon," said Kevin. "Especially if you need some bait for the evil souls. I'm sure if I sat around in the woods they'd come to me, I'd just need to make sure Deputy Stevens is nearby to keep me from running to the bad guys again."

"Looking forward to seeing you there, Kevin," replied Deputy Stevens. "You know I've got your back when you do come up."

"Okay, then, that lets me know which members are staying here, and I assume the rest of you are all coming to Havenswood Valley?" asked the sheriff. There were collective yeses given in response. "Right, figured that would be the case. Does anyone have questions for Eleanor regarding her offer to support The Voyageurs and our members? This would be the best time to speak up if you want her to talk more specifics."

"I'd be happy to explain to the group, Sheriff, about my offer," said Eleanor.

"Perfect, I'm sure everyone would appreciate that," he replied.

"Thank you. As I said before, each offer is the same for everyone, depending only on your time commitment. Those participating part-time will be offered $25,000.00 per year for five years. Those of you that will be working on this full-time will be offered $50,000.00 per year for five years. The time period and support won't end until you decide to move on to do something else, or for full-timers if you need to cut back to part-time. For bookkeeping purposes, I've contacted my attorney and C.P.A. to help set up a small corporation. The paperwork should be available soon and then we can all review how we would like to vote in the officers. I'm also working on some company basics such as health coverage, transportation and communication. I have the feeling that no matter when we accomplish our task for Havenswood Valley, there will be other people we can help in our area. Long term I'm hoping to establish a company that will be available to help people in ways not readily available to the average person."

"Mrs. Hamsteen! Oh my gosh!" exclaimed Roxie.

"Eleanor, are you sure about this?" asked Robert.

"Alright, I'm changing my mind, I'm in one thousand percent!" added Axel.

"Thank you, but let me assure you, this is going to be hard work, and you'll earn every penny!" she laughed. "What made this an easy offer to extend was seeing how much you all care about this project, and about each other. This is a special circumstance and I value each and every one of you for what you bring to the table. Collectively we are a fantastic group and I'm sure we'll accomplish great things together. There's nothing better than having a purpose in life that helps others, and I'm really looking forward to The Voyageurs performing incredible feats in the coming years."

"You're an angel, Eleanor, to be so concerned for your friends and your fellow human beings," said Norma. "I'm so glad to be a part of this."

"Me, too," said Kevin. "Karen and I are excited to be staying."

"I guess what we need to do now," said the sheriff, "is to finalize everyone's time status. Karen, would you mind putting together a checklist for Eleanor with everyone's name and what their time involvement is going to be, as well as where they'll be living? You already know a few, and you can put me down as part-time, living at my home. As Karen works on the list, let's talk about logistics; how and when we're all going to get settled into our housing."

Karen made quick work of the list, getting everyone's choice of residence and their time status. The full-time group was made up of Marcus, Roxie, Axel, Karen and Kevin. They would be moving into Hamsteen Manor, while the rest of the group would keep their current jobs and residences. Only when there was an event or meeting would the part-timers stay at the manor, except for Stanley and Norma. Stanley still planned to write and Norma preferred Prairie Falls over Havenswood Valley, so much so she confirmed to everyone that she would be opening a Tres Azure store in town. Stanley would move back into his regular room and Norma would stay until she found a place of her own in town.

For the next hour The Voyageurs planned how the group would travel to Havenswood Valley. It was decided a caravan of three vehicles was the best fit. The sheriff, Roxie and Robert would be in the department's SUV. Deputy Stevens would drive a Hamsteen Manor car with Marcus and Axel and the third vehicle would be Stanley's, with Reynolds as his passenger. Cell phones were to be set with speakers on and the vehicles would stay together the entire drive, always on alert for any sign of the Sinergy. Departure would be no later than noon the next day, allowing just enough time for each local member to get their gear together, also done in small groups. The sheriff would drive the trio to their homes, Deputy Stevens taking Stanley to his home. It was going to be a full morning of preparation and everyone was feeling the excitement, along with some nervous tension, growing.

There was also a candid discussion on how to explain to family and friends about what in the world they were doing with their lives, mainly for the five full-time members, but also for the part-time members as they, too, were putting in a significant amount of time with The Voyageurs. It was decided that a small business office would be set up in downtown Prairie Falls under the name P.F.I., for Prairie Falls Investigations. Eleanor said she owns a few business properties and had one location that was a perfect fit as a somewhat false front for their real business. This would allow The Voyageurs' members to talk about their new line of work, investigating any kind of mystery or situation, yet still be able to hide the details of their work on the Sinergy. They were all very encouraged about the direction The Voyageurs was moving, even though they knew a very real danger was right in the path of their future.

"Don't you think it's a little weird Edgar never told Eleanor about his brother and sister? Or that his mom was still alive? What kind of family is that?" asked Axel from the back seat. He, Marcus and Deputy Stevens were driving north to Havenswood Valley in an SUV from Hamsteen Manor. Theirs was the lead vehicle in the three car caravan.

"Some families just don't mix well together," answered Marcus. "As the saying goes, you can pick your friends, but you can't pick your family."

"We see a lot of people on their own in our area," said Deputy Stevens. "Somebody is down on their luck and may think it's a place they can start over. Unfortunately, sometimes they make the same poor decisions that put them out on their own to begin with and end up back in jail. All of a sudden there are family members coming in to bail them out and friends trying to help get them back on their feet. Edgar just had a part of his life that he kept private. Happens all the time."

"Well, I hope Mrs. Hamsteen doesn't feel left out. They just told her they'd take care of all the arrangements and that was that," added Axel. "Tough way to start the day."

"At least there will be a funeral she can attend, maybe she'll get some answers then," replied Marcus. "And I thought we had a crazy morning. I gave my parents a pretty thorough explanation of what we're doing when we stopped to get my gear, but it was the condensed version and I know I left some stuff out. That was easy compared to Eleanor getting a knock on the door from people you had no idea even existed!"

"In a way it might be a relief for her," said Deputy Stevens. "She was suddenly under a lot of pressure, which she seems to handle very well, but all the same I bet she's relieved to have the funeral off her plate."

"Yeah, I know, just weird," said Axel. "So, my parents were kind of shocked about my news. I called them and said I was hired by a new company in Prairie Falls to do investigations and they thought I was getting into police work. I said not a chance, no offense, Deputy, so I let them know it was more like finding lost or missing people for families needing help. I just couldn't tell them the truth yet, they'd have me locked up. Again, no offense, Deputy."

"None taken," Deputy Stevens replied. "You're pretty funny, Axel. The Sheriff's Department could use a guy like you around, smart when you need to be but relaxed and quick with a joke when the time is right. Most of the time we get recruits that are way too heavy-handed. It takes a while to educate them about the real world, not the one they see on TV. Think about it. I'll mention our talk to the sheriff."

"Uh, thanks, but I don't think I'd look very good in a deputy uniform," Axel replied.

"Oh," laughed Deputy Stevens, "There're lots of other positions in the department where you'd fit in just fine. And no," he laughed again, "I wasn't picturing you in uniform, either, Axel. No offense."

Just behind the lead vehicle, Sheriff Anderson was driving the department SUV. Robert was riding shotgun, Roxie sat in the back seat.

"Roxie," asked Robert, "how'd your parents take the news?"

"Actually they were fairly supportive," she replied. Roxie had been living on her own for a few years, and her parents knew that if Marcus and Axel were involved it was a safe bet their daughter would be in good hands. They were confident in her and her two best friends. "I told them we were heading back up to the cabin to work with the Sheriff's Department on some missing persons files we had found on our last trip, which I thought was pretty close to the truth."

"Close, sure," said Robert. "And the fine details?"

"Well, I did let them know I have a new job with a start up company and that surprised them. I've been working for the same company for some time and I think they feel this might be a short term job that doesn't go anywhere. They're just concerned I'm going to mess up a good thing for something that sounds like it was thrown together kind of quickly."

"Your parents sound like they're looking after your best interests, Roxie," said Sheriff Anderson.

"I know, I really do have great parents," she said. "They do want what's best for me. I'm learning a lot being on my own."

"Never stop learning, Roxie," said Robert. "Otherwise life gets real boring, real fast."

"Some parts of these roads are getting tough to maneuver," Stanley noticed. He and Steven Reynolds were in the final car of the caravan, and having never been this far north it was tough to judge their driving speed. "How much longer before we enter Havenswood Valley?" asked Stanley.

"That's pretty common this far north," answered Reynolds. "The road starts to wind through the forest more and the hills near town slow travel time. That's why we can't see the other cars right now. Just be careful. We're in no hurry." Reynolds' cell phone suddenly rang and startled them both.

"Hello, Reynolds here. Hi, Robert. Yep, can't be more than a minute behind you. Sure, okay, we'll meet you at the cabin. Thanks for checking in."

"I wasn't ready for that call!" Stanley said. "Made me jump when the phone rang."

"Me, too," agreed Reynolds. "Robert was checking in on us, making sure we were heading to the cabin and not downtown. There's a road we'll turn on about a mile ahead, comes out of nowhere since it's before town and there's not much around so we'll have to keep a sharp eye out for it. Zachary Road."

"You're right about nothing around, I figured there'd be cabins and some stores around here but I haven't seen anything for miles. And the forest is so dense," said Stanley. "About a mile you say? Then it's a sharp eye out for Zachary Road." Stanley slowed the car down in this unfamiliar territory. The thick growth made it look like a place you wouldn't want to be on your own after dark. "What's that?" asked Stanley. "Is that a loose boulder?"

"Where?" asked Reynolds. "Oh, geez, that's moving right onto the road!"

"What the heck is it?" Stanley demanded.

"It's a huge bull moose and it's turned toward the road! Slow down, Stanley!"

"It's not headed to the road! It's going to ram the one on the other side!" yelled Stanley.

Instead of the two Bull Moose running at each other, they turned and began running head-on at Stanley's sedan.

"This is crazy! We're being attacked!" screamed Reynolds. "Stanley!"

The impact came on the left side, Stanley's side, of the vehicle. He had made a choice and tried to drive off the narrow two lane road on the right side, protecting Reynolds from a direct impact with a moose. But just when what should have been the moose on the right nailing Stanley's driver side door, both mammals morphed into one large, dark, Sinergy blob of power and hit the vehicle like a mallet smashing a croquet ball across a lawn and into the weeds. The car was no match for the lateral force and it careened down the short grassy buffer between road and forest. In a single roll it was pinned, roof to tree trunks, against a strand of red pine.

The Sinergy was on the offensive even before The Voyageurs had made camp, and they meant business!

CHAPTER
41

"We can't believe it either, Karen," Marcus was on his cell phone speaking to a shell-shocked and tired Karen, her morning coffee not getting into her system fast enough. The team at Hamsteen Manor had been up late the previous night discussing the Sinergy.

"But how do they keep finding out it's us in the cars? This is crazy!" she said.

"I know," said Marcus. "They've got intelligence we have no idea about. At least Stanley and Reynolds are okay. It sounds like they'll probably be released later today. Stanley's car had, like, a dozen air bags go off so they barely felt a thing, I think they got more bruised from the air bags than the accident."

"Thank God for that, really. I think He's starting to watch out for us," said Karen, "and I'll take all the extra support we can get! So now what are you guys going to do?"

"Sheriff Anderson will be here in a few minutes, and then we'll set up our plans," answered Marcus. "I'm excited, but nervous, like before a race. I know once we get started I'll be ready to push as hard as I can. Hey, I see the sheriff's car pulling into the driveway. One of us will check in with you guys later. Be careful down there!"

"You guys be careful, too!" Karen replied. "I don't want to get a call about anyone else getting hurt! And take extra care of Roxie! I know she'll want to go toe to toe with the evil spirits!"

"Will do!" Marcus said. "Talk with you later, and let us know as soon as you hear anything about the stones. If we can get more we'll take them right away."

"Okay," Karen replied. "Norma has some great connections and thinks she can get answers for us quickly. Bye!"

Sheriff Anderson walked into the cabin and saw everyone was ready for a quick update. The attack on the car was another confirmation this was a deadly serious endeavor, yet the looks on their faces told him they were up to the challenge.

"Good morning and thanks for getting up early. I'm not going to beat around the bush," the sheriff stated. "This is a war we're in. Everyone have their Wearing Stones on? Good, because Stanley and Reynolds had put theirs in the trunk, wrapped up for safekeeping during the drive. The rest of us had ours on, not sure if that was the reason they were hit, or if it was just because they were the last car in our caravan. Either way, keep 'em on at all times."

"Sheriff, I just talked with Karen," said Marcus. "She said Norma has a good lead on someone that may know about the stones."

"Good, that could be a big help," said Sheriff Anderson. "I have to be at the mayor's office later this morning so let's get started. As in any investigative case that has us searching for lost or hiding suspects, you need a list of possible locations. Eleanor has sent me one from her research, although it's not very detailed since she doesn't know the area, and I have one from the work Robert, Norma and I have done over the years. I also brought a few maps of the region we can use to plot potential search areas."

"So, are we looking for the Sinergy or their entry point?" asked Roxie.

"Good question," replied Sheriff Anderson. "We are looking for both, so again, like an investigation, if we find where they're coming in, we should be able to track the Sinergy activity more closely. I'd like for you to divide into two groups, one working on Eleanor's info, the other on the work we've done up here. Axel, if you and Roxie would go through our information that would get some fresh eyes looking at our data. Robert, if you and Marcus can work on plotting the locations from Eleanor's research that would help with our mapping. Either I or Deputy Stevens will bring Stanley and Reynolds back this afternoon. The doctor said they're fine but he wants one more test done. They should be good to go at noon. Goal this morning is to put some red dots on the maps from what you all figure out. Then we'll go about setting up how to check each spot as a possible entry point location. Any questions?"

"When was the last time Havenswood Valley had a mysterious death or missing person?" asked Marcus.

"About two months ago we found a body under a railroad trestle. He had been beaten up pretty bad, but it was as if he was thrown from a vehicle, not punched. No one came forward to claim the body and to this day he's a John Doe. Sad to say but he was one of about twelve total over the past three years in our dead and missing files."

"When do you think we'll be ready to go searching?" asked Axel.

"Very soon," replied the sheriff. "We'll do our best to choose a few locations that look most promising and then try those. Small steps at first, then we'll tackle more spots. Right now I've got to go and see what the mayor is all fired up about. I'll be back later, good luck!"

"That was quick!" said Roxie as the sheriff made his way down the steps of the cabin.

"He's a very busy man," said Robert "and with all the unexplained deaths he's feeling the pressure. It's not fair, but every time they find another body a few people get scared and think someone new should be in charge. If they only knew how wrong they were."

"Sheriff Anderson isn't like any sheriff I could imagine. He's a regular guy working really hard to protect his own, which I guess every sheriff does, but he just seems to be more normal than I expected," said Axel. "I like him and his deputies, too."

"Me, too," said Roxie. "We lucked out having him around. Really glad he didn't bust us and just take the tubes when he found out about them."

"Well, then, why don't we all get started," suggested Robert. "Roxie, why don't you and Axel work on the big table, Marcus and I can work at the kitchen peninsula."

"Works for me!" said Marcus.

While the cabin group was being very diligent in their efforts, trying to match up dead and missing persons events to their locations, Sheriff Anderson was knocking on the door of the Havenswood Valley Mayor, unsure why he had been summoned to come by. There had always been tension between the two, due to a game of stalemate the mayor had played regarding a number of important Havenswood Valley issues. People were beginning to point fingers and blame the two men for their lack of action on civic priorities. Maybe the power outage the town recently experienced put Mayor Turner on track to make some concessions and start the process of fixing the infrastructure in town.

"Good morning, Mayor!" the sheriff said in a dry and slightly sarcastic tone. He walked tall into the room after being approved to enter by the secretary in the foyer. Inside the well apportioned office was Mayor Turner, sitting comfortably in an overstuffed leather chair behind his desk. In fact, everything in the room was overstuffed; walls of Chamber of Commerce plaques showing the mayor glad-handing with local business owners, photos of the mayor with celebrities of all kinds that happened to pass through town during vacation or on tour and anything he had that looked like an award or prize. Too overweight to comfortably stand and provide a welcoming handshake, the mayor smiled smugly, snorted a comment and looked like he was already bored with whatever the discussion topic would be.

"Anyone out of power today?" Sheriff Anderson asked.

"Hilarious, Sheriff," the mayor responded. "You practicing for your second career? Besides, you know as well as I do it was the city council's fault for not approving the funds to repair that part of town, but as Mayor I end up with all the blame." He looked around the room as if he was watching a small bird flying from wall to wall, "Is it warm in here?" he asked.

"Actually, kind of cool in here, I'd say," the sheriff answered. The mayor's oversized stature meant the room was normally much colder than most of his visitors would like. He pressed the intercom, "Alice, will you come in here and check the thermostat, I think it's broken."

"Feels just like everyday in here to me, Mayor Turner," Alice said as she gave the thermostat control the once over. She was at the mercy of a boss who got what he wanted, when he wanted it. "Alice, get me a cool glass of water then, will you, please?" He added the please mainly because Sheriff Anderson was in the room, he wanted to appear respectful in front of company.

"You're looking a little flushed, Mayor," said Sheriff Anderson. "You feeling alright?"

"As a matter of fact, I am not." The mayor stood up, loosened his collar and wiped his face. "I was feeling just fine until you walked in. Maybe I'm allergic to you!" he huffed. Mayor Turner was definitely flushed, his heart rate gaining speed and the sweat on his face looked as if he had just finished a long walk on a very hot summer's day. The ceiling fan was spinning rapidly above the mayor's desk, yet had little effect on his red line status. "Listen, Sheriff, I asked you to come here today to let you know I've heard about something going on out at Washburn's cabin. Is that official sheriff's business or are you getting involved in some kind of private affair?" He fanned himself with a notebook, set it down and took a long drink from the glass Alice had brought to him. "Doggone if I don't think I'm going to faint!"

"Alice, why don't you call for an ambulance, no siren or anything," said the sheriff. "If this man is about to have a heart attack I'd rather it be at the hospital, not the city hall." As Sheriff Anderson sat the mayor back down into this overstuffed chair, Mayor Turner moaned with pain, his eyes began to roll and the limpness in his body made it very tough to keep him in a sitting position. As Alice hung up the phone he said to her, "Alice, I'm going to grab a couple of men to see if they can help me get the mayor to the front door for the ambulance. Stay here with him and if he gets worse, scream for help. I bet there's an AED in the building that we can use if he goes into cardiac arrest. Turner, you still hear me?"

"Whaaad youuu saaaaay?" he drooled the words in a low moan.

"I hope he can hang on," said Alice, "at least until the ambulance gets here. Go ahead and get help, there should be a wheelchair in the custodian's closet."

"You keep a wheelchair on hand?" asked the sheriff.

"Don't ask," replied Alice. "We get all kinds in here."

Five minutes later the ambulance pulled up to a half smiling mayor. "I'm feeling much better," he grumbled to the EMT's. "Maybe it was just gas!" he smirked as they approached him, first aid cases in hand and a look in their eyes that said they were trained to make sure the mayor did not expire on their watch.

Back inside the foyer of the mayor's office, Sheriff Anderson and Alice were discussing what had transpired. "Sure looked like he was having a heart attack, Sheriff," said Alice. "I thought he was a goner!"

"Me too," he replied. "By the time I got out to my car to radio for backup, he was being wheeled right back into the building! Where is he now?"

"They took him to the hospital anyway," she replied. "After a few minutes talking with him the EMT's told me they wanted to get the mayor in for a few quick tests. He could be back home later tonight, unless they find something."

"Well, good luck then," the sheriff said. "A near heart attack might be just the thing to get him thinking about a healthier lifestyle. I know he's single, but that's no excuse to eat out every meal and not take care of yourself. He's got a whole town depending on him, plus the charity group he's involved in. I've got a deputy heading to the hospital sometime later today, I'll make sure he checks in with him. Even though he never agrees with anything I do, he's still the mayor. At least until the next election," he smiled.

"He's the third mayor I've served," said Alice, "and I'd like to start on mayor number four next term," she laughed. "Not that I'm wishing Mayor Turner ill will just to make my job easier, but I'm ready for a change."

"You and me both, Alice," the sheriff replied as he headed outside to his vehicle.

"They're all yours, Deputy," said Doctor Evans as he signed off the patient charts at the nurses station. "These are two very lucky men, you might want to have them buy you a couple of lottery tickets," he joked.

"Thanks, Doc, we just might do that. While we're here, I would like to check in on the mayor, if you think that would be alright," the Deputy asked. "Sheriff Anderson told Alice we'd see how he was doing."

"Sure, he's doing fine and he should be released in a few hours," answered the doctor. "Room 212, Nurse Nelson will be in there. Let her know I said you could stop in."

Stanley and Reynolds followed Deputy Stevens into room 212, "Knock, knock," said the deputy, announcing their entry. "Hello, Nurse Nelson. Just thought we'd stop in and say hi from the department and Alice. How's the mayor?"

"He's doing as well as expected," she sighed. "Not the best patient, if you know what I mean," she whispered. "You've got five minutes, then I'm back to scoot you out. The mayor needs - oh, no! Now what?"

The room was suddenly shattered by a high pitched alarm of loud beeps sounding every two seconds.

"Nurse!" the mayor gasped. "It's happening again! Get me a doctor!"

The emergency signals had alerted the nurse's station and Doctor Evans was already heading down the hallway to room 212, two nurses at his heels. Nurse Nelson spoke with authority, "Deputy! Hold down the mayor for me. I've got to give him a shot of adrenaline, STAT!"

The three men listened to her directive and moved quickly to keep the mayor still. At first it was like wrestling a bear, but within seconds the mayor was turning into the same flush faced, sweaty mess that he was earlier in the day. He had no choice but to succumb to their force as he turned limp and barely coherent, the needle sinking easily into his arm.

"Get, away, from, me," he slowly groaned. "You're... killing... me." His eyelids closed as the doctor and additional nurses rushed into the room.

"Out, right now!" commanded Doctor Evans. "We need room to work here! Go!"

They left at once and began walking down the hallway, unsure of exactly what had transpired. Once outside the hospital they began to talk about the incident.

"Whoa!" Stanley said. "Was he having a heart attack?"

"Maybe, that's what they thought was going on this morning," answered Deputy Stevens.

"Did you hear what he said to us?" asked Reynolds. "What did he mean saying that we were killing him?"

"Don't take it personally, things people say while in distress sometimes turn rather nasty," replied Deputy Stevens. "His eyes seemed ready to roll back and his heartbeat was skyrocketing. I'm pretty sure he was talking about the shot the nurse was giving him. He might have thought we were crazed bad guys trying to pin him down for a dose of poison."

"He sure looked like he meant it," said Reynolds. "Let's call back later and ask the nurse to give us an update."

"This may sound weird since he's the mayor and all," said Stanley, "but does he have many friends in town? It was awfully empty in his room today. We've seen more people come and go for patients with much less life-threatening maladies."

"For a man in his political position he does seem pretty lonesome," answered the deputy. "He lives by himself and other than his official duties as mayor, I don't recall reading much about him in the local paper. I do know he's good friends with Jericho Brown, the guy that runs a program for the homeless. Let's drive by the center and let him know the mayor's not doing too well, maybe he'll stop by and visit him later at the hospital. It's on the way to the cabin."

"Don't let him fool you, Stanley," said Reynolds. "This town's so small everything's on the way," laughed Reynolds.

Of course it didn't take long before the three men were pulling up to the front of the Havenswood Valley Shelter. Located on the west side of town, the building looked as solid as they came, back in the early 1900's. Large tan bricks, some nice stonecutting work, and a few decorative touches would have put this building out of the range of any non-profit in a larger town. In this region it was another timeless reminder of a construction style that may never be repeated. It was also very vacant when Jericho Brown came searching for a site to house the homeless. He had transplanted from Cleveland and was looking to replicate a program he had started there, this time on a smaller, less stressful level. It was said he had lost his wife and two children in a car accident as she drove them to school one day and he felt he needed a fresh start. Jericho was a strong, stoic man searching for salvation by helping those in need, an elixir that also helped keep him going, day by day.

As they entered the building the small foyer opened into a larger area filled with comfortable seating, tables for eating, a couple of computers, and no televisions. The people inside looked relaxed and at home. Deputy Stevens recognized one of the staff. "Hi," he said, "remember me? Deputy Stevens from the Sheriff's Department?"

"Oh, hi, Deputy, nice to see you," said Hazel. "Can I help you?"

"Looking for Mr. Brown," he replied. "Won't take but a minute, is he around?"

"Yes, he's working in the back loft," replied Hazel. "If you walk straight through it will be right after the kitchen. It might be blocked off, so just holler up to him," she smiled.

"Thanks, appreciate that," he said. They made their way to the back of the building, looked up and saw Jericho shuffling some things back and forth in the loft area above another open seating area. There was a stairway leading up to the loft, however a rope was laid across from the banister to the wall at the first step, a sign hanging down with the word closed on it. Deputy Stevens yelled up to Jericho, "Mr. Brown! Hello, it's Deputy Stevens from the Sheriff's Department, can we come up?"

"Hello, Deputy!" he replied. "I'm pretty busy, what is it?" Jericho looked to be in his late forty's, and very fit. However today he was stumbling around, partly due to the load he was carrying.

Stanley noticed Jericho was looking like he needed a rest. "Is he okay? I think that man needs a break," said Stanley. "He looks like he's going to faint and I sure don't want to get a complex about people getting sick around us!"

"We just came from the hospital," said the deputy. "I'm sure you heard about the mayor? He looked to be having a heart attack this morning so they took him in for some tests!"

Jericho stopped in his tracks, set down the box he was holding and looked down at Deputy Stevens. The deputy felt a chill run up his spine.

"Yes, I know. What condition is he in now?" asked Jericho.

"We're not sure," answered the deputy. "We left him at the hospital and he was looking pretty bad, kinda like this morning."

"You don't know? How could you leave him there in that condition?" Jericho's voice was loud and edgy.

"He was in good hands, Mr. Brown," said Reynolds. He didn't want the deputy to take all the heat on the news. Besides, Reynolds had run into Mr. Brown a few times and he felt like they had some kind of a connection. "You can call the hospital if you'd like to know more, we're going to call in an hour to check on him."

"Yes, of course he was in good hands, thank you, Mr. Reynolds. Thank you," said Jericho.

"You feeling okay, Mr. Brown?" asked the deputy. "You seem a little under the weather up there."

"Oh, I'm fine, don't worry about me," he said. "It's just a really busy time at the shelter, so I'm feeling run down, that's all. Is there anything else?"

"Other than you look like you need a lunch break?" asked Reynolds.

"I'm fine!" he stressed, in a more than a unpleasant tone, finally sitting down on a bench, leaning against a railing as if about to pass out.

"He's getting worse by the minute, Deputy," Stanley said so only his friends could hear.

"Okay, we'll go. Just wanted to let you know about the mayor in case you want to check in on him," said the deputy. "So long, and good luck with the shelter!"

Mr. Brown slid down in a heap on the floor as soon as the men turned to walk away.

"Stevens, let's get one of the staff to go back with us and check on Mr. Brown, and another one to wait out front for the ambulance," said the deputy. "Tell them to keep it on the down low, I don't want Mr. Brown to know what's going on until the EMT's get here."

"Good idea," replied Reynolds. "I see a couple I know right up the hallway."

They hustled up to the front, Deputy Stevens already on the phone with the ambulance company and explaining the details of the call. He told them it may be nothing, or it may be a heart attack on the way and was assured by the 911 operator it was best to call before something happened. Help would be there in a few minutes, no fan fare. Stanley and Reynolds had two staff members running after them back to Mr. Brown and they found Jericho still slumped on the floor, trying to get back up on the bench. As soon as he saw the men he gave up and lay prone on the floor, eyes rolling back as he passed out.

It was a chaotic few minutes but as the three men of The Voyageurs walked out of the homeless shelter to their car, they knew a potential disaster was averted. The ambulance was rolling Code 2 to the hospital, yet they felt uncomfortable leaving the scene.

"What's in the water up here?" asked Stanley. "Two middle aged men looking like they were going to drop at any minute? This town needs a health check up."

"The mayor, he really needs to address his health," said Reynolds, "but I thought Mr. Brown looked fine. Maybe he's got the flu."

"We might have overreacted," added Deputy Stevens. "That's alright with me, I'd rather have a laugh about it later than be attending a funeral just because we didn't want to be embarrassed. Although now we have to tell The Voyageurs what happened and I'm sure we'll get some grief about it."

"No worries," said Reynolds. "I'm just glad to be alive myself, thank God. Stanley's car had so many airbags, that and having our seatbelts on saved us during one heck of a barrel roll. Everyone at the cabin still on board after hearing about Stanley and me being attacked?"

"Oh, yeah," answered Deputy Stevens, "more than ever. They want to hear all about it from you two, but right now they're trying to pinpoint locations to search for the entry point. Once we find it then we'll stake it out for activity. I'm sure everyone is secretly thinking about how the stones are going to work. It's not like we have directions on how to work these Wearing Stones, or the Sealing Stone. Norma may have a lead on someone that can figure out what they are without blowing our cover, but other than that the parchments were somewhat vague on what to do with them."

"And how will we know they work?" asked Stanley. "What kind of effect on the Sinergy are we looking for? If we get close to a Sinergy with a Wearing Stone will they just vaporize into thin air?"

"Hey!" yelled Reynolds from the backseat of the department's SUV. He had startled the other two and Stanley turned around quickly, expecting another dangerous encounter! Deputy Stevens was looking out every window and into every mirror on the vehicle, wondering if Reynolds had seen something coming at them.

"What?" they asked in unison, both of them impatient and shaken.

"What Stanley said, I've got an idea," Reynolds said with a look of inventive excitement from ear to ear. "Head to the college. I need to get into the science lab, it's in the Edison building, south side of campus."

"The science lab? You planning on experimenting on the Sinergy?" asked Stanley.

"Yes, yes I am! This could work, it could really work!" Reynolds answered, eyes wide open and all over his face, a classic look of scientific Eureka!

"Now this looks like an investigation moving along at full speed!" exclaimed Sheriff Anderson as he entered the cabin. Looking around he saw the great room table covered with papers, books, snacks and coffee mugs. The kitchen peninsula had the same paperscape, with more pages taped to nearby cabinets, showing about a dozen locations in the greater Havenswood Valley area, six of them with large circles of red marker ink. The sheriff smiled. This was his idea of the perfect combination of research and teamwork; two very important ingredients for successfully breaking a case wide open. "Who can update me on where we are?" he asked.

"That would be me, Sheriff," replied Kevin.

"I hear you, just can't find you," Sheriff Anderson said.

"Right behind you on the monitor. We hooked up Hamsteen Manor with the cabin and have been trading tons of information back and forth. We've been able to identify and map out 11 possible Sinergy gateway locations, six of them being our first round of the places we think most likely to produce our target," said Kevin.

"With all the research that's been done by you and Robert up here and Eleanor in Prairie Falls, we had an easy time figuring out the most likely areas to focus on," added Roxie. "In picking the final spots, we picked areas with water because of what was said in the parchments, along with our own experiences with Passage Creek and the pond at Hamsteen Manor."

"That's great work, everyone," said Sheriff Anderson. "Kevin, how are things going at the manor?"

"Middle of the road, just the way we like it," he replied. "Edgar's funeral is in two days, and Eleanor's family and friends have realized she's going to be fine, so the phone calls and visits are back to normal. Something we have not discussed is the information Norma found on the stones. She just got back so I'll let her fill everyone in."

Norma sat down in front of the computer camera, smiling as she laid out the information she wanted to relay to The Voyageurs. "Hello, everyone. I had a very interesting meeting with a friend of mine this afternoon. As you know it was about the stones and I would like to pass along what I've learned. Ready to take some notes?" she asked.

"Fire away, Norma," replied Roxie.

"Okay, then, here we go. The stone is a mineral called zircon, and I know that sounds like something from a science fiction movie, but these stones actually go all the way back to the time of Moses and the early days of Jerusalem and come in a variety of colors. For centuries these stones have been used in place of precious jewels like diamonds and topaz, as well as a replacement for colored gems. Like most stones, zircon comes in different grades. Zircon is found in some of the most exclusive jewelry collections in the world."

"Wow," you could hear Karen say in the background.

"Yes, Karen, some of the pieces I saw were just amazing. The stones are usually mined in Sri Lanka, but are also found around the world in places like Russia, Norway, Burma and Cambodia. Zircon is very dense and has radioactive elements, so it is a perfect candidate for radiometric dating, a way to tell how old something like these stones are. Because of those properties scientists have declared zircon the oldest object on Earth, dating back 4.3 billion years!"

"Dang!" said Axel, "that is some old rock!"

"Did you say radioactive?" asked Robert. "How radioactive?"

"Nothing that will cause any problems for humans. It's called, let me check my notes, it's called a metamict zircon gem," answered Norma. "It's clarity may be altered over time, but only in the green or brown stones. They are rare, especially in the type of condition ours are in, and have become scarce. So between your Wearing Stones and the rings we are having made, be very protective of them. We have a limited collection of a unique, rare stone, let's not lose any of them!"

"Thank you, Norma," said the sheriff. "You seem to have great information on the stones. If you'd email a copy of your research to Roxie, it would help those of us here digest it better."

"No problem, Glen, I'll send it right over," Norma replied.

"So, we have an update on the stones," the sheriff continued, "and I'm sure whoever put them in the tubes chose wisely. Let's move on to the areas you've chosen to search. Deputy Stevens, Reynolds and Stanley will be here shortly. The deputy called in and said they had made an extra stop but were now on their way."

"Glen," Robert started, "we've got six good leads, based on all the information we had, to look at. No particular order, but here they are. First one is the C & L trestle bridge area, just northwest of town. Second is Passage River along the cabin property, third is kind of a mixed bag of places downtown; Pike Park, The Old Depot and the Steely Hotel. After that we have where the natural spring feeds into Iron Rock Lake, Brackett's Bluff and Voyageur River where it flows over the glacial potholes. Marcus, Roxie and Axel would be one group, Reynolds, Stanley and I would be the other. You'd handle the trio and Deputy Stevens could cover my group. As of yet we haven't divided up the spots, but we should do that now. Any suggestions?"

"Well, let's see," said the sheriff as he walked over for a closer look at the map. It had been marked up with notes and color codes and was spread out on the table. "I don't want Marcus' group going out too far, so let's have them cover the Passage River and Passage Creek spots and also the stream at Iron Rock Lake. Fresh eyes on these water areas will be good. Robert, having your group out at the trestle, around town and at the Bluffs will give us an advantage of having searchers that really know the area."

"Sheriff?" asked Kevin. "Once we look at all eleven places, if we haven't found our target, what if we switched areas of the two groups instead of trying to find completely new targets? Maybe one group will find something the other did not."

"That's a smart strategy, Kevin," the sheriff replied. "We use that approach often, especially when leads have run dry, and we go over the original information again. I'll let each group set up their own plan for tomorrow, our first day of exploring. Allow one day for each area, and for this first round of exploration, everything will be done in total daylight. No searching until after sunrise and you'll need to be back here before sunset. There wasn't anything said in the parchments about needing to be out in the dark looking for the Sinergy passageway, although I'm sure once we find it the only option we may have of chasing the evil souls back into their domain is to do it at night."

"Looks like the rest of our group is here. Isn't that Deputy Steven's car?" asked Marcus.

"Yep, that's Steven's all right," he replied. "Nice to see Stanley and Reynolds out of the hospital." He watched as the three men went to the back of the vehicle. "Guess they have some things in the trunk to bring in."

"Pretty sure we got all their stuff from the wreck, maybe they stopped for more food!" suggested Axel.

The sheriff's sixth sense had raised the interest of the group as to what exactly was in the trunk and Roxie was the first to comment, "That doesn't look like a grocery bag, Axel."

"Not unless the local grocer now sends you home with a very large duffle," added Robert. "I'm thinking soft-sided gun case."

"Then why is Reynolds carrying it?" asked Marcus. "Shouldn't the deputy be handling weapons?"

"Reynolds is a good outdoorsman, Marcus," replied Robert. "He's fired just about anything that has a barrel or a bow, and by the size of the case it's gonna take an experienced marksman to handle it."

The three men had made their way up the steps and were now entering the cabin as Axel stood on the porch, holding the screen door out of their way. "Welcome, gentlemen," he said. "Please be sure to check your weapons with the sheriff, he's the one inside with the uniform on."

"Before we get an explanation of what's inside that carrying case, let me just say it's good to see you two out of the hospital and looking as if there was never a car accident," said Sheriff Anderson.

"Thank you, Sheriff," replied Stanley, "and thank goodness for modern auto technology!"

"That's for sure," added Reynolds. "It was no worse than a bumpy ride at the state fair, but the needles and tests they gave us at the hospital, that's another story!"

Stanley and Reynolds went on to explain the details of the accident. How they were driving along, nearly at the turn off from the main road to the cabin when the moose appeared. There was no doubt the Sinergy had attacked them, but the story unveiled a couple of very important questions. How many of the Sinergy were as strong as the two that sent them tumbling into the ditch, and why didn't the Wearing Stones have any effect?

"It sounds like they were tipped off, that they knew we were coming back," offered Reynolds. "As far as the Wearing Stones, I'm not sure they would have worked no matter if we had them dangling from the rear view mirror. They moved so fast I can't imagine how something like these small stones could have deterred them."

"Well, so far that's the only sign of the Sinergy we've seen. It's been quiet here and at Hamsteen Manor," said Robert. "Looks like you've got something to share with the class, Reynolds, how 'bout we see what you've brought?"

"Sure, now's a perfect time, but I'd like to ask if we can disconnect from the internet for the time being," Reynolds asked. "No offense to our friends at the manor, but with all the on-line piracy these days I just can't afford for any information to find its way onto the web."

"I completely understand," replied Kevin. "We'll sign off for now and when you guys want to reconnect just give us a call. Good luck!"

"Pretty top secret stuff?" asked Axel.

"Kind of. It's being worked on at the college science department, which is a public institution, but you need clearance to get access and authorization to use it," replied Reynolds. "Fortunately I can grant both without anyone else knowing what's going on. At least for a while we can use this and the other two professors won't worry about me having it. We've all checked it out from time to time so we could do some field trials."

"Well, then, why don't you go ahead and show us what you've got, Reynolds," the sheriff asked with a hint that he was anticipating the unveiling as much as anyone in the cabin.

"First, I'd like to let you know this is an experimental item and my idea about us using it may be totally off base, so don't get your hopes up, yet," said Reynolds. "Second, we can't discuss this outside of our group. With everything you've all been through, I trust you explicitly and I'm confident no one will talk about this. Besides, if you do the feds may show up at your door someday. The back story on all this is that a few years ago we had a visit from a government agency that I can't reveal to anyone, and yes, black suits, dark sunglasses, the typical stereotype agent look. They brought us a few first generation prototypes they had started working on, but were about to lose funding for, when they happened upon an extremely small project we had posted on our web site. There were only three of us on the project and the visit from the feds scared the crap out of us. Not that we were doing anything wrong - it was just freaky that they found us, and even more scary was the fact they wanted to help with funding. They even provide some of their own highly advanced technologies for us to work with."

"But if they were going to lose funding, how did they get you money?" asked Marcus.

"We wondered the same thing and we asked that exact question," replied Reynolds. "The short answer, they said, is that there is always funding available. Sometimes you just need to cover the project up by moving it around, or change the people involved. They got us rolling forward faster than we ever would have on our own."

"From the moment they left we were in another stratosphere," Reynolds recalled, "one that allowed us to dream that anything, any thing, really is possible. Of course from what some of you have seen through your encounters with the Sinergy you already know that." Reynolds carried the long case to the big table. "I knew I could trust you all, which is why I brought it here. No one, other than the two professors I work with, know the tiniest clue about our advancements, or about our funding from the feds. They ordered us to accept their terms, or get nothing. We chose to have something and we've kept our mouths shut ever since. They are encouraged by what we've come up with, and to our benefit the funding has improved. We've even received a few bonus checks in the mail."

"I sure hope there isn't anything alive in that case," Roxie said as she backed away.

"That would be so cool!" responded Axel. "A programmable computer chip inside a killer snake!"

"Uh, almost, Axel," said Reynolds. "Here, let me take it out." Steve Reynolds, biologist by day, secret inventor by night, unzipped the long case and laid it flat to the table, bringing to light the hidden experiment.

"Uh, not what I expected," said Stanley.

"Kind of underwhelming, Reynolds," said Robert.

"You said you got a bonus for this?" asked Axel. "I think the feds might be knocking on your door for their money back."

"Very funny, and we've heard worse wise cracks from the feds, so don't worry about offending me," replied Reynolds. "I'll save you a few comments; Is that a kaleidoscope or a telescope? I've seen hair dryers that look more threatening! One of my favorites was from the new agent that asked if it made smoothies."

"You've got to admit, it looks pretty harmless," said Sheriff Anderson. "Was that part of your design strategy?"

"Not at first," Reynolds began to explain, "but we built it from the inside out and never gave much thought to the physical looks. We just wanted it to work and after a while we gave up trying to make it look cool. It ended up looking like a toy and that's not such a bad idea as far as keeping it out of the bad guy's hands. Most people would walk right by this if they were looking for a laser beam nano-particle transporter."

"A what?" asked Roxie.

"We call it a laser beam nano-particle transporter, or NPT for short," answered Reynolds. "The idea to try it on the Sinergy came to me as Deputy Stevens and Stanley were talking about how the Wearing Stones would affect the Sinergy, which we have no way of knowing since that was somehow left out of the parchments."

"That's true," added Robert. "We're in the dark about how to use these things at all. So why do you think your toy gun can work on them?"

"Stanley said something about vaporizing the Sinergy and it made me think about Betty. That's what we call her, er, this." Reynolds picked up the 55" long, six inch diameter cylinder, its weight of fifteen pounds causing him to steady his arms to keep the transporter from swaying too much. "It's really a simple concept, but it's loaded with space age technology." He rested the butt end on the table and angled the cylinder at forty-five degrees to provide a better view for his audience. "We put a product in the chamber, here," as he slid back a piece to expose the inside of the load chamber, "and turn on the exciter switch. I know, get the jokes out of your system, I've heard these, too."

"You mean people have asked you to install an exciter switch on someone?" asked Axel.

"I think your exciter needs to be switched off, Axel," said Roxie.

"Yep, heard them all from the feds," said Reynolds. "They really thought their jokes were funny, God bless 'em. Anyway, inside the chamber a reaction is brought on by the vibrations of the exciter elements, which in turn leads to nano-particles becoming loose inside the chamber. The machine is developed to pull these nano-particles from the chamber via the laser beam and transport the particles to the target. Depending on the type of laser, it could be used for delicate work on skin, and with a much smaller version of the machine it could be used on deeper tissue and organs that need medicine to kill infections. Like cancer cells, or vital organs that need healing done in a way that regular surgery can't be used on."

"That's beyond incredible, Reynolds. Does it work?" asked the sheriff.

"It does! The advancements in science over the past five years are amazing. Light sensitive lasers, chemical treatments, it's all happening so quickly. We were lucky enough to get in at a time that was perfect for our program." Reynolds picked up one of the extra Wearing Stones that was lying on the table. "The idea that came to me in the car was this." He held up the necklace and continued speaking, "I think we can put one of these Wearing Stones into the chamber of the NPT, turn on the exciter elements and get some nano-particles of the stone to transport right at the evil souls of the Sinergy!"

"Lord God Almighty, Reynolds," said Robert, "you've got a gun that'll kill those son's a bitches!"

"You guys nervous?" asked Axel.

"Of course," replied Roxie. "I get the feeling we're going to be sitting ducks if we find the Sinergy's entry point. We have no idea how strong the Wearing Stones are, or what we should be doing with them."

"Yeah, no kidding," said Axel.

"Well, I'm feeling good," Marcus shared. "I woke up this morning and felt super energized. Today, something happens!"

"Great, just when I thought we'd be able to do some sight seeing and call it a day," Axel lamented. "Now I've got to worry about being killed by the Sinergy!"

"Don't stress out," Marcus replied. "I don't have any thoughts about us getting hurt. Sure, we'll probably get a good scare before this adventure is over, but I'm counting on all of us getting through this just fine."

"Maybe you're right, Marcus," said Roxie, "but this is different from what you've been able to see and feel in the past. This is something from another dimension."

"I know, Roxie," Marcus replied. "It is different, for sure. But I've been training for this my whole life; learning how to interpret the things that pop into my head, figuring out how to prepare and react. I am so ready for this!"

"Don't get me wrong, I trust you, Marcus, you know that," said Roxie. "It's just that the stakes are bigger this time, and we're going into it against an enemy, not just reacting to something taking place. I know deep down that we'll be okay, and I don't mind being kind of nervous - that will keep us on our toes!"

"Speaking of keeping on our toes, here comes the sheriff," said Axel. "When are Kevin, Karen and Norma supposed to pull in?"

"Around 9:00 am," answered Roxie. "I hope they don't have any problems on the drive up here."

"Morning," Sheriff Anderson said as he walked through the front door. "How's everyone doing today?"

"Very ready!" Marcus replied.

"He's feeling it, Sheriff," Axel added. "We're gonna have to watch him like a hawk. He has a habit of heading into action before the rest of us know that anything's going on!"

"Alright, then," said the sheriff, "let's make sure we keep the lines of communication clear at all times. Marcus, do your best to update us ahead of any change of plans, okay?"

"I don't know if that's possible, Sheriff," said Roxie. "He's used to handling things on his own and taking charge in crazy situations."

"My favorite" recalled Axel, "was when Marcus convinced about ten guys to come into the bar, off the sidewalk smoking area where they were having a great time, and two minutes later an SUV plowed into the tables they had just been sitting at. I don't recall much after that because those same guys ended up buying us drinks for the rest of the night!"

"I'll admit to being somewhat overzealous in the past, but now I'm on a team, Sheriff," Marcus said. "I've never had this kind of support and from what we've already seen, it's going to take all of us working together to beat the Sinergy."

"Glad to hear that, Marcus," replied the sheriff. "I see Deputy Stevens and Reynolds are just pulling in, where's Robert and Stanley?"

"Robert went out to walk around the cabin and Stanley is doing some writing in his room," Roxie answered.

"Robert's out on his own?" asked the sheriff.

"Yep, all by my lonesome self," replied Robert as he walked in from the kitchen. "Not much to see this morning, don't think even the squirrels are hanging around these days. Something's got 'em off their regular routines."

"Morning, Robert," said Sheriff Anderson. "Good to know you're keeping tabs on the place. Any sign of the Sinergy?"

"Nothing out of place as far as I can tell," he replied. "Maybe they're waiting to see what we're up to."

"We're not up to anything, much," joked Reynolds as he walked into the cabin with the long, NPT carrying case in hand. "This is just a little science experiment!"

"Yes, and the moose that crashed into my car were just a couple of optical illusions," added Stanley as he entered the great room.

"Glad to see everyone is in a good mood this morning, tight situations bring out your true self," said the sheriff. "It's good to hear some humor to break the tension instead of arguing, and let me tell you I've seen good people go bad real quick when it's game time."

"Hey," exclaimed Roxie, "Isn't that Kevin's car coming up the driveway?"

A few minutes later The Voyageurs were nearly at full force inside the cabin. Everyone but Eleanor Hamsteen was present, as she had stayed home to attend the funeral for Edgar and to provide any support she could from the manor. Kevin, Karen and Norma had a very boring drive north, thankfully, and had brought the tubes, parchments and the extra Wearing Stones. Two Wearing Stones were left for Eleanor and Katrina, and two were at the jeweler, being made into rings. The setting would be based on the Sealing Stone; a slightly rounded slice of the Wearing Stone, surrounded by a gold rim. Stanley had led the way on a crest design for their group that would be inset on each side of the ring. The inside of the band would have The Voyageurs engraved, along with the year.

"I can't believe we're here without all our friends," said Karen. "It feels weird."

"Welcome to my world, Karen," said Norma. "Everything feels weird," she laughed.

"Glen," Robert said, "now that everyone is here, how 'bout we get this show on the road? What's the final verdict for today's plans?"

"Thought about that a lot last night. Here is what I propose," answered Sheriff Anderson. "Marcus, Axel, Roxie and I will keep to our route, starting with the stream at Iron Rock Ridge, then Passage River and finish up here checking out two stretches of Passage Creek. I'll be riding one of the department's four passenger ATV's that we'll trailer out to our first area and, by their choice, the others will be on foot. Something about getting a run in while we search that I agreed to. The four-wheeler will be equipped with a few weapons, first aid equipment, radio, food, water. In other words, loaded."

"And if you need to make a quick exit, Sheriff?" asked Norma.

"Whatever mode of transport we use, at some point we're all going to be on foot checking out our assigned places, and we're all going to be in danger if we run into the Sinergy. I agreed to this and I'm confident a single ATV is as good an option, maybe better, than four separate ones."

"Besides, isn't today kind of a quick pass through the areas to get an idea of which ones to go back to and spend more time on?" asked Kevin. "That's one of the reasons the three of us came up here, to help go through all the notes you bring back, analyze them with the past research, then make suggestions for the follow up."

"Yes, Kevin, that's right. We'll get a feel for each area, see if anything stands out, and then rank them in order to revisit as a group," answered the sheriff. "Today we have three goals. Number one is checking out the spots that have been designated as the best potential places to find the Sinergy's entry point. Number two is new, and that's letting Reynolds and the cabin crew; Kevin, Karen and Norma, experiment with the NPT. Our third goal is to meet back here for dinner, get an update from Reynolds on the NPT, and make our decisions on which areas we all go back to and search more in depth."

"What about monitoring the Sinergy, Sheriff? When do we start searching for them?" asked Marcus.

"If we're going out looking for their home," suggested Stanley, "I think we're already looking for them, Marcus. We've got to remember the entry point is also the passage back to their world. I, for one, have imagined it to be more like a bee hive, and if we disturb it, the entire colony may come after us!"

"Geez," Roxie sighed, "that's a terrible image!"

"Holy crap," Axel said. "That would really suck."

"Yes, Roxie and Axel," said the sheriff, "Stanley's scenario would be one heck of a terrible consequence."

"But it could happen," Norma stated. "We have no idea what these evil souls are capable of. We've only seen a glimpse of their powers."

"Listen, let's not get ahead of ourselves here," Robert interjected. "One thing at a time, and make sure you don't get yourself in over your head. Maybe we'll be surprised by a few things, but then again maybe these Wearing Stones will give us advantages, too. We just need to take this one step at a time, folks."

"Good advice, Robert," said the sheriff. "Okay, it's nearly 10:00 am and that's our go time. We have cell phones and radios for communicating, try contacting the group leaders first with any news. If there's trouble, get out of the area and head back here at once. Otherwise, let's plan on meeting right here by 4:00 pm. Any last-minute questions?"

"Just in case we run into a nest of evil souls," Axel said as he looked at the sheriff, "you got a hemi in that ATV?"

It was a great way to end their morning meeting, the group laughing as they began gathering their supplies for the day. Deputy Stevens, Robert and Stanley were first to head out. The department SUV kicked up dust as it headed along the two lane highway that would lead them to their first stop, Brackett's Bluff. Sheriff Anderson, Marcus, Axel and Roxie were not far behind. Sheriff Anderson's department quad-cab pick-up was pointed to the highway with the ATV sitting on the trailer, loaded and ready for service.

"Ready?" asked the sheriff.

"Oh, yeah," replied Marcus.

"You bet!" said Roxie.

"Oh, we're ready," said Axel, "just not sure what we're ready for!"

"What a beautiful day," Roxie declared. "It's hard to imagine the reason we're here is so awful."

"Not for me!" Axel championed. "We're here to save the day! I'm feeling like a Super Hero!"

"The shape you're in?" replied Marcus, "maybe Super Zero!"

"Really, Marcus?" Axel countered. "Sure you're ready to push it at the end of our run today? I may be in better shape than you think, and I wouldn't want to leave you too far behind."

"The only behind in play will be you looking at mine as I sprint away," Marcus joked.

"Very funny, guys, but you might want to save your fartlek workout for when it really counts," suggested Roxie. "Like when you're being chased by the Sinergy."

"That's a smart idea, Roxie," said Sheriff Anderson. "I know you guys are ready to go, but let's make sure our work is done before you challenge each other to a, well, whatever that fart-thing contest you were talking about is."

The sheriff's comments broke up the three runners-turned-investigators and they had a good laugh. After they contained their laughter, they explained the meaning of a speed-play workout to Sheriff Anderson.

"Oh, I see," he said. "Might be a great way to get in shape, but the Swedish language just doesn't seem to mix well with our American style English."

After a fifteen minute drive, Sheriff Anderson turned off the main road and into the trailhead.

"How far to the potholes?" asked Marcus.

"About a half mile," the sheriff replied. "Once we get clear of this parking area the trail really thins down. During the summer it's well travelled, but the park system never trims back the growth of the trees and brush very much. They want to keep it as natural as possible. That means you'll be feeling closed in until we reach the bend in the river where the potholes are, then it widens out and we can search that area more thoroughly. Remember, today we take a good look, but our goal is to get to each location, rank them and go back as one large group to really dig deep. Any questions?"

"Yeah," Axel laughed. "How fast will that ATV go with all four of us on board?"

With that rhetorical comment left hanging in the air, the foursome began their adventure with Marcus leading the way at a modest running pace. Low grasses flourished between the trail and the river, and dotted along this strip were willow and birch trees, spaced to offer glimpses of the ruggedness looming high above the far bank of the river. The land side of the trail offered a selection of tall trees, blue spruce, maple and pine. Large boulders were placed randomly as if they were in a game of marbles being played by Paul Bunyan. It was northern Minnesota at it's most natural state, with all the accents; mossy tree bark, lichen on granite, wood duck nest boxes, the river rock remnants of an early settlement foundation and across on open field, the skeleton of an abandoned pick-up truck, rusted to a dark chocolate brown from years of sun and snow.

Sheriff Anderson, scanning the trail from his seat on the ATV, thought to himself how lucky he was to have such dedicated members as part of The Voyageurs, and how quickly this whole team came to be. It had taken him and Robert, and then Norma, many years to gather information on what was causing the homicide and missing person numbers to rise in Havenswood Valley. Then, out of the blue, along come these three and in what seemed like just a few days, here they are searching for an enemy he had no idea truly existed until just recently.

"Well, that wasn't so bad," Roxie said. They had arrived at the bend in the river and as they looked across the water they could see the ripples from the potholes.

"I don't think I'd want to try this at night," offered Axel. "I think I'd get a little creeped out."

"You'd be fine, Axel," said Marcus. "You've camped and hiked enough to feel comfortable after a night or two."

"Maybe in a regular camping area," he replied. "All I could think about was Sinergy souls popping up as we ran along the trail. What easy targets we would be!"

"Speaking of targets," Sheriff Anderson said as he climbed off the ATV, "let me suggest how to survey this area. When you walk out to the exact bend in the river you'll be able to see clearly into the water almost all the way to the far bank. It's about forty feet wide at that point and narrower everywhere else. Let's divide up and start from there. Roxie and I will head south, Marcus, you and Axel will head north." He explained how to go over an area and notice details an untrained person would likely miss.

"I think I've got this," Roxie said proudly as she gazed over a ten meter circle around her. "I'm going to find something here, I just know it."

"Keep the same review system for every square foot of the area you are looking over. It's all about finding a system that allows you to move forward without missing a section and then doing it over and over again."

"Let's hit some potholes!" cheered Axel.

As the four searchers began making their way to the bend in Passage River, three other members of The Voyageurs were starting to explore the Brackett's Bluff area of Havenswood Valley, heading out along the trail that meandered along the base of the bluffs. The actual Brackett Bluff was a projection in the middle of a half mile long stretch of exposed, glacially deposited top soils that normally support tree and groundcover growth between the granite rocks and boulders. The slope and southern exposure of this specific land area led to erosion and eventually, the bluff.

"You know," Robert said, "I've been walking these bluffs my whole life and they haven't changed one bit, and here I am all wrinkled and slow and losing strength. We really are just a piece of dust on this Earth, aren't we?"

"That's funny. My grandpa used to tell me stories about these bluffs, how he and his brothers would come out here and hike around, drink beer and shoot guns," Deputy Stevens said. "I never thought much about it till just now, but one of the last stories he told me was something to do with coming out here around Halloween one year with a bunch of friends. I think they were all fairly young, in their twenties. Anyway, he and his last surviving brother laughed about getting scared, but it was the first and only time I'd ever noticed a look in their eyes that said something else happened that night. Something they weren't talking about."

"Did you ever ask him about it?" inquired Stanley. "If something did happen?"

"No, never did. He died shortly thereafter," replied Deputy Stevens, "and I didn't have a close enough relationship with his brother to ask him. Heck, I was in my late teens and probably blew it off as me seeing something in the way they reacted to each other that wasn't there. But now, now I look back and would bet something really did happen that night."

"Well, let's keep that in mind and see if you can work with Eleanor and figure out when your grandpa was there and if there was an incident at the Bluffs," said Robert. "It's worth a try."

"Sure, that's a good idea," replied the deputy. "Thanks, and I'll see if I can talk to Uncle Paul, grandpa's brother, about the bluff incident."

"Good luck, Deputy. By the way, since I'm new to the bluffs," said Stanley, "what's the plan here, other than not falling off the edge of the trail?"

"That's a good plan to start with," said Robert. "Let's try not to end up like Billy Brackett; crumbled and battered at the bottom of the cliff."

"Yeah, that sounds like a good goal," laughed Stanley. "That's how the bluffs got their name?"

"Yep," answered Robert. "During prohibition, everyone was looking for places to make booze. There was a camp in the woods up there," he pointed behind the outcropping of the cliff, "and one night 'ol Billy got up and took a long leap all on his own. Nobody ever came up with a reason why, other than he must have been drinking a bad batch of liquor."

"Or, maybe he and the deputy's grandpa saw something up there that got under their skin," offered Stanley.

"So, do we head up there?" the deputy asked as he was looking at the cliff.

"That's my best guess for a place to check out," said Robert. "We can catch the ravine trail just around the corner. It's steep but well traveled so we shouldn't have any trouble."

"I'm sure Billy was thinking the same thing when he set up his still," laughed Stanley.

The three men made their way along the trail, kicking up some dust, looking around for any clues that the Sinergy may frequent the bluffs. It was secluded enough, especially at the top. People usually stayed along the trail, hiking out a mile or two then coming back. There wasn't anything of particular interest, the flora and fauna being typical for the region, but the bluff's size did call out for a visit by all. Most residents responded one time or another while they lived in Havenswood Valley. It was an attraction with more notoriety than it was probably due, but then again in a small town it doesn't take much to get noticed, and tales about ghosts and illegal booze grow more interesting over time.

"Halfway?" Stanley huffed. He was tired.

"I'd say so," answered Robert. He too, was feeling the exhaustion setting in. "Not as well traveled as I remember, and a lot steeper than when I was young. Guess it has changed," he joked.

"About two hundred feet, cliff top to bottom of the bluff," stated Deputy Stevens. "Trail we're on is longer," he slowed his pace, "guess we don't need to rush it."

"What the?" Robert exclaimed.

"Over there! Look at the rocks!" yelled Stanley.

Down the other side of the ravine a dozen or more football sized rocks were rolling to the bottom of the bluff as if racing to see which one would crash onto the trail floor first. They seemed to jockey for position, pushing and bumping their way until they hit the trailhead, split open and careened to a dizzying stop.

"That didn't look normal," Stanley pronounced. "That did not look normal!"

"Hang on, Stanley," Robert calmly said. "We're out here telling stories and getting anxious about the Sinergy. Everything is going to look suspicious."

"I don't know, Robert, I've got to agree with Stanley," said Deputy Stevens. "If I didn't know better I'd say those rocks were shot out of a cannon, not dislodged from the side of a hill, and not thrown down by somebody up on top of the bluff." The three men looked up and down the ravine. Nothing moved, and nothing could be seen at the top of the bluff where the rocks must have come from.

"If you two don't mind, I'd like to say this is one area we need to come back to as a group, hopefully with Reynold's gun," Stanley said.

"Today was supposed to be a recon of the areas," added Deputy Stevens. "I'm good with your suggestion, Stanley. I don't need to see the top of the bluff and I really don't want to have any granite stones raining down on us. Let's head down and drive over to the bridge."

"Can't say I disagree," Robert added. "No sense in overdoing it our first day. Besides," he smiled and continued, "we wouldn't want to take all the excitement away from our other members."

"They're beautiful," said Roxie. "I've seen some of these along the St. Croix River, but those are all above water. They look so different below the surface."

"Hypnotic," Axel said as he stared at the ripples the lips of the taller potholes generated. "Sheriff, do people go diving into them?"

"Oh, yeah," he replied. "People have been swimming in these for decades. Not much found in them, they're pretty shallow, maybe eight feet deep for the one in the middle. I've learned over the years the geology of the area filled in around them with small rocks and debris, and the potholes themselves have filled up with silt and gunk, but were cleaned out about ten years ago by a local college biology department."

"Well, they look pretty cool anyway," said Marcus. "I could see how they would attract attention."

"And smallies!" Axel added. "I bet they bite like crazy in the spring. We should try fishing here some time, Marcus."

"Sure, Axel," he replied, "right after we seal the Sinergy's escape hatch, unless it's at the bottom of one of those potholes. In which case I'll never want to lure anything out from them, not even small mouth bass."

"Until then," said the sheriff, "I'd like to get started on our review of the area. Let's keep our search limited to a quarter mile up or down stream, and about twenty-five feet from the edge of the river. Phones on, radios on, eyes wide open. Stick close to the rivers edge on your way out, then move away from the edge on your way back here. Should take about thirty minutes each way. Let's set a time of fifty minutes to meet back here. Okay?"

"Got it, Sheriff," answered Axel. "On our way now, let's go Marcus."

"Be careful!" Roxie called out. "I know they'll be alright," she said to Sheriff Anderson, "it's just a habit."

"And a good one at that," he replied. "Those are two sharp, young men, but reminders are never a bad thing. You ready to start?"

"Yes, and excited to look at the river like a real detective!" she said.

"One thing I've learned," said Sheriff Anderson, "is that once you start doing investigative work you'll never really look at things, or people, the same way. We get down to the details that separate our viewpoint from that of the average citizen."

"During investigations or all the time?" asked Roxie.

"Well, for some it is all the time," he replied. "We need to look at the big picture, of course, but without dialing in the final aspects of anything we do, well, nothing gets finished. Can't see the forest for the trees kind of thing."

"Got it," Roxie replied. She and the sheriff began their trek down the river at a very slow pace, stopping often to ask each other if a certain area looked like a potential spot for the Sinergy's entry point. Roxie was nervous today, even though Marcus and Axel were pumped up about finally getting out and searching, she knew they would soon have to confront the Sinergy at their most powerful spot, and that meant the members of The Voyageurs would be at a disadvantage. "You think we'll find anything, Sheriff?" she asked.

"Robert says we're going to find it," replied the sheriff. "He said he's got a feeling like never before that a reckoning between the Sinergy and The Voyageurs is close at hand."

"Really?" Roxie asked.

"Yes, and he's very serious about it." The sheriff stopped and stared at a section of the river on the far side of where he and Roxie stood. "He said so much has happened in such a short time he's convinced we'll find their entry point." He stared a few seconds longer at the brush on the other side of the river, gave a shrug and started to walk on. "His biggest concern is not being there when it happens. He's afraid you three are going to get into trouble and if anything goes wrong, well, he just couldn't take it. I know it would break his heart if anything happened to you three, anyone really, but you've all grown on him and he wants to keep you out of harm's way. Like we all do, of course, but Robert's got a deeper vendetta against this thing than anyone else does. With Robert, it's very personal."

"We sure like Robert," Roxie replied. "It's ironic but after what happened to Edgar we want to make sure he's being careful." She bent down to pick up a stone that looked as if it had been polished and cleaned just for her. "Nature is truly amazing, I look at the beauty of this simple stone, and then in the same moment remember I'm here trying to find the home of an incredibly dangerous element in our world. Such amazing differences from the same planet, it's too bad."

"Don't get discouraged, Roxie," the sheriff responded. "There's plenty of wonder in the world and lots of great people to keep things in check, like you and Marcus and Axel. You three give me and the others hope that our world will continue to move ahead and become a better place for everyone."

"Thanks, Sheriff, and back at ya," Roxie replied. "We never thought we'd be hanging out with such a diverse group of people, but we love it. Hey, look at that stack of rocks ahead," Roxie came to a stop and pointed at a three foot tall, somewhat triangular shaped collection of rocks, heaped together about twelve feet from the edge of the river.

"Interesting," Sheriff Anderson said. "Let's take a look."

"So far," Axel announced, "this is kind of boring. When's lunch?"

"Very funny. Anyway, we just got started, what'd you expect?" Marcus answered.

"Don't know, just want to know how it's going for everybody else and if we're the only ones with nothing happening," Axel said.

"That could be a good thing," Marcus replied, "especially since we're on our own. Wow, check this out!" Marcus stepped into the river and about two feet from shore and bent down to picked up a very small snake, about six inches in length. "I've never seen one of these in the wild! It's a Redbelly snake, pretty cool."

"Sure, if you like that sort of thing," Axel said. "Me, I'm more of a hunter than a gatherer."

"I know, big game hunter. Hey, nothing wrong with that," Marcus said. "Okay, little guy, time to head home." He set the tiny reptile down. "They don't get much bigger than this, maybe eight inches on average. Tough to make it in the woods being that small."

"Speaking of surviving in the woods, you think these Wearing Stones work?" Axel asked.

"Hard to say, we've never tested them," Marcus replied.

"Axel, Marcus, can you read me? Over." It was Sheriff Anderson on the walkie-talkie.

"Sheriff, this is Axel and I read you loud and clear." Axel loved his status as an outdoor gear nut and had the walkie-talkie at the ready. "What's the situation? Over."

"We're about two hundred yards past the bend in the river where we started," the sheriff replied. "Found a stack of rocks and want you two down here as soon as possible to take a look at this with us. Over"

"On our way. We'll run over and be there in a few minutes. Over." Axel looked at Marcus. "Cool! Let's get rolling! If it wasn't for all these trees we could probably see them from here."

"Let's go!" Marcus took off at tempo pace, Axel matching his gait, stride for stride.

"What is it?" Marcus asked the sheriff as he and Axel came to a stop near the neatly stacked river rocks.

"Not sure, Marcus," Sheriff Anderson replied. "So far we've just been looking in and around the stack, thought you two should get here and take a look. We'll give you a few minutes and if you don't see anything I think we'll take some pictures and then dismantle it."

"Too bad Reynolds isn't here, he might be able to tell us how long the stack has been in place," Marcus said.

"Looks pretty fresh," Axel remarked. "There isn't any moss or other growth that would suggest it's been stagnant in one place. I'd say it's been built fairly recently."

"You're probably right," said the sheriff as he clicked off a dozen photos. "Maybe a scout troop put it up for training. Let's take a few rocks off the pile and see if there's anything inside."

"Marcus, I'll hand the rocks to you and let's try and keep them in order so we can put this back as we found it, just in case we're disrupting someone's training," suggested Axel.

"Sure, good idea," Marcus replied. "Roxie, will you help me keep these in order?"

"No problem!" she said.

"Okay, starting from the top. Here's the first rock," Axel said. He pulled off three more and as Marcus and Roxie were laying out the large stones in order, Axel stopped and stared inside the pile that now resembled an open volcano. "Whoa, what do we have here?"

"What is it?" asked the sheriff.

"Seems like someone has hidden a small treasure for their friends to find," Axel replied. "Shall we check it out?"

"Mind if I take a look?" asked the sheriff. He stepped to the edge of the structure and peered into the open crater. "Hmm, looks like a small pouch, just big enough for a secret stash or a game reward, depending on who's playing. You never know how someone might be transferring drugs these days. Let's see what's inside." Sheriff Anderson reached into the pile and pulled out a small, tan colored leather pouch - about the size that would fit a deck of playing cards.

"Sounds like something's inside!" Roxie announced.

"Kind of heavy," reported the sheriff. "I'll just pull open the bag and take a look inside." He grabbed the drawstrings, loosened their bind around the opening of the pouch and pulled the small bag open. "Hmm," he said, "never would have thought this would be inside!"

"What is it?" pleaded Axel.

Sheriff Anderson opened his left palm and with his right hand poured a small bit of the contents of the pouch into his open hand.

"Is that what I think it is?" Axel asked.

"I think so, Axel," the sheriff replied. "Looks like zircon to me."

"Wow, this is weird," Axel said. "Who would have known to leave us these?"

"And what are we supposed to use them for? These are pretty small chips," said the sheriff.

"Really small, almost like shavings," suggested Marcus.

"Let's dig into this pile, see if there's anything else, and then get the heck out of here!" Roxie suggested. "I get the feeling we're being watched."

"I'm sure we're being watched," Marcus said, "but at least someone's out to help us for a change."

"I'm with Roxie," Axel said. "Let's dig through this pile then move on to our next spot. I think we found what we were supposed to find, let's not get greedy."

Ten minutes later, after a thorough dismantling of the rock pile led to nothing more than a couple of frogs, the three runners flanked the ATV on a quick run back to the sheriff's SUV and trailer. They were very apprehensive about their find, yet excited and eager to tell the rest of the team that someone was watching out for them.

"Yes, Deputy, go ahead and meet us back at the cabin," the sheriff said as he spoke into the handset inside the SUV. "Change of plans so we can go over something we found at the river. Meet us there ASAP. Over"

"Ten-four, Sheriff, see you at the cabin shortly. Over." Deputy Stevens replied.

Axel looked at Roxie, his eyes bright and a huge grin on his face.

"What are you smiling about, Axel?" she queried.

"Me? Oh nothing, just that we've discovered another treasure on our first day looking for a secret passageway, and the fact that there's somebody else that's got our back." Axel stared out the window, "I wonder what the regular people are doing today? You think anyone has a clue what goes on around them, just slightly outside of their normal life?"

"Sounds like Axel's world just added a couple of planets to his personal solar system," the sheriff said. "I think you'll like the view, Axel, just don't get nervous when you're hit with new challenges. Life will move at a much faster clip for you now, for all of you."

"I think we're ready, Sheriff," he replied.

"You were ready weeks ago," the sheriff said. "You just needed to open yourselves up to this adventure one step at a time, at your own pace."

"At our own pace," Roxie repeated. "That's how we train, guess it's only natural that's how we live."

"Sheriff," Marcus began, "have any of you ever thought there was someone watching over you?"

"Not once, not until today," he answered. "This is a huge step, I just wish I knew the next one to take."

"I may know what that next step is, Sheriff," Marcus answered, "and I have the feeling Reynolds is going to be leading the way."

CHAPTER 46

"How are you, Eleanor?" Norma spoke into the computer monitor microphone. She wasn't used to having two-way image conversations like this and kept combing her hair back with her fingers, thinking she was in front of a large TV audience.

"Oh I'm doing just fine, Norma, but I miss you all. Suddenly it's very quiet down here," Eleanor replied. "How are you and what's new in Havenswood Valley today?"

"I'm anxious. Our two search teams just returned from their first outings not more than five minutes ago," Norma said. "Glen, Roxie, Marcus and Axel found something they want to show us right away. It sounds pretty important so we wanted to see if you were available, too. Can you see the great room? That's where everyone will be."

"Oh, yes, very clear. Thank you for thinking to include me. Is everyone well?" asked Eleanor.

"Yes, everyone is doing well. Looks like we're going to get started. Let us know if you want to ask a question," said Norma, "I'll make sure to have the volume turned up so we can hear you."

The team was ready and Sheriff Anderson started the meeting with a question no one expected. "Is there anyone outside of our membership that has knowledge of our activities?" he asked, and then added a clarifier. "Down to the detail of what we were doing today, anyone?"

"Nobody could know what we were doing today, Glen," answered Robert.

"What about the fact that one of our vehicles was attacked on our trip up here?" Sheriff Anderson continued. "Nobody feels that one of us, whether on purpose or by accident, may have leaked crucial information about our movements?"

"No way!" exclaimed Axel. "We've kept everything super tight, Sheriff."

"I agree with Robert and Axel," added Kevin. "Even when Karen and I were in Arizona we never said a word to anyone. It had to be the Sinergy tracking us."

"Well, I agree with you three, and I'm sure the rest of our group does, too," replied the sheriff. "The Sinergy is a worthy adversary and we all know we've got our work cut out for us. However," he continued, "there is a new twist that was discovered today and it appears to put us in a much better position to battle our enemy."

"We're all ears, Sheriff," said Norma. "What in the world did you find out there today?"

"Why don't I let Roxie tell you what we found along the river. Roxie?" asked the sheriff.

"Sure!" she replied as she stood up to address the group. "The sheriff and I had been searching for what seemed like a pretty short time, still on our way out on the course we chose. Following near the river trail we took on the way out, Sheriff Anderson and I saw a mound of rocks that had not been there earlier, and I mean earlier as in about an hour before. We called Marcus and Axel to join us before we started to dismantle the mound, well, it was actually a pyramid shape, we took some pictures. Then just like it was planned for us, we're taking apart this pyramid shaped pile of river rocks about two feet high! Oh my gosh," Roxie took a deep breath, "my heart is pounding just thinking about it!"

"It's okay" said Marcus, "you're doing great."

"I'd be excited too, Roxie," said Stanley. "One rarely gets to discover true artifacts!"

"Right. Thanks, guys. So, we peel off a few of the rocks and near the bottom we see a small leather pouch, kind of what you would think would hold some old gold coins," she explained. "That's when it got really weird. I thought we'd find a note from someone playing a joke on somebody else, but this was meant for us. Sheriff Anderson reached in to grab the pouch and since we had no idea what was inside, he volunteered to open it."

"Here's the bag, Roxie," Marcus said as he handed it to her.

"I'll pour some of it out on the table," she said, and then emptied a portion of the contents for everyone to see.

"What the heck?" said Robert.

"This is definitely for us, not a joke for somebody else," said Stanley.

"How in the world did they know? This is scary, Glen," added Norma.

"I don't know how they knew," Reynolds said, "but these are just what the mad doctor ordered!"

"What do you mean, Steve?" It was Mrs. Hamsteen, asking a question over the computer hook up.

"Well, Mrs. Hamsteen, I think these small bits of zircon will be a much better sized unit to use for Betty, I mean the NPT. They should react faster in the chamber and enable me to pull the micro chemicals out through the laser to the targets. Someone gave us silver bullets for our Sinergy-killing gun."

"I knew it!" exclaimed Marcus.

"You're saying someone outside of our circle knows what we are up to?" asked Eleanor.

"And that we have the laser gun?" added Norma.

"That's pretty scary, Sheriff," stated Karen. "Are we being watched?"

"I'm thinking it's more like watched over," he replied.

"So why not just help us, why all the secrecy?" asked Kevin.

"I've been wondering the same thing," answered Sheriff Anderson. "I've dealt with many anonymous informants over the years and the number one reason they don't come forward is the fear of being hurt by the criminal. I can't say I blame them, but this is something that feels very different."

"Yes, Sheriff, very different," added Stanley. "I would wager that whoever planted these stones knows a lot more than we do about the Sinergy. And maybe the size is for another reason than the NPT, since that's such a secret. We might need to figure out another use for these small pieces."

"Stones certainly have different uses by size," interjected Norma. "Some are for decoration, some for ceremonial use, and some for potions and cultural recipes."

Robert offered an idea. "Suppose the zircon people have also been watching, or even fighting, the Sinergy and happened to see us at the cabin, or out in the woods, or even in Prairie Falls. I get the feeling they're farther down the road on this matter but don't have time to get involved with our mess, which means they have something much bigger on their plate."

"Or maybe just the opposite," countered Marcus. "For argument's sake, let's say they've had some interaction with the Sinergy, were beat back, and are now hiding from view. The only thing they discovered was the zircon as a weapon of some sort and they've passed it along to us in hopes we'll have better luck than they did."

"I think it's from water fairies that found it in the river and gave it to us for earrings!" Axel joked and got the group to relax for a minute.

"Well, I don't think Axel is correct, but Robert and Marcus both have solid views we should talk about. So first, Deputy Stevens," asked Sheriff Anderson, "how about you, Reynolds and Robert take a few of these smaller zircon stones and figure out a way to test that laser gun? If you can try it here, that would be best, but I can understand if Reynolds wants to use the lab at the college."

"Sure thing, Sheriff," replied Deputy Stevens. He turned to Reynolds and Robert, "Let's head outside and decide the best plan of action," then made his way to the front door, not waiting a second for the other two men.

"Guess we're going outside," Robert chuckled.

"Right behind you," added Reynolds.

"I've got to head outside, too" Marcus announced. "Sorry, it's the third time my mom's called in the last ten minutes. Something's up." He stepped through the doorway and onto the porch.

"Marcus, it's Mom," came the voice on the cell phone. Anna Jennings sounded nervous. "Where are you?" she asked. "Who's with you?"

"Mom, I'm fine, relax," Marcus could sense the anxious temperament of his mother. "I'm up at the cabin in Havenswood Valley with everyone."

"Everyone is there?" she cried.

"No, not everyone. Really, we're fine. The sheriff and his deputy are here, and so is Axel and Roxie, Kevin, Karen and a few others from our group." He tried to sound convincing but at the same time wanted to know what had made his mom so upset. "What's going on, Mom, is everyone at home safe? Is Dad alright?"

"Oh, Marcus, yes, I'm sorry, we're all fine, I'm just lost for words right now. Listen to me, son, this is very important. I know your group is very smart and you've already been through a lot, but I just got a call from my friend that found the first cabin rental for you kids. She's a nurse at Havenswood Valley Hospital, and called to ask if your group was in town. She said someone from the cabin was just at the hospital and that you were all in danger. I can tell you for sure, Marcus, she was as upset as I am now."

Marcus sat down in one of the Adirondack chairs and began to be mesmerized by his mother's words. The group figured he was going to be a while so they continued on.

"Ok, then, so we have the laser gun being tested, a couple of theories of why we were presented with the stones, and still no solid lead on the entry point of the Sinergy," the sheriff said.

"Are we at a dead end?" asked Roxie.

"Not exactly," Stanley offered. "At a time like this we need to make something happen. It's how we deal with quiet times that shows how we will handle the crazy times. If we just sit and wait, nothing will happen or it will pass by without us noticing."

"I agree with Stanley," Eleanor said, rather loudly, into the computer microphone. "In my research I've found that activity is the primary resource to finding an answer. We must search out our enemy to find them."

"Or as we say in my fishing boat," Axel added. "You can't catch a fish if your lure isn't in the water."

"Glen," laughed Norma, "I think it's time we get ready for action. Your team is ready to go!"

"Oh, hey, Marcus," Kevin said as Marcus came back into the room, "everything cool with your mom?"

"Yeah, she's fine," he responded, "just totally freaked out for us." It wasn't what he said, but how he said it that shut down the free flowing banter that had just filled the room. Marcus looked dazed, his thoughts spinning from the story his mother had relayed to him.

"Marcus," asked Roxie, "what's the matter? What did your mom say?"

"Dude," Axel said, "what's going on?"

"She got a call from an old friend, the nurse at Havenswood Valley Hospital that found us our first cabin rental. The day

Deputy Stevens, Stanley and Reynolds went to visit the mayor, she was on duty in his room. She saw the whole episode go down, when he started feeling bad, when he yelled at you to get out. At first she thought it was a reaction to his health, then later she heard something that scared the heck out of her and she realized it was the visitors he was trying to get out of the room."

"Marcus, take your time, son," Norma said. "No need to rush."

Sheriff Anderson had his notepad out, pen in hand. "Marcus, take a breath and try and tell us exactly what your mother said, in the order she said it."

"It's just, well, she only knows half the story but felt it was important enough to call my mom. When I add in what we know, holy crap, are we in a bizarre world or what?"

"Well said, Marcus." Stanley stood up and walked to the kitchen for a glass of water. "I can't think of a more apt way to put our situation."

"Go ahead and tell us about your conversation," Karen prompted.

"Well, her friend, Nurse Ann, knew we stayed at the cabin about this time each year and tracked my mom down." Marcus began to relax and explained what happened. "It was nearly 10:00 pm and Nurse Ann came into the room to check on the mayor, and now also Jericho, as he had been put in the same room. Everything seemed fine as she pulled the privacy sheets closed around the beds. She pulled the door open to leave but saw her clipboard on the far countertop. The door closed with her still in the room and as she was about to grab her clipboard, Jericho began to talk. She heard everything clearly through the privacy sheets."

"It's now or never, Turner. We've got to leave town or stop those cabin people dead in their tracks."

Nurse Ann froze in place.

"I know, I know," replied Mayor Turner. "But we're so close to making this area a productive breeding ground, I can't imagine leaving."

"If those kids and the sheriff figure out we're the ones they're looking for, it's going to be hell to pay trying to get free" Jericho replied. "Especially now that they have found the stones."

"They still don't know of our escape route," Mayor Turner replied. "However it may be only a matter of time before they find it. Our weaker members have no idea how to manage themselves in this world and it will lead to the death of us all here in this ugly outer world if they mess up and panic."

"Maybe your death, but I'm not letting any earth creature take me down," Jericho said. "I'll let the Wisps eat the stones and I'll head back."

Nurse Ann was beginning to panic at the thought of being discovered. What in God's name were these men talking about? She had to remember it all, but at the same time she needed an escape route.

"Listen, if they don't know we're the leaders we can stay clear and let the others try a few more times to take them out," Jericho said. "If they fail, then it's up to us to finish the job. Once they're all out of the picture we'll take a break, just like we always do, and then start up again with a new army. See if they can spawn here and build us a decent size following. We've been here this long, may as well try it again."

"You're right," the mayor replied. "Besides, seems like every place else is taken."

"I said lights out!" Nurse Ann banged on the door as she pulled it open, acting as if she had just burst into the room. "How are you two going to get any better if you don't get some rest?" She was amped up and caught the two patients well off guard. She ripped back both privacy sheets.

"Just as I thought, not a sleepy eye between you!" She continued in a forceful manner, "Time to get some rest! Good night, gentlemen!" She pulled the sheets back, made a slight detour to grab her clipboard and was out of the room and running down the hallway before the mayor and Jericho could utter a word. She had worked her impromptu plan to perfection.

"Wow, that's one brave woman," said Karen.

"No kidding," Kevin added. "What a great idea, and to make it so convincing. Good for her!"

"We're glad she made it out safely," said the sheriff. "That's a ton of incredible information, Marcus. Say, Kevin, would you please go out and have the others come back in? We need to bring them up to speed on this ASAP."

"She also said they've both been discharged Who knows where they are now or what they are working on," Marcus said.

"You guys had your Wearing Stones on when you met with the mayor and Jericho!" Axel exclaimed. "They work!"

"Yes, Axel," the sheriff answered, "it appears we have done our first two successful tests of the stones."

"Glen," Robert started to say as soon as he stepped into the cabin, "Kevin's talking crazy talk. Says the mayor and Jericho are the leaders of the Sinergy!"

"Apparently not crazy talk, Robert," Norma answered. "A third party intervention gave us the play by play of a hospital conversation between the two and we are more than sure it's true."

"Sheriff," Deputy Stevens said, "should we call for more units?"

"Not yet, Stevens," he replied. "Let's see what we come up with for a plan, first."

"I have a plan for myself," Eleanor offered. "I'm going to get the rings finished and up to you right away. I'm also going to start research on Mayor Turner and Jericho. Anything I dig up I'll let you know at once. Good luck and I hope to have information to you all soon. Bye for now!"

"Bye, Eleanor," said Norma as she turned to the group. "Once she gets an idea in her head, she's off and running!"

"Alright, everyone, this situation has just taken a huge leap forward. In my work we call this a break in the case, and this one just busted itself wide open!" The sheriff looked very serious. "Right now the mayor and Jericho are plotting ways to take us out, so if anyone wants to head south, no problem, I completely understand. Any takers?"

"I think we should work on a plan that involves all of us, Glen," Robert said and then looked around the room. "No one is going to leave."

"You're right, Robert, just had to ask," the sheriff replied. "Okay, here's the set up. Four teams of The Voyageurs; Marcus, Axel and Roxie are a team. Robert, Norma and Stanley are a team. Deputy Stevens and Reynolds are a team, and Kevin and Karen will join me as a team. Always together, never leave anyone behind or in a vulnerable position. Got it?"

The members of The Voyageurs all nodded in agreement.

"Reynolds, let's start with you," the sheriff said. "Have you had any luck with the laser?"

"Not yet. Didn't have enough time to warm it up," he replied.

"Let's get that thing humming. You and Deputy Stevens head back outside and get that gun operational, I have the feeling we'll need it much sooner than later." With those foreboding words still hanging in the air, Reynolds and the deputy left the cabin for the pole barn. "The rest of us are going to set a trap for our enemy, the same way it happened before," said the sheriff. "Same bait. Kevin, Robert, do you mind sitting in the grassy area again? You two seem the best at attracting the Sinergy."

"I'm good with that," Kevin answered.

"Fine by me," replied Robert.

"Norma, you and Stanley will be responsible for watching over Robert," the sheriff advised, "and that means he doesn't leave the grassy area. If he so much as stands up, you're on him. If he begins to walk in any direction, as if under the influence of the Sinergy, you tackle him and tie him to the two of you. Whatever it takes, you can't let him get away." He turned to look at Karen. "Sister, you and I are going to have to keep a close eye on Kevin, same rules I just explained to Norma and Stanley."

"What about us, Sheriff?" asked Axel. "We're ready, too."

"Oh, I know that," the sheriff chuckled. "You three are going to be out in front scouting for the Sinergy and then let us know when to expect them."

"Cool, we're the scout team!" added Axel.

"Couldn't have a better trio," replied the sheriff. "We'll all have walkie-talkies, so make sure to keep in touch at all times. You see anything out of the ordinary, let us know." The sheriff sat down at the table and looked hard at the carvings. "Who would have thought this old table held such secrets."

"Maybe we'll discover even more, Sheriff," Norma said. "You never know what may come from an encounter with the enemy."

"Very true, Norma. It will be dark in about an hour, so let's get outside and work on the details. Everybody, grab all the zircon you have and anything else you think may come in handy once the Sinergy arrives. Marcus, you bring the Sealing Stone."

"Uh, not that I'm scared," said Karen, "but I am getting nervous about all this. What's our back up plan, Sheriff?"

"So far we've beaten back the Sinergy every time," he replied, "so I'm counting on our history to hold true. Besides," he continued, "I've always wanted to give the mayor a piece of my mind, and now I get to figure out a way to stop him, whatever he is, from hurting anyone else again."

"Don't worry, Karen," Roxie said. "We're stronger now than the last time the Sinergy attacked us."

"For sure!" added Marcus "The zircon is a huge plus to our side. If just being near the stuff made the mayor and Jericho ill, once we figure a way to expose them to the stones they could be dead in a matter of minutes."

"Whoa," Kevin said. "How are we going to explain their deaths to anyone else?"

"Simple," replied Stanley, as everyone turned to him to hear his explanation. "When they come to attack us, they won't be in the form of the human shapes they have taken."

"That's right," added Norma. "They will be the Singery, not the mayor and Jericho."

"So if we finish off the Sinergy," Kevin continued, "the mayor and Jericho just disappear without a trace?"

"My feeling is that we'd end up finding their bodies in their beds, or some other comfortable place they use for their transition from human form to Sinergy," said Norma.

"Very common thought," added Stanley. "My research in Europe showed many similar instances reported throughout history where human bodies were found dead without any trace of a malady. The evil inhabitant left for a night out and never returned."

"You guys are freaking me out," Axel laughed nervously, "I know we've talked about stuff like this, but tonight it's real. How 'bout we just figure out how we're gonna take out whatever Sinergy shows up and then tomorrow we find out who it was?"

"Good point, Axel." Sheriff Anderson looked around the room and realized it was tense, yet focused. "Okay, like Axel said, let's just focus on what it is, not who it is. We've probably already battled the mayor and Jericho at some point and didn't even know it."

"Remember," Norma interjected, "they're not human, they're just in a human form to help them maneuver in our world. Don't get hung up on emotions. They sure won't."

"They're just a target we need to hit," said Robert. "And I'm damn ready to hit them as hard as I can."

"Then let's do this!" Marcus said with a power in his voice that showed he was ready for the fight. "Axel, Roxie, everyone, grab your gear like the sheriff said and let's meet at the fire pit." With that he left with his backpack full of the items he felt they would need including the Sealing Stone. Axel and Roxie were right behind him, the rest of the group quickly pulling their gear together.

"Hey, Kevin," Axel asked as they were walking to the fire pit, "did you ever think a trip to the cabin would be this crazy?"

"Oh I don't think this is crazy, Axel," Kevin laughed, "I think it's totally insane!"

Marcus, Roxie and Axel were the first to gather at the fire pit, dressed in clothing to keep them warm in the 46' evening temperature. The three have many memories of gathering around a blazing fire during their group trips to the cabin, but this night would be very different.

"You're pretty amped up, Marcus," said Axel. "Are you getting a feeling about tonight?"

"Yeah, I am. Didn't mean to be so obnoxious in there," he replied, "but I think we're going to have a rough go of it out here. So far we've just had to do enough to get the Sinergy to leave. Now we have to do way more than that."

"You think that means we have to kill them?" asked Roxie.

"Whatever they are, they have to be stopped," Marcus replied. "I guess that means we have to kill them, yes."

"Weird," Axel said flatly. "I hunt all kinds of animals and this is the first time I'm at a loss on what will work. We're really just pulling this one out of our butts, aren't we?"

"Maybe you are," laughed Roxie, "but I'm using what I've got in my pack, and the stones."

Marcus was actually smiling now, bordering on laughter "If you think what you pull out of your butt is going to stop them, you better get checked out by a doctor, Axel."

"You two are so twisted," he answered. "I need some new friends."

"You three all set?" asked the sheriff. His approach brought the three back into focusing on the matter at hand.

"We are, Sheriff," Marcus replied. "What are your thoughts on where we should be?"

"Well, I was going to ask you the same thing," he said.

"North side," offered Axel. "That's where I'd start. It was the direction we saw movement the very first night, and it was where Kevin was headed when he was being pulled in by the Sinergy."

"It's also where the wolves came from that attacked the moose," added Roxie.

"I'd agree with that," said Marcus. "We can start at the northeast corner and work our way west, toward the creek, then come south as we head back to the cabin."

"Yep, that's a logical approach," said Sheriff Anderson. "You won't be too far away at any one time and the north end does appear to be the direction of choice for our enemy. I brought the portable base camp walkie-talkie monitor, and everyone will have their own hand-sets. Just keep in touch with us at all times. Even if things are boring out there I want to hear your voices. Channel nine for everyone. Keep your headlamps handy, too."

At this point the rest of The Voyageurs had gathered around the fire pit.

"Look at us," said Norma, "three threes."

"Trees?" questioned Axel.

"Threes, she said," Stanley corrected. "As in everything comes in threes."

"Exactly," replied Norma. "We have three groups, each with three members."

"Except for Deputy Stevens and Reynolds," said Karen.

"True," replied Stanley. "Maybe they are the odd men out."

"I don't know," said Kevin. "That laser gun Reynolds has should count for something."

"Two's, three's, on my own, doesn't matter to me," said Robert. "Let's get this hunt started."

"Right, let's get rolling," Sheriff Anderson said. "First, let's review what's worked in the past for us. Who can tell me what we've had success with in fighting off the Sinergy?"

"I remember the shotgun being fired when we were being attacked at Hamsteen Manor," Marcus offered. "And also here on the night Kevin was being pulled in. We ended up agreeing it was the vibration of the pellets that did the trick."

"Loud music!" Axel added. "Same as Marcus said, on the night Kevin was heading into the woods. I think we said the sound waves were what worked."

"Music was also used the night the three of us drove down from Havenswood Valley to Prairie Falls, Glen," said Norma. "You had your external music system going as loud as possible."

"Those are all correct, as far as my recollection goes," agreed Sheriff Anderson.

"Light, I remember light being a part of our battle on Kevin's night, and again when he and I were in the desert," Karen exclaimed. "The lights, oh, and the loud exhaust pipes from the motorcycles, I never thought of those! Light and vibration!"

"I took the liberty of bringing a few fire extinguishers to our party," said Robert. He peeled down the burlap of a bag containing the four he had brought to the fire pit. "They don't look too mean, but one of these things saved my life not too long ago, so I'm kind of partial to them."

"If you say they work I'll be glad to carry one wherever I go!" said Axel.

"I've carried a lot of things on my trips, but this is a new one for me," said Stanley. "Exactly how did one of these work for you?"

Robert explained how he had grabbed a fire extinguisher as a last resort while being attacked in the basement of Tres Azure, that it was a stroke of luck he was even able to pull the pin and squeeze the handle, much less that the mixture turned the evil of a Sinergy minion into a puff that blew out the window.

"You know, I'm not sure it went out the window on its own accord," Robert said thoughtfully. "Looking back, it may have turned to dust and just been sucked out the window. Well, either way I'd keep one handy, and be close enough to make it work."

"So now that we have our weapons," Karen said, "what's the plan Sheriff Anderson?"

Karen was still nervous, but with good reason. She had seen the Sinergy in Havenswood Valley, Prairie Falls and near her home in Scottsdale, Arizona. Karen was still all in, but she didn't want anyone to put their lives on the line without knowing exactly what the plan was. She eyed Sheriff Anderson with a look that said as much, and he knew it was a fair question.

"I'll be frank with you. For everyone else in Havenswood Valley, it's just another fall evening. Cool temps, starry sky and nothing out of the ordinary going on, but we all know that's really not the case. Looking out into the woods here, I can't imagine how in the world we're going to really end the terror of the Sinergy, but I know we've turned it back without our best weapon, the zircon stones. Tonight the plan is to do what's worked in the past," shared the sheriff, "entrapment!"

Sheriff Anderson was in charge of a task that had been in the making for over twenty years and had changed the course of his life. "We're going to toss our bait out just like Axel would when he's casting for a largemouth bass. Just before the strike we're going to move in and take the prey before it takes us. Simple as that."

"You mean laser the prey!" announced Reynolds as he headed to the fire pit.

"Sheriff, we need one of these for the department!" Deputy Stevens added, talking as if he was nearly out of breath. "This thing is beyond awesome!"

Reynolds and Deputy Stevens had come into the group with grins splashed from ear to ear, totally excited with the results the chips of zircon had provided as fuel for the NPT.

"I take it the testing has gone well?" the sheriff asked.

"The NPT works like a charm with the zircon chips, it's like they were made for it! Works better than any material we've tried in our lab," said Reynolds. "I can't wait to write up the results for my team!"

"Boys and their toys, doesn't get much better for them than that," Roxie sighed and looked at Karen and Norma, both well aware of the fondness men have for their weapons. "How many bursts from the laser will it take to bring down a Sinergy?" Roxie asked, wanting to be taken seriously. "You have a gauge for that on your laser?"

"Uh, no, I don't," answered Reynolds. "That's something we'll have to field test."

"Oh, like when Kevin and Robert are sitting ducks in the middle of the field?" Karen responded.

"Hey, that's not fair," Axel said. "No one would know that answer. We just have to assume it's going to work much better than the stones did on the mayor and Jericho."

"I don't think it's fair we assume anything when someone is putting their life on the line," Karen shot back. "Especially now that we know they're really coming after us."

"Alright now, it doesn't do us any good to challenge each other. Let's figure this out," Sheriff Anderson said. "Reynolds, what are your expectations with your laser?"

Steve Reynolds was not nearly as excited now that he was holding a weapon of unknown power that would be defending Kevin and Robert as they sat waiting to be attacked. "Well," he said slowly, "with the rate of transfer Deputy Stevens and I witnessed, I'd say we can hold a Sinergy at bay with the first burst, and from then it's just counting the time it takes to refuel. Guessing about thirty seconds for the second burst."

"Okay, that's fair," the sheriff said, "but I'm going to change it up. Robert, we'll just have you in the field with Reynolds stationed here at the fire pit. Everyone else will be set up in a semi-circle with one or more of our weapons. When I give the signal, Reynolds will fire the laser and we can see how it works. How much zircon do you think you'll need?"

"From the short test, I'd say this stuff has an extremely long chamber duration rate," Reynolds answered. "I'd guess we have enough to burst 24 hours a day for a week, maybe two. I just need more field testing to be able to formulate a more accurate answer."

The teams were then divided up into areas around the grassy field, with weapons and stations assigned to each pair. Between the shotguns, search lights, alarms, fire extinguishers and music, they would be ready for battle.

"One last thing," Sheriff Anderson said, "Robert will have a small box with the extra Wearing Stones, and another one that contains the Sealing Stone. Any time you want to pull them out, Robert, you go for it. Don't wait for my orders if you feel uncomfortable out there, but when I do yell for you to open the boxes, don't hesitate a second. Got it?"

"Sure, Glen," Robert agreed. "I won't play the hero."

"Darn right you won't!" Karen added, with a hint of a smile. She felt better knowing a plan was in place that wouldn't jeopardize Kevin and that Robert was being watched over with great care.

"Axel, Roxie, we should get going," Marcus said. "It's time to head out on the trail."

"Good luck!" Roxie said as the trio headed up the path and away from the cabin.

"You guys be safe out there," Stanley called back. "I hope you have your running shoes on!"

"You bet we do! Ain't no Sinergy monster going to outrun us tonight!" Axel yelled.

"This is the only part of the plan I don't like," Sheriff Anderson said. "But we've got to have some scouts and those three are the best fit for the job."

"Don't worry, Glen," Norma said. "We've seen those three in action and I'd bet on them versus the Sinergy any day."

They watched for another minute as the trio made their way into the woods. Two shotguns, a fire extinguisher, high beam light, one hundred decibel alarm and their Wearing Stones made for an odd looking array of weaponry. It was rag-tag at best, but the best they could muster.

"I'm hoping they don't see a thing, that the Sinergy comes to the cabin," Sheriff Anderson said. "That's my hope, that they come back and it's all done and over."

"They're pretty amazing kids, Glen," Norma said. "They just might surprise us all."

"Hey, Glen, I'm ready for the chopping block!" Robert said with a laugh. "Bring on the Sinergy!"

"You're way too anxious, Robert," he replied. "Don't think you're going to take them all by yourself, now. You'll have to share the battle with the rest of us."

"Only if you can keep up with me!" he laughed.

The trio of Marcus, Roxie and Axel had been walking for ten minutes and were approaching the northeast corner of the trail, at which point they would then turn west along the wooded section of Robert's land and head to Passage Creek. The night was calm, a light whisper from the leaves and tall grass was nearly all they heard.

"Anyone else thinking it's really quiet out here?" asked Roxie.

"For sure," answered Axel, "no crickets, nothing."

"Might just be the time of year when not much is going on," offered Marcus.

"Or maybe everything is in hiding from the Sinergy," replied Roxie.

"What was that?" Axel said, his voice raspy, his throat suddenly dry and tight. He had heard the rustle of brittle leaves about twenty yards into the woods.

"It's over there," Marcus pointed. "Get down," he directed and the others joined him in a low crouch on the trail. They instinctively moved to the edge of the trial, working to find a pinch of cover to blend in with.

"I see something! Look, over there. By the tallest spruce," Roxie said as quietly as possible. "Oh my gosh! It looks like a mountain lion!"

"It is," Axel confirmed. "Not the biggest one I've ever seen, but they're strong and fast no matter the size."

"What about those two?" Marcus said as he pointed out a pair of mountain lions about fifteen feet behind the first one. They were walking in tandem and appeared to be slightly larger than the first. Moving without a sound they appeared to be in no hurry, yet moving with purpose. They passed out of sight and the three Voyageurs members knew what to do.

"There were three of them, Sheriff," Marcus said on the walkie-talkie. "One on its own, then two more following close behind. That's all we've seen so far."

"Thanks for the update, Marcus," the sheriff answered. "We'll be ready for them and let you know how it goes. You three head to the creek now and be very careful. If they are Sinergy then I'm sure more will be coming."

"Will do, Sheriff," he replied. "Good luck!"

"Don't you want to go back to the cabin and help?" asked Axel.

"Of course," answered Roxie, "but we have to be the eyes and ears out here and give them a heads up."

"I know, it's just tough to miss out on the action," Axel said. "I sure hope that laser gun works."

"Me too," Roxie said.

They walked the dirt path, stopping at the slightest sound or movement. Halfway to their destination Marcus began to feel uneasy. He had admitted to Axel earlier that his senses were telling him something was going to happen, he just didn't know what.

"Guys, I'm thinking we need to be super careful out here. More than we were thinking," Marcus said. He looked around and although nothing was out of the ordinary at the moment, he knew something was not right.

"Do you think we should go back to the cabin?" asked Roxie.

"No, not yet, but let's keep closer to the woods. It hides us better." He replied.

"You sure we don't need to go back?" Axel asked.

"Something's going on, but not at the cabin," he said as if in a trance. "C'mon, let's keep moving."

"Sheriff, I'd like to make a suggestion, if I may," Stanley offered.

"Sure, Stanley, what's on your mind?" the sheriff answered.

"If we have enemies on the way," he said, "there really is no need to place bait out in the open. I think we should have Robert come back to us here by the fire pit."

"You'd make a great officer, Stanley, I was about to call for everyone to join us here." Sheriff Anderson continued, "I'll get Robert, you start the word to quickly gather here. I don't want anyone on their own if those are Sinergy on the way. Let's go."

Stanley rushed to tell the others as Sheriff Anderson hustled out to get Robert. Gathered together at the fire pit, Sheriff Anderson gave new instructions for setting up their defense. The trucks were repositioned, and each member was given new instructions for handling an attack. They felt ready, but not sure for what.

And then, as if on cue, the first mountain lion walked into the clearing at the north end of the grassy area.

"Hey," Axel said, "up there, past the old rock fence on the right. It looks like something moving through the woods."

"I see it," answered Roxie. "Do you think it's a Sinergy? And does it look purple to you guys?"

"Looks like really dark red to me," said Marcus. "There goes another one!"

"Holy crap!" Axel said. "There's a couple more from the other direction. They look like blobs moving across the ground. No real shape, and not very fast."

"Guys, maybe it's time we head back to the cabin," Marcus suggested. "Something's going on and we need to let the sheriff know this might be more than we can handle."

As soon as Marcus stopped talking there was a new sound from the woods. It began as if the wind was calling them to join the masses heading into the woods, a delicate invitation. It turned into a siren of a tall waterfall, caressing down a hillside and into a pool of water. The trio stood silent, each straining to decipher the sound and the direction of its origin. More shapes began to appear in the woods, some coming down from the treetops, floating into an area that held the colors of each as if it were a rainbow colored pond. Purple, deep red, neon green, yellow and blue. Bright hues, yet all colors found in nature.

"No one's going 'Kevin' on us, are they?" Axel asked, wondering if anyone was being pulled in as Kevin had been.

"Not me," answered Roxie, "but I do want to be a little closer."

"Me either, and I've changed my mind about going back. Let's move over and get a better look," Marcus said.

They took a few steps, and as they moved around a group of thick trees they stopped dead in their tracks.

"No way!" Axel stated.

"Incredible!" Roxie gasped.

"This is it!" Marcus whispered. "The entry point!"

Marcus grabbed Roxie's left hand, and nodded to her to reach out and grab Axel's left hand as Marcus guided them across the path and into a patch of birch trees for some cover and yet still be able to keep on eye on things. They stopped behind the birch and crouched low to the ground.

"You were right, Marcus," said Roxie. "Something big is going on tonight, and not at the cabin."

"The cabin is just a distraction," offered Axel. "Whatever is going on over there, that's the main event."

"You guys remember that spot?" Marcus questioned. "It's the old nasty tree that's all gnarled up and smelly. Remember when we checked it out on our last trip here?"

"You're right!" Axel exclaimed, "I didn't even notice that."

"So that really is it?" asked Roxie.

"Yeah," answered Marcus. "I'm betting that's their way into our world, but right now it's exit time. Those mountain lions must be the mayor and Jericho and one of their minions. Figures they'd go for king of the forest instead of a lowly moose this time."

"Guess they want to leave in style," Axel mused.

"Let's get the stone and stop them from leaving," Roxie blurted out without really thinking. Marcus and Axel just stared at her for a few seconds, and then the three made an amazing plan - something that was so crazy it would only work if everything went perfectly! It was a deadly gamble.

"Why not, for if not us, then who?" Axel said with as much seriousness as he had in his body.

And with that Marcus was off, running as fast a pace as he dare go on his way to the cabin. He'd have to save some energy for the return run, knowing he'd have more weight in his pack. The motivation of winning this battle with the Sinergy was all he needed to be swift and quiet on the trails. He'd be approaching the cabin in what would feel like no time at all.

"Sheriff, this is Roxie. Come in. Over." She turned the volume down on the walkie-talkie.

"Anderson, here. Over."

"Sheriff, we found the entry point," Roxie announced in a hushed voice. "We found it and it's being used for all the

Sinergy to escape. There are dozens of them heading down a hole in the base of an old tree near the rock fence. Over."

"Don't get too close. If there are that many there you could be overwhelmed. We have one of the mountain lions in sight right now, but it's just sitting at the end of the field. Why don't you sit tight until we see what happens here. Over."

"Sheriff, this is Axel. Marcus will be there in a couple minutes. You need to give him the Sealing Stone without the mountain lions seeing it happen. He's going to be on the creek side of the field. Have Norma bring it to him right away, then we'll get it over the hole before the mayor and Jericho can make it back. We don't think they're going to fight, they're just stalling so the other Sinergy can escape. You've got to keep them busy until we get the Sealing Stone in place. Over."

"I'll give it to Marcus, but you have to promise me you'll only try it if there's a clear and open shot at getting it sealed. No hero stuff, you hear me?" Sheriff Anderson commanded.

"Loud and clear," Axel answered. "You just hold them in place with that laser gun and we'll do the rest. Marcus should be there by now, do you see him? Over."

"Yes, I do. He's hiding along the west side, and it's a good thing. The other two mountain lions have just wandered in and are sitting behind the first one. Gotta go. Good luck! Over."

The others had heard the entire conversation on the base monitor, and Robert had already given Norma the Sealing Stone. She looked at Stanley and motioned for him to make some movement along the far side, closer to the cabin. Kevin and Karen joined him, hoping to give Norma a more discreet exit to Marcus.

"I don't know what the range is on the NPT, Sheriff," Reynolds said. "This is going to be a first."

As those on the far side became more active, Robert held the switch for the spot light and motioned to Norma. He hit it with three quick flashes, right at the eyes of the mountain lions, hoping to blind their vision for a moment. Norma took the opportunity and rushed to Marcus, who took the Sealing Stone and disappeared into the darkness without a sound. The mountain lions growled, pawed at the air and stood up. They looked and sounded upset, walked in a couple of circles then sat back down.

"I especially don't trust the first one," Deputy Stevens announced. "That's the one that will rush us first. Reynolds, your laser hot?"

"Oh yeah, I'm ready!" he replied.

"Sheriff, I think we need to make an offensive move here. Let's see what this thing can do," the deputy said.

"No need," Sheriff Anderson replied. "We've got one coming our way all on its own!" The first mountain lion was indeed making its way. Slowly, not directly, seeming to be stalking them in plain sight.

Norma was now in the truck bed ready to hit the spot lights, Karen in the other truck ready to blast the sound waves. Robert, Stanley and Sheriff Anderson each held shotguns at the ready, fire extinguishers were placed near everyone, and of course each member of The Voyageurs had their wearing stones on. They knew the stones worked, thanks to the mayor and Jericho, but in every battle something changes, something causes the playing field to be tipped in one direction over the other. They prayed silently this was their night to gain an advantage.

"Oh, Marcus, you look terrible, are you hurt?" asked Roxie.

"I tried to put the stone in my pack without stopping, bad idea," he replied. "I nearly killed myself when I fell because I was trying to keep the stone from hitting the ground. My forearms are toast from the gravel."

"Dude, you must have been running six minute pace to get back here so quick," said Axel. "We're doing a 5k next weekend!"

"Yeah, sure, whatever," Marcus said. "All three of the mountain lions are sitting in the field by the cabin, just hanging out. What's been going on here?"

"Same, only it's a lot less busy," Roxie answered.

"I think their plan was to get out quick," said Axel. "Except for the mayor and Jericho."

Marcus looked at the spot where just a short time ago brightly colored blobs were gathering and then disappearing into the earth. There was a slight glow to the area.

"Should we move on with our plan?" Marcus asked. "I'm feeling recovered and it looks like the action has stopped. Maybe there's still some light glowing, do you two see it?"

"Oh, yeah, I see it," answered Roxie. "I think it's their slime trail."

"I'd second that," Axel added. "Wait, there goes one more, an orange one."

"Alright, let's get our gear out and double check our list," said Marcus. "We better hurry though, before the mayor and Jericho try and escape."

"They're going to be really pissed," Axel laughed. "I can't wait to see their faces, and then BAM! We hit them with the laser!"

"Except we don't have the laser, Axel," said Roxie.

"Right, forgot about that part again. Dang, we need two of those guns," he replied.

"If the laser works, they're going to head this way as fast as they can. Remember, we're just here to seal off the source and then run like crazy back to the cabin," Marcus reminded them. "Like the sheriff said, no hero stuff!"

"And that goes double for you, Marcus," Roxie said with as stern a look as she could muster.

Deputy Stevens and Reynolds took a few paces into the field. It had meandered to the middle of the field, roughly forty yards from the fire pit. As Reynolds took aim, the group stood as if in prayer. Most were.

"Is there a power setting on that laser?" asked the deputy.

"Just on and off," Reynolds replied.

The mountain lion crouched down, as if ready to pounce. The two at the back of the field took a few steps closer, then sat on their haunches. Knowing the battle was to begin, they would view the action as spectators. The mountain lion leapt as if propelled upward from the ground, its elongated stride eating up nearly five yards with every lunge.

"I'd say it's 'On' time!" yelled Deputy Stevens.

The only person that would be able to say exactly what happened next was Reynolds. The fact that he had remembered to put on protective eyewear gave him the distinct advantage of being able to see his target, hit his target and maintain the laser in the right place. The mountain lion didn't have a chance. A slight glance to the eyes of the mountain lion and the mammal was blind. Then, as the NPT beam of transported zircon particles hit the body, the stiffening of muscles set in, followed by a slowing of the heart and a tightness in the lungs. It was over before it had started. This Sinergy attacker turned from beast to bile in less than a minute. A mass of fluid started to seep onto the grass. Thick as motor oil, it would take time to soak into the soil.

Loud roars emerged from the remaining two mountain lions. They raised up like wild horses on their hind quarters, then, as if their minds were playing games on them, the members of The Voyageurs saw the two furry felines morph into their named enemies, Mayor Evan Turner and Jericho Brown.

"Norma, I want you, Karen and Kevin to get inside my truck, now! Stanley, you and Robert post yourselves at the front of the truck. Reynolds, you and Deputy Stevens step over here. We're going to be in the front and pray to God Almighty that laser works as well on these two as it did on that first one."

"Very impressive!" yelled Mayor Turner. "That was a startling display you put on. I've never seen anything like it. Government issue, Sheriff?"

"Just a little something we cooked up here in Havenswood Valley. Special order just for you!" he yelled back.

"Don't worry about us," the mayor shouted. "Just came to say goodbye and thanks for all the wonderful memories. It's been easy to live off the land, so to speak. We've quite enjoyed the flavor of your people, if you know what I mean!"

"You bastards!" yelled Robert. He broke from the truck and walked at the two figures, unloading his shotgun as he went. Deputy Stevens pulled him back after Robert's shotgun chamber was empty.

"You are so predictable, Robert," Jericho yelled. "You're such an easy target, we could never bring ourselves to finishing you off completely."

"Let's get this over with, Reynolds. Follow me," the sheriff said. They began walking right at the two Sinergy figures.

"It's not hot yet," Reynolds whispered to the sheriff. "I don't think it will work."

"Act like it will, that's all I need!" he replied. "How close do we need to be?"

"Thirty yards, just like the last one," Reynolds replied. "The zircon won't travel any farther."

They were in the middle of the field when the mayor spoke again. "We'd love to stay and talk about old times, but our exit visa is about to expire," he laughed. "Good riddance to you all! May your people continue to destroy each other until your world is ruined beyond repair."

"Hey, Norma, just so you know," shouted Jericho, "your mother was my favorite!"

The two Sinergy members turned and disappeared into the woods beyond the field, just as the NPT was ready for another blast.

"It's ready, Sheriff!" Reynolds said.

Robert had already gotten behind the wheel of the sheriff's truck, everyone else was in the crew cab as they pulled to a stop and picked up the sheriff and Reynolds.

"Can we get there in time?" asked Norma.

Nobody wanted to admit how anxious they were feeling, least of all Robert. "Those two sons a bitches better not mess with our team!" he said.

"We'll get there in time," Kevin said. "Those three can take care of themselves until we do." He was praying inside, asking God to help save his friends from the evil that was headed their way.

"Yuk!" Roxie said. "This stuff is super gross. I sure hope it isn't poisonous."

"Glad we brought gloves," Axel replied. "At least we don't have to actually touch it."

"C'mon, let's get the stone on," Marcus ordered. He knew there wasn't much time. They had jumped from their hiding place down the path and ran quickly to the gnarly tree, thankful it was clear of any Sinergy. Roxie was the lookout, Axel was clearing what appeared to be the passageway that had earlier been filled with transitory Sinergy members. Marcus held the Sealing Stone in his hands.

"Is it ready? Do you see the shape of the stone?" Roxie asked. She was peering into the forest, thankful nothing was moving their way. One hand held a super charged light, the other a one hundred decibel alarm, both ready to go! Three fire extinguishers stood nearby, along with two fully loaded shotguns.

"No, not yet," Axel said. "I feel the edges, though, yep, I definitely feel the rim of the hole. Feels like a really hard stone, not the base of a tree."

"Okay, let's try this," Marcus said and he moved in to cap the entry point. "Damn! It won't seal."

"Here, let me twist it," Axel offered. "Like trying to fit a new part on an old car engine. Sometimes it just takes a different set of hands."

"Guys!" Roxie screamed in a quiet yet desperate voice. "Two more are coming, and they're big!"

"I bet it's the mayor and Jericho," said Marcus. "Wow, look at the deep red color they are! Axel, give me the stone and I'll keep working on it. Roxie, you grab a fire extinguisher and get ready to move back. Keep the alarm ready. Axel, make sure you have that spotlight and a shotgun ready, and stay in front of Roxie. Okay, now step back before they get here. I can hide inside the tree until I get this in."

"No way, Marcus," Axel said. "We're not stepping back without you! This ain't no practice round - this is the real thing. You're coming with us!"

"Move!" Marcus yelled, startling his friends. "Now, before they see you! Don't argue with me, I've got the stone and as a last resort I can run with it and let them escape, then we seal it off."

Axel and Roxie stepped back into the nearest trees, close at hand but hidden from view. Marcus tried to seal the stone but centuries of growth had wreaked havoc on the edges of the hole. The saving grace was that the slime from the Sinergy members had cleared most of it away, and Marcus just about had it sealed; he could feel it sliding into place.

"Taking up some nighttime landscaping are we, Marcus?" It was Mayor Turner's voice, but as Marcus looked up all he saw were two dark red outlines of what had been the mayor and Jericho. "A little late in the season to be planting, is it not?"

"Marcus must have a green thumb," said Jericho. "No, that's not his thumb, that's a Sealing Stone he's got there. Another impressive bit of warfare from the earth creatures."

"I'd be glad to give you a piece from our collection," Marcus offered, his voice stronger than he felt. Now that the two leaders of the Sinergy were in their true forms and right in front of him, he was feeling overwhelmed. He countered with all the courage he could bring. "Oh, wait, that's right! You'd end up in one of our hospitals again. Flat on your back like the weak sauce that you really are!"

"Brave words from a man so helplessly stuck in a hole," said the mayor. "Now why don't you take your little green rock and step back while we disappear forever. Isn't that what you want?"

"I don't think so," Marcus answered.

"Well, have it your way," Jericho said confidently. "We only have a few minutes until your friends arrive and we'd like to be gone by then. So if you won't cooperate, we'll just call back a batch of those that have recently gone down the hole. I'm sure they'd give their lives here on this awful surface called Earth by moving you out of the way, in exchange for allowing the two of us back to our world."

"Too late, losers! Your passports have just been canceled!" Marcus shouted. He stood up and pushed down with his right foot in the center of the old gnarly tree base. There was a loud click that sounded like a granite boulder cracking in half. A deep reverberation followed that rippled through the valley floor.

"You fool!" yelled Jericho. "You will die for this!"

CHAPTER
49

They had come together as friends, and in a moment of utmost danger, they were willing to die for each other as family. When the ripple hit Axel and Roxie, they jumped from the trees. Roxie pointed the decibel alarm in the direction of the Sinergy, then pulled a fire extinguisher up to her waist, aimed and fired a cloud of white powder at the enemy. She acted as if this concoction was as lethal as any weapon on Earth, not knowing if it would have any effect at all. She was totally committed to the battle!

At the same instant Axel had leapt to Marcus' side, shotgun blazing with round after round; his high output spotlight strapped across his chest. On his back were a laser flashlight and a fire extinguisher. He was there to win, no other option had a chance to alter his focus!

Marcus had already pulled his shotgun up, wishing it was something more dangerous to the Sinergy. He had battled them before, but never the top two members. They were going to need help but until backup arrived he was focused only on how to destroy his enemies.

The plan was to gather inside the trunk of the gnarly tree, since it held the Sealing Stone; the object they hoped would be their best protection against the Sinergy. There they stood, shoulder to shoulder blasting pellets, spraying foam and hoping their eardrums would not burst from all the noise!

The enemy had been caught off guard, but their essence allowed them to absorb nearly everything sent their way. They seemed stuck, but not mortally injured. If they could just hold them until the rest of the group arrived, they might have a chance of destroying the leaders of the Sinergy!

Roxie began to pull her wearing stone from around her neck, Axel did the same. It only took a couple of tugs and they were off, the two then threw them at the Sinergy, and it worked! The mayor and Jericho were definitely affected. Their dark red shapes became more like masses than figures, and there was not a sound coming from either.

Roxie was on the third fire extinguisher when she saw Marcus give his shotgun to Axel. "What are you doing! We have to keep this up!"

"No hero stuff!" Axel yelled.

Marcus fell to the ground, found the edge of the Sealing Stone and pulled with all his might. Nothing! He jumped up and stepped hard on an edge to try and flip it up. Still nothing! He lay back down and felt all along the edge of the rim, and that's when he found the hole he was looking for. He had felt it when he had been trying to put the stone in place. Now he knew what it was. Thank God he didn't toss his wearing stone! He pulled his from around his neck, took the cord out from the middle and then placed the wearing stone into the hole. It worked! He easily lifted the Sealing Stone from the hole and ran at the two weakening Sinergy blobs, the Sealing Stone now glowing from the slime. Axel was out of ammo, Roxie had but a puff of foam left. Axel turned his spotlight beam to hit the stone and prisms of green light filled the forest like a kaleidoscope!

Marcus and Axel worked together to focus the strongest beams of light as best they could on the Sinergy. Luckily, it had the effect the trio from The Voyageurs had desired for so long. Whatever they were made of, or whoever's bodies they had stolen, what were once the human forms of Mayor Turner and Jericho Brown were now blobs of melting slime, helplessly pooling onto the forest floor.

They could hear the truck racing up the road, its headlights shooting into the openings between the trees. Marcus lowered the Sealing Stone, Roxie dropped the fire extinguisher, her arms suddenly aching from the effort. Axel was snapping his fingers near his ears, testing his hearing after all the shotgun blasts.

"You really think this is the last of them?" asked Roxie.

"I sure hope so," answered Axel. "I do know I'm going to ask Mrs. Hamsteen for a raise!"

"What about you, Marcus?" Roxie inquired. "Is this the end?"

"I'm not sure. Maybe, but it's a big world. We got the bad guys out of Havenswood Valley, but are there other places that need a Sealing Stone?" Marcus picked up the Sealing Stone to put it back in place. The sheriff's truck had nearly arrived when Marcus pushed down the stone once more. No ripple this time, just a snap into place.

The trio looked at each other as if disappointed not to feel the movement.

"Holy crap!" yelled Roxie. Suddenly there was a man standing not four feet from them. He looked unassuming; medium build, dressed in blue jeans, plaid shirt, a ball cap, and hiking boots, as if he was camping in the woods. The three victors stood in place, even Axel was held speechless. Something about the man rendered the three friends to be on alert, yet instinctively they understood he was there to help, not harm.

"It only sends out the Tundra Wave once," the man said. "The shock you felt when Marcus snapped the Sealing Stone into place?" he continued, hoping they were hearing what he was saying. "We call that a Tundra Wave. Pretty common in North America, not so much in Africa. Such different geography."

"Your friends are about to arrive, and unfortunately I don't have time to talk with all of you just yet. I can see by the looks on your faces; Marcus, Roxie, Axel, that I've caught you off guard. Sorry to surprise you. Your team has done well, very well in fact, and with such limited resources! But this is just the tip of the iceberg. If you truly want to get involved with battling this enemy, there's much more you can do. I've been asked to extend an invitation to your group for a visit to the headquarters of C.R.U.S.T. Something you've never heard of, yet you have all most recently become highly qualified to join."

"Hey," Marcus blurted out, breaking free of the momentary spell the three were under. "You left us the zircon, right?"

"Correct, Marcus, that was me. Just a little something to help with your laser gun," he answered. "Besides, maybe someone will figure a way to beat back cancer with that thing. So, again, excellent work by your group on this one, but we really do have a lot more to accomplish. What you've been doing here in Havenswood Valley is like trying to protect sand castles on the shore of a beach. C.R.U.S.T. would like to teach you how to slay the monsters of the deep blue sea. Think about it, and do keep this offer and it's considerations within The Voyageurs circle. I'll be in touch."

Acknowledgements

Jeanette Siddons; my incredible wife and on-site support crew. Her exceptional patience with my writing, along with her gentle nudging of options and ideas, proved we can accomplish anything together. Jeanette kept me going with lots of encouragement and allowed me the time to write without feeling guilty.

Beverly Siddons; amazing sister-in-law and aspiring writer. Skilled in writing and grammar thanks to her education and teaching career, Bev gave me great hope that I was onto a good story. Her editing and support were invaluable, and helped keep my head in the game and the project moving forward.

Malcolm Citron; the best father-in-law and with a heart of gold. His command of the English language and help with grammar were helpful keys to me staying on track. I really enjoyed having this project as a way to keep in regular contact with him.

Paula Keeler; my sister and biggest fan. She was always supportive while reading the chapters and provided me with just the right motivation when I needed it. Her continued belief in my success kept the fire burning and she was a wonderful part of my initial group of readers. Paula is an awesome sister!

Dave Forsberg; running partner and a patient listener. He was always kind enough to let me ramble on about the book as we trained for marathons. Dave hadn't read a word of the book but continued to provide great motivation for me to keep writing.

Sarah Hawkins; a family friend that happens to have a masters degree in Library and Information Science! Sarah provided an excellent edit with valuable insight as the project was wrapping up. I know she has a very bright future ahead of her!

To my editor.

The adventure that has been the writing of this book is very similar to the commitment it takes to train for a marathon, my other favorite endeavor. As with marathon training, my writing effort would never have made it this far without support. In the case of this book, my saving grace was working with Vicki Bauman as my editor.

Vicki not only dove in with passion, her expertise and attention to detail was incredible. She cast a net and harvested word, grammar and content errors, and provided manuscript changes to tighten up the story. Vicki kept the project moving, providing motivation to help me finish as fast, and as strong, as possible. I look forward to working with Vicki on my next book!

To my family and friends.

Many thanks to my family and friends for all of your support and encouragement over the past few years! It was a blessing to know you were in my corner! I'm so happy to be able to share this with you!

Mal and Nan,
Jeanette, Jackie and Bill, Spencer, Harrison,
Al and Bev, Brent and Heather, Brian and Katie,
Ray and Elena, Lindsay,
Paula and Mike, Abraham, Malina and Josh,
Theresa and Tom, Sarah and Josh, Tess,
Gary and Jill, Connor,
Carolyn and Gary, Blake, Breanna, Austin,
Troy,
Bob and Sandy,
Dave, Bryan, Stan,
Vicki,
Sarah.

To my long time friend, Darrell. I hope you enjoy my first novel.

Brian James Siddons began putting pencil to paper as a teen, writing poems and songs, never thinking about having anything submitted for publishing. His penchant for writing has been apparent over the years, and he finally took the step toward authorship after he explained the idea for this book to his wife, Jeanette. She wholeheartedly supported the project from the very start.

"The Voyageurs-Discovery In Havenswood Valley" was written back-to-front, and is based on a final scene that Brian had envisioned years before. A lover of Halloween, Brian and his son, Harrison, had finished putting away their yearly front yard holiday display when he decided to sit down and write out the ending of this book. From there it was on to the prologue and eventually the start of the story.

Married to Jeanette since 1985, they have three children; Jacqueline, Spencer and Harrison, and live in Andover, Minnesota. Brian and Jeanette were born and raised in Southern California, and have found Minnesota a fantastic place to raise a family and build life long friendships.